Preface

Secret Sacrament was conceived in October 1993, in a room in one of the residence halls of the University of Iowa, in the United States. I had won a writing fellowship to go there to take part in the International Writing Programme at the university. The fellowship was one of those extraordinary gifts that comes just once in a lifetime. It arrived when I was burnt-out by long years of labouring alone in my studio, when my creative cup was empty, and I was hungering for encouragement and company. I had already glimpsed the young man, hero of a new book, but I had no energy for him or his story – whatever it was to be.

From the moment I arrived in Iowa I felt renewed. There is indescribable richness when thirty people from around the world – from countries including Slovenia, Saudi Arabia, Russia, Egypt, Colombia, Ukraine, Cote d'Ivoire, Finland, Kenya, Zimbabwe, Bangladesh, and Honduras – meet together to share stories and songs, poems and laughter, food and philosophies. It was a rare experience, inspiring and utterly enriching. Out of it, out of that wondrous time in America, came *Secret Sacrament*.

But the book was not born easily. It went through several drafts, all written during a time of grief in my life; and the main character, Gabriel, became not only a healer in the book I was writing, but a friend in whose company I found solace and strength. Equally important to me was the encouragement of friends who read the early drafts, and whose suggestions and

3

SHERRYL JORDAN

wise advice helped give birth to the version of the story first published here in New Zealand in 1996.

Then, in 1999, the book was accepted for publication in the United States, and an American editor, Antonia Markiet, made suggestions for further changes. Her insight and deep empathy with the story and its characters opened to me new themes I had not explored, or had too briefly hinted at. Finally, three years after its first publication, and under Antonia's excellent guidance, the story became what it was always meant to be. It remains unchanged.

There is one other friend to whom I am forever grateful, who deeply influenced this story. That friend is my mother, who died in 1994, while the very first draft of *Secret Sacrament* was being written. I was with her as she journeyed between this world and the next, and what we shared during those last minutes was the greatest gift she ever gave me. The scene in this book of Myron's death, and what he and Gabriel experienced in the Valley of the Shadow, is taken almost word for word from my own diary.

This month is the eighth anniversary of my mother's passing on. It is a fitting time to be writing this preface for the UK edition of the story that is dedicated to her.

Sherryl Jordan
Tauranga,
New Zealand
September 2002

SACRAMENT

SHERRYL JORDAN

CHUSTER

First published in Great Britain by Simon & Schuster UK Ltd, 2003
A Viacom company

1 3 5 7 9 10 8 6 4 2

Simon & Schuster UK Ltd
Africa House
64-78 Kingsway
London WC2B 6AH

A CIP catalogue record for this book is available from the British Library

ISBN 0689837097

Typeset by SX Composing DTP, Rayleigh, Essex
Printed and bound in Finland by WS Bookwell

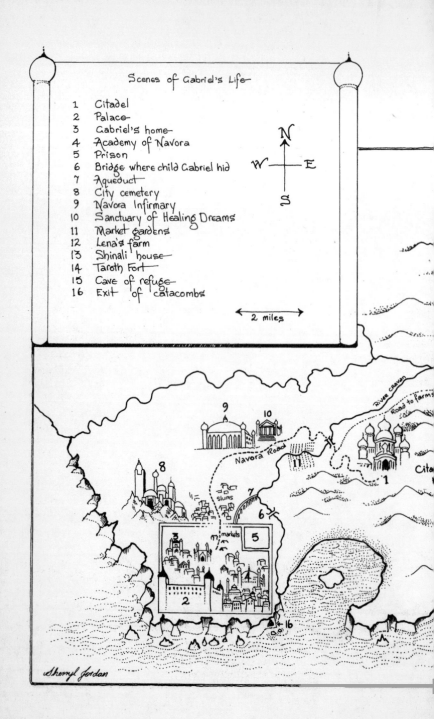

Scenes of Gabriel's Life

1 Citadel
2 Palace
3 Gabriel's home
4 Academy of Navora
5 Prison
6 Bridge where child Gabriel hid
7 Aqueduct
8 City cemetery
9 Navora Infirmary
10 Sanctuary of Healing Dreams
11 Market gardens
12 Lena's farm
13 Shinali house
14 Taroth Fort
15 Cave of refuge
16 Exit of catacombs

2 miles

Sherryl Jordan

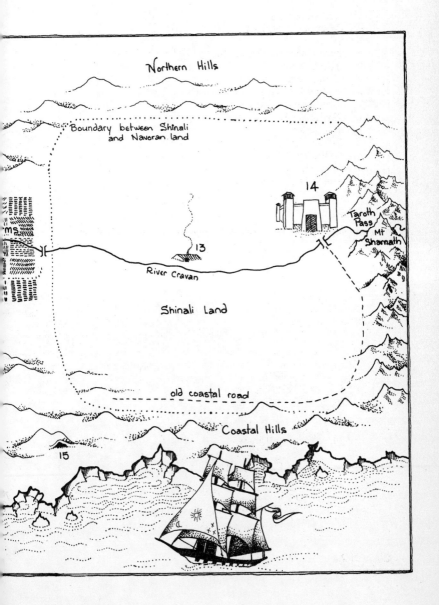

Northern Hills

Boundary between Shinali
and Navoran land

14

Taroth
Pass

Mt
Shamath

ms

13

River Cravan

Shinali Land

old coastal road

Coastal Hills

15

Chapters in Secret Sacrament

Main Characters

Gabriel	A healer, gifted with the ability to interpret dreams
Petra	Empress of the Navoran Empire
Salverion	Grand Master of Healing
Sheel Chandra	Master of Mind-power and Healing Through Dreams
Amael	Master of Herbal Medicines

(Sheel Chandra and Amael: Teachers at the Citadel)

Hevron	Gabriel's tutor at the Academy of Navora
Lena	Gabriel's mother
Myron	Gabriel's brother, younger than him
Imri	
Darien	
Jayd	
Subin	

(Imri, Darien, Jayd, Subin: Gabriel's siblings in order of birth)

Jager	Gabriel's father
Egan	Jager's brother, uncle to Gabriel

Ferron	Gabriel's servant and friend at the Citadel
Eva	Myron's girlfriend
Topaz	Surveyor; Lena's friend
Jaganath	High Oracle and chief adviser to the Empress; Gabriel's enemy
Nagay	Commander of Navoran navy
Kamos	Commander of Navoran army; Gabriel's enemy
Sanigar	Prophet and astrologer; Gabriel's enemy

} Advisers to the Empress

Kanyiida	High Priest; Gabriel's enemy
Cosimo	High Judge, friend to Salverion and Gabriel
Ashila	Young woman of the Shinali people. A healer, loved by Gabriel
Oboth	Elderly chieftain of the Shinali people
Tarkwan	Elder son of Oboth
Moondarri	Tarkwan's wife
Yeshi	Tarkwan's younger brother
Zalidas	Priest of the Shinali
Thandeka	Ashila's mother; a healer
Razzak	Commander of Taroth Fort
Darshan	The name Gabriel uses when hiding from the Navoran authorities

Secret Sacrament

1 Broken Images

TREMBLING, THE BOY crouched in the shadow of the bridge. He pressed his hot, wet face against the ancient stones, and fought to stop the waves of nausea that swept through him. Behind him towered the vast outer wall of the city, crimson-drenched in the sunset. From cobbled roads far beyond the wall came the rumble of chariot and wagon wheels, and the neighing of horses. The whole city of Navora seemed to vibrate and boom within its walls, like a mighty heart preparing for the night. There was something ominous in that quiet thundering, and the boy shrank from it, pressing himself harder against the bridge. He discovered a deep crevice in the stones, and squeezed himself into it. Hidden, safe for the moment, he wiped his grubby hands across his eyes and enjoyed a momentary respite from his troubles.

Glancing behind him, he saw the darker stones of the ancient north-east corner of the city, marking the outer confines of the prison. The stones in these mighty prison ramparts had only slits for windows. On the wide crests of the walls guards walked, crossbows gleaming as the sunset struck them. The boy shivered, thinking of the stories he had heard about the inside of that place. People never came out, it was said, except to be buried or beheaded.

Turning from the prison, he scanned the evening skies and the deserted banks of the River Cravan. The setting sun struck his eyes, changing their vivid, translucent blue to violet. His fair hair shone with red-gold lights, and clung around his wary face in long, damp curls. Satisfied that he was alone, he settled more comfortably into his hiding place and listened to the river gurgling over the rocks as it tumbled, close to the shadowed east wall, on its way to the sea. He could smell the sea, if he sniffed hard; could smell the rank odour of the oyster shells piled two hundred years deep along the beach, and the salty air blowing in from the ocean. He loved the sea, and loved the times his father took him out on the oyster boats. It was wonderful to watch the young men and women dive deep, deep into the murky waters, and come up again with string baskets full of rough oyster shells. Some of the oysters would be sold for food in the marketplace, but many would be left in piles on the beach to putrefy. Much later Gabriel would sit on the beach with his father and watch the people remove the precious pearls from the soft rotting flesh.

'These little stones,' his father had once said, holding one up into the sun, 'these are what began this great city of ours. One day, over two hundred years ago, a great navigator came to this land, and he found barbarian fisherfolk dwelling in caves under the cliffs, living off whatever the sea could provide. The fisherfolk traded with the navigator. For knives and bows and arrows, they gave him some of the strange, pale pearls they fished from the sea. The navigator took the pearls back to his own country, and told of the distant land they came from, with its beautiful harbour and clean blue waters. Then other people sailed here, built a village on the harbour edge, and fished for the pearls themselves, trading them with passing ships. They became very wealthy, for the pearls were much prized. More people came, and more, and took over the harbour and the coast. The tiny village became a town. But the barbarians didn't want

to share their fishing waters, and there was war between them and the newcomers. The barbarians lost and were driven away from the coast. The new town flourished. And now look at Navora: the largest port in the world. Centre of all trade, all knowledge, all wealth. Centre of the Empire. And at the heart of it, a little pearl. Never forget that, Gabriel. It's what's at the heart of things that matters.'

Gabriel did not forget. But lately he had heard his father say that the oyster beds were becoming depleted, and the oyster business would not last much longer. Gabriel's mother wanted to go inland to farm or grow an orchard, but his father was determined to put his wealth into trading ships, and to sail to alien lands. There was seldom harmony between his parents now, and Gabriel and his three younger brothers were in trouble more times than they were out of it. They had learned to creep about unseen and unheard, but this evening they had landed in trouble with a crash that had shaken the whole house and brought the slaves running.

The boys had been playing with a ball inside, and Gabriel had got excited and thrown it so hard it bounced off a wall and toppled a marble statue from its pedestal. The statue had broken into pieces on the polished wooden floor. It was only a small image of the Empress Petra, but Gabriel's father treasured it. He had always said that if a slave ever broke the statue, the culprit would pay for it with his life. He had not said what would happen if one of his own sons broke it, and Gabriel did not stay to find out. He had fled to this forbidden place outside the city walls, where even his father would never dream of looking for him. In this dangerous, desolate place, the river stank from the city's sewage, diseased beggars came to die, and women abandoned their unwanted newly-borns. Here the city's rubbish

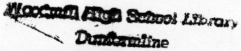

found its final home or was washed in the river's flow out to the beaches beyond, where it rotted in the sun, was picked clean by gulls, or was sucked out to sea by the tide. For one wild moment the boy thought of throwing himself into the river, risking drowning in the oceans rather than discipline from his father. He struggled to stand, but his quivering limbs shook so much, he sank back into the shadows, defeated. He began to sob again, very quietly. Then he heard a sound and held his breath.

Someone was moving down by the river. Small stones, dislodged, were tumbling down the steep bank. Someone was moving slowly, furtively. He crouched deeper into his nook, his heart pounding so loudly he thought the newcomer must surely hear it. But after a while the stealthy sounds stopped, and he heard only the swift flowing of the waters. Slowly, in total silence, he peered out around the old stones of the bridge.

A woman was down by the river, washing her hands and wrists in the water. She crouched in shade, for the sun had almost set behind the city. The river and opposite rocky shore were indistinct in the dusk. Past the shore the land rose steeply to the hills, purple as the night deepened, their upper slopes brushed with gold from the sun's last rays. On the highest hill, surrounded by the green of gardens and vineyards, shone the Citadel, institute of the most advanced knowledge in the world. Above it a full moon ascended, the colour of apricots. A few stars were out.

The woman still crouched by the water, washing. In the waning light Gabriel could see that a chain or rope dangled from her wrists. She wore a single long brown garment, dull and roughly woven, unlike the shining silk and bright linen the city women wore, and her black hair fell unbound to her waist. For a few minutes she crouched there, washing her hands and trying to remove whatever it was that had tied them.

From high on the rocky path leading from the city came the sound of men's voices and boisterous laughter. The woman leaped to her feet, and Gabriel cringed into his nook. He heard the men drawing nearer, talking and chuckling. Their voices were slurred, and they stumbled often on the uneven ground. There was a sound of someone falling, and glass breaking on rock. A man swore, and others laughed. Then one of them mentioned the woman, and there was laughter again, as well as a few lewd comments. The men came nearer, and Gabriel could hear their boots slipping on the stones, and their heavy breathing as they struggled down the rocks to the river shore. As they passed his hiding place, he closed his eyes and held his breath. The odour of wine and stale sweat came to him on the still air. He heard them go on down to the water's edge. He heard the woman cry out, and stones scattering as people raced over them. The men were laughing and swearing. The woman yelled at them in an unknown language, her voice strong and defiant. There were sounds of running again, and stones being thrown. Then the woman screamed, and the men cheered. There was the sound of a sword being drawn from its scabbard.

From the summit of the prison wall a guard shouted. The men by the river were silent. The woman called out once. The boy gathered up his courage. He looked upward, ready to call for help. But at that moment the guard was joined by another, and the two walked away to a different part of the prison roof. After a while the noises by the river continued. The male voices became low and brutal.

Gabriel covered his head with his arms. He could hardly breathe for terror. The sound of his own heart thundered in his ears, and he was certain the men would drag him out, too, and murder him. After a time he uncovered his ears and listened again. But they had not murdered her; the woman was still alive, for he could hear her groans and sobs. She was saying the same thing over and over again, her voice high and anguished: 'Kaath sharleema . . . Kaath sharleema . . .' The men were mainly silent, but every now and again there was rough laughter, and the men applauded one another and used words Gabriel had never heard before. And all the time the woman moaned and begged, and said her strange words.

As the boy listened, sweat ran down his forehead and into his eyes and trickled down his body until his woollen tunic was wet. He was trembling again and wanted to vomit. He wished he could not hear, and he was afraid not to. The sounds went on and on, until the night was black except for the cold silver splendour of the moon. Still the boy hid, not moving a muscle lest the men find him. He remained motionless in his hollow, even long after the men had staggered back up the rocks and vanished through the narrow door at the base of the city wall.

The dawn sky was orange above the hills when the boy slid out of his hiding place and began to creep across the stones towards the city wall. Then he stopped. The woman was still down by the river. She was moaning softly, sobbing and saying things in an alien tongue. He crept down to her. Then he stopped a short distance away, horrified.

In the glimmering dawn he saw that she was lying on her side, curled into herself. She was naked. They had cut off her long hair, and what was left stood up like dark spikes. She was quivering all over. Her back was bruised from the rocks, and her legs were smeared with blood. The boy moved around to stand in front of her. She heard him and cried out. Then she saw that it was a child, and she reached out a hand towards him. Her hands, too, had blood on them, and one of her arms was bent crookedly against her body. Bone protruded through the skin.

'*Sharleema*,' she whispered.

Her hand was still outstretched, pleading. Her skin was deep olive, and she wore armbands of bone. Knotted tight around her wrists were the frayed remains of a rope. Her arms were stained with blood. Glancing at her face, the boy saw that her eyes were black and beautiful. Her features were unlike those of the women of the city. There was a wild, dark beauty about her, and the boy realised, with a shock, that she was of the Shinali people, the barbarians who lived beyond the hills. He saw that her throat had been scratched with a knife, and blood trickled into the hollows of her shoulders and neck. Above her left breast was a strange spiralling mark, coloured deep blue, and the stylised image of a bird.

'*Tortan qui, sharleema*,' she entreated him, her voice breaking.

He backed away, stumbling. His feet were in the water, sinking into soft mud. He looked down and noticed, under the murky flow, the gleam of something white. He stooped and picked it up. It was a carving of some sort. Bone, threaded on a piece of severed leather thong. When the woman saw what he had found, she gave a frenzied cry and lunged towards him, gripping his ankle. She wept, saying things in her strange language. Terrified and bewildered, he pulled free and raced up the rocks to the city wall. Her agonised calls followed him. He did not stop. Sprinting along the narrow path at the top of the rocks, he fled through the same doorway the men had used earlier.

Along the dim streets he raced, sobbing and panting as if demons were after him. There were few people about. He sped between the deserted stalls of the fish and vegetable markets, past the narrow alleys where the poor lived, and along the wider streets to the wealthier sector of the city. Here high walls guarded the courtyards of the rich, where fountains played and small trees in urns cast shadows over cobblestones. There were no gardens in Navora; the city was built of stone, on stone.

He came to his own wrought-iron gate and hammered on it. An elderly slave came out, his face creased with anxiety. Seeing who it was, the slave almost laughed in his relief. 'Thank God you're alive, master!' he cried, drawing the bolts and swinging the gate open. 'Your mother's beside herself with worry. Your father's been out all night looking for you, with sentries.'

Panting, Gabriel ran across the courtyard and sat on the seat between the pillars of the grand front porch, to remove his muddy sandals. Then he pushed open the front door and crept in. Shadows enveloped him, cooling his feverish skin. He stole between the great pillars of the foyer, past the grim marble bust of his grandfather, and the terrifying stuffed owl on the wall with its outstretched wings and menacing claws. He crept on, past the huge murals depicting Navoran ships being unloaded at the wharves. For a moment he stopped to look up at the pictures, glimmering and ghostly in the dawn. The ships towered over him, their misty sails furled, their dark hulls seeming to heave on the shadowed tide. On the wharves their cargoes gleamed: precious silks, golden urns, statues, cages of exotic animals and birds, and heavily shackled slaves. Looking at the manacles on the slaves, Gabriel thought of the woman's hand reaching out to him, and the rope on her bleeding wrist. The painted slaves, too, were dark-skinned, their eyes large and beautiful and afraid. In the semi-darkness the images on the wall blurred and changed, looming and vanishing like people in a dark mist. The eyes of the slaves were fixed on him, moving when he moved, pleading with him. It seemed that even their voices called to him. Suddenly he cried out and ran.

Finally he reached the hall leading to the bedrooms. On one side of the hall, by a window in a small alcove, a lamp burned. His parents stood there, waiting. One of the city sentries was with them, his smooth bronze breastplates and helmet shiny in the lamplight.

Gabriel's mother gave a relieved cry and moved towards him, but her husband gripped her wrist, restraining her.

'Where have you been, Gabriel?' he asked. His face, always impressive and severe, was more fierce than ever. His red tunic and trousers were dark as blood, and jewels winked on his wide belt.

Gabriel tried to speak but could not. His breath came and went in deep, painful gasps. He shook his head.

'We've been searching for you all night,' said his mother softly. 'I've been so worried.'

'Silence,' said his father. 'You go to bed now, Lena. There's no more need to worry. I'll deal with the boy.'

'Please, be easy with him,' Lena begged. 'It was an accident.'

'It was no accident that he stayed out all night,' muttered his father. 'Now leave us.'

Gabriel watched as his mother went down the hall. She did not notice as the sentry bowed to her; her head was held high but she walked slowly, as if she were unspeakably tired. He dared not look at his father. He stared at the sentry's high boots, and noticed the horse, symbol of the Empire, embossed in red on the brown leather.

'I'm glad to see the lad is safe, sir,' the sentry said. 'I'll go now, and call my men back from their search.'

'I'm sorry I've wasted your time,' said the father. 'It seems he had run away, as I suspected. I'm happy to pay you for your trouble. Would five hundred hasaries be enough?'

'Please don't even think of it, sir. We only did our duty.'

The sentry bowed, and a slave stepped forward to show him out. Gabriel waited, his head bent, his heart thudding in his chest. He could feel his father's grey eyes boring into him.

For a long time Jager did not speak but stood looking at his son with an expression of contempt. At last the man said, 'You made a fool of me, son. I've had twenty sentries out looking for you. You've piled wrong on top of wrong. But first things first. Come.'

He led the way along the hall, towards the schoolroom where the family tutor taught the boys to read and write and do maths, and where they learned the great Navoran creed and the history of their Empire. Outside the room was the pedestal on which the statue had been. The pieces were still on the floor where they had fallen hours before. Jager opened the schoolroom door. 'Pick up every bit,' he said. 'Put them on the table in here.'

With trembling hands Gabriel obeyed. Carefully he placed each piece on the table. Each fragment he tried in vain to join with the part it belonged to; he tried to join the two halves of the beautiful head, the hands to the shattered arms, the legs to the cracked body. It was no use; they fell apart again on the dark wood of the table, glowing and lovely as living flesh, each piece a witness to his wickedness.

'You're a great disappointment to me, Gabriel,' said his father. 'You're seven years old, and you still haven't learned integrity. You're a coward. You wouldn't even stay here to tell me what you'd done. You let me find out from your mother. Have you no courage at all, no sense of what is honourable? You're Navoran. Do you know what that means?'

Gabriel wiped his nose on his sleeve.

'It means you bear responsibility for your actions,' said his father. 'If you make a mistake, you do your best to right it, or you take your punishment like a man. You don't run away and hide. Look at you – you're filthy. Your tunic's torn. Your feet are muddy.' He hesitated, then asked in a low voice, 'Were you down by the river?'

Gabriel nodded.

For a while the father did not speak. When he did, his voice was shaking and deadly quiet. 'I never thought you'd go there, Gabriel, not after what I'd told you about that place, not after all my warnings. You don't know how lucky you are to be alive. Were you alone there? Did you see anyone?'

The boy lifted his face. He opened his mouth to speak but had no words for the horror he had seen. Instead he wept, and Jager made an impatient sound.

'You have to learn obedience, Gabriel,' he said. 'This isn't just for the statue. It's for wasting the sentries' time, and mine. It's to teach you to be strong, to be a true son of Navora. Also, it's for distressing your mother. Take off your tunic and bend over the table.'

While Gabriel did as he was told, he heard his father go to the cupboard and take out the bamboo rod. He waited, hands clenched, his face pressed to one side against the table's smooth wood, his eyes on the gleaming shards of the broken statue. And all the time his father whipped him, he saw only those fragile, ruined pieces, glowing and warm in the morning light like real flesh, the slender arms broken, the hands outstretched towards him, the beautiful eyes tormented and full of grief and pleading. He wept in agony and guilt, and when he could not stand the pain any longer, he cried out words of which he did not know the meaning. Then his father shouted something furious and hit him harder. And it was only later, when he found himself lying on his bed with a cool sheet laid over him, that he realised he held in his right hand the alien bone carving on the leather thong, and it had cut his palm and his fingers were slippery with blood.

All day he lay there, dozing. The first time he woke, he felt his brother Myron leaning over him. 'I tried to tell Father it was my fault,' Myron whispered, 'but he knew it was you, because you'd run away. I wish you hadn't. I can't stay; Father said we weren't allowed to see you.' Myron's voice broke as he wept, and he kissed Gabriel's cheek before he crept out.

Several times Gabriel's mother came in. Gently she washed his back, and he smelled herbs and wildflowers she had added to the water. Though her tender ministrations were agony to him, he made no sound, pretending to remain asleep. Once he thought he heard her softly crying. And once she lifted his head and offered him a drink. It tasted bitter, and he guessed it was drugged. He slept again, drifting in and out of painful dreams.

When he awoke the midday sun was streaming through his window. He stared at it, narrowing his eyes so they were almost shut and his lashes made shadows like tawny grasses shimmering in the light. He felt the smooth surface of the bone carving in his hand, and timidly opened his fingers. He expected the bone to glint at him like an accusing eye; instead, to his amazement, it gave him comfort.

Dreaming, he lay in long grass on a wide plain. The wind was warm and sweet on his face. High above, an eagle soared in a cloudless sky, and nearby a river rushed, gurgling, across shifting stones. He could smell sheep, their wool warmed by the sun. Somewhere a woman sang, her voice rising and falling on the wind as smooth as a silken flag. Her words were foreign, yet he knew she sang of a summer's day, and of the earth laughing. The song moved across his soul, easing it. Never had he felt so much at peace, so much at home.

When he awoke the dream was still with him, holding him warm in its power, the smell of wool and wind and grass still vivid and strong. He realised he was cradling the bone carving against his cheek. He lifted the bone into the sun and watched it swinging there on its short thong. The etching was filled with blood, and Gabriel wiped his thumb across the bone, smoothing away most of the redness. What remained coloured only the lines engraved in the creamy surface, and for the first time he clearly saw what the carving depicted.

It was a design made up of an eagle and a man. Only the man's head was shown. His face, etched in profile, was strong and steadfast, almost fierce, and his eyes seemed to look beyond, to places ordinary people could not see. Behind his head, worked so that his long hair flowed and became the feathers of the outstretched wings, was an eagle in flight. It was a striking design, skilfully executed, and wonderfully blending the images of bird and man.

Gabriel pressed the carving against his aching forehead. The bone was smooth and cool, and seemed to vibrate softly against his skin. Instinctively he knew it was old, very old, and precious. He closed his eyes. He heard his brothers running down the hallway outside his room, their footsteps muffled on the narrow strip of thick carpet. The sound was prolonged, became deep and haunting, like the throbbing of drums. He heard the rushing of a river, and men shouting. The sounds faded. An old man was chanting, his voice grating and cracked like stalks of grain falling on dry ground. Thunder rolled, rain hissed on to the parched earth, and cool water ran deliciously over his naked skin. Inside an earthen dwelling a fire roared, and fish sizzled on hot stones, smelling good. Again the odour of wool, and the sound of women singing. Then a curtain rattled on its wooden rail, and the enchantment was shattered.

It was Gabriel's mother, drawing his curtains now because it was evening and the air was chill. Gabriel slid the bone beneath his pillow. He longed for the dream images, the solace and the joy. Desolation swept over him, as if something unspeakably precious was gone.

'How are you feeling now?' asked Lena gently, sitting near the foot of his bed.

He did not reply.

She sighed and looked down at her hands, tensely clasped on the soft blue linen of her robe. She was again carrying a child, and her long dress flowed loosely around her. Her hair, tied back in a knot, was chestnut brown.

'There's something you have to understand, Gabriel,' she said. 'You're a very special child. Your father is one of the most honoured merchants in Navora. You're his eldest, his heir and future hope. But the city's full of desperate, unhappy people, and some of them do terrible things to get money. You must never wander the streets at night, never go outside the city walls, never go down by the river. We've told you this a hundred times. I worried so much about you, last night. I thought you had been kidnapped. I couldn't bear that. Do you understand what I'm saying?'

He shook his head, distraught. 'I'm not special. Father says I'm a coward. He says I run away, instead of facing my responsibilities. He says I'm not a true son of Navora.'

'Strength isn't always a matter of muscle, Gabriel. And, in a way, you were brave to run. But there are times to run, and there are times to stand firm. You'll learn the difference as you grow up.'

'I'm not brave,' he said, choking, tears streaming down his cheeks. 'I ran. I shouldn't have. I shouldn't have left . . .'

'Hush, hush,' she said, stroking away his tears with her hand. 'It's all right, it's over now. Try to sleep some more.' She smoothed back his damp, disordered curls and caressed his face. When he was quiet she stood up and went out, closing the door behind her.

He lay on his side crying, hot with guilt. Afterwards he took the bone carving out from beneath the pillow and looked at it again. Slowly, like a dawn, peace came to him; a Shinali peace, full of the sweet scent of the grasslands and the grand freedom of the skies. With that clear, unquestioning trust that only children have, he opened his heart and accepted it. Sighing deeply, he curled his fingers around the bone, held it close against his heart, and lay for a long time staring into the gathering dark.

2 Healing Dreams

THE YOUTH WAITED at the top of the mausoleum steps, staring down at the open ancient doors and the musty dark beyond. Though he stood in bright sunlight, and his black funeral clothes sucked up the summer heat and made sweat run down his back, he shivered. He looked across the stone steps at his mother. She appeared calm and assured, but she was very pale, and there were deep shadows under her eyes. Her youngest child, her three-year-old daughter, Subin, dragged on her hand and whimpered in the heat. Beside them, lined up in single file on the steps, were her other four children, all sons. In silence they waited, while the funeral bier bearing their father was carried up through the winding stone paths of the huge city cemetery. All Navora's dead were interred here, in family crypts hewn out of the rocky hillsides. On the lower slopes were the simple caves where the poor were buried, but where these mourners stood, on the highest ground, were the stately tombs of the wealthy, adorned with carved obelisks and statues. There were no plants or trees, and the dark stones glinted in the sun and threw back the heat like a furnace.

Gabriel wiped his sleeve across his face, pushing back the heavy curls. Glancing at the other mourners on the path behind him, he saw mainly uncles and aunts and cousins, and close family friends. Among them were several distinguished citizens: dignitaries from the palace; a famous astronomer from the

country of Sadira, tall and majestic and olive-skinned, and now a
Master teaching at the famed Citadel, and the commander of the
Navoran navy. They too looked uncomfortable in their formal
clothes, their faces flushed but dignified. In spite of the hot day
the commander was in full naval uniform, his heavy cloak falling
in deep blue folds to his black boots. He wore several jewelled
rings, and priceless stones fixed his cloak to the shoulders of his
tunic. The front of his tunic was richly embroidered with the
sign of the horse, cleverly intertwined with the Empress's
initials. He was an imposing man, a famous navigator and
warrior, and one of the most powerful people in the Empire.

The heat intensified. High above, gulls wheeled and
screamed in the blazing skies. Elsewhere in the cemetery
children laughed, the sound echoing and incongruous in the
solemnity. There was a scuffle farther down the path, and the
mourners heard men labouring, heavily burdened, up the steep
slope. Gabriel looked straight down the steps, his eyes
narrowed, his expression suddenly tense. As the bier was carried
past him he noticed the sickly odour of embalming liquids,
precious oils and spices, and he glimpsed his father's face, stern
and resolute even in death. He tried not to think of the rest of his
father's body, the lower half crushed by a marble block that had
fallen while being unloaded at the wharves; tried not to think of
his father carried home, wrapped in an old boat sail that dripped
with blood, with the slaves wailing and sobbing; tried not to
think of his mother's screams, or of his own horror and
powerlessness in a household suddenly devastated.

The bier disappeared into the cavernous dark below, and
Gabriel glanced at his mother. She saw his tension, the beads of
sweat across his upper lip, and she smiled a little to encourage
him, and nodded.

As eldest son, he led the way down into the hollowed earth. From brilliant light he passed into utter darkness; from birdsong and summer warmth into silence, ominous and cold and suffocating.

Slowly he grew accustomed to the dark. Immediately in front of him was the stone sarcophagus, its huge lid propped against one side. Beside it stood the bearers, his father's six brothers, stern and straight as they held the bier. Beyond them, indistinct in the dimness, loomed the stone coffins of previous family members, some richly carved and bearing statues of those interred within. Gabriel looked away from them and concentrated on the living. His relatives stood close by, and the more important family friends. They stood very still, the shadows pitch black around them, their faces glimmering in the torchlight. In the hollowed stone even their breathing seemed loud, and their fine clothes rustled like moths' wings against the dark.

A priest stepped forward and said an old Navoran prayer, and the body of Jager Eshban Vala, merchant and navigator, was lowered into the stone coffin. Other people made speeches and placed gifts in the tomb, or messages from those who could not attend but who wished to honour the dead man. The navy commander said a few words, and placed across Jager's body the Navoran banner that had flown from his ship when he won a great victory for the Empire. The banner was gold with a scarlet horse, and was splendid. Then one of the palace officials read a eulogy written by the Empress Petra herself, in which she called Jager one of Navora's most faithful and worthy sons. "'You brought to our city not only wealth and foreign splendours,'" the palace envoy read, "'but you brought to it the greatest glory there is – the presence of a true Navoran. In you we saw a man who not only loved the ideals and dreams that first made our Empire great, but who lived them. You were an honest Navoran, a brave navigator, and a wise and discerning merchant. We all are richer because you lived."'

Then Lena said a few words, her voice steady and low in the echoing dark. She leaned over the stone, kissed the tips of her fingers, then placed them against the dead man's cheek. All the children went up to the coffin and either whispered a few words or pressed a special gift into the folds of their father's shroud. Then it was Gabriel's turn. Always the eldest son spoke last, then drew the shroud over the departed before the lid of the sarcophagus was forever dropped in place.

He stood at the foot of the coffin and looked down at his father. Torchlight flickered over Jager's face, giving the waxen skin a warm and golden sheen. Yet there had been no warmth in Jager; not that Gabriel had ever seen. As he looked at the hard mouth, firmly closed, he thought of all the times he had longed to hear words of approval or encouragement, and received only criticism. He looked at the permanent frown carved between his father's brows, and tried to forget the image of Jager in his office, annoyed at being interrupted; tried to forget the impatience, the sarcasm, the fault-finding even when Gabriel had shown him something of which he was proud. Never had he made his father proud. Always there had been only a devastating struggle to please, and bitter failure. It occurred to Gabriel, with a rush of unbearable grief, that his father had never hugged him, never once given him the smallest sign of tenderness or love. Fighting down the hurt, he began speaking aloud the famous tribute paid by all first-born sons to their dead fathers.

'With all my heart, I honour you,' he said, his voice coming out nervous and high. He hesitated, and one of his cousins giggled. Quivering, feeling as though his throat were full of dust,

Gabriel went on: 'With all my heart, I shall honour all that you have . . . have left to me. I shall do my utmost to live . . . utmost to . . .'

He stopped, unable to speak the words. How could he live out his father's ambitions for him when he hated the whole idea of taking over the shipping business? How could he swear it, breaking the vow in his heart before his lips even spoke the words? Despairing, horrified at what he was doing but unable to help himself, he deliberately missed out the greater part of the eulogy and went on with a safer bit. But the next part, filled with gratitude for a father's love and guidance and encouragement, also stuck in his throat. So he stood there in the glimmering dark, his gaze fixed on the dead man's face, and said nothing. People began to whisper. Lena stepped towards him, but one of his uncles spoke first.

'Leave him, Lena. He's not a child. He's fourteen, and the man of the family now. He can do it.'

Gabriel bent his head. They waited. The torches spat and sizzled in the stale air, and somewhere a rat squeaked. Outside, in another world, birds sang, and the children shrieked with laughter among the tombs. At last Gabriel lifted his head. 'Goodbye, Father,' he said, and abruptly bent down and drew the pale cloth over the stern face. Breaking into the shocked silence, the priest said a last prayer, then Lena gathered the youngest children around her and led them out into the sun. Gabriel followed, feeling severed from them, and shamed. As they went up into the sunlight, blinking in the sudden glare, the darkness behind them boomed as the stone lid was dropped on to the sarcophagus. With all of his being Gabriel longed to run back, to say all the things to his father he had never said, but too many people pressed from behind, and going back was impossible.

His brother Myron, a year younger, came and walked beside him. They did not speak, but Myron walked so close their shoulders touched, and he made the secret sign they had used when they were small, to encourage one another when they were in trouble: he made a fist with his right hand, the little finger and thumb extended like the horns of a defiant bull. Gabriel saw the sign, and his eyes met Myron's for a moment. But even Myron's brotherly support could not wipe away the scandalous silence where a son's homage should have been, or the sound of the uncles' boots heavy on the stones behind him.

In the house he expected the reproaches to begin the moment he got in the door. But no one spoke to him. They all went into the spacious dining room, and slaves handed out goblets of cooled wine and tiny fruit pastries. People talked in subdued tones about the heat, and there was some discussion on the rising prices of fresh fruit and vegetables, and whether or not the Shinali would sell some of their land so more market gardens could be developed. Then one of the aunts said how wonderful all the funeral orations had been, and there was an onerous silence. Feeling as if all eyes were on him, Gabriel went and stood by the open door to the courtyard, and looked out. Behind him the talk resumed, and there was polite laughter at something one of the uncles said. It seemed an age he stood there, wanting to flee. Then one of his aunts called to him. He went over, trying to look nonchalant.

'Gabriel,' she said, her fingers fluttering towards the low table with its bottles of wine and empty goblets, 'it really is time the slaves started serving the funeral feast, and your mother's not here. I don't know where she is. Would you go and find her, dear? Some of us have a long way to travel back. If we don't eat soon, we'll miss out. This really is turning out to be a very disorganised day, isn't it? Not at all your conventional funeral.'

'I'm sorry, we don't get much practice at funerals,' Gabriel replied. The aunt looked perturbed, and he hurried out to look for Lena.

It was cool in the entrance hall, for the slaves had left the front doors wide open, and a breeze swept across the polished stone floors and up the long stairs. Perhaps Lena had gone to her room for a moment's quiet. As he passed his father's office on the way to the stairs, he heard voices and stopped. The office door was not quite closed, and he could clearly hear his mother.

'I won't agree to it, Egan,' she was saying, her voice raised in anger. 'I've just lost my husband. I'm not going to lose my eldest son as well.'

Gabriel halted just outside the door, his breath caught in his throat.

'You won't be losing him,' said Egan, quietly, reasonably. 'You can visit him whenever you like. It's the only way, Lena. The boy's spoiled. If you don't do this for him, he'll never amount to anything. He's already made a total disgrace of himself.'

'No, he hasn't! He didn't forget those words today. He chose not to say them. He couldn't say them and mean it. He was being honest, and even Jager wouldn't blame him for that. You don't know what Jager was like, always putting him down, never –'

'Jager was a hard man, I know, but he was also fair. If he put Gabriel down, it was because the boy had already let himself down, was already a grief and a disappointment. Today's shameful exhibition wasn't the first. What about all the other times he failed – the times his father wanted him to study commerce and navigation at school, and he refused. Or else he failed the exams deliberately. Gabriel's got a good brain in him – he must have, he's Jager's son – but he's self-willed and defiant and aimless. What's he going to do with his life – play around with plants and microscopes, and read books all day?'

'He doesn't play around. He passed exams with honours, in biology and anatomy,' said Lena. 'His tutors say he's gifted in certain –'

'Gifted? The only gift he's got is his inheritance, which is in grave danger of being thrown away. He's not wasting his life on biology. He's got a great vocation ahead of him, and he has to take it. There are twenty ships out there owned now by him, and he has to learn to manage them. There are trade centres in major ports all over the Empire, all his now. Until he's old enough, Jager's shipmasters will carry on, but the time's going to come when the business has to be taken over by someone in the family. That has to be Gabriel. And if he's not properly trained for it, he'll throw away everything his father ever built up. I won't stand by and watch that happen. Jager broke his heart over that boy. He often said the only disappointment in his life was his eldest son. He was going to send Gabriel to the Academy this year to study business and navigation, in a last attempt to make a decent son of him. I'll see that wish is carried out.'

'What about Gabriel?' cried Lena. 'What about his wishes?'

'Has he got any?'

'I don't know. I don't know what he wants. But I do know he doesn't want to take over the family business.'

'Every other lad in Navora would give anything to have what Gabriel's got. He's going to be grateful for it, Lena, if I have to beat it into him. If he stays here, you'll spoil him. He's coming to live with me, and I'll see that he studies the right things at the Academy and is fit to inherit everything his father left to him.'

'What about Myron? Or one of the others?'

'Myron wants to join the army, you know that as well as I do. The others are too young; too many years lie between now and when they would be qualified. The family business goes to the eldest son, Lena. You're not selling it.'

'I don't think it's any concern of yours.'

'Damn it, it *is* my concern! I loved my brother, Lena. When we were boys together, he used to say he would own a fleet of ships and travel all over the Empire to bring back riches to make Navora great. He sweated blood to make that dream reality. I won't stand by now and watch you sell it to some greedy investor in a foreign country, who doesn't give a damn about Navora. I won't let you sell it because a spunkless brat cares nothing about shaming his family name and his father. If you won't knock sense into him, I will.'

There was silence, and Gabriel heard heavy footsteps crossing the room towards the door. He fled, taking the stairs three at a time. In his room he slammed shut the door and crouched against it, breathing hard, fighting back tears of helplessness and hate and rage.

A long time he stayed there, dreading the sound of footsteps. But none came, and after a while he crossed the room and sat in the sun on the window seat. He reached up and removed something he wore on a leather thong around his neck. It was the Shinali amulet.

He sat and looked at it, his body tense, his hand shaking. He still suffered guilt for not helping the Shinali woman that awful night; yet in the tranquil beauty of the bone carving that had been hers, and in the Shinali dreams that haunted him, he found a kind of forgiveness, a peace. Sunlight slanted across his palm, turning the alien bone to gold. It shone against his skin, he could have sworn the light came from within the bone, and it was warm, warmer than the sun could make it in these moments. He closed his fingers around the carving and leaned back, his eyes shut, conscious of the sun soaking deeply into him. For a few glorious moments he forgot the discord downstairs, forgot everything but the warmth and the quiet and the indescribable calm that lay within his hand. It was a peace beyond his understanding, beyond suffering and regret and guilt; an inexplicable gift reconciling him with a woman, a people he did not know; a gift he embraced with all his soul, without knowing why.

Images, sensations floated like half-forgotten memories in his mind: a great plain, dazzling under the sun; the scent of summer grass, heady and sweet; a sense of lying in it, his face against the sun-beaten earth, the heat soaking into his body. Wood smoke drifting across the ground, and the bleating of sheep. The inside of a house, the roof thatched with grass, and smoke rising through a central hole. And peace, peace so awesome and profound it almost had the power to wipe away his pain.

He felt as though he were outside time, lost elsewhere in a world between reality and dream where strange memories drifted, became briefly his, and vanished again. It frightened him, yet at the same time drew him, gave him joy, made him complete. Dozing, he dreamed of a dim Navoran house, of long passages with dark, locked doors. The passages became a great maze, bewildering and frightening. Desperate, lost, he searched for a door that would open. But they all remained closed. From behind some came sounds: human voices, sails snapping in the wind, and the thunder of the sea. Despairing, he ran on. At last he came to a golden door. As he pushed it open, light flooded over him. Suspended in the brightness were things he loved: books on anatomy, the microscope his father had brought back from a far land, the faded charts illustrating the human heart and organs, and healing plants. He saw hands moving over human skin, the movements quick and sure. The fingers held a needle, were sewing up a wound. His hands? The images blurred, changed. Hands binding cloth around a wounded arm. The pungent odour of ointments, the cloth stained with juice of leaves and roots. He had a feeling he knew what they were, knew exactly what was being done. Wood smoke again, and a knife, its blade shimmering with heat, held above a deep cut. Blood everywhere. The blade plunged deep, the smell of human flesh searing –

With a jolt, he awoke. There were footsteps on the stairs, on the carpeted floor outside. His door burst open, and Myron came in.

'Mother wants you,' said Myron.

Gabriel blinked at him. 'What?'

'Mother wants you. She's been arguing with Uncle Egan. I didn't know she had so much spit and fire in her. All the guests have left, except for our uncles. Mother thought you'd gone with us. Uncle Egan's been waiting for us to get back, so he can see you.'

Gabriel glanced at the window and saw that it was sunset. He stared at Myron, and noticed that his brother's curls, long and red-gold like his own, were damp, and that he had grass stains on his white sleeves. 'Where have you been?' he asked.

'Swimming in the river, with our cousins. I came to ask you if you'd go with us, but you were asleep and I didn't want to disturb you. Are you all right? You've been up here for hours. You're not sick, are you?'

'No. I'm fine.'

Myron noticed the Shinali bone in Gabriel's hand, and picked it up. It was familiar to him; he had often seen Gabriel with it, and he was the only one to whom Gabriel had told the story of that awful night. Frowning now, Myron turned the carving to the day's last light, stared at it hard for a few moments, then studied Gabriel's face. 'I've just noticed something,' Myron said. 'This face on the bone . . . it looks like yours.'

'Your imagination's almost as good as mine,' said Gabriel, taking the bone back and putting it around his neck again.

There were footsteps on the stairs, and little Subin came in. 'Uncle Egan wants to see you,' she announced to Gabriel in imperious tones. 'Right now. And Mama says you've got to get me and the others ready for bed, Myron.'

Gabriel sighed and stood up.

'Good luck, brother,' said Myron, and together they held up their right hands in the sign of the courageous bull.

In the dining room, slaves were clearing away the remains of the funeral feast. Discarded cushions, bright against the polished stone floor, were still scattered around the low table. Lamplight cast a rosy glow across the half-emptied bottles of wine and the remaining goblets. Egan and three of the other uncles were at one end of the table, reclining on the cushions, talking. Lena was standing by the door to the courtyard, her back to the men, looking out at the silver-blue twilight. As Gabriel entered, she turned around. She looked remarkably cool for someone in the middle of a family dispute. Calmly she picked up two cushions and placed them at the end of the table opposite the uncles. 'Sit down, Gabriel,' she said, her voice gentle. 'Would you like a glass of wine?'

It was the first time she had offered him alcohol, and he

nodded as he sat down, though his stomach churned. It occurred to him that he had missed his father's funeral feast: another unpardonable offence.

One of the slaves placed a glass of wine in front of him. It was gold-painted glass from Amaran, brought back by his father on one of his first voyages, and worth a fortune. Still half in his dreams, Gabriel had a disturbing feeling of incongruity, as if the priceless glass were out of place, and instead there should be a pottery bowl, simple and unpolished. He shook the feeling off and glanced down the table towards his uncles. They looked severe in their dark funeral clothes, their usual jewels left off today, their long hair tied back, making their faces seem more angular than ever. All were intimidating men, tall and impressive like Gabriel's father, with the same severe look and irascible temperament. Only Egan had red hair and blue eyes, like Jager's, the rest were swarthy and brown-eyed. As Gabriel sat opposite them, he felt alienated, insignificant. He marvelled that his mother, who had never opposed his father, could defy these brothers and yet look poised.

'Do you wish to explain today's performance, Gabriel?' Egan asked, in heavy tones.

Gabriel shook his head and sipped his wine. To his surprise, it was delicious. He gulped the lot and felt Lena touch his arm. He looked at her, and she smiled with her eyes and shook her head slightly. A slave refilled his glass, and he decided to leave it for fortification later in the battle.

'What I can't understand,' said Egan, 'is how you could forget the most important address of your life – your homage to your dead father.'

'I didn't forget it,' said Gabriel.

'Do you care to explain, son?'

'No. And I'm not your son.'

The uncles muttered, and Gabriel reached for his wineglass. Lena put her hand on his arm, checking him. 'Answer them, dear,' she said. 'They'll never let it go otherwise.'

'It's none of their business,' Gabriel whispered, too loudly.

'It is our business,' said Egan. 'As Jager's eldest brother, I'm responsible for you now. If you stay here with your mother, you'll end up a discredit to your whole family. You need discipline. Today was the last time you'll ever dishonour your family name and cause your mother shame. You're coming to live with me. You'll go to the Academy and study navigation, seamanship and geography. When you're eighteen, you'll accompany me on one of your father's ships, and start learning everything you need to know to take over the family business. By the time you're twenty, you'll be man enough to do it on your own. Go and pack whatever you need. We're leaving tonight.'

'We'll hear what Gabriel wants,' Lena said. 'If he doesn't agree to this, I'm not forcing him to go.'

'Do you know what you want, Gabriel?' asked Egan, his lips curling derisively. 'Have you any idea at all what you want – which illustrious enterprise you want to spend that great inheritance on? Tell me, Gabriel. What noble dreams smoulder behind that rebellious look? What deserving ambitions? Name me one. Just one worthwhile goal. Or else go and pack your things.'

Trembling, Gabriel stood up. He did not know whether it was the wine or the afternoon's strange visions, but he felt suddenly more sure and at peace with himself than he had ever felt in his life. He thought of the dream with all its closed doors, and the one that alone stood open.

'I do know what I want,' he said, lifting his chin and looking straight at them. 'I want to help people.'

'God forbid!' cried Egan, mockingly. '*You,* help people? What'll you do – give away your inheritance to the poor? Open a home for the impoverished? Buy a bakery for beggars?'

'Hear him out,' said Lena quietly. 'You asked Gabriel what he wanted, and he's telling you.'

Gabriel stood very tall and still, his face radiant in the lamplight. The dream, the hands, the heated knife, the torn flesh sealed and healed and restored, filled his heart. He was so sure, so fiercely resolute, the uncles dared not laugh, though his next words astounded them.

'I'm going to be a healer,' he said.

ꝺ Preparation

THE PATIENTS LAY on their narrow beds and waved their hands languidly at the flies. It was unbearably hot, and most of the sick had kicked off the sheets that covered them. Some lay naked, uncaring, wishing someone would draw the curtains over the wide windows, to block out the infernal sun. Others groaned with pain or called for water. Nursing help was voluntary, and rare; the sick were washed and fed by their families. Relatives also supplied the bedding, which was seldom washed; infected wounds were common, and diseases spread easily. Medicines, bought with temple donations, were in short supply.

The ward was the only one in a small infirmary attached to the Academy of Navora, where the city's destitute were treated free. The physicians were the teachers of healing and their students. The hospital was hopelessly short-staffed, and there were beds only for the desperately ill. Men, women, and children lay adjacent to one another, and the only people with privacy were those with infectious diseases, isolated behind curtains at the far end of the ward. Only the tutors and senior students entered that isolation area, because of the danger of bulai fever. This plague raged through the city every six or seven years, killing everyone who caught it, each time wiping out a third or more of the population. Six years had passed since the time the fever had last struck, and everyone was wary.

A group of people entered the ward, and heads lifted from

damp pillows as patients looked hopefully in their direction, longing for the water-bearer or visitors. The newcomers were the students of medicine and their tutor of surgery, a short, balding man called Hevron. The students were excited today, as it was the Empress's birthday and they were looking forward to the celebrations in the city that night. The atmosphere of the ward suddenly changed as the young people passed between the beds, their clothes vivid whenever the shafts of sunlight fell across them. They went to the far end of the ward, where they were each given a pouch of medical instruments, and instructions from their tutor. It was simple work, for they were first-year students; they were to change dressings, lance boils, or remove stitches from those surgical patients whose wounds were now healed. They were each given the names of several patients and told to call the tutor if they were unsure about anything.

From their beds the patients watched, hoping for the more gentle students to be assigned to them. Most of them hoped for the youth with unruly red-gold hair and brilliant blue eyes, but he was assigned to only one patient, an elderly woman in need of a great deal of care. She was a tiny person, ugly and cantankerous and tough, and known simply as Edyth. She had been attacked one night and slashed several times about her head and upper body. When she saw that it was Gabriel who was to remove her stitches, she cackled triumphantly at the people in the other beds, and made a rude gesture to them with her left hand. It was bandaged, but not as thickly as her right hand, which was covered to the wrist and oozing blood.

Gabriel put a clean cloth on the edge of the bed, set out the instruments, and examined the cuts on the woman's face. They were well healed, and the long rows of stitches were ready to be removed.

'Are your hands still painful?' Gabriel asked, carefully wiping her face with a dampened cloth smelling strongly of antiseptic herbs.

'No,' she lied. Her hands had been badly cut as she had tried to defend herself, the fingers almost severed.

'Hevron will come and have a look at them later,' Gabriel said. He added, gently, 'Are you sure you wouldn't like something for the pain, Mother?' He used the term of respect usually reserved for elderly women of the aristocracy, and Edyth chuckled at the title, hugely amused in spite of her agony.

'I can bear a bit of hurt,' she said. 'Don't stand there frowning like that. I might get the idea you're worried about me. Are you here to take the sewing out of my face, or to watch me die of old age?'

Gabriel picked up the scissors. The old woman relaxed back on the rolled blanket that served for a pillow and watched the youth's face as he removed the sutures from her cheeks and jaw. He had an expressive face, forthright and honest, with a strong, well-defined brow, slightly aquiline nose, and decisive mouth. She guessed, correctly, that he was eighteen years old. He felt her watching him, and for a second his eyes flicked from his work, and his gaze met hers. His eyes were translucent, intense, almost unsettling. Very slightly he smiled, then was absorbed in his work again, his fingers quick and light as moths on her skin. Her skin was damp, her sweat rank against his nostrils. She had no family to care for her, and she had not been washed since the night she was brought in, ten days ago. She could walk to the latrine, but her bed was stained from sweat and blood. Her own clothes had been burned, and she wore a grey shift donated by the priestesses of charity at the temple. Even the shift was dirty now, stained from soup she had not managed to drink properly without help. Half her teeth were decayed, and her breath was repellent. Gabriel fought nausea as he leaned close to remove the more difficult stitches, though he never betrayed it.

'How are you going to manage when you get out of here?' he asked.

'As I always have,' she replied sharply. 'By my wits.'

'Where do you live?'

'At the palace.'

He grinned. 'I've heard that silk sheets aren't very warm on cool nights,' he said. 'I'll get you some blankets. When did you last have a proper meal?'

'Not since I've been in this torture-house. The Empress doesn't realise I'm here, I think.'

'I'll bring you some food, too, later on today. And I'll give you a wash, and change your bed.'

'Do you feed and wash all the crones who come in here, that you feel sorry for?'

'Only the beautiful ones.'

Unexpectedly she laughed, and he almost nicked her skin with his scissors. 'You'd better keep still,' he warned.

'I'm glad you appreciate true beauty when you see it,' she said, still cackling. 'Princess of the rubbish pits, that's what they call me.'

'Why?'

'That's where I live – when I'm not at the palace, of course. It's amazing what you find there, what other people call rubbish.'

'Food, you mean?'

'That, and other treasures. I find them and sell them.'

'That's how you live?'

'I make a few hanas, enough to eat once in a while.'

'Is that why you were attacked? You'd found something of worth?'

'You could say that. A cup. I'd found a cup, only one little crack in it. The boys decided they wanted it.'

'You suffered all this, for one cracked cup?'

'It was a lovely cup.'

He bent his head low again, concentrating on the stitches around her eye. The ones nearest the lid he left for Hevron to remove. While he worked, Edyth peered at his clothes, searching for jewels or signs of affluence. She noted the simple brown thigh-length tunic and the white shirt with its flowing sleeves and cuffs neatly edged with blue. He wore no rings, and there was no money bag attached to his wide belt, only a small knife in an embossed leather sheath. The handle was metal set with a dark green stone. If the stone was a real gem, it was the only sign of wealth. His trousers were a lighter brown, homespun of fine wool. He looked plain compared to his colleagues.

'Have you got a rich relative paying for your training here?' Edyth asked.

'You're a nosy old crone, aren't you?' he said amicably.

'Just curious. You're not stuck-up like the others. If you have got it, you don't flaunt it.'

They did not speak again for a while, and the only sounds were the snip of the scissors as Gabriel cut the silken threads, the droning of the flies above the beds, and the murmuring of other voices in the ward. Suddenly the voices stopped. Even the patients stopped talking. Then Gabriel heard Hevron hurrying to the door of the ward, heard him say, with a graciousness and warmth never used with his students, 'Greetings, Grand Master! Greetings! What an honour, to have you here!' He was obviously bowing low, for his next words were muffled. For the first time

Gabriel halted in his work. Straightening his back, he turned and looked where every person in the ward was looking.

In the doorway, resplendent in his crimson, gold, and white robes, stood one of the Masters from the Citadel. Hevron finished paying homage, and the Master shook his hand in the Navoran way and spoke to him. For several minutes they talked, their voices hushed, and the students slowly returned to their work.

Gabriel's fingers trembled slightly against Edyth's cheek, and his face was flushed. 'Has he come to see you?' Edyth asked, eyeing him shrewdly.

'No. He's here to tell Hevron who's been chosen to study at the Citadel. They pick only the best students from the top universities in the Empire. It must be someone from here, this year. That man is Salverion, the Grand Master of Healing. He's the greatest healer in the Empire. They say he can stop pain just by moving his hands over a person, that he can even do major surgery, and his patients feel nothing. He teaches that skill to his disciples at the Citadel. I'd give everything to be one of them.'

'Hevron says you're his best student. I heard him discussing you with one of the other tutors.'

'Hevron's always telling me I'm too soft. You must have been mistaken.'

'I may be half blind and beautiful, but I'm not deaf.'

Gabriel continued working in silence, acutely aware of the great healer at the other end of the ward. With all his heart he wished he could meet him. He stole another glance behind him and realised that the Grand Master had gone. Sighing, he turned to Edyth again, and began taking another row of stiches from her cheek. Shortly Hevron arrived, and watched in silence as Gabriel finished his task. Then the youth stepped aside, and the tutor unbandaged the wounded hands. The bandages were foul with green pus, and stank. When the hands were revealed Gabriel stepped back, unable to conceal his horror.

Hevron examined the hands carefully, then said, with compassion and regret, 'I'm afraid we have to amputate, Edyth. Gangrene has set in. It will spread, unless it's totally removed. If it's not dealt with now, eventually you'll lose your arms and suffer a lot more pain than you're in now. I'll remove just the three affected fingers on your left hand. As for your right . . . Well, I'm sorry, but that will have to come off at the wrist.'

'When are you going to do it?' asked Edyth in a flat voice, her face expressionless.

'We'll give you something for the pain, and do it in an hour,' said Hevron.

'Will Gabriel help?'

'Naturally. He's my best assistant, and we'll be as quick as possible. Bring a strong decoction of valerian, Gabriel, and give it to her. Stay with her till it takes effect, then come and get me.'

They both left, and Edyth lay back, her eyes closed, her dour face more twisted than ever in her efforts not to weep. Shortly Gabriel returned. With infinite gentleness he lifted her head and pressed a goblet to her lips, but she grumbled and spat as the bitter potion went down her throat, and she cursed him as he lay her down again.

'No wonder half your patients die,' she growled, 'when you give them that kind of muck to drink.'

'You're not going to die, Edyth.'

'Might as well. Can't earn my keep, with no hands.' She turned her face away and told him in coarse language to leave. He stayed where he was, smoothing back her hair and stroking the agonised furrows on her brow. She felt him slip something beneath her blanket.

'I hope that's not money,' she hissed. 'I don't want your pity.'

'It's my knife.'

'How thoughtful. I'll be able to slit my throat.'

'It's to sell. The handle is silver, and the stone an emerald. It's antique, very valuable, so don't let anyone offer you less than a thousand hasaries for it. You'll be able to rent a room somewhere, and have enough for food for a few months. You might find someone to share the room – free rent, in return for looking after you.'

'Damned fool,' she muttered, weeping at last. 'More money than sense.'

'You're probably right,' he said, smiling.

It was late in the afternoon when Gabriel went home. The day was still hot, and he walked slowly. Suddenly he remembered that Hevron had wanted to see him again, but he had forgotten in the busyness of comforting Edyth after her ordeal, and washing her, and giving her some broth. It was too late now to visit the tutor, so Gabriel resolved to see him first thing in the morning.

The marketplace was still busy, and Gabriel wished he had some money for an apple or a drink. It was a colourful place, bright with red and gold awnings stretched over the stalls. Flags and ribbons, stained with yellow dust, fluttered in the warm puffs that occasionally swept down the humid street. The air was rich with aromas of hot baked bread, sweet pies, and fruit and vegetables fresh from the gardens outside the city. Less appealing was the stench of rotting oyster shells carried in by the breeze from the beach, and the human sweat from the milling throng. Beggars limped among the shoppers, and small thieves darted close to the wealthier customers, looking for loosely tied money bags. Buyers and sellers shouted as they bargained, and live chickens squawked from bamboo cages. Priests went about selling tiny marble replicas of the new Navoran temple, chanting blessings for any who would buy.

Leaving the tumult of the market sector, Gabriel went up a lane to the business area. Here the streets were narrow, the buildings high and close, blocking out the sun. In spite of the shade, the air was stifling. Climbing a flight of wide, ancient steps to an upper street, he came to the crest of a hill. Looking across the rooftops he saw the sea far below, stained brown where the city's sewage and the River Cravan entered the harbour. A steady breeze blew in, rank with the smell from the beach. A ship was leaving, its yellow sails painted with the Empire's symbol of the red horse.

Gabriel thought of his father, and the old regret ached in his heart. It was four years since that momentous day of Jager's funeral, and the loss of him, the loss of the possibility of ever receiving love from him, still hurt. Shutting the pain away, Gabriel left the old business area of the city. As he crossed the city square in front of the marble temple, he passed a colossal golden statue of the Empress Petra. The statue and the city square were new, recently built by the Empress as her eternal gift to the Empire. Not protesting that taxes had been raised to meet the cost of the so-called gift, the city's prosperous came here every day to recite prayers and to leave offerings in the money urns. They were here now in crowds, to celebrate her birthday. Pressing through the throngs, Gabriel came at last to the grand streets of his own neighbourhood. At his home the gates were open and his seven-year-old sister, Subin, waited between them, crouching down with her arms around her knees. She leaped up when she saw him coming and raced to meet him, waving frantically.

'There's a man here to see you!' she cried. 'He's got a letter for you. It's got a blue seal and a green ribbon around it, and he wants to give it to you his own self.'

'He's probably from the lawyer's office, with something about my inheritance,' he said, picking her up and carrying her over his shoulder. Giggling, she tried to talk while he jogged through the gateway and across the courtyard to the front door.

'Mama gave him a glass of wine. Father's best. He's waited a long time.'

'I wish I'd got home sooner,' Gabriel remarked, setting her down unceremoniously on a cushioned seat between the stone pillars, and sitting beside her to remove his shoes. 'What does he look like?'

'Old.'

'Any more useful details?'

'He's got a mole on his eyelid.'

'That narrows the field. It's not one of the lawyers.'

He went inside, and the house enveloped him in shadows, wonderfully cool.

'They're upstairs,' said Subin, skipping behind him.

He hurried up the stairs, feeling his shirt wet under the wide belt, and he decided to visit the city baths later. His mother waited in the hallway at the top of the stairs, in the small alcove with the window overlooking the sea. She wore a simple long green dress with a gold sash and looked cool and tranquil, but he noticed that her hands were clasped tightly together in front of her, and her fingers were tense. In one of the carved chairs beside a small table sat the visitor.

Before he looked at the man's face, Gabriel saw the long crimson robe with its rich gold-embroidered hem and the white tunic embroidered with seven silver stars, sign of the Citadel.

4 THE CALLING

SPEECHLESS WITH ASTONISHMENT, Gabriel bowed low. 'Greetings, Grand Master,' he managed to say at last, wishing his voice were steadier. Raising his head, he looked into Salverion's face. He saw eyes steel-grey and discerning, yet full of gentleness and affection, and a smile that enveloped him like a warmth. It was impossible to judge Salverion's age. His hairline was receding, and his waving hair was white, yet his face was almost without lines. Gabriel noticed a small mole on his right eyelid and another on his clean-shaven chin.

'Greetings, Master,' he said again, flushing scarlet, guilty for staring too long.

'I'm sorry if my visit is a shock to you,' said Salverion softly. 'I did ask your tutor, Hevron, to tell you to expect me. Did he not mention it?'

'He told me to see him before I came home, but I . . . I'm afraid I forgot, Master. I'm sorry.'

Salverion smiled again. 'I wanted to deliver this to you myself,' he said, handing Gabriel a small scroll.

Gabriel's fingers shook as he undid the ribbon and broke the blue wax seal, imprinted with the seven stars. He unrolled the parchment and read it, unaware of Subin leaping about him or of his mother telling the child to be still. Three times he read it. When he looked up his face was a shade deeper, and he looked confused. 'I think there's been a mistake, Master,' he said.

'No mistake,' said Salverion. 'Read the letter aloud, my son, so your mother knows what is in it.'

In a voice still shaking with disbelief, Gabriel read the words.

To Gabriel Eshban Vala: Greetings.

The Grand Masters of the Citadel have elected you to join the priesthood of those who search for the highest in wisdom, understanding, and truth. Should you agree to join us, you will take the Healer Vows, and study all the arts in that calling. We exhort you to think on this matter with great carefulness and prayer, being fully aware of all your gifts and obligations. Your commitment to us would be absolute, for the term of seven years. Should you decide you cannot make this pledge, we will understand.

May God shelter you in all peace.
Salverion Shon Avilah,
Grand Master of Healing.

For a while there was total silence. Then Subin whispered to her mother, 'Is he going away with that man?'

'I don't know, dear,' said Lena softly, hugging the child and smoothing her auburn curls. 'I don't know. Gabriel has a lot to think about, and he and the Grand Master must have a lot to discuss.' Firmly taking Subin's hand, Lena bowed to Salverion. 'Would you like me to bring you more wine, lord?' she asked.

'No, thank you. But it's excellent wine, and I enjoyed it.'

'We'll leave you to talk.' She bowed again and left.

Gabriel and Salverion heard them going down the stairs, and Subin's voice, piping and loud, asking, 'Why was that funny old man wearing a dress?'

Gabriel covered his face with his hand, embarrassed, but the

Grand Master chuckled. 'The refreshing honesty of children,' he said. 'Please sit down, Gabriel, and relax. I'm here as a friend.' When Gabriel was seated, Salverion continued. 'Please know that you are not obliged in any way to accept our offer, and that if you decide against it, no one will think any less of you or dispute your decision. The commitment we demand is total, and seven years a long time. You have tonight and tomorrow morning to think about it.'

'I don't need time to think, Master,' said Gabriel.

'I would like you to take the time, anyway. If you decide not to come, send me a message by noon tomorrow. If I don't receive a message, I shall send a chariot for you at nightfall. There are certain things you need to know, before you make your decision. Perhaps you have heard of the kind of healing we do?'

'I know you have the skills to wipe out pain, Master.'

'That is true. We work in the regions of the human mind and spirit, as well as in surgery and medicine. That's why the training in the Citadel is a sacred calling, and our disciples are healer-priests bound by laws of secrecy and honour.'

'The letter you gave me mentioned vows, Master,' said Gabriel. 'Would the vows apply only during my training at the Citadel?'

'The vows are for life. You would always be a healer-priest, so long as the wisdom was imprinted on your mind.'

'I could never marry, then?'

'We would never demand that no one marry, only that during the seven years of training their time remains consecrated wholly to learning, and that their first loyalty is always to us. Why, my son? Are you betrothed, or wishing to be?'

'No. There's no one. Only my family.'

'You'll be able to keep in touch with them by letter. I'm afraid you may visit them only under special circumstances. No one may visit you; outsiders are forbidden to the Citadel. There is not a great deal I may tell you, unless you do join us, but are there any other questions you would like to ask?'

'I can't think of any right now, Master. My mind's a bit scrambled, I'm afraid. This is the last thing on earth I expected.'

'God often gives us the things we least expect, my son. Sometimes I think he delights in surprising us.' Salverion stood up, and Gabriel walked with him out to the gate, where a chariot waited. To Gabriel's surprise, the Grand Master embraced him warmly as he said goodbye. Then he was gone, his chariot rattling on the cobblestones, the seven silver stars on the sides of the chariot burning in the rosy sun. Gabriel watched until it vanished around a corner in the street, then he went back inside.

From the kitchen doorway the slaves peered at him, wide-eyed with curiosity and awe. Then bedlam broke loose as Subin and his youngest brothers came stampeding down the stairs, shrieking his name and a dozen questions. Above them stood Lena, very still and calm, her face shining with tears of wonderment and pride.

The streets were deserted, since most people had already begun their feast. The Empress's birthday coincided with the Festival of Plenty, and the citizens celebrated both events in a frenzy of overindulgence. They would eat until midnight, then surge out into the streets for the festivities. There would be musicians, dancers, magicians, and street performers; vendors selling pastries and sweets, and stalls giving away free wine from the palace. Heavily guarded, the Empress would come and walk down the main avenues. The people would go wild. But for now the city was peaceful, waiting, while the people feasted.

*

Hurrying through the sector of the city where only the elite lived, Gabriel headed in the direction of the west city wall. He loved running on the wall in the evening; the sea breeze was always cool and exhilarating, the solitude guaranteed. Few people ran in Navora; most exercised, as Myron did, in the city gymnasium.

The city walls were ancient, built in the early days when Navora was only a small town defending itself against the marauding barbarians from the hills. The renowned Navoran army had tamed most of the barbarians by now, and parts of the walls were falling into ruin, but on this seaward side the walls were intact, wide, and safe enough to run on in good weather. The north wall, facing inland, had been partly pulled down to make way for the expanding city, its stones used to build the aqueduct that carried water to Navora from the upper part of the River Cravan, before it became contaminated with the city waste. Beneath the aqueduct were the houses and slum areas, spilling over the arid ground towards the hills. Eastward, beyond the hills, was the plain where the Shinali people lived. They were the most peaceful of the native tribes, and eleven years ago had signed a treaty with the Empire. Though the treaty held strong, there were few dealings between the barbarians and the Navorans. Only the army went through Shinali land, on its long marches to settle trouble in far provinces, or to subdue hostile tribes and bring back new supplies of slaves. But on the highest hill overlooking those grasslands, standing between the barbarians and the capital of the mighty Navoran Empire, was the Citadel.

It filled Gabriel's thoughts as he ran. Often he had gazed at its shining walls, a hopeless yearning in his heart to learn what was taught there – the remarkable methods of healing, the skills that banished pain. Now they were within his reach.

Breathing hard, he stopped halfway along the coastal wall and looked down at the cliffs plunging steeply to the sea. Far to his left were the towers and ramparts of the palace, with banners flying. The palace stood on the south-west corner of the city, on a rocky point of land safeguarded by impregnable cliffs. Looking out to sea, his eyes narrowed against the light, Gabriel watched the sun go down. The evening was glorious, its peace approaching holiness.

Gabriel raised his arms and spoke the famous Navoran prayer, recited since he was a child, but spoken now with deepest significance: 'Sovereign Lord, give me wisdom to know your dream for me. Give me courage to live that dream. Give me strength to fulfil the task before me, knowing it was designed for me alone. Give me peace in the knowledge that I have been given everything I need. So that what I do has value in your sight, give me love. Make me a worthy son of Navora.'

He lowered his arms, and for a long time stood on the sea wall staring at the ocean, unaware of it, or of the moonlit night, or the glittering, turbulent city behind him. A hundred different emotions swept through him, indescribable joy alternating in moments with uncertainty and fear. Behind him in the great city the celebrations had begun. Suddenly someone slapped his shoulder, and he turned to see Myron.

'I heard the news,' said Myron. He looked strained, his expression a mixture of gladness and pain. Then he and Gabriel were embracing, hugging each other hard. 'Oh, brother! I'm so proud of you!' cried Myron. 'I can hardly believe it – you, an Elected One!'

'I can hardly believe it, either. I'm scared, Myron. I'm half drunk with joy, but I'm scared, too.'

'You'll be all right. You'll love it there. They say the Citadel is the most beautiful place, far better even than the palace. You'll have the best tutors, the most gifted people in the Empire for company.'

'But they won't love me like a brother,' said Gabriel, hugging him again. 'You'll write to me, won't you?'

'You're not going to prison,' said Myron, trying to sound cheerful. 'There are bound to be times when we can see each other. The healers from the Citadel often visit the city to treat the aristocracy. I bet by this time next year you'll have felt the pulses of all the prominent women in Navora. More than their pulses, probably. I could be envious.'

'No need to be,' said Gabriel, releasing him. 'You know what the pampered rich are like. I'd rather give my services to the poor.'

'It's a bit late to decide that. You're more likely to end up being private physician to the Empress herself.'

They fell silent, listening to the sound of the sea booming on the rocks far below, and the clamour in the city streets. In the skies behind them fireworks exploded, and the colours flashed across the steel scabbard of Myron's sword. He wore it whenever he was in the streets and knew well how to use it. He trained every afternoon in the Navoran gymnasium. In the moonlight his face, like Gabriel's, was strong and resolute, with that almost fierce expression they had inherited from their father. They looked very alike; even their hair was the same, long and coppery and curling. They could have passed as twins, except that Gabriel was taller and of a slighter build.

Walking back along the wide summit of the wall and down a flight of steep steps, they entered the crowded streets. They jostled their way through, avoiding the vendors who tried to sell to them, and the wild whirling of the performing dancers. In one square, experts were dancing the Navoran fire-dance, men and women in pairs, taunting one another with flaming torches. At times the dance was frenzied and impassioned, at times slow and enticing. The brothers watched, fascinated, then moved on, struggling through the crowds.

Suddenly a great cry went up: 'The Empress! Long live the Empress!' The people rushed about, shrieking, working themselves into hysteria. Temple bells, brassy and echoing, pealed out across the uproar.

Swept helplessly in the throng, the brothers found themselves in one of the major streets of the city. Torches blazed on walls, and flowers hung in garlands across the roadway and from every terrace and window ledge. Palace guards and soldiers lined the road, at times beating back the revellers with the flats of naked swords. Watchful bowmen stood on balconies and in upper windows, their bows ready and fitted with arrows.

Almost crushed in the crowd, clinging to Myron's sleeve, Gabriel could barely see the procession as it came. But he heard the music, the singing of the slaves, and the roar of the crowd sweeping towards him like a wave as the Empress approached. Then he saw her, lifted high on a golden chair with a purple canopy, her robes pure white and her face aglow in the lamplight. Only a moment he saw her, before she was borne away, but it was long enough to fill his heart with joy, with the reverence that there, before him, was the epitome of everything Navoran – of everything that was highest and best in the world. A huge pride went through him and he wept, overcome by the thought that tomorrow she would hear his name and know that he, out of all the sons in her Empire, was chosen to study medicine at the great Citadel. He passed his hand over his eyes, but not before Myron saw his emotion and gave his shoulders an understanding squeeze. Then, silent, they returned home, Myron's hand on the hilt of his sword.

The atmosphere at the next evening meal was a strange mixture of gaiety and sadness. Little Subin wept constantly, convinced she would never see her oldest brother again. Myron was his usual stalwart self, teasing the younger ones, and entertaining the family with the latest gossip from the gymnasium. Every now and again he looked at Gabriel, his eyes full of affection and pride. The others did not fully comprehend the magnitude of the honour given to Gabriel and were more concerned with the hurt of losing him, and the fact that he would no longer be able to take them fishing in the Cravan or sailing in the harbour. They joked and argued as they always did at mealtimes, but there was a sadness underlying the talk. Lena did her best to keep the conversation light and cheerful, but she, too, dreaded the sound of the Citadel chariot outside the gates, and the call of the slave to tell Gabriel it was time to go.

Gabriel ate little but spent most of the time looking at the faces around the table, loving them, imprinting them perfectly on his memory. In seven years they would all be changed, perhaps beyond recognition. Subin would be fourteen, a young woman almost old enough to be betrothed. The child next to her, Jayd, would be as old as Gabriel was now, an apprentice to a carpenter, unless he changed his ambitions. The next two brothers, Darien and Imri, thirteen and fourteen now, would be working. The oyster business would have collapsed totally by then, so they would probably have their own farms, since they shared their mother's love of the country. No doubt they would be married, too, with children. And Myron . . .

As he looked at Myron, an awful foreboding went through him. Myron looked up and caught his gaze. 'What are you thinking, brother?' asked Myron, smiling. 'Thinking how much more peaceful life's going to be at the Citadel?'

Gabriel fought to put the fears aside, to make his voice normal. 'I'm thinking how strange it'll be, coming back,' he said. 'Some of you won't be here. You'll be married.'

'Maybe none of us will be here,' said Lena. 'We might be living in the country. The Shinali are selling some of their plain, and we're buying it for vegetable gardens and farms. If we grew our own wheat and barley, we wouldn't have to import it. We need more wool, too; the sheep farmers up the coast can hardly supply us with enough any more. I wouldn't mind being a sheep farmer.'

'If you sell this house, there'll be another argument with the uncles,' warned Gabriel. 'There was enough strife when you sold the family business – especially when you used some of the money to pay my tutors' fees at the Academy. This house is the last property left that was Father's. Are you sure you want the uncles up in arms again?'

'Actually, I rather enjoyed the fighting,' said Lena, a spark of lively defiance in her eyes. 'I've spent all my life pleasing everyone but myself. It's time for my dreams, now. And it was worth the strife, wasn't it? Worth the war with the uncles, to see you tonight – an Elected One going to the Citadel. And it would be worth fighting them again, to live in the country. I've always wanted to do that, ever since Jager sold the oyster business.'

'Farming's boring!' cried Jayd, and there was a noisy argument about the virtues and drawbacks of country life. In the middle of it a slave came in, bowed to Lena, and announced that the chariot was here. Immediately there was silence.

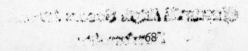

'I guess it's time,' said Gabriel, attempting cheerfulness. He could not bear the looks on their faces. As in a dream he helped one of the slaves load his chest of most treasured belongings on to the back of the chariot. He greeted the driver, then turned to say goodbye to his family. All the household slaves were there as well, and he embraced them fondly, for some of them he had known all his life. The goodbyes with his family were painful. All his brothers cried, and Subin clung to him so tightly, she had to be dragged away by her mother.

Last of all Gabriel bade farewell to Myron, embracing him hard, neither of them able to speak. Then he climbed up on to the chariot and held tightly to the bronze rail that ran along its front and sides. The driver shook the reins, and the chariot rattled and jolted over the cobblestones. Barely able to see, Gabriel looked behind him. For as long as he could he watched their pale faces, turned up towards him in the clear summer night. Then the chariot rounded a bend, and his home and family were lost to sight. Forcing his emotions under control, he faced the road ahead.

Before long they were in the city outskirts. The last houses flashed past, then the impressive Navora Infirmary, famous for its modern surgical techniques, and the mysterious Sanctuary of Healing Dreams. Then the buildings were gone, and the road wound through forested hills and cultivated fields. Through the darkness Gabriel could just make out the gardens where vegetables were grown to sell in the city marketplaces. Watchmen's torches made flares of light among the guarded vegetables, and irrigation waterways glimmered under the moon.

The road began to wind upwards. Looking ahead, Gabriel caught glimpses of the Citadel tower, luminous as pearl, between the trees. It was surrounded by high walls, and little could be seen from the road. But as the chariot drew near, the mighty gates in the Citadel walls swung wide open, revealing the buildings within. Gabriel's breath caught in his throat.

The Citadel soared into the sky, its towers and turrets moon white among the stars. At its heart was a magnificent domed tower, with huge golden doors lit by dozens of torches and flanked by slender spires. Surrounding its lofty walls were the lower buildings, their gold-tiled roofs glowing in the moonlight. Never had Gabriel seen anything so high, so unutterably beautiful. It seemed to lean against the universe, a shining link between this world and the cosmos, hallowed and breathtaking. Gabriel could not tear his eyes off it; it overwhelmed him with its peace, drowned him in its whiteness. Terror and elation tore through him. Before he was even inside the gates, he felt with all of his being that the Citadel had claimed him and possessed him, and that his life was no longer his own.

5 Vows

OVER THE RIM of his plain pottery goblet, Salverion scrutinised his new disciple. He saw a young man looking more assured than he had looked yesterday, though Gabriel's slender fingers trembled as they held his goblet of wine.

'I cannot tell you how pleased I am that you decided to join us here,' said Salverion. 'What decided you, in the end?'

'It just feels right, Master,' said Gabriel, and immediately wished he had said something more intelligent. Did he have to make a fool of himself so soon?

Salverion asked, 'You live by your intuitions, Gabriel?'

Gabriel's face reddened, and he felt those steely eyes probe his soul. 'I'm afraid I do, Master.'

'Why afraid?' asked Salverion, gently. 'Our intuitions are our wisest guide. In what way do yours guide you?'

'Mostly in dreams, Master. All my life I've had clear dreams, and over the years I've worked out what they mean. For example, I've realised that wind is a symbol of change, while a corridor of closed doors means to take care about a decision. An open door signifies the right choice.'

Salverion nodded, understanding. 'We did well in choosing you,' he said. 'Our ways of healing will come naturally to you. Most of our healing here is intuitive, accomplished through the mind. The skills we teach are ancient, very potent, and imparted only to the disciples in the Citadel. The highest skills are for the prevention of pain and the promotion of rapid healing. We work not only through our own minds, but through the minds of those we seek to help. The skills, if misused, could give a person incredible power in the world, and control over whomever he chose. That's why your training here is a holy calling, and you are a healer-priest bound by solemn vows. You will learn all the known powers of the human mind. You see, Gabriel, healing is a matter of the spirit, and that our medicines and scalpels and hands cannot touch. The heart of our work is to encourage the spirit of each one who needs to be healed. Love is a far greater healing force than anything else on earth. I have a feeling that is something you already know.'

Slowly Gabriel smiled, and the smile was like a light on his face. They were silent for a time, and Gabriel studied the Grand Master, marvelling at the man's perception and generosity of spirit, the gentleness in his voice, the almost childlike candour in his face. He looked like a philosopher, a man without anger or guilt or bitterness; yet there was a deepness in his eyes that made Gabriel know he had suffered.

'Do you teach all the Wisdoms, Master?' he asked.

'My brain would not be enough to contain them all,' said Salverion, with a chuckle. 'Nor would one lifetime be enough to impart them. There are seven Wisdoms taught here at the Citadel: the Wisdoms of Healing, of Science, of Music, Art, Literature, Religion, and Astronomy. For each Wisdom there is one Grand Master, acquainted with all the arts to do with that Wisdom. And under him are several Masters, each an expert in a particular branch of that Wisdom. For example, in the Wisdom of Healing there are Masters of surgery, of medicine, of healing by touch, of dream healing, of acupuncture, and of other secret arts. Then there are the disciples. There are over a hundred of you altogether, from all places in the Empire, and at various stages of learning.

'This year you were the only one elected for the healing arts. I have twenty-two other disciples, but they have been with me two years or more, and work now with the Masters of Healing, perfecting their skills. During this first year you will be with me. I will teach you the basics and give you an overall view of what you have ahead of you. Our work together will be mainly practical. Nearly every day we go to the Navora Infirmary. Sometimes we stay overnight there, if the weather is inclement and travel difficult, or a patient requires our constant attention. Then we share a small lodging attached to the hospital. I hope you won't mind. Also, I am frequently called to families in Navora, and you'll accompany me on all those visits. The people are invariably of the wealthy class, though they may not pay us in gold, only in gifts.'

Gabriel sipped his wine and tried to fathom everything he had just heard. He noticed that the goblet from which he drank was very simple and realised that, although Salverion was one of the most illustrious men in the Empire, wealth meant nothing to him. Even the Master's clothes were unpretentious, just a simple long rust-coloured tunic with a yellow hem and a belt made of linked bronze discs. Under the robe he wore a blue shirt and trousers, not particularly well matched with the rusty red. He wore no jewellery, and his sandals were made of undecorated leather. He might have been any ordinary Navoran relaxing in his home.

For the first time Gabriel looked closely at the room, and was surprised at its simplicity. They were in the small sitting room of Salverion's private apartment, made homely by furs scattered on the floor and over chairs. Rustic hangings decorated the walls, and there were shelves crammed with scrolled books. There were small statues, pieces of pottery, and a number of wooden animals. Some of the artworks were simple and unpolished, obviously made as gifts by grateful patients, and treasured by the Master. A bronze lamp burned on a stand between the chairs in which Gabriel and Salverion sat, its oil aroma filling the room even though the door was open to the patio. The night wind carried in the scents of warm summer grass, citrus, and recently watered soil. The earthy fragrances were intoxicating after the stone courtyards and streets of Navora.

'It's beautiful here,' remarked Gabriel. 'I've never lived away from the smell of stone.'

'I believe it's important to have a refuge to come back to, after the demands of our work,' Salverion said. 'I'll take you to your apartment shortly. I hope you'll be pleased with it. Your chest has already been taken there. Your rooms are fairly bare at the moment, but tomorrow you'll be given the first of your monthly stipends, and you can purchase whatever you need. You're supplied with a thousand hasaries each month. Your room and food are free. You will also be given a horse, for travel. I hope the money we offer will be sufficient.'

Gabriel tried not to look astonished. 'I'm sure it will be, Master,' he said. 'But I'm afraid I've never ridden a horse before.'

'You'll be trained,' said Salverion. 'If you need anything from the city, your personal keeper will go for you to make your purchases. His name is Ferron. You'll meet him tonight. He's utterly trustworthy and dependable and will be your keeper for the seven years you are here.'

'Is he a slave?' asked Gabriel.

'There are no slaves here. But he was a slave; I acquired him four years ago and freed him. He's a superb artist and in his spare time illustrates charts and documents for the Great Library. He's also a skilled swordsman.'

'Will I have much time on my own? I prefer solitude.'

'Ferron has rooms next to yours and will attend you only if you call him. He has a kitchen, and will prepare all your meals. He won't be a nuisance. All our keepers are chosen with extreme care and are very tactful and discerning. Many are freed slaves, here by their own free will. But the hour is late, and there's much I have not yet explained. It will have to wait until the morning. Have you any last questions?'

'What happens in the morning, Master? And what time do I have to wake?'

'At dawn Ferron will wake you, and take you to the central tower, which is over the Great Library. I, and all the Grand Masters, will be waiting. There will be an initiation ceremony. You'll bathe and be given new robes and will make your vows.' He noticed a sudden tension in Gabriel's face and added, with a smile, 'Don't be anxious about anything, my son. Ferron will explain everything, and you will be guided at every moment.'

Getting up, Salverion went out of the open door on to his patio and looked up at the night sky. Gabriel stood beside him, breathing deeply in the balmy air. An owl swooped low over the garden, hooting mournfully, and he thought of the stuffed owl in the foyer at home, of his childhood with its fears and agonies and longings, and of the awesome road that lay ahead.

Except for the lack of furnishings, Gabriel's room was identical to the Grand Master's own sitting room. Though the room was almost bare, a lamp burned on a low dining table, its welcoming glow falling across a supper of fresh and dried fruits, cheese, and a crusty loaf of bread. There was also a goblet and a small bottle of wine. A curtained doorway led to the combined bedroom and study, where the bed was made ready with rich covers and tasselled pillows. Gabriel's chest stood at the foot of it.

In the sitting room wall opposite the curtained door was another door. It was closed. It was, Salverion had explained, the door to Ferron's rooms. Gabriel stood outside it for a few moments, then hesitantly lifted his hand and quietly knocked.

The door was opened by a young man not much older than himself. His eyes were the colour of light jade, with very thick dark lashes. His skin was olive coloured and flawless, his face handsome. Long hair, blue-black and waving, flowed to his shoulders. He was from the eastern part of the Empire, Gabriel guessed, brought over as a slave after one of the Navoran conquests. For a few seconds they stared at each other, then the keeper bowed low.

'Please don't do that,' said Gabriel, embarrassed. 'I just wanted to thank you for the meal, and for everything else you did to prepare my rooms. They feel like home already.'

'It was my pleasure to do that, sir.'

'Do you have to be so formal? My name's Gabriel.'

Ferron looked surprised, but he nodded.

'Would you like to have a meal with me?' Gabriel asked. 'Salverion said there were things about tomorrow that you'd explain. We could talk while we eat.'

Ferron's surprise turned to astonishment, though he tried to smother it. 'It's not usual for keepers to eat with disciples,' he said. He had a heavy accent, but Gabriel could not place it.

'We've got seven years here together,' Gabriel said. 'By the end of that time you'll have seen the very worst of me, and I hope, the best. I'd feel easier about that if you were a friend rather than a servant.'

Slowly Ferron smiled. 'If that's your wish.'

'It is. So won't you get another plate, and eat with me?'

Ferron nodded and went into his sitting room. Looking through the doorway, Gabriel glimpsed walls covered with paintings, all scenes from a country unfamiliar to him. He was still staring at them when Ferron came back, a pottery plate and cup in one hand and a cushion in the other.

'Did you paint your walls?' Gabriel asked, sitting down on his own cushion by the table.

Hesitantly, as if not quite comfortable with the arrangement, Ferron placed his cushion at the table across from Gabriel and sat down. In answer to Gabriel's question, he said, 'Yes. I'm employed here as an artist as well as a keeper. Though I painted my walls for my own pleasure, of course.'

'They're beautiful,' said Gabriel, offering him the bowl of fruit. 'The pictures are of your country, I guess. Where are you from? Sadira?'

'Amaran.'

'My father was a merchant,' said Gabriel. 'He often went to Amaran, brought back glass and metalware. He said Amaranians were a nation of craftspeople. Were you an artist in your own country, before you came here?'

'I was only a child at home, before the Navoran army overran my country. I was twelve when I was enslaved. Eshtemoh, my brother, was eight.'

'Have you seen him since?'

Ferron shook his head. He began peeling an orange. There were scars around his wrists, much lighter than his skin.

'Where were you before you came to the Citadel?' Gabriel asked.

'I was in the palace for five years, before Salverion gave me my freedom and offered me a place here.'

'What's the Empress like?' asked Gabriel, pouring them each a goblet of wine.

Ferron thought for a while before he answered. 'From a slave's point of view, terrifying. But I think you'd get along well with her. You have a direct and honest look. She likes people around her to be confident and to look at her straight when they speak to her. She doesn't tolerate indecision, or clumsiness, or fear. Challenging, for a nervous slave.'

'Challenging for a nervous novice healer, too,' said Gabriel, and they laughed.

'Salverion told me that you're a skilled swordsman,' remarked Gabriel.

'We have an excellent gymnasium here, if you like exercise.'

'I do. I run every day, if I can. I'd like to run later, barefoot, on real grass. I've never done that before.'

'If you do go outside,' said Ferron, 'please stay on the lawn just outside your own rooms here. I'm afraid the rest of the Citadel is forbidden, until you've taken your vows.'

'How many of us will be taking our vows?'

'Only three tomorrow. There are several others elected, but they come from other parts of the Empire, and their ships haven't arrived yet.'

'Will you be there, at the ceremony?'

'No. Don't worry; Salverion will explain everything. You won't make a blunder.'

'That'll make a change,' said Gabriel, and thought Ferron looked amused.

After the meal Ferron showed Gabriel where the washrooms and latrines were, further down the spacious pillared porch connecting all the apartments. Later, when Ferron had cleared away the remains of the meal and returned to his rooms, Gabriel went outside into the garden. The night was humid, the grass warm and slightly damp beneath his bare feet. He longed to go for a run but remembered Ferron's request that he stay here. He walked a short distance out into the garden and noticed lamps between the trees, lighting the leaves to gold. Beyond the garden the smooth lawn ran down to a high wall built of white stone. Narrow steps were cut into the wall, leading up to a gap in the stones near the summit, obviously used as a lookout in times past. Gabriel glanced behind him but could see no one. Quickly, exulting in the beauty of the night and the softness of the grass beneath his feet, he ran across the lawn and climbed the steps. Reaching the top, he leaned on the stone barricade, and looked down.

The view was breathtaking. Before him, lucid under the silver moon, lay the Citadel fields, gardens, orchards, and vineyards, all contained within high walls. Past those walls, out towards the east, were gently rolling hills and shadowy valleys. Beyond them stretched a great plain, bordered on the far side by mountains. The plain shone with prairie grass, and a silver river ran through it: the Shinali lands.

Involuntarily Gabriel touched the bone carving that lay against his chest. His heart hammered, and his throat went tight. For a long time he stared at the grasslands, blue and serene under the moon. But he saw, too, the face of a woman, dark-skinned and beautiful, and her hands reaching out to him, imploring, pleading. Guilt and nameless longings swept through him. Still with his hand on his chest, caressing the amulet, he went back down the steep stairs to the lawns and the lamp-lit garden. Later he slept in his unfamiliar bed, his fingers still around the Shinali bone.

He dreamed of the silver river, and of paddling through the waters in a log canoe. He was sitting close behind a man whose naked back was brown and strong and who wore bone beads in his hair, and they chanted together as they paddled, their canoe swift and purposeful in the sunlit waters, between the singing lands.

Gabriel came up out of the water, his heart pounding, his eyes blinded by the light that flooded down from the shining tower above. Dimly he was aware of the Masters about him, quietly chanting; of someone drying his body and hair with a soft towel; of someone else putting a long crimson robe on him; of a sash being tied about his waist, and sandals being strapped on his feet. He glanced over his shoulder at the glittering golden pool and the shaft of sunlight that streamed down into it. On the other side stood the other two initiates, waiting. Looking up, he saw the soaring marble walls of the tower and the vast dome above, its pinnacle lost in light. Someone gave him a scroll of parchment on which were words, beautifully written. Dazzled, he could hardly see them.

'They are your vows, Gabriel,' said a voice. 'You will say them aloud.'

Gabriel stared at the words wavering like flames across the white. So much light . . .

'Gabriel?' The voice was Salverion's. Gabriel blinked and saw the Grand Master standing in front of him. Salverion was smiling a little, his expression questioning. 'Have you a difficulty with the vows, my son?'

'No, Master.'

'When you're ready, just read aloud what is written. Take all the time you need.'

Gabriel looked at the parchment again and saw that the words were now clear. In silence he read the vows through several times, accepting them, making them a part of his life. Only then did he say them aloud.

'In the Name of Sovereign God, I swear that I shall honour the sacred laws of compassion and respect for all life. I swear that I shall bow to the will of the Grand Masters, for as long as I live in the Citadel. I swear that I shall hold sacred in my heart all skills that I learn here, and never disclose them to another person; neither shall I use the Wisdoms for anything other than the free and loving service of healing. And, within the sacredness of that service, all secrets told to me, and all matters concerning those I heal, shall remain with me alone. I will never do anything to any person without his or her permission, or the permission of relatives. Above all, I swear that I shall do my best to love every one I meet as if that soul were myself.'

As with one voice, the Grand Masters chanted their own vow to love and serve and support him. The parchment was taken out of his hands, and the seven Grand Masters came up one at a time, introduced themselves, and said a few words to him. They all were elderly, all smiling and warm and unassuming. He had the absurd feeling that they were honouring him, not he them, and he wanted to bow low in front of them, but instead found himself shaking hands with them in the Navoran way, with his right forearm raised and crossed with theirs at the wrist, and with hands clasped tight.

The Grand Masters were all dressed, as he and Salverion were, in long crimson robes embroidered heavily with gold about the hems and short sleeves. But over the red the Grand Masters wore knee-length white tunics, embroidered on the chest and back with the seven stars of the Citadel. They wore different coloured sashes, and Gabriel guessed there was a colour for each of the seven Wisdoms. His own sash was green, the same as Salverion's: the colour of life and healing. The other initiates were also in crimson, one with a silver sash, and one with a sash of turquoise. Gabriel wanted to go and greet them, but they were engrossed in conversation with their Grand Masters. He began to feel cold, and was shivering as the Grand Masters drifted away, the other new disciples with them, leaving him alone with Salverion beside the pool.

Narrowing his eyes against the light, Gabriel gazed at the vast library all around him. 'There's so much wisdom here,' he said, marvelling.

'All the wisdom of human souls,' said Salverion. 'This is the greatest library in the world, Gabriel.'

'How is it that there's so much light? It's unreal.'

'The light that comes down through the tower is concentrated,' explained Salverion. 'Our astronomers designed a series of large lenses and mirrors, and placed them high in the tower, in such a way that the sunlight is caught and magnified and reflected down. The pool diffuses the heat, though the water gets very warm in summer. The light is always intense, aside from in the darkest days of winter. This harnessing of the natural light saves our having to burn lamps except in the dimmest corners of the Library, and reduces the risk of fire.'

'Fire would be fatal, wouldn't it?' said Gabriel, gazing about him at the untold rows of priceless scrolls.

'If there is a fire, of course the pool itself is a ready supply of water to quench the flames,' said Salverion. 'Within this Great Library there are actually seven libraries, one for each Wisdom. I'll show you the libraries and how they're arranged, then I'll show you the rest of the Citadel.'

For several hours Gabriel followed the Grand Master through the libraries, along corridors, up winding stairs, and through ancient doors into rooms that overwhelmed him with their vastness and beauty. The Citadel was built entirely of white stone, and everywhere were carved pillars and vaulted ceilings so lofty and graceful they seemed almost fragile. Every building was designed to catch the solar light; brilliant rays poured down from unexpected places, and Gabriel glimpsed small windows high in the curved ceilings, and guessed there were mirrors placed there, too, to reflect down the sun. The soaring walls, the spacious rooms, the statues and artworks and painted frescoes, were all radiant.

The buildings were arranged around a central courtyard garden. On one side was the Great Library, on the opposite side the living quarters and administration rooms. The connecting buildings were the centres of learning. Salverion led the way along one of the pillared stone porches bordering the courtyard. Morning sun poured through the open archways, and Gabriel saw the gardens set out in geometric patterns, with fountains and sundials. Along the inner walls of the porches were doors to the learning centres and cushioned seats where a few disciples sat studying in the sun. Above stretched the magnificent porch roofs, vaulted and carved.

Some of the rooms were secret, closed to all save those who taught and studied there, but Gabriel saw the art and music rooms, the superb theatre where musicians performed, and the recreation room with its massive fireplace where, in the bitterest winter days, disciples and Masters relaxed and drank mulled wine. 'It's not all hard work here,' Salverion explained, with a smile. Then he took Gabriel to the healing rooms, where he met the other Masters of healing, and the other healer-priests.

The Masters greeted him as if he were a son, enfolding him in their arms and welcoming him with words of blessing and affection. All the Masters were charismatic and memorable, but there was one with whom Gabriel felt a special affinity. He was Sheel Chandra, the Master of Mind-power and Healing Through Dreams. He was a tall dark-skinned man of about sixty, charming and compassionate, with an accent so heavy Gabriel could hardly understand him. But with Sheel Chandra he felt an instant, powerful kinship and trust.

The only Master with whom Gabriel was not totally at ease was the Master of Surgery, Kes. Kes was one of the younger Masters, aristocratic and tall, and slightly reserved. He was the only Master Gabriel felt had expectations of him, and therefore with Kes he felt tense.

Then he met the twenty-two other healer-priests, disciples of Salverion. They were all older than himself, some by several years, and from diverse parts of the Empire. Like the Masters, they greeted him with wholehearted warmth and affection, shaking his hand in the Navoran way. Many embraced him, and he found himself enfolded into a strong fellowship, wholly accepted and valued and loved. Afterward Salverion took him away to the quiet courtyard garden, where they sat in the sunlight to talk.

'I hope you'll be at home here,' Salverion said. 'If ever you have a problem, I hope you feel you can talk with me. For you, I'm always available. And Ferron will explain anything you want to know. You won't have to work too hard, this first week. Take time to look around the Great Library, and the orchards and vineyards. The Citadel is almost entirely self-sufficient: we make our own wine, grow all our own fruit and vegetables, keep bees, and grow grains for flour. You'll like the estate, I think.

'I have to go to the Navora Infirmary now. I don't expect you to accompany me today. When you're ready, Ferron will prepare you a light midday meal. Have this afternoon to yourself, and buy some furnishings for your apartment. If you've time, ask Ferron to take you to the stables, and choose a horse you feel comfortable with. You might have time for a riding lesson. Tomorrow you will come with me to the Infirmary for a few hours. I have a tumour to remove. You'll assist me.'

They stood, and Salverion embraced him, briefly. 'Please don't look so alarmed about the surgery tomorrow,' the Master said. 'You're only helping. I won't leave you loose and alone with a scalpel among my patients' vital organs. Not for a long time yet.'

6 THE SILKEN SNARE

SWEATING AND FRETFUL, Gabriel tossed in his unfamiliar bed and tried to shake off the nightmares that troubled him. In his dreams he was trapped in white silk, beautiful and fine but wrapped tightly around him like a shroud, stifling him. He awoke breathless, drenched with sweat. His right shoulder ached from a fall from his horse, and he was thirsty and feverish. He threw back the bed covers and lay naked in the moonlight, grateful for the night breeze that came in through the open window, sweet with fragrances of unfamiliar blossoms. Outside, far in the Citadel fields, a sheep bleated. The sound was comforting and earthy, and Gabriel's fears subsided. He rolled over and drifted into sleep again. A tapping sound disturbed him, and he muttered in his sleep and tried to shut it out. But it became louder and insistent, and then someone shook his shoulder. He mumbled and buried his face in the cushions, thinking he was back home and Subin was trying to get into his bed, as she did when she was afraid at night. Then he heard Ferron's voice, urgent and low.

'Gabriel! Salverion wants you. He's been called to the palace, and he wants you to go with him.'

Instantly Gabriel was sitting on the edge of his bed, blinking in the light of the lamp Ferron had lit. 'What's wrong?' he asked, reaching for the crimson robe Ferron had picked up from the chair, shaken smooth, and was already holding out to him.

'It seems that the Empress is sick,' replied Ferron, noticing the tension in Gabriel's face, and the damp hair around his forehead. 'Are you well?'

'Bad dreams,' said Gabriel. 'What's wrong with her? I won't have to examine her, will I?'

'I have no idea,' said Ferron, showing Gabriel how to tie his sash. 'You wanted to know what she was like, now you'll find out for yourself. Where are your sandals?'

'I don't know,' said Gabriel, dragging a comb through his dishevelled hair.

'Perhaps you should tie your hair back when you're visiting patients or helping Salverion,' suggested Ferron. 'I put a green band on your table, for that.'

At last Gabriel was ready, but intensely nervous and pale. 'You'll be all right,' said Ferron, holding Gabriel by the shoulders, and inspecting him. 'Salverion waits for you by the main gate.'

'I don't have to ride that infernal horse, do I?' asked Gabriel, fresh anxieties rushing over him.

'There'll be a chariot waiting to take you. Go – quickly!'

With his heart thumping, Gabriel left his apartment and ran along the pillared porch way, then out through the high arched door that led to the outer courtyard. He hurried across the smooth moonlit lawns towards the main gate, and found Salverion just outside. A chariot waited, its driver stifling a yawn.

'Sorry to disturb your sleep, Gabriel,' said Salverion, as they climbed into the chariot and gripped the rail. 'But I never attend the Empress Petra alone.'

'Doesn't she have her own physician?' asked Gabriel, bracing himself as the chariot bounded forward, beginning the swift descent down the winding road through the Citadel hills.

'She does, but occasionally she calls me, for no other reason than that she wants to. And what the Empress wants, no one argues with – not even a Grand Master.' Then he smiled, seeing Gabriel's apprehension. 'Relax, we won't be doing major surgery. She's probably got a toothache, or simply can't sleep. She's rarely sick, she's as strong as a horse. Speaking of horses, did you go riding?'

'I attempted to,' said Gabriel. 'I achieved a few bruises.'

'You have my sympathy. What have you called that carefully chosen stallion of yours?'

'Rebellion,' said Gabriel, with a grin. 'Master, how am I to address the Empress? What do I do when I first see her?'

'You call her Your Majesty, or Lady. Whichever seems appropriate. Either title is correct. When we first enter her presence we both bow, at the same time if possible. I'll whisper instructions. Then I shall question and examine her, while you stand at a discreet distance. Her own physician will have already set out anything I may need, and, if I ask you to do so, you pass me what I ask for. You'll probably feel a bit superfluous, I'm afraid. The Empress usually ignores my assistants, so it's unlikely you'll have to make conversation with her. If you do, speak only when she has spoken first. Don't look so apprehensive, Gabriel. She's just a human being, with faults and fears and pains like the rest of us. She's actually very lonely.'

'But she has a consort.'

'It's a marriage of convenience, to seal a pact with an important nation. He's a morose and inhibited man, that's why he's seldom seen in public with her. The Empress lives in her own quarters at the palace, and there's no heir to the throne. She has few female friends, and the men she knows are all in high places, all wrangling among themselves for power, and using her to further their own careers.

'The Empress looks on me as a friend more than a healer, and it may be that tonight she simply wants to talk. Regardless of the topic of conversation, or how private it is, you must remain quietly in the background. Remember your vows, and never repeat anything you hear.'

The chariot sped on, the rumble of its wheels and drumming of horses' hooves like thunder in the deserted city streets. As they passed between the mighty gates of the palace, the skies were beginning to lighten. The chariot stopped, and Salverion and Gabriel got down. Gabriel followed the Master through an expansive courtyard, then up wide steps. A slave met them, and they were led deep into the interior of the palace. A number of slaves were already up and about, changing flowers in urns or cleaning floors.

They came to a set of doors inlaid with precious stones. 'Her private suite,' whispered Salverion. 'Lower your head.'

Gabriel obeyed and passed through a curtained doorway into another room. He felt Salverion's hand on his arm, telling him to stand still. He waited, not daring to look up, aware of the rich red of soft carpets, subdued lamplight, and the strong smell of incense or flowers. The presence of the Empress filled the room, and with every nerve Gabriel was aware that here was the heart of the great Navoran Empire, the ultimate authority on earth. Quivering with fear, he had an almost overpowering impulse to fall flat on his face.

'Bow.' The whisper was so low he barely heard it, and the Grand Master had already bent over when Gabriel began paying homage. He waited several seconds, until Salverion stood upright again, then he dared to raise himself and look at the Empress.

She was sitting on a carved throne overlaid with gold and

softened with cushions of purple velvet. A lamp burned on a table nearby, casting fiery lights and deep shadows around her. In the dimness she looked younger than he expected, twenty-five perhaps, with black hair waving loose about her shoulders and down her green embroidered robe. Her face was lovely, with compelling violet eyes and red, full lips. She was elegant and poised, but there was a tension about her that reminded him of a beautiful predatory animal, languid for the moment, but quietly conscious of its power. He realised she was looking straight at him, her magnificent eyes clear and curious. He flushed scarlet, and it seemed an age before she turned her gaze to Salverion and greeted him.

'My dear Salverion. It's so good of you to come,' she said, reaching out a slender hand sparkling with rings and jewelled bracelets. Her voice was deep and alluring.

Salverion bowed low again and kissed her fingers.

'It's a delight to see you again, Lady,' he said. 'Though it would be a greater delight if you were well.'

'I'm not too ill,' she said. 'I have a toothache, and the mixture Osric put on it hasn't helped. I need your magic touch more than your forceps, I hope.'

'Which tooth is it, Lady?'

'I don't know exactly. On the lower right, at the back.'

'Will you turn to the light, please, so I can see?'

She tilted her head, and Salverion bent over her. After a few moments he straightened. 'I cannot see anything obviously wrong with your tooth, Lady,' he said. 'It may be that you have an infection in it. There's no need for it to be removed yet. I'll prescribe some salve to put on it, and something for you to take.'

'Will you stop the pain for me, in the meantime?' she asked.

'Of course, Lady. Would you sit upright, please, and make

your spine as straight as you can? Relax. Close your eyes and breathe calmly.'

Gabriel watched as Salverion's hands moved over the Empress's face and the top of her head. She was wearing a golden chain around her head, with an emerald that hung over her forehead. Carefully the Grand Master removed it, placing it on the table beside her throne. Then he massaged her brow and the hollows of her cheeks. When he had finished, she opened her eyes and smiled at him.

'You're a wonderful man,' she sighed. 'I should have called you yesterday. I didn't want to bother you, and I thought Osric's potions would help.'

'You could never bother me, Lady,' he said. 'I am at your service any time.'

Her eyes went past him, to Gabriel. 'So this is your latest Elected One?' she asked.

Salverion beckoned Gabriel over. 'Your Majesty, this is Gabriel Eshban Vala,' he said.

Gabriel bowed again. The Empress studied him, her head tilted slightly back, her eyes half closed and pondering. 'You're Jager's son, aren't you?' she asked.

'Yes, Your Majesty.'

'You look very like your father. He was a handsome man. I always admired him; he was one of the 'old' Navorans, who loved justice and honesty. He was deeply loyal to the Empire. He used to bring me back silks and rare spices from the east. Why did you not continue his business?'

'I wanted to be a healer, Your Majesty.'

'Gabriel is a gifted young man,' said Salverion. 'He wrote an impressive essay on the human heart and blood vascular system, for which he won the Navoran High Honour. And his tutor at the Academy says he has great steadiness and skill when he assists with surgery.'

'I shall remember that, if I ever need the knife,' the Empress said. 'Tell me about your essay, Gabriel.'

Salverion excused himself, glanced encouragingly at his disciple, then went to the table at the far side of the room.

Gabriel swallowed nervously. In spite of the warm night, he trembled.

'What made you first interested in anatomy?' prompted the Empress.

'It's a strange story, Lady,' he replied. 'I was about ten, I think. I went to the kitchens one day to get something to eat, and one of the cooks was preparing a dish made up of animal hearts. I wanted to help, and he gave me a heart and a small knife. I cut the heart open, and immediately I wanted to know what the chambers were inside, what the valves were, and where the veins and arteries came from and went to. It seemed so intricate, that heart, it was like a whole world to me. It was wonderful.'

'And that sense of wonder lasted, and brought you all the way to the Citadel,' she said. 'Isn't it amazing how things that happen in our childhood, even little things, can have such influence on our lives?'

'That's very true, Your Majesty,' he replied, thinking of a wounded Shinali woman.

'Do you believe in destiny, Gabriel?'

'I'm not sure.'

'What would have happened if, on that day you went to the kitchen, the cook was preparing something else instead of heart? A vegetable dish, say. Would you have been a gardener now?'

He looked amused, intrigued by the idea. 'I never thought of that, Lady,' he said.

'Perhaps you should,' she replied. 'I think you might have some extraordinary talks with the philosophers and religious Masters at the Citadel – if our friend over there doesn't make you work too hard.' She glanced laughingly in Salverion's direction. He went on mixing his concoction, his back to them, as if he had not heard.

The room was growing lighter. Gabriel looked up at the tall, narrow windows and the beams of sunlight beginning to spill in.

'I suppose you must go with Salverion to the Infirmary today,' the Empress said. 'I hope my interrupting your sleep won't spoil that famous steadiness and skill of yours.'

'Not at all, Lady. You didn't interrupt my sleep; it was already disturbed.'

'Missing a lover, perhaps?'

He reddened. 'No, Lady. I had dreams.'

'I have dreams, too,' she whispered, leaning forward, her face shadowed from the lamp. 'Are your dreams vivid, Gabriel? Do you remember them when you wake?'

'Yes.'

'What were you dreaming about this night?'

He looked at her and saw that she was intent and interested, her violet eyes glowing softly in the grey dawn.

'I dreamed that I was wrapped tightly in fine silk, like a shroud,' he replied.

'Do you know what it meant?'

'The silk signified splendour, probably the Citadel. I think perhaps the dream expressed a fear that I might not live well there, that I might fail in some way. There was also a feeling of entrapment, which I don't understand. It could mean that I'm afraid of being utterly committed to one place for seven years. Or maybe it meant that, because I'm at the Citadel now, everything I knew before has come to an end; a kind of dying, perhaps. I'm not certain of the meaning. I hadn't thought about it until this moment.'

'Death is very ominous and final, Gabriel.'

'Death in dreams means only an ending, and a beginning in something new.'

'How do you know that?'

'I don't know how I know, Lady. I just know that I know.'

Salverion came back and handed Gabriel a tiny bowl with a pungent mixture in it. 'May I put this on your tooth, please, Lady?' Salverion asked.

She opened her mouth and turned to the light again, and Salverion applied the mixture with a long thin spatula. 'Please don't speak for a while, while that sets,' he said. Then he took the bowl and returned to the table. They heard him stripping leaves from fresh plants, and chopping up roots. A fragrance like lemon permeated the room, stronger than the scent of flowers.

Gabriel noticed a mural on the wall behind the Empress's chair, and he moved forward to examine it. It was a painting of the city of Navora beneath sombre, stormy skies, but a shaft of light broke through the clouds and lit the towers and the highest buildings, bathing them with unearthly radiance. So lost was he in the painting, Gabriel did not notice that he leaned with his hand on the arm of the Empress's chair. He was totally unconscious of everything else in the room, until he felt a hand brush his wrist. Even then, he was not fully aware of it. Only when the fingers travelled lightly up his arm, stroking the inside of his elbow, did he realise what she was doing. He remained motionless, hardly breathing, hardly able to believe what was happening. The fingers moved on, gliding over his skin to the edge of his sleeve, then underneath the linen and on, sliding over the sensitive inner flesh of his upper arm as slowly and sensuously as a snake. He looked at her face and saw that she was watching him, her eyes smiling, teasing. He did not know what to do. To remove his arm would dishonour her; in submitting, he dishonoured himself. He remained perfectly still, every nerve taut, his flesh frigid under her touch.

'You have amazing eyes, Gabriel,' she said, her voice very low. 'A Visionary's eyes.'

'I don't think so, Your Majesty.'

'You dare to contradict your Empress? People lose their lives for that.' Her voice was light and jocular, but he suspected she was serious.

'People don't lose their lives, Your Majesty. Their lives are taken from them, or else they lay them down themselves.'

'And which will be your fate, Gabriel?'

'I'll lay mine down, Lady.'

Her eyes narrowed, and a subtle smile played about her mouth. In the increased light, Gabriel saw that she was much older than she had seemed at first. Her face was smothered with heavy makeup, and under it her skin was blemished and lined. Her hair, which had looked so dusky and luxuriant before, was grey at the roots, and he realised it was dyed. And her eyes, instead of being teasing and good-humoured, were hard and dangerous now. For a split second he felt as if he were looking not at her, but at something horrifying behind or within her, something evil and predatory and powerful. Gently but firmly he withdrew his arm, then stepped back a pace so she could not reach him.

'That's a marvellous painting, Your Majesty,' he said, looking again at the wall behind her and striving to keep his voice casual.

'Yes, it is,' she replied. 'It was done for me by an Amaranian

slave. His name is Ferron. You've probably met him; Salverion bought him from me. Well, didn't buy him, exactly; in a moment of extreme gratitude I promised Salverion anything he asked for. He asked for my favourite slave. He was an exquisite youth, and I always regretted letting him go. But Salverion won't give him back now. He can be very stubborn, your Grand Master, even towards me. I hope you won't imitate him, Gabriel.'

Gabriel kept his gaze fixed on the painting and dared not reply. Fortunately, at that moment Salverion returned.

'I have your medication prepared, Your Majesty,' he said. He was standing a short distance away, on the other side of her chair. A covered bowl was in his hands, and his face was expressionless. 'Have your physician put this on your tooth four times a day, Lady,' he said. 'It contains lobelia and prickly ash and will alleviate your pain immediately after it's applied. It will also relieve any inflammation about the root.'

'Thank you, my dear Salverion. And thank you for bringing your new disciple. We had an interesting chat. I very much approve of your choice.'

'Thank you, Your Majesty.'

Salverion bowed low, and Gabriel bowed with him. As he lifted his head, Gabriel glimpsed the Empress's face. She was smiling at him with a taunting, lascivious smile. He wanted to run as he backed slowly away, his mind and emotions in chaos.

'Our patient is a man with a thyroid tumour,' explained Salverion, as he and Gabriel put on fresh white aprons and scrubbed their hands. They were in the small washing room adjoining one of the large operating rooms at the famous Navora Infirmary. 'He's Wymar, thirty-four years old, and has had the tumour since he was fifteen,' went on Salverion. 'He's here from

Sadira, with his wife and their four children. They're a close family, and I expect Wymar to recover fully and quickly, with his loved ones supporting him. He's well prepared for this surgery, and I talked to him again only this morning. I've also given him some medicine made from the opium poppy.

'The tumour is exceptionally large and already compressing his windpipe. If I block the nerves in his throat so that all feeling is gone, it will further affect his breathing and swallowing reflexes. So I'll relieve what pain I can, but he will feel some sensations. We'll have to be as quick as possible. The operation should be straightforward: the tumour moves freely, and should be easily severed. I'll make a large horizontal incision, and give us plenty of room. You'll be holding back the layers of skin and muscle and other tissues, and tying off the bleeding vessels. Sponge away all the blood, it's vital that all bleeding is controlled. Use the hot oil to seal off the smaller veins. Watch for the great vessels, especially the two thyroid arteries. We never cut anything unless we're absolutely sure we know what it is.' He added, with gentle amusement, 'And please try not to look so apprehensive, you'll panic the patient.'

'Sorry, Master,' said Gabriel. 'I'm not sure I'm ready for this.'

'*I'm* sure you are. From what Hevron told me, you've helped with this kind of operation many times. This will be just the same, except that our patient will be peaceful. I have every confidence in you, but if you are unsure about anything, ask. I don't care how insignificant the question seems. Are you ready?'

Gabriel took a few deep breaths and nodded, and they went into the operating room. Built of pale grey stone, the walls and floor of the room were polished and spotless. The furniture and equipment shone. Lamps hung low over the workplaces, and, as in the Citadel, ingeniously placed mirrors reflected sunlight into vital areas. All the windows were glassed to keep out dust and insects. After the impoverished, squalid conditions at the Academy infirmary, the room was superb. But Gabriel had little time to admire it.

Wymar lay waiting on the operating table, his chest raised by a pillow under him, his head tilted back. The tumour in his throat was large, deforming his neck. Salverion introduced Gabriel and explained that he was going to assist.

'He's young,' whispered Wymar, his breath whistling in his throat.

'So he is,' said Salverion, 'and talented as well. I have no doubt that we shall both manage better with his help. How are you feeling this morning?'

'Afraid, Grand Master.'

Patiently, Salverion explained again what he would do, all the while stroking the man's hair as if Wymar were someone especially dear to him. 'You have nothing to be afraid of,' Salverion said. 'You'll feel only sensations of pressure and pulling as we cut the skin and hold back muscles and tissues, then the release as the tumour is removed. If you feel sick, or the sensations become actual pain, lift your hand with your fingers spread, so I know. I'll relieve your distress immediately. Please don't touch our hands or try to speak. Breathe slowly, and count to five with every breath in and every breath out, as I taught you. Have you any questions?'

The man shook his head. 'Then just relax,' murmured Salverion. 'Begin your slow breathing. I'll put pressure on certain nerve pathways that will dull the feeling in your neck and throat. Close your eyes if you wish. I shall be touching the back of your neck and your face. You may feel heat and numbness, but no pain.'

Gently, Salverion placed his hands over Wymar's face.

Other people came in and arranged themselves in a semi-circle on the far side of the table. They were student physicians and surgeons from other parts of the Infirmary, here to see the Grand Master at work. Gabriel felt suddenly awkward and inexperienced. But he soon forgot the audience and watched, enthralled, as Salverion's hands moved over Wymar, dulling his feeling. Nothing special was done, it seemed, apart from gentle pressure in certain places, but Wymar visibly relaxed, and his breaths became deep and serene. Salverion removed his hands, and for a while stood with his eyes closed, praying.

When the prayer was finished, Salverion said to his disciple, 'Forget everyone and everything but what we do. We are simply two healer-priests, you and I, doing our best for a fellow human being in difficulty. Now let us begin.'

A table stood at Gabriel's left, covered with a clean white cloth spread with instruments, silk and tendon threads, needles, and all else necessary. Gabriel picked up a scalpel and handed it to Salverion. The Master divided the skin and the tissues underneath, and Gabriel wiped away the gathering blood. He glanced at the patient's face: incredibly, the man was tranquil, his lips moving slightly as he counted with each breath. Salverion's knife moved again, slitting muscles, revealing the tumour. Gabriel picked up strong threads for closing off the bigger blood vessels, and had them tied before Salverion sliced the vessels with his blade. Sometimes a frown creased Wymar's forehead, or his breathing altered, and Salverion talked to him, his voice calm and gentle.

The world beyond Gabriel's hands ceased to exist. In perfect harmony he worked with Salverion, intuitively knowing what the surgeon wanted and when he wanted it, his motions swift and sure. The Master's skill was breathtaking. Gabriel had thought Hevron was clever, but the movements of Salverion's hands were smooth and unfaltering and beautiful. Watching him work was like witnessing a dance of healing over the wounded throat, and at times Gabriel could have sworn he saw light flowing from the Master's fingertips. He rejoiced to be working with him, to be a part of that healing.

He was almost sorry when it was over, and the wound was closed, the sutures firm and neat. He did not hear Salverion congratulating him or the spontaneous praise of the people who had watched. His eyes were on Wymar as the man lifted his hand and tentatively examined his own neck, feeling the unfamiliar flatness and normality, the long miraculous scar. Wymar looked astonished, then his face became full of wonder and thankfulness and supreme joy.

The look on Gabriel's face was the same.

Later that day, as their chariot wound upwards through the twilit hills on the way back to the Citadel, Salverion said, 'I very much enjoyed working with you today, Gabriel. I know it's early yet in your training, but you show an aptitude rare in someone your age. Why did you want to be a healer?'

Glancing at those steely eyes, seeing their discernment and understanding, Gabriel came very close to telling him. But at that moment the chariot bounded over the crest of a hill, and he saw, far below, the wide Shinali lands, and there tore across him a guilt too deep to confess. He looked the other way, towards Navora, and said, 'I wanted to do something useful with my life. Also, I've always been interested in anatomy.'

'You enjoyed surgery at the Academy?'

'I hated it, Master. I thought it was brutal, though I knew it was for the ultimate good.'

'You still consider it brutal?' asked Salverion, with a curious smile.

'The way you work can't be compared with other surgery,' Gabriel replied. 'It's not just that your patients have no pain. There's something more to the way you operate. Something powerful and sacred. I'd give my life to be able to heal like that.'

Salverion gave him a tender, solemn look. 'You have given it,' he said.

When Gabriel was back in his rooms, he changed into his trousers and went for a run through the Citadel gardens. They were radiant in the evening light, and the grass was warm and lush beneath his bare feet. In the orchards the apple and pear trees were heavy with fruit, and the vines in the walled vineyards drooped with clusters of purple and green grapes. Gardeners were still at work in the vegetable gardens, hoeing in the cool of the evening, their forms wrapped in clouds of shimmering dust. They looked up, surprised, as the lone runner went past. Gabriel waved at them, and they called out greetings and waved back. He ran on through the farms where the animals were kept, past soft-eyed cows in a walled field, and hens foraging in the grass. To his right were the outlying vineyards, where long irrigation canals glinted in the sun.

He ran up a small hill towards the east and stopped on the summit to look across the Shinali lands. The plain and the distant mountains were purple. On the foothills just before the edge of the plain sheep were gathered, and a Shinali shepherd was with the flock. The Shinali was too far away for Gabriel to see clearly, and he did not know whether it was a man or a woman, or even a child. But he thought of the woman by the river, and the strange Shinali visions that came to him in sleep, the joy and wonder of them mixed with childhood guilt. Suddenly he realised that the shepherd's arm was raised, and the Shinali was waving to him. Gabriel glanced behind him: there was no one else. He looked back at the Shinali. Slowly he raised his hand and waved back. The shepherd waved again, then began striding down the golden hillside towards home, driving the sheep before him.

Smiling, Gabriel touched the bone carving he wore and watched until the shepherd had gone from sight. Then, astonished by the joy that suddenly swept through him, he turned and jogged back to the Citadel.

The days sped by. Gabriel had never been so satisfied or happy. His mornings were free at first, and he spent them studying in the Great Library, or riding Rebellion in the Citadel hills. In the afternoons he worked with Salverion, discovering a deep unity between himself and the Grand Master that left him feeling humbled and amazed. In the evenings he went running through the Citadel farmlands and looked out at the Shinali lands, his fingers enfolding the bone amulet around his neck. Afterwards he sat in his room near an open window, with moths fluttering around him, his head golden in the lamplight, and wrote long letters home. Every day mail arrived for him: letters from his tutor and friends at the Academy, drawings from Subin and the younger ones at home, lively epistles from Myron, and loving notes from Lena.

The incident with the Empress he managed most of the time to forget, convincing himself that it had been nothing – only a whim, a casual act, probably totally imagined on his part. But whenever he was called at night to go with Salverion to the home of someone taken ill, or to an urgent case at the Infirmary, his heart lurched, and his dreams were haunted by a mocking figure in jewels and soiled white silk, who pursued him through Navoran mansions once excellent and glorious, but which were ruined now.

7 THE DREAM

SUMMER'S FRUIT RIPENED on the boughs, and in the scorched fields the animals gathered in the shade, or around their water troughs. Every evening in the Citadel gardens, water spilled along the irrigation canals, and the precious herbs and vegetables flourished. But in the surrounding hills the grass withered, and the earth dried and hardened and waited for rain.

In the Navora Infirmary, Gabriel worked long days with Salverion in the operating rooms. Only the most difficult and painful operations were performed by Salverion, Kes, and the experienced healer-priests from the Citadel. The rest of the work was done by the Infirmary's full-time surgeons, whose patients did not have the benefit of the release from pain by gifted hands. Gabriel never got used to hearing their distant cries.

Every day he and Salverion examined all the patients who had symptoms similar to those of the dreaded bulai fever. Salverion had prepared for the plague, having a large sanatorium built out on an island in the harbour, where victims of the disease could be totally isolated. Also on the island was a crematorium, so that even the dead could not carry the lethal infection back to Navora. So far the sanatorium had remained vacant, but all people with fevers were carefully examined.

Interspersed with the Infirmary work were the visits to the homes of the elite in Navora, whose wealth and influence gave them the right to call on the Grand Master of Healing. Many of the families were Salverion's personal friends, and after the healings he and Gabriel were given fine dinners and even finer gifts. Many of Gabriel's gifts he sent home to his mother or Myron. Most of his monthly stipend he sent anonymously to Hevron, knowing it would be used to improve conditions in the Academy infirmary.

Occasionally he spent mornings at the Citadel, preparing ointments, medicines, and poultices with the good-humoured Amael, Master of Herbal Medicines. But as much as he enjoyed the work with herbs, he longed to work with Sheel Chandra in the mysterious and powerful art of dream healing. When he expressed this wish to Salverion, the Grand Master replied, 'The knowledge Sheel Chandra teaches is the most advanced and sacred and will be given to you when you are ready for it, probably in your third or fourth year here. In the meanwhile, take one step at a time. You're learning all the dimensions of healing, remember; not only healing of the body, but also healing of the emotions and the spirit. Any physician can chop out a tumour or mix a medicine, and hope for the best. Only a healer-priest can release the hidden energies already in the body, and direct healing like a light to wounded memories and nerves and flesh. Much is learned only through prayer, meditation, and mind-power. Such things cannot be hurried.'

Several things could not be hurried, Gabriel discovered: not deep learning, or the pain of separation from family, or a horse when it was feeling obstinate.

'I'm leaving Rebellion here tomorrow,' he announced angrily to Ferron one evening, when he got home. 'I'm running to the Infirmary. It'll be more pleasant, more dignified, and probably quicker.'

He collapsed into a chair, and Ferron smiled and handed

him a glass of cool apricot juice. 'I told you what to do when he gets stubborn,' he said. 'His previous owner always gave him grapes. You don't give him grapes. Every now and again he protests.'

'I refuse to give in to him,' said Gabriel.

'Sounds like a deadlock between two stubborn animals.'

'While it's a deadlock, I'll jog to my work.'

'In that case I hope you're not too tired,' Ferron said. 'You have to go to the city now, I'm afraid. Today there was a message from the palace. An official came early this morning, and said the Empress wants to see you. Alone.'

Gabriel slowly put his drink down on the table, and the glass rattled a little on the polished wood, before he let it go. 'I'm not going,' he said. 'Send a message back to her. Tell her I'm ill.'

'I can't do that! No one refuses the Empress, Gabriel – not even a healer-priest.'

Gabriel sat biting his lower lip, his face strained and white. Suddenly he stood up, went into his room, and changed into his running clothes.

'Can you tell me what's wrong?' asked Ferron, from the doorway.

'No,' said Gabriel, pulling on his shoes. His hands were shaking. Watching him, Ferron felt a surge of anger, almost of contempt. Then he remembered that Gabriel was only eighteen, no more nervous and panic-stricken than Ferron himself had been the first time he was summoned to attend the Empress on his own. 'She doesn't bite, you know,' Ferron said, smiling a little. 'Not often, anyway.'

Gabriel looked up, pure terror on his face. He was so pale, Ferron thought he was going to vomit. 'The old witch won't get near enough to try,' Gabriel said, standing up. Ignoring the shock on Ferron's face, he ran out through the open door into the gardens and vanished between the trees.

Four times he ran around the perimeter of the Citadel grounds, never stopping, running hard, on the last lap almost sobbing with the pain. He got back to his rooms breathless and drenched with sweat, and found Salverion waiting for him.

The Grand Master waited while Gabriel got a towel from his room, wiped his face and neck, and collapsed in a chair in the sitting room. Only when the youth's breathing was normal again did Salverion speak.

'Is it true that you're refusing to see your Empress?' he asked.

'She's not my Empress,' said Gabriel.

'What do you mean by that?'

Gabriel did not answer.

'Is there something you should tell me?' asked Salverion.

Gabriel remained silent.

Losing patience at last, Salverion stood up and began pacing angrily. 'I didn't pick insolence as one of your faults, Gabriel,' he said. 'So what is it? Fear? Cowardice? Some kind of senseless defiance? By God, she *is* your Empress! She stands for everything you believe in, for all that's excellent and great in our Empire. If you can't honour her for that, then at least respect the fact that she holds ultimate power on earth. When she commands, we obey. We do not run away like frightened children.'

He stopped in front of Gabriel, saw that Gabriel's face was stormy and mutinous, and that he was near to tears. Salverion flung himself into a chair, and ran his hands through his white hair. 'I don't understand what's got into you, Gabriel,' he said, his voice quieter now. 'You have to go to the palace. If you don't, you'll devalue the reputation of everyone at the Citadel, and embarrass me and all your Masters. Worse, you'll incur the Empress's wrath – and that is no small thing.'

'What about *me*?' said Gabriel hoarsely, his eyes averted. 'I'm allowed to be devalued and embarrassed, so long as everyone else is all right?'

'Would you like to explain yourself, my son?' Salverion asked, softly.

It was a long time before Gabriel answered. When he did, his voice was so low that the Grand Master had to strain to hear it. He listened, white-faced, while Gabriel told him of the incident with the Empress. 'And that's why I don't want to see her again, Master,' Gabriel finished. 'You can call me a coward; you can dismiss me from the Citadel. But she's not my Empress, not the Empress I believed in and loved all my life. She doesn't stand for anything excellent, anything Navoran. I don't honour her and I won't obey her.'

Salverion sighed heavily and looked suddenly very old and tired. 'I knew the Empress had certain weaknesses,' he said, 'but I never thought they would entangle my own disciple.'

'I'm not entangled,' said Gabriel, 'and I never will be.'

'No. I know that,' said Salverion. 'And if things do become difficult for you – if there is conflict between you and the Empress, I'll speak to her myself and support you to the end. But please think on this calmly, and don't despise the Empress because she has one fault, born out of her deep loneliness. There's much in her that is strong and good and worthy of respect. She's not the only woman in the world to want beautiful young men.'

'She's the only one who can command them, though,' said Gabriel. 'That's an abuse of her power. It makes her corrupt.'

Salverion said gently, 'Not one of us is perfect, my son. Even the Empress. But she isn't totally corrupt, any more than you and I are corrupt because of our shortcomings. Go and see her. But take Ferron with you. Make sure he waits for you just outside the Empress's room, and is within calling distance. See the Empress, treat her illness, if that is what's required, but make sure her own physician is present. If he's not, decline to treat her until he is. I wouldn't attend her without someone else present, and she can hardly blame you for keeping to the same code of conduct. You know enough to treat her usual minor ailments. If you're not sure, ask her physician. If she's not ill . . . well, your own conscience must guide you there. Remain courteous, and leave as peacefully as you can. If politeness and composure are not possible, flee. Ferron knows a secret way out of the palace. Hide in the hills for a few days, then come back here, but not by the main gate. By then I'll know which way the palace winds blow.'

'And if they blow against me?'

'We'll discuss that if the time comes. But please don't think of the worst yet. It may be that the Empress simply wants to talk to you, or that she does have some complaint she feels you can deal with without my supervision. Be calm. Ferron will guard you – with his life if necessary. Maybe you'll be back in a short time, laughing at these fears.'

Lightly, the Master touched the top of Gabriel's head, as if blessing him. 'Come and see me when you get back,' he added, 'no matter what the hour.'

The Empress smiled and handed Gabriel a golden goblet of white wine. There was no slave in the room, and she had poured the wine herself – a rare honour for a guest. He took it in both hands and bowed his head as he thanked her for it. He had not seen her standing before; she was surprisingly tall and slender. Her long dress was of the softest silk, the same violet as her eyes. Her hair was plaited and adorned with amethysts and silver ribbons. In the lowered lamplight she looked younger than he remembered her, gracious, less threatening. Even so, he shook, and his throat was so dry he could hardly speak.

'Come and sit down, Gabriel,' she said.

They were in the same room as before, but this time she was sitting not on the great carved throne but beneath the windows on a divan spread with luxuriant cushions. She indicated for him to sit beside her, so he did, as far from her as he reasonably could, and slightly facing her direction.

The Empress Petra relaxed, leaning with her left arm on the back of the divan, her cheek resting on her hand. Sipping her wine, she studied the healer-priest. He looked excellent in the Citadel robes, princely and beautiful. This time his hair was not tied back, and it was tousled, rippling gold against the crimson.

'You're enjoying your work with Salverion?' she asked.

'Yes, Your Majesty, thank you.'

'Which healing art do you find the most satisfying?'

'I haven't learned them all yet. But I've enjoyed the surgery more than I thought I would.'

'Don't you find it strange, being the youngest of all the healer-priests?'

He grinned nervously and sipped his wine. 'I never think of my age, Your Majesty. It still puzzles me when patients look alarmed.'

The Empress laughed: a warm, throaty sound. 'Salverion says you are an exceptional person. And I know you are, in more than healing ways. I haven't forgotten the talk we had when you were here before.'

He said nothing, but his fingers tightened around the golden cup.

'Did you ever fully understand what your dream meant?' she asked. 'The one with the white silk?'

'Yes, I did.'

'Can you tell me?'

'I'm sorry, I'd rather not, Your Majesty.'

There was a long silence, and he drank more wine. Suddenly it occurred to him that the wine might be drugged, and he lowered the cup, staring uneasily into its gleaming depths.

'Would you like something to eat?' she asked.

'No, thank you. We ate before we left.'

'We?'

'I came with a friend, Lady.'

'You were afraid to visit your Empress alone?' Her voice was light, mocking.

'No. But the Grand Masters prefer us not to ride in the city alone at night.'

'And they are wise, with so much crime in our streets. Have you talked with the philosophers yet, at the Citadel?'

'With some of them, Your Majesty. But so far my learning has been mainly with Salverion, in the Infirmary. I'll study more in the winter, when travel to the Infirmary won't always be easy.'

'Does that mean you won't be able to visit me, either, in the wintertime?'

'It does, Your Majesty.'

'I should have been making more use of you these summer months, then.'

'I've been very busy.'

'I know. That's why I waited. There were several times I

wanted to see you, but I waited until now, when my need was most urgent.'

Gabriel stared down at his hands and fought to remain calm. It took all his will just to remain seated there beside her.

'I have a dream,' said the Empress. 'The same dream, night after night. It worries me. It's not a bad dream, and I'm not frightened in it, but I know it's significant. I've asked my physician about it, and the philosophers and astrologers here. But they don't know. They guess, they all tell me different things – mainly what they think I want to hear. Nothing they say feels right to me. Even my most skilled augur, Jaganath, is uncertain. I need to know what the dream means, Gabriel. I trust you. You're forthright and honest. If I tell you my dream, will you tell me what it means?'

'I'm not a seer, Lady.'

'But you know what dreams mean.'

'Only my own dreams. I know what my dream symbols are, and from those I can work out meanings – sometimes. Not always. I can't promise I can help you.'

'I understand. Shall I begin?'

He nodded, and she took a deep breath. 'This is my dream: I'm sitting in a room that is totally empty but for a pile of stones on the floor. Then I see a hand moving across the stones. It's not my hand; it's someone else's. I don't see the person, only the hand. The hand sorts out the stones; some are precious jewels, but some, though they look like jewels, are only coloured glass. I can't tell the difference, but I know that the hand can. The hand divides the stones into two piles, the jewels and the glass. Then a strong wind comes, and mixes up the stones again.

'A prince comes and sits down by the stones. He sorts them into two piles, then gets up and walks out. An old woman comes in, sees the two lots of stones, and goes out again weeping. She is very distressed. Suddenly the stones are mixed up again. A prophet comes in and sorts them into two piles, gets up, and goes out. The old woman comes in again, looks at the two piles of stones, and goes out weeping. The same thing happens a third time, only this time a madman comes in. He's dressed in rags, and dribbles everywhere and mutters to himself. He sorts out the stones, and when the old woman comes in, I think she'll go wild with despair. But this time, when she sees the two piles, she sings praises, and goes out dancing. I feel very surprised by her reaction. The stones remain in their two piles, and I know they are right. So what does it all mean, Gabriel?'

For a long while he stared at the floor, seeing nothing, his eyes almost closed. 'It's to do with evaluation,' he said at last. 'The precious stones and the coloured glass must be divided correctly. Your dream is to do with discernment, with knowing what is true and what is false.'

'Whose discernment? Mine? Do I have to make a decision?'

'No. It wasn't your hand dividing the stones. It was someone else's. Someone else is the judge. The wind signifies change. Wind always blows something away, brings in something new.'

A slow smile spread across the Empress's face. 'Go on, Gabriel. You're making a great deal of sense, so far.'

He was silent for a while. The Empress waited, watching his face, seeing his eyes brilliant and fixed on something far away she could not see. He was very still, relaxed but intent, as if he were listening or trying hard to remember something.

'The prince and the prophet are similar,' he said. 'They would both seem to be good valuers of the stones. But the old woman is Wisdom. She sees that they have made wrong judgements, and she grieves. Then the madman comes. He's the odd one out. He doesn't symbolise insanity; he symbolises the one who is different, the unexpected one, the one you would not think would show the greatest discernment. But he's the one the old woman, who is Wisdom, is most pleased with. He's the right one to divide the stones. I would say, Lady, that your dream means you are looking for someone with discernment, someone to decide between true and false. The right person is not the one you would logically choose.'

He took a deep breath and looked expectantly at the Empress. She was gazing at him with wonder.

'You have the Vision, Gabriel!' she cried.

He blushed deeply. 'No, Your Majesty. I'm just very good at guessing.'

'You have the Vision. Your interpretation of my dream is more fitting than you know. You've just told me things about Navora, and about our politics, that no one else in this city knows yet – except me and my advisers and those scheming astrologers. I was right to call on you. I would have made a huge mistake if you hadn't come here tonight.'

Finishing his wine, he put the cup on the table nearby. A sudden sense of unease disturbed him. 'Lady,' he said, 'if you intend to take my interpretation seriously, to act on it, please first discuss it with Sheel Chandra, or Salverion. As I said, I've only interpreted my own dreams, at times when I've needed guidance or confirmation about important matters in my life. But your dreams – they help you rule an Empire. They're too important for me to interpret, without training or true understanding. Please promise that you won't act on what I've said, without discussing it with one of my masters.'

'I'm not accustomed to making such promises,' she said. 'But your humbleness is refreshing, after the self-conceit of my usual advisers. I will take care, that I do promise you. Now, how can I thank you?'

'No thanks are necessary, Lady,' he said, relieved. 'My dream interpretations, like my healings, are free.'

'Not to me, Gabriel. Give me your hand.'

For a few seconds he hesitated, then held it out. She removed a ring from her middle finger, and put it on him. The ring was small, and she tried it on him twice before it slid on to his little finger. He examined the ring, and noticed that it was a snake forming the first letter of her name.

'Only ten people in the Empire have a ring like that, Gabriel,' she said. 'It's my pledge-ring. You may use it once in your life, when you need my help. When you send me that ring with a request, whatever you ask I will do. That's my solemn pledge, and I swear it in the name of God. The pledge-promise is greater than all laws and transcends all other commands. But you may ask only one thing, and the pledge-ring will not be returned to you. Use it wisely.'

'Thank you, Your Majesty,' he said hoarsely. The Empress was silent, and he realised there was nothing more to be said. He stood and bowed low in front of her. 'Is there anything else I may do for you, Your Majesty, before I go?' he asked.

'I haven't dismissed you yet.'

'I'm sorry, Your Majesty,' he stammered, his face scarlet.

'Your impropriety is forgiven. You may leave.'

'Thank you, Lady.' He bowed low again, not daring to meet her eyes, and began to back away. Panicking, he did not know if it was proper to turn his back on her as he walked out, so he walked backwards several paces, then bowed again, and turned and went away. Outside the guarded doors of her suite Ferron was waiting for him, his face anxious.

'Is everything all right?' Ferron whispered, and Gabriel nodded.

A slave met them and showed them out through the lamp-lit rooms and inner gardens to the courtyard. On their way out they passed a very tall, middle-aged man in long emerald robes richly embroidered in cerise with stars and mystical symbols. He was extremely handsome, with a cultured face and elegant bearing. He was so impressive that Gabriel stopped, and he and the man regarded each other for a few moments. Then the man bowed low.

'You must be Gabriel, Salverion's disciple,' the man said in silky tones. He smiled, and his black eyes glittered. His skin was olive coloured and flawless, his black beard carefully oiled into tiny ringlets. 'Greetings. I am Jaganath, Spiritualist and High Oracle to Her Majesty.'

Gabriel too bowed. 'Greetings, Lord Jaganath. It's an honour to meet you. I've heard of the great skills you have in prophecy and divination.'

'Though not great enough for Her Majesty at the moment, it seems,' said the Oracle softly, his smile fixed and too charming. 'You'll put me out of business, Gabriel.'

'I don't think so, lord. My skills this evening were guesswork and good luck.'

'We shall see,' said Jaganath, and glided past.

'Well?' Ferron shouted, when they were on their horses and cantering through the city streets. 'What happened? And what was Jaganath talking about, saying you'd put him out of business?'

'She wanted me to interpret a dream,' Gabriel said, laughing with the relief that rushed over him. 'Oh, God! I feel as if I've been let out of prison!'

'What do you mean, you interpreted a dream for her? You're not a dream healer yet.'

'I'll explain it all later. While we're in the city, can we visit my home? I'd love to see everyone again.'

'You don't need my permission, Gabriel. I'm only your keeper.'

But Salverion's face rose in Gabriel's mind, and he remembered the Master's anxiety. He sighed and urged Rebellion on towards the highway to the Citadel. The horse was in a rare mood for a gallop, so Gabriel and Ferron raced, leaving clouds of moonlit dust behind them on the road.

At the Citadel, though it was well past midnight, Gabriel knocked on Salverion's door. Immediately it was opened, and Salverion stood there fully dressed, and looking extremely anxious.

'She only wanted me to interpret a dream, Master,' said Gabriel, smiling, holding out his right hand. 'She gave me a pledge-ring, see?'

Salverion was stunned. 'You interpreted a dream for her?'

'I told her what I thought it meant. She and I talked about dreams before. I happened to mention that I know what mine mean. She thought I could help her find the meaning of hers. Which I did, I think.'

'Is she going to act on what you've told her?'

'I gather so, from what she said. But I did ask her to discuss my interpretation with you or Sheel Chandra first. I warned her that I might be wrong, that interpretation is only a knack I have, to understand my own dreams.'

'It's not a knack, it's a gift. But you were wise to ask her to consult one of us. Your interpretation, if the Empress acts on it, could affect our Empire.'

'I know, Master. That's why I warned her.'

'The High Oracle, Jaganath, won't like this. He'll look on you as a threat, when he finds out.'

'He already knows. I met him as we were leaving. He was polite enough, like a python before it strikes.'

'You understand him, then. He's a dangerous enemy to make, Gabriel. He's her chief adviser, which makes him one of the most influential men in the Empire. His powers are formidable, and he uses them to manipulate people and events, and to further his own ambitions. Beware of him.'

'I'm a healer-priest, just beginning,' said Gabriel lightly. 'I'm hardly likely to be a threat to the Empress's High Oracle.'

Salverion smiled, but his eyes, as he watched his disciple go, were deeply troubled.

'I hope you don't spend all your spare time studying, Gabriel,' said Salverion one evening as they were riding back to the Citadel. They rode slowly, for it had been raining heavily that day, and the road was slippery with mud and yellow leaves. 'I worry that you work too hard.'

'I don't,' Gabriel assured him. 'Ferron sees to that. He drags me off to all the plays and poetry readings, and all the musical events, as well as the art and science exhibitions. I've never been so inspired in all my life.'

'I heard a musical event last night,' said Salverion, straight-faced. 'It went on until dawn, was very noisy, and most of the singing was off-key and not at all inspiring.'

A slow blush spread upward over Gabriel's face. 'We celebrated Ferron's birthday, Master,' he said. 'Some friends came for dinner. I'm sorry we disturbed you.'

'You didn't. I've learned to sleep with my fingers in my ears. I forgot it was Ferron's birthday. I usually give him something. Talking of gifts . . . that's a rather splendid sapphire you have fixed to your cloak. From the Empress, for another dream wisely interpreted?'

'For another dream interpreted, anyway, Master. Whether I

was right or not is yet to be seen.' He hesitated, frowning. 'I hope she checks my interpretations with her advisers before she acts on them. I always ask her to test what I say, and to have it confirmed by you or Sheel Chandra. It worries me that she never does. I wish she wouldn't depend on me in this way.'

'You don't have a choice, since she demands your help in these matters. Obviously she trusts your opinion. And I must say I'd rather trust your interpretation of royal dreams, than Jaganath's. He'd tell any tale to further his own ambitions. Have you seen him again?'

'Not to talk to. But the last time I saw the Empress, Jaganath was in the room. He was sitting in a far corner, just watching and listening. He never spoke, and left before I did.'

They came to a rise in the road, and stopped. Before them lay the Shinali lands, wreathed in mist. It was just on dusk, and in the orange skies a few stars were already out. Across the quiet evening came the bleating of sheep. Far out on the plain, from a shadowy place by the river, rose a thin column of pale smoke.

'Do you know much about the Shinali people?' asked Salverion.

'No, Master.'

'I couldn't help noticing, that first morning when you had your ritual wash in the holy pool, that you were wearing a Shinali amulet.'

Gabriel made no comment, but all his being grew tense. Salverion, watching him, saw that he struggled with painful emotions. 'Do you want to tell me about it, my son?' he asked, gently.

Gabriel shook his head. Salverion waited, and after a time Gabriel said, his voice broken and low, 'It was the great wrong of my life.'

He said no more, but his eyes, fixed on the Shinali lands, were full of anguish.

'I too have done great wrongs,' said Salverion. 'I've done things I regretted and left undone things I should have done. Both have caused unbearable guilt. But I've discovered, over the years, that sometimes we are given another chance, a way to right the wrong. Sometimes it's this atonement that shapes our destiny, redeems us, makes us the people we were born to become.'

Still Gabriel was silent, and Salverion followed his gaze to the Shinali plain. 'You're not the first healer-priest to have a bond with the Shinali,' he went on, still with gentleness. 'Amael, our Master of Herbal Medicines, visited them once to exchange knowledge with their healer. They're a gentle and spiritual people, the Shinali. They're sheep farmers and hunters, though they were formidable warriors when they were called to be. They fought hard to keep that plain, and it remains the only part of their vast homeland that we didn't take. The treaty guaranteed them the plain forever, but already the Navoran authorities want part of it. It's flat, fertile, and – according to the authorities – mostly unused. I hear talk in some of the houses I visit, and it worries me. There will be conflict again. Destiny hasn't yet finished with the Shinali; there's a chapter in their history yet unwritten. And in ours.'

'What do you mean, Master?'

'There's a prophecy known only to those at the Citadel. Many years ago it was seen in a vision by three of the Citadel Masters, all separately, but at the same hour. The Shinali will rise again, be reborn as a great nation. They'll reclaim their lands, wipe out much of Navora as we know it. But the best of our civilisation will remain, and for us too there will be a rebirth, a new beginning. We'll join with the Shinali, become a unified people, living side by side in harmony, with a simpler, purer life. That age will be called the Time of the Eagle.'

'What do you mean, a "purer life"?' asked Gabriel. 'Surely we have a perfect life now, with the Empire as it is! How can it all be torn apart?'

'I wish it were all perfect, my son. But there's a great deal of corruption, and the Empire has committed huge wrongs against the Shinali, and other peoples, in its rise to power. The cleansing will be for our good. The prophecy is of hope and harmony, of things as they were always meant to be. I believe that the Citadel is one great part of our Empire that will remain, but it will be open to all people of all nations, men and women together. Maybe Shinali will study there too, enriching our wisdom and arts.

'And there's another part to the prophecy that I find intriguing. The catalyst to the changes, for us and for the Shinali, will be a Navoran. One man who will bring about the rise of the Shinali nation, and the undoing and eventual rebirth of ours.'

'He'll be a traitor, this man?'

'No – though he may be accused of that. He'll be a deliverer, Gabriel, the beginning of a great and necessary reformation.'

Salverion turned his horse back to the road, and they went on. Gabriel's mood lifted, and he talked about Amael, and his work with herbs. He spoke, too, of Sheel Chandra, and how he longed to work with him in the art of healing with the powers of the mind.

'That will happen sooner than you think,' said Salverion, smiling. 'I've already spoken with him about you. You begin work together tomorrow.'

'Tomorrow? But I thought I couldn't work with him until my third or fourth year!'

'I said you would not begin work with him until you were ready. Anyone who can interpret dreams for the Empress is ready to study with Sheel Chandra. I don't think you realise this, Gabriel, but you have the Vision. My understanding of this is limited; Sheel Chandra is the one you need to learn from now.'

Gabriel looked astounded. 'I didn't think it was the Vision, Master,' he murmured. 'I thought it was just ordinary intuition.'

'So it is, but developed to an extraordinary degree.'

'I'll miss working with you, Master.'

'And I shall miss you. But it's only for a few months, then we'll work together again. I'll need you in the Infirmary later in the winter, when it's full of people with winter ailments. But we haven't been so busy lately, and now is a good time for you to do something different.'

'What will you do, Master?'

'I'll operate in peace for a change, without your interminable questions, and I'll do a few things I don't normally have time for. Tomorrow I'll visit the prison.'

'I didn't realise you went there.'

'I've never mentioned it, because the visits are not compulsory for you.'

'Why do you go, Master? Why not some of the physicians from the city?'

'Many do, though the work is voluntary because prisoners have no rights, not even to medical care. I go because seeing the prisoners keeps true my perspective on human life.'

'You go to the prison alone?'

'A prison guard is always with me.'

'I mean, don't you want any help? I'll go with you.'

'Thank you. But I've already made arrangements for Sheel Chandra to see you tomorrow. Besides, this visit won't be busy;

the prison is half empty now. We have a new High Judge in the Navoran Court. A man called Cosimo. He's re-examining the evidence from some of the old trials, and many prisoners have been released.'

'They were wrongly imprisoned?'

'Yes. That's just one part of that corruption I mentioned. Over the past few years, justice hasn't always served the people; it's served the powerful few in high places. Whether a person was judged guilty or innocent often depended not so much on evidence, as on whether he wore silk or rags.'

'And everyone just accepted it?' cried Gabriel, appalled.

'Not everyone. There are a few who had the courage to stand up and challenge the system. They died of obscure poisons, or met with fatal accidents, or ended up in prison on trumped-up charges. One way or another they've been silenced.'

'This new judge must be taking a few risks.'

'Oh, he is. But he's not the sort to be easily intimidated.'

'You know him?'

'I've met him several times. He's become a friend, actually. He has a medical condition he's asked me about. It's because of this condition that the majority of people thought he would never be chosen as judge, though he's a man of integrity and has a remarkable knowledge of the Navoran laws. The Empress had three men to choose from. The other two had admirable qualities, and everyone expected her to appoint one of them. But, against all advice, she chose this man, and he's proving to be the finest High Judge we've seen in a long time. We have justice in the Navora court again. What are you smiling at, Gabriel?'

'I'm pleased that Her Majesty made the right choice,' said Gabriel.

'So am I, though she defied Jaganath over it.'

'Does that matter?' asked Gabriel. 'He's only her adviser.'

'He's a great deal more than that. He has tremendous power, can control dreams and create illusions. I suspect he even uses demons to manipulate people. He has a strong hold over the Empress and, through her, influences much that happens in the Empire. I tell you this in strictest confidence. But it may help you to understand Petra, and why she bends so often to his will. In her own soul she's a wise woman, with a strong sense of justice and a deep love for the old values Navora was built on. Free of Jaganath, she would rule very differently and restore those values – which she is beginning to do, with the appointment of the new judge. I don't know who or what gave her the strength to stand against Jaganath, but I'm glad it's happened at last.'

'This condition the new judge has, Master . . . can you tell me what it is?'

'Yes. He's blind.'

'Can you cure his blindness?' asked Gabriel.

'I can, but whether I will or not depends on him,' said Salverion. 'I have the feeling that he would rather remain the way he is.'

'Why would he want that?'

Salverion smiled and asked, 'Isn't justice meant to be blind?'

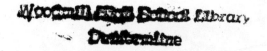

8 Temptation

DEAREST GABRIEL, Myron wrote, Greetings from my new home! Well, it's not truly my new home, but I'm living here for a while, so I can continue my sword practice at the Navora gymnasium. I'm living with Eva's family. I can tell what you're thinking, brother, and you can wipe the grin off your face. There's no creeping about between the rooms after dark, believe me. Her father's very religious and had wanted Eva to be a priestess at the temple. He's given up the priestess idea, thank God, but he's clinging to the notions of innocence and celibacy. I have a challenging time even stealing a kiss from her. However, I live in hope. And I scheme a lot.

No doubt Mother's already told you about her new home in the hills. You'd love it; the house is built of wood and smells like a forest. Mother's planted winter vegetables and plans to farm sheep for their wool. She's very happy and spends quite a lot of time with the surveyor who marked out the land. It was bought from the Shinali and is on the edge of their plain. The Navoran authorities bought enough land for ten farms, though they wanted more. The farms will all grow produce for the Navoran markets. There's a flour mill planned, and a proper road being made between the farms and the city.

The other day I met a friend who was recovering from a chariot accident. He had broken a leg and ruptured something inside – his spleen, whatever that is. But he said you were his healer when he was in the Infirmary. It was a while ago, before the winter. He described what you did for him, how you healed him after the surgery by moving your hands over him, just above the wounds. He said it was strange, and it frightened him at first, but then the pain went and he could feel forces of some kind flowing through him, like warmth. He cried when he told me. It almost made me want to go and leap head first out of a racing chariot, just to have your healing. I can't tell you how proud I am of you, how much joy I have thinking of this wonderful work you're doing. Surely nothing in the world could be greater than giving another human being life.

Thank you for all your letters. I'm glad you're enjoying your training with Sheel Chandra. He sounds an amazing man. I can't imagine why you have to spend so much time meditating, but no doubt it's to do with the mysterious dream healing. I wish you could tell me more about that kind of work, but I know you're not allowed. I try to give myself nightmares, so I can sleep in the Sanctuary of Healing Dreams and let you chant prayers over me. So far I just have nightmares about chasing Eva and catching her father instead, but I don't think they qualify me for a sleeping place in the sanctuary. Mother says it's a place for people with hurts or fears so deep, they can't bear to think about them when they're awake, and they must sleep in the sanctuary and be healed through their dreams, while healer-priests pray for them. She seems to know quite a lot about it; did she ever sleep there? Sometimes I think she must have been very unhappy with Father. I hope she marries the surveyor. I've met him and like him very much. So do the others, especially Subin, who wheedles cakes and little pet turtles out of him. She misses you. So do I. I think of you every hour,

with love,
Myron.

Smiling to himself, Gabriel read the letter through several times. Though it was afternoon, the lamps were lit, and they gleamed on his high boots and fur cloak. Under the cloak his crimson winter garments were rich, each of the thick quilted shoulders embroidered with seven silver stars.

There was kindling wood in his fireplace, and a supply of coal in a basket on the hearth, but the fire had not been lit. A brazier burning in the middle of his room had scarcely taken the chill off the air. Outside his window the garden was white with snow, and the trees were almost bare, their last leaves ragged and dark against the azure skies. But behind him, glimmering in the lamplight, were the summer hills Ferron had painted on his wall, and a flock of sheep and a Shinali shepherdess.

Reluctantly he placed the letter down on the table and put out the lamps. Over the metal brazier he placed a heavy lid, so the flames would die out. There was a sudden stamping outside his door, and it was flung open. Freezing air whipped into the room as Ferron entered, slamming the door shut behind him.

'The chariot's waiting,' Ferron announced, shaking snow from his cloak, and stamping his boots hard on the mat. 'Are you sure you don't want me to come with you?'

'I'm positive. I just hope the child isn't seriously sick. I shouldn't be going without Salverion. Why does he have to be out at dinner, tonight of all nights?'

'Why, tonight of all nights, is it Jaganath's child that gets sick?' asked Ferron. 'Be careful, Gabriel. The man's evil. He hates you. You're doing his work and stealing his influence. I wouldn't be surprised if he injured his own child just to lure you there.'

'What for – so he can harm me as well?' said Gabriel, half laughing. 'You're too suspicious, Ferron.'

'You don't know him. I do. For years I've watched him. He's corrupt, powerful, and dangerous. They all are – he and his soothsayer cronies. They run the Empire.'

'You sound like Salverion,' said Gabriel, grinning as he

picked up his leather bag of medical instruments and essential medicines. 'I promise I'll treat the child and come straight home. Will you have supper ready for me?'

'Of course. Take care.'

In the long porch ways the air was brittle with the cold. Gabriel pulled up the hood of his cloak, wrapped his scarf about his throat and the lower part of his face, and hurried along to the arched door that led to the main gate. In the courtyard someone had wiped the snow off the sundial, and its bronze surface shone. The fountains were frozen into stillness, and the trees were stately and dark, their branches bending under the weight of the snow. All else in the garden was pristine white, unutterably peaceful. But in spite of the serenity, a deep uneasiness fell over Gabriel. He stopped and for several moments stood staring at the white garden, his lips moving in a prayer for protection and safekeeping. Then, feeling more at peace, he went out to the waiting chariot.

The child lay writhing in her bed, her skin wet with sweat. Her right arm ached where the snake had struck, and breathing was difficult. She tried to sit up to call for her mother, but no sound came, and she collapsed back on the silken pillows, distressed. Ten years old she was, with her father's dark skin and blue-black hair. Her eyes were green, for her mother was a red-haired slave. She became aware of her father bending over her, stroking her hair. His lips on her cheek were hot, and she turned away, whimpering.

'Just a little longer, Syana, and the healer will be here,' Jaganath whispered. 'Lie still, else the poison will only run faster through your veins.'

Syana obeyed, though tears slid down her cheeks, and she

trembled from fear and pain. She tried to look up, but her eyes would not open properly, and she saw only a blur of dark skin, and two deep spots that were her father's eyes. Then there was a different voice speaking, and someone golden and scarlet bent over her. Her shift was moved aside, and cold fingers gently brushed her shoulder. She did not mind that the hands were cold; she was burning up and welcomed the touch, like cool water flowing over her. She closed her eyes and lay very still. The unfamiliar voice, quiet and calm, was asking questions. And she could hear her father's answers, though sometimes the pain got bad again, and her arm cramped and ached, and she could not hear what was said. Then cool hands were on her again, easing the pain, binding her arm firmly but gently, so she could not move it. The stranger was talking again, telling her that everything was all right and she would soon be well. She relaxed and let the hands heal her, not caring about anything except breathing.

'It was a little black snake,' Jaganath told Gabriel. 'It had two yellow spots on its head. The child was playing in the courtyard, and knocked over a potted plant. The snake must have been sleeping underneath it.'

Gabriel checked the child's mouth and saw that her gums were bleeding. Gently he asked her if she felt nauseated, and she nodded slightly. He asked her to open her eyes wide, but she could not, and he knew the poison had been enough to begin paralysing her. Every vein in her body still carried the venom, and she needed the deepest kind of healing – the kind that called forth the body's own energies and powers to cleanse and restore and heal.

Gabriel stood up. 'I have to ask you to leave, my lord,' he said to Jaganath. 'What I have to do requires all my concentration, and I can't be distracted. Would you please send me Syana's mother?'

'There's nothing she can do to help you that I cannot do,' said Jaganath.

For a moment Gabriel was at a loss. How could he tell Jaganath that his energies were disturbing, even destructive? That everything in the man repelled him, and that healing was impossible in his presence?

'For this kind of healing I must have total peace,' Gabriel said, carefully. 'I'm sorry, but your forces and mine are different.'

'Then I'll leave, and you may be alone with her,' said Jaganath.

'I'd like her mother present.'

'Very well, since you insist.' Jaganath turned and went out, and Gabriel put away the unused bandages and washed his hands in a silver bowl of water that had been placed on a table for that purpose. There was a soft sound behind him, and Syana's mother came in. She saw Gabriel, and her green eyes widened in surprise.

'You're the healer-priest?' she asked.

'Yes, lady.'

She blushed deeply at the title he gave her. 'I'm not Jaganath's wife,' she said softly. 'I'm one of his slaves. Will Syana live?'

'Yes. The venom is seldom fatal. But it's caused some paralysis and bleeding in her mouth and stomach, and she's in a lot of pain. I need to give your daughter mind-healing, to pray for her. It takes a while, and I mustn't be disturbed while I do it. But I wanted you present. And I need your permission.'

The woman nodded.

Gabriel turned back to the child. She was barely conscious,

but she sobbed sometimes from pain, and her breathing was still laboured. He had done all for her that an ordinary physician would have done, but it was not enough. He stood for a few moments praying, gathering his strength and preparing himself. When he was ready he leaned over the child, his hands either side of her small shoulders, his forehead close to hers. He closed his eyes, aligning all his mind, all the forces of his body and soul, with hers. He was hardly breathing, no longer mindful of his own body. His whole world became the child; became her energies, her torment, her battle to survive.

He was acutely aware of her brain, of all the delicate nerves and blood vessels of her head. Beginning at the top of her head and following the contours of her skull and brain, he imagined healing light. Through all her head it flowed, around the swollen tissues and veins of her eyes and face, through all her tortured nerves, down even to the taste buds and the surface of her tongue. He envisaged every major blood vessel and poured the white light through, cleansing and healing, negating the bleeding, the forces of the venom. Then he renewed her thoughts, casting out the fears and hurts, restoring her peace, and making strong her wavering will to live. Briefly he explored the images he saw there; he glimpsed a favourite doll and a pet monkey in a cage. There were impressions of her father, lofty and terrifying. And a snake, a tiny black snake with yellow spots on its head, gliding out of an upturned basket of toys. The snake image was dominant, made sharp by fear. He saw the reptile raise its head, preparing to strike. Gabriel's breathing, like the child's, became quick and afraid. It took all his will to wipe out the snake, to replace it with silver light that comforted and healed.

Praying, he poured the light through her neck, easing the

paralysis in her windpipe as she breathed, then on to her shoulders and arms, making the light very bright around the wound. Every muscle of her arms and hands he saw filled with healing; every chamber in her thudding heart, her lungs, the marrow of her bones, her intestines, and the vital organs that strove to deal with the invading poison. The light rushed, swift and strong like a river, through all of her, overwhelming the venom, fighting it on a huge scale and in every minute cell of her being. He baptised her with it, bathed her in it, until she was reborn, restored. And only then, when her breathing was easy and her sweat had dried and her pain had gone, did he stand up.

Very slowly he stood, and he said nothing for a while but watched her face while she slept. Her mother stood with him, her shoulder against his. She hardly touched him, but he staggered and almost fell. She took his arm, leading him to a nearby chair. He sank on to it, his head bent.

'Would you like a glass of water, sir?' she asked. He nodded without raising his head, and she hastened to get it. But it was Jaganath's hand that offered him the goblet, and it was not water, but wine. Gabriel sipped it cautiously, longing for water. Well he knew the vulnerability after this kind of healing, the emptiness that left him defenceless and open to outside forces. He had a niggling fear that Jaganath knew his weakness at this time and intended to exploit it. He struggled to gather his scattered forces, to be alert.

Jaganath bent over the sleeping child and lightly brushed her face with his fingers. For the first time in that long afternoon, her eyes opened fully and focused properly on his face.

'Where's Mama?' she asked.

'She's with our guests, dear heart,' he replied. 'But she was with you while you were healed.'

Syana leaned up on one elbow and looked at the young man sitting in the chair. He grinned at her, and his smile was like her brother's, warm and full of humour. She smiled back. 'Am I allowed something to eat?' she asked.

'Anything you like,' Gabriel replied. 'But you should drink plenty of water, too. It will cleanse your body, chase out the last of the poison.'

'It's already chased out,' she said. 'I had a dream. I was swimming in a sunny lake, only I was turned inside out, and the water went everywhere.' She giggled. 'Even in my bones.'

Gabriel stood up and smoothed her hair gently back from her face. 'You might like a bath,' he said. 'We'll ask your mother to give you one.'

Syana nodded and lay down, a blissful expression on her face. 'I didn't know I had a lump in my ribs that went in and out,' she said, making a pumping motion with her hands. 'Did you know?'

'I was vaguely aware of it,' he said. 'I think it was your heart, Syana.'

In the hall outside, Jaganath offered Gabriel a velvet bag heavy with precious gems. 'For healing my favourite child,' he said. 'What you did was like a miracle. Even Salverion could not have been more skilful.'

'I don't want payment, thank you,' said Gabriel.

'None at all?' asked Jaganath, his lips curled disbelievingly. 'Is that because of those absurd vows they force you to take?'

Gabriel did not reply, and Jaganath gave a humourless laugh. 'They have you under their control, don't they, healer-priest? Still, I accept that you won't be paid. Allow me instead to give you dinner. No – do not protest! I insist. As it happens, I have some important guests who would very much like to meet you.'

'Thank you, but I'd like to go back to the Citadel,' said Gabriel.

'I said I insist.' Jaganath's tone was velvet-smooth, but his eyes were like flint. 'I will not have it said that my daughter's healer was allowed to go away with no reward, not even a dinner. Come.'

He led the way along gleaming black marble floors to the dining room, rich with silken hangings, glorious lamps, and luxurious cushions. The room was firelit, colourful, and warm, yet to Gabriel it felt deathly cold, and he longed to run from it. Instead he bowed politely as he saw the other guests. They were indeed important; they were four of the Empress's most influential advisers, next to Jaganath himself. Three of them Gabriel had seen before at the palace; one he knew from childhood days.

The men were seated on cushions at the low table, but they stood as they were introduced, and Gabriel went to them and shook their hands in the Navoran way. There was Nagay, the commander of the Navoran navy, who had attended the funeral of Gabriel's father. He had not altered; he was still handsome and imposing, with an easy smile and great personal magnetism. As he shook Gabriel's hand, he said, in his gravelly voice: 'You're Jager's son, aren't you?'

'Yes, I am,' said Gabriel. 'I met you four years ago. You were at my father's funeral.'

'Of course. It was a sad day for Navora, that. And for you. If I remember rightly, there was a commotion over you not wanting to take up Jager's business. Your decision was the right one, obviously, since you're an Elected One now. I offer you my congratulations, as much for your determination as for your ability. Jager's brothers would have been daunting opponents.'

'They were, my lord,' said Gabriel, his unease diminishing under Nagay's disarming smile.

The next guest was Kamos, commander of Navora's army. He was a formidable man, not unlike the navigator in appearance, but without Nagay's magnetism. He was blond and tanned and still as muscled as if he had fought his latest battle only yesterday. A distinguished warrior, he was responsible for most of the treaties signed between Navora and foreign nations over the past fifteen years. Now he lived at the palace and was known for his decadence and the considerable influence he had with the Empress. With Nagay, he advised her on all matters to do with foreign nations, and wars were waged on the basis of what he said.

There was Sanigar, esteemed astrologer. He was short, with a bald head and a benign, innocent look. Believing in the influence of the stars, the Empress seldom made a decision without first consulting him. 'It's good to meet you at last, Gabriel,' he said in a soft, effeminate voice. 'I have heard many things about you, all remarkable.'

There was nothing Gabriel could say to that, so he turned to the fourth and final guest. The intensity of this man struck Gabriel like a blow, and he felt the man's energy flowing from him as they shook hands. He was Kanyiida, the High Priest from the Navoran temple. Like Jaganath, he was very tall and dark and charismatic, and his eyes, an unexpected blue, were perceptive and disturbing. Gabriel knew nothing about the High Priest, except that he had tremendous control over the Navoran people. Gabriel could understand why. Feeling awed by the man's presence, he shook hands, then sank gratefully on to the thick cushion Jaganath indicated to him. It was not a good place; he was alone on one side of the table, with Jaganath on his right, and the other four opposite him. He felt alienated, like the accused in a court. As he thought that, he realised that the only influential adviser absent was the new High Judge, Cosimo.

'We have already finished the main part of our meal,' said Jaganath pleasantly, 'but I will have the slaves prepare for you whatever you wish.'

'Just fresh fruit, please, and some water,' said Gabriel. The little wine he had sipped in Syana's room had affected him more than he would have believed possible; the golden utensils and platters of round cheeses on the table were hazy, and the lamps were overbright. There was a confused buzzing in his head, which he knew was a forewarning. He rubbed his eyes and tried to gather his wits.

'I hear that you're studying already with the great Sheel Chandra,' said Kanyiida, in a deep, rich voice. 'Salverion must be very pleased with your progress.'

How did the High Priest know what he was doing? Puzzled and suspicious, Gabriel said nothing.

'Your work with Sheel Chandra must be very satisfying,' said Sanigar in his soft voice, 'especially considering your visionary gifts.'

'All my work is satisfying, my lord Sanigar,' said Gabriel.

'You're happy, then, at the Citadel?' said Sanigar. 'Even though it inhibits you?'

'What do you mean, lord?'

The astrologer shrugged apologetically, his bald dome gleaming softly in the lamplight. 'Well, it seems to us that you are being held back,' he explained. 'In spite of your abilities, it's obvious that Sheel Chandra has not yet taught you all you need to know about dream interpretation.'

'I'm sorry, but I can't discuss my training,' said Gabriel. He picked up a small knife and began peeling an orange. The knife was silver, and about its handle wound a silver snake with opals and emeralds in its scales. He thought of the snake that had bitten the child, and something bothered him, niggling in the back of his mind. There flashed across his memory the picture of an upturned toy basket, and a black snake slithering from it. Yet what had Jaganath said, about a pot in the courtyard? He frowned, trying to remember, and, as he thought, he glanced upward.

On the wall in front of him was a mural depicting various mythical creatures from Jaganath's religion. At the heart of the mural was a being half animal, half human, and it was staring directly down at him with bright black eyes. The hollows in its gaunt cheeks were shadowy, and its gums and pointed teeth were prominent, the lips curling back from them as it smiled. There was something terrible and fascinating about it. While he stared, the face seemed to change: the features clouded and the skin dissolved and another face peered out, a different one, cunning and powerful and too hideous to endure. He cried out. The knife slipped, and the blade, razor sharp, sank deep into the ball of his thumb. The cut stung, bitter with the orange juice. The slave offered him a bowl of water and a clean cloth, and he dipped his hand in the liquid, turning it instantly scarlet. Then he held the cloth hard against the cut, staunching the flow of blood.

'So, you recognise demons when you see them!' murmured Jaganath, looking amused. 'Don't be alarmed, my friend. Demons can be very useful accomplices. And they inhabit only one of the many dimensions open to us, if we have the Vision. But you don't yet fully understand visionary things. The Citadel Masters are very cautious, and there is much they won't explain at first. This is understandable, considering the limited talents of most of their disciples. But you're exceptional, Gabriel. Potential like yours cannot be restrained or denied. Already the Empress has opened a new door for you, for that greater power you have. It disturbs and grieves me that you are not adequately helped by your Masters. I have the greatest respect for Sheel Chandra and Salverion, but in holding you back they're doing you a grave disservice.'

The slave filled Gabriel's goblet with water again, and he drank it thankfully. His head was beginning to clear, though his feelings of disquiet and danger were stronger than ever.

'Lord Jaganath,' he said, hoping he sounded calmer than he felt, 'I appreciate your concern, but I won't discuss my Masters or my training. You don't know what I'm learning, so you can't comment on it.'

'But I do know what you're learning,' said Jaganath. 'Or, rather, I know what you're *not* learning. I don't think you realise the enormous responsibility of dream interpretation. Are you told about the hidden dangers, the risks?'

'I am aware of the responsibility,' Gabriel replied. 'I've always asked the Empress to check my interpretations with my masters. Since she doesn't, I hoped she checked them with you.'

'Ah – but she doesn't,' said Jaganath. 'She trusts only you, in the understanding of her dreams. And dreams are subtle, ambiguous. Interpretations – especially the wrong ones – can cause destruction and death. In fact, in your last dream interpretation, you did cause a death. That's why we're so concerned.'

Gabriel went cold. 'I don't know what you mean, lord.'

'Haven't you heard?' asked Jaganath, his sleek eyebrows raised. 'That last dream you interpreted for Her Highness. What was it now? The pile of grain, with a rat sitting on top, eating it. Was that right?'

Gabriel nodded. It was the dream he had interpreted while Jaganath was in the room.

'Yes. That dream. You told the Empress it implied that something precious to her was being stolen.'

'That's true,' agreed Gabriel. 'That's what the dream did imply.'

'It's most unfortunate that you weren't more precise. She took you to mean that the city treasurer, who had held that highly honoured position for fifteen years, was robbing the Navoran treasury and secretly adding to his personal wealth. She had him beheaded yesterday. We're still grieving, for he was an old friend of ours, and his wife and children are distraught. It was such a little dream, such an easy interpretation, such a monstrous result. I hope you were right, Gabriel.'

Gabriel went white. 'I didn't tell her the corn signified the city wealth,' he said. 'I told her I thought it meant her health, her well-being. I warned her to think carefully about the dream, and I urged her to discuss it with Sheel Chandra. If she did not, I can't be –'

'Keep calm, my friend,' said the High Priest soothingly. 'We are not blaming you. But you must realise that a man has been executed because of one of your interpretations. You've made solemn vows that direct and control your healing powers. But in your dealings with the Empress and her dreams, you have nothing to guide you, nothing to stand on, no experienced teachers to help you. In your dream interpretations, you're free. And the consequences, as we have seen, can be catastrophic. You already realise you need guides in this – but you need guides who are close to Her Majesty, and who are well informed in matters of the Empire. For all their extraordinary gifts, your Masters at the Citadel remain secluded and unaware of worldly things. This isn't their fault, but they can't possibly guide you wisely in your dealings with the Empress. This is why the Empress has never discussed your dream interpretations with them, despite your advice; they could be no help.'

'It would be a sensible move, to consult with us,' agreed Nagay. 'You don't know the Empress, Gabriel, and when you tell her what you think a dream means, you have no idea what she'll do with that knowledge. Honesty is a noble thing, and the advice of a true friend is to be valued above all else. Your own father taught me that, and doubtless it's what he told you as well. But sometimes the truth must be tempered with discretion and experience. I wish you'd let us help you in your new position with the Empress.'

'It isn't a new position,' said Gabriel. 'I'm a healer-priest, not a dream interpreter. I'd be very happy if you could persuade Her Majesty not to call on me again.'

'We'd all be very happy if we could persuade the Empress to do what we want,' remarked Kamos. 'But the truth is, she does what *she* wants. We have no choice but to jump when she cracks the whip. And, whether you like it or not, she's claimed you as her personal analyser of royal dreams. You may continue with your lofty position on your own, or accept the advice and help of those a good deal wiser and older than yourself. I know which I would rather do, when people's lives hang on what I say.'

Gabriel toyed with the handle of the silver knife, and glanced at the door. 'I'll consider it,' he said.

'That is all we ask,' said Jaganath, beaming. Leaning forward, he pushed a platter of bread rolls and cheese towards Gabriel, and a silver jug of wine. 'Now eat, please. Relax, enjoy good conversation and the company of friends who care about you.'

To Gabriel's relief, the conversation shifted from himself to politics. Musicians came in and began softly playing, and the music made Gabriel relax. Then he heard the Shinali mentioned, and his nerves went taut again.

'I had an omen last night about the Shinali,' Sanigar was saying. 'It was a vision, a sword raised between us and the barbarians. What have we done wrong, to upset them?'

Kamos sniggered, his big teeth glinting in the rosy light. 'What have we done right?' he asked. 'If we're not knocking off the chieftain's one and only daughter, we're wheedling our way on to their precious land. Now we're thinking of repealing our treaty with them altogether. No wonder you saw a sword, my friend.'

'It's eleven years since the incident with the daughter!' said Kanyiida. 'Surely they're not still bleating about it!'

'They have long memories,' said Kamos. 'We thought they'd have forgotten about the woman by now, but they haven't. We've had a hellish time just buying enough land for ten farms. They still want nothing to do with us, and they cling to that old treaty like it's the pledge of gods. But we're one step ahead: the treaty allows us to cross their land whenever we wish. We shall wish to again very soon – right through that monstrous hole in the dirt they call a house. A few of them will get trampled, I should think.'

'Is that the only purpose of the little jaunt?' asked Sanigar. 'To trample on a few barbarians?'

'We're going to restore Taroth,' Kamos replied. 'It was our friend Jaganath's idea. It's time the Shinali remembered who's in control.'

As Gabriel listened, a great fear crawled through him. Taroth was the ancient fort in the mountains on the far side of the Shinali land, built in the early days when Navora was first established and was being attacked by the native tribes from the deserts further east. The fort stood near the only pass through the mountains and guarded the Shinali plain and the hills that were the only land access to Navora. The army had not occupied Taroth for fifteen years.

'I think we've talked enough about the Shinali,' said Nagay, with an uneasy glance at Gabriel. 'Perhaps you could amuse us with a small demonstration of your powers, my lord Jaganath. I'm sure Gabriel would be more interested in that than in the future of a race of savages.'

'Ah, yes, a demonstration!' cried Kamos. 'Maybe you could contact Gabriel's father, Jaganath. That'd give the lad a thrill.'

Gabriel glanced at Jaganath; the High Oracle was watching him, his black eyes full of insight and cunning.

'If you don't mind, lord, I'd like to leave now,' said Gabriel.

But before anyone could move, Jaganath snapped his fingers, and a slave extinguished all the lamps but one. That one light glowed softly on Jaganath, but the rest of the room, apart from the dying firelight, was in darkness. Immediately there was silence. Gabriel stared at the High Oracle, and the hair tingled on the back of his neck. Jaganath was falling into a deep trance. His body swayed a little, and his eyelids fluttered, then closed. His head fell back. His throat was strong, the muscles in spasm as he struggled with extreme emotions. In the dim lamplight his long black ringlets and oiled beard shimmered with fire, and his skin had an unearthly sheen. Yet Gabriel saw only obscure shades and felt an appalling cold.

Strange sounds came from Jaganath's throat, as if he were being forced to speak. 'I see a boy running,' he said, his voice halting and guttural. 'He's running, running as if demons are after him. I see him at home. Lying stretched across a table, being whipped.'

Gabriel stood up, knocking over the bowl of fruit. His face was white.

Jaganath continued. 'There's a message from your father, Gabriel. Jager . . . Jager says he had no idea of your distress, that night. He deeply regrets that he beat you. He loves you, Gabriel. He always loved you. You were his favourite son, his eldest.'

'He never told me.' Gabriel's voice came out strangled. 'He never told me; I don't believe it.'

'He wants to tell you now. You can have a whole new relationship with your father, Gabriel. He wants it. He wants to talk with you often. Don't disappoint him. He's waiting for you.'

'No!' Gabriel stooped and felt in the darkness behind him for his cloak and bag. He swept them up and turned towards the curtained door and the long hall where lights still burned.

But Jaganath said, still in that strange, unearthly tone, 'There's a Shinali woman, too, who wants to talk with you.'

Gabriel froze. Very slowly, he turned around. His face was ashen and drenched with sweat, and sweat ran down inside his clothes. He shook his head and tried to speak but could not.

'I see a Shinali woman,' said Jaganath, 'with her hands reaching out to you. She cries for help, but you don't give it. You run. And I see her fall on the stones. She dies. She dies. But what is it, now? Ah! the voice is clear! "Tell the child," she says. "Tell the child to feel no guilt."'

Gabriel went back and sat down. He leaned on the table, his head buried in his arms.

Jaganath sighed deeply and after a while opened his eyes. The only sound in the room was the sputtering of the solitary lamp, and the agonised breathing of the young man.

'Dear friend, you must not distress yourself,' said Jaganath, with great gentleness. 'The woman has forgiven you. Do you know who she is?'

Without looking up, Gabriel shook his head.

'She was a chieftain's daughter. Eleven years ago she came here to learn about our ways, as a peace-sign between us and them. She was to stay in Navora only a month, and then return to her own people. But she was kidnapped. Someone wanted a ransom for her, knowing the Empire would pay anything to keep the peace between Navora and the Shinali, who were still a significant tribe then. But before the ransom price was paid, she escaped. You saw what happened to her on her way to the Shinali lands. But you were only a child, Gabriel. And all is forgiven, all is well. All is well.'

Gabriel raised his head. The High Priest was looking at him, his face smiling and full of love. 'What torment you have lived in, my dear friend!' Kanyiida cried, tenderly. 'I'm astonished that Sheel Chandra never helped you.'

'He didn't know,' said Gabriel.

'What a great sadness,' mused Sanigar. 'If he had even the smallest measure of the Vision, he would have known. He would not have let you suffer any longer. You see the enormous good that can be done, when the Visionary gift is fully used? When we have the authority to tear through the veil between this world and the next, and make a connection across the grave? Imagine how much you could do for the depressed, the grieving, the hurt.'

'At the moment, even with all the wisdom of a healer-priest, your power is not enough,' said Jaganath to Gabriel. 'Your power stops at death. Yet death is the only certainty in life, the ultimate reality. But you don't learn anything about it. How limiting that is, my friend! You can work miracles for the sick, but in the end they all die. And you can do nothing, not for them or for those who mourn for them. In the last great human experience, you're impotent.' The High Oracle's voice dropped, became silky and seductive. 'But I can change that, Gabriel. I can give you authority that goes beyond death, to the Other Side. I can give you the skill to see beyond the veils of death and to bring back visions of those who dwell there. I can give you the power to communicate face-to-face with the dead. Your patients would worship you for it. The help, the comfort you would give them would be boundless. It's the ultimate authority, command over the dominions of death.

'What you learn at the Citadel limits you. You know that in your heart, Gabriel. You weren't meant to be limited. You have a great gift, but it will never be fully used, not as long as you allow yourself to be restricted, to be bound by laws and regulations. There's no reason why you can't be the disciple of two men. Give me just a few hours a week, and I'll give you power such as you never dreamed was possible. I'll lay dominions at your feet. All you have to do is pledge yourself to me.'

Gabriel raised his eyes. Jaganath was smiling a little, self-assured, too shrewd. *How do you know?* Gabriel thought. *My worst memories, my deepest hurts – how do you know?*

Suddenly, like a revelation, the understanding hit him. It was so obvious, so clear, he was astounded he had not realised it before. He almost laughed in his relief.

'I think I know how you do it, lord!' he said. 'You don't see spirits at all! You search memories, and see the images in people's minds. You do nothing I can't already do myself!'

Jaganath looked faintly surprised. 'No wonder Salverion loves you,' he murmured. 'You're an excellent student. Misguided and a little confused, but excellent.'

'I don't think I am misguided, lord,' replied Gabriel, with anger. 'You despise the Masters for the limitations they place on me, because I have to ask a person's permission before I walk in their memories. You don't have those restrictions. You use your power secretly, without anyone's consent, and you use what you see to intimidate and –'

'Be very careful, Gabriel,' warned Nagay softly.

But Jaganath taunted, 'What else, Gabriel? What other evil do I do?'

Words burned on the tip of Gabriel's tongue. Again he saw the images in Syana's memory: the upturned toy box in the playroom, the snake concealed there, where Syana was bound to disturb it. He thought of Salverion at Cosimo's for dinner, conveniently unavailable; of himself called here alone to a healing he could not refuse, and of this timely gathering and its portentous offer. He longed to accuse Jaganath but dared not.

'You may have the Vision, Gabriel,' Jaganath mocked, 'but you don't have the nerve to use it. You're a coward and a fool. I wouldn't waste my time with you. Go on – run back to your sympathetic Masters and your hallowed Citadel and your safe little virtues and vows. But I tell you this: the day will come when you'll interpret another dream and cause another death – and that death will be your own. You'll wish, then, you'd allied yourself with me.'

Gabriel picked up his cloak and bag from where he had dropped them on the floor and walked out. Only a slave followed and guided him through the black marble corridors to the front door. Not waiting for the chariot to be called, Gabriel strode out into the darkness, heedless of the cold that struck his skin like ice, and walked the whole way back to the Citadel.

In the dining room, Jaganath had the slaves light the lamps

again, then dismissed them. Kamos glanced at his host, and poured himself more wine, splashing it over the table. 'Well, that wasn't exactly a successful evening, my lord Jaganath,' he said. 'Instead of winning the talented Gabriel to our side, we've accomplished exactly the opposite: we've driven him away. We must be losing our touch.' He raised his dripping goblet. 'To the lovely Petra. And to her precocious new adviser; may his life be brief.' He added casually, 'We could arrange for it to be brief.'

'You're a drunken fool!' hissed Nagay, standing up and leaning over him, his dagger drawn. 'He may be young and naive, but he is an Elected One!'

'Sit down, Nagay,' said Jaganath. 'We've already lost our judge and our treasurer; we're not losing our army commander, too.'

'Not unless he drowns in his own vomit,' hissed Nagay, sitting down and sheathing his dagger. 'You should have him replaced, Jaganath, when you're emperor.'

'Maybe I will,' said Jaganath, smiling.

Kamos clicked his tongue and wagged a hairy forefinger in Jaganath's face. 'Be very careful, Your future Majesty. If that Elected One continues to twist similar messages out of Petra's dreams, you and I – and all of us, for that matter – may well have our glorious plan exposed before its time. To say nothing of having our necks exposed to the executioner's blade. And if that happens, gentle Majesty, you will need me and my army, rather rapidly.'

Jaganath lifted his arm and gripped the army commander's wrist. 'I don't *need* you, my drunken friend,' Jaganath said softly. 'You need me, remember, when the wine can't keep your demons at bay, and you crave peace from them, and I'm the only one with the power to give it to you. Remember that. Threaten me again, and I swear your demons will take physical form and strangle you.'

Kamos fell back into his chair, looking sickly.

There was silence for a long time. Then Jaganath said, 'You may be drunk, Kamos, but you do have a point. It would be most expedient if our young healer-priest did meet with a fatal accident.' He added, in a voice as smooth as a sword being withdrawn from its scabbard, 'And such an event is not impossible.' He smiled, selected another grape, and crushed it between his teeth.

9 Into Infinity

'THERE ARE ONLY two people sleeping in the sanctuary tonight,' Sheel Chandra said to Gabriel as their chariot rolled through the snowy hills towards the Navora Infirmary and the beautiful Sanctuary of Healing Dreams. 'There's an elderly man who is trying to come to terms with an incurable disease. There is also a woman. She's had a hard life and suffered a great deal and is now destitute. For many months she's been ill. The physicians at the Academy treated her, and she's over her disease. However, she suffers intolerable depression and was advised to seek healing in the sanctuary. I would like you to work with her. As always, protect yourself carefully; her dream images may be distressing, even shocking. And there will almost certainly be pain.'

It was late afternoon, and already the sun was setting. The air was clear and cold, and Gabriel wished he had walked to the sanctuary, for he had been inside all day. Often he walked this road, preferring the exercise to the harsh jolting of a chariot, or battling with Rebellion. He did not run in the winter, as the road was treacherous with ice. He was the only one from the Citadel who travelled this way by foot and was well known for it.

Against the sunset the Sanctuary of Healing Dreams gleamed pale gold, its splendid pillars and terraces lit by fiery lamps. On the top steps Gabriel stopped and looked along the frozen road towards Navora. The city lights glimmered in the dusk, and the long road was marked with chariot and wagon wheels, the tracks dark and criss-crossed on the snow. Between the sanctuary and the road were parklike grounds, the smooth lawns overshadowed by the huge pines around the gate. As Gabriel turned to follow Sheel Chandra into the sanctuary, he noticed a figure standing on the steps a little way off to his left. It was a youth, wearing a long black cloak almost identical to Gabriel's. To his astonishment and joy, Gabriel recognised him.

'Myron!' he called.

But Myron remained staring up at the deepening skies and did not hear. The younger brother cupped his hands over his mouth, warming them on his breath, then pulled his cloak tighter around him. For a while he stared along the terraces towards the long road and the city, his gaze passing through Gabriel as if he were not there. Myron was smiling slightly, as if something had recently pleased him. Then he ran lightly down the steps towards the trees. A terrible foreboding fell over Gabriel, and he called out again, but Myron vanished.

Gabriel felt a gloved hand on his shoulder and turned to see Sheel Chandra watching him, his black eyes searching and concerned. 'What's wrong?' the Master asked. 'What vision was it?'

'My brother,' Gabriel said.

'You must pray for his protection before you begin work here,' said Sheel Chandra.

'I'm already doing that,' Gabriel replied, walking up into the lamp-lit sanctuary.

Only a short way along the road, in a private room in the Infirmary, Myron sat on a bed and held the hand of the girl who lay there. 'Are you sure you're not in pain?' he asked anxiously. 'I can go and tell the physician to give you more medicine.'

She shook her head, her auburn curls tumbling on the blue pillow. 'Don't fuss, Myron. I'm all right. It's only broken ribs. I can go home tomorrow. And you should go now; it's getting dark.'

'I don't want to leave you yet,' he said. 'And I'll be safe. I have my sword.'

'You're not immortal, you know. It's dangerous in the streets at night, and you've a long way to walk.'

'Are you trying to get rid of me, Eva?' He leaned down and kissed her, his hand roaming in the warmth under her blankets. 'They've bandaged you up,' he said, disappointed. 'How restricting.'

'It's meant to be.' She giggled, and winced. 'I'm not supposed to move too much, or take deep breaths.'

'You just lie there, then, and I'll do enough deep breathing for both of us.'

'Stop it, Myron! Get off the bed! Someone might come in!'

'They all think you've gone to sleep.' He lay on the top of the bed beside her, cradling her gently in his arms.

'The physician might come,' she whispered. 'Maybe your brother. I don't think even he would approve of this.'

'I'm being remarkably well behaved, at the moment. Besides, Gabriel isn't here. He's in the Sanctuary of Healing Dreams tonight.'

'How do you know?'

'He told me in a letter. He's there for ten nights. I want to call in on my way home and ask if I can visit him. It's eight months since I saw him last. I have a hankering to see him again.'

'And I thought you were staying late because of me.' She sighed.

'I am,' he said, softly nibbling her ear. 'If you weren't here, I wouldn't be here either. Thank God for icy stairs, and a woman too busy blowing kisses to watch her step, and – at last! – a private boudoir, solitude, and a hundred stone walls between us and your father.'

'I'll remember not to blow you kisses again,' she said, 'since they get me into so much trouble.'

'This isn't trouble,' he murmured, his lips on her cheek. 'This is bliss.'

She turned her head and kissed him. 'It might be bliss for you, but it's pain for me,' she said. 'I'm sorry, but I'm very tired.'

'If you want me to, I'll go.'

'Do you mind?'

'Of course I mind. I'm devastated. I've spent months scheming for this opportunity.' He got off the bed carefully, so as not to disturb her, and buckled on his sword. He had taken it off when he arrived to visit.

'That crimson tunic suits you,' she said, watching him. 'You're a gorgeous man, Myron Eshban Vala.'

'Not gorgeous enough, or you'd be head over heels in love with me.'

'But I am,' she said, smiling. 'You swept me right off my feet.'

'True. All the way down the stairs,' he said, bending to kiss her again. 'Skip the acrobatics next time. Try to fall in love less dramatically.'

Eva laughed, holding her ribs.

He grinned, flung his long black cloak around his shoulders, and blew her a kiss as he left.

In the sanctuary, the woman lay on the mattress on the polished wooden floor and waited for the healer-priests to arrive. She was in a circular room, and there were white pillars all around the edge, with lamps flaming on stands between them. A brazier burned close by her bed, its smoke fragrant with incense. She glimpsed slaves moving silently about, tending to the lamps and braziers and making sure there were enough blankets for the people who would sleep here tonight. There were only herself and an old man lying on the other side of the room.

A slave brought her a heavy woollen blanket, and tucked it gently around her. 'Are you warm enough?' he whispered.

She nodded, though she was shivering.

'Is there anything else you would like?' he asked. 'A drink, perhaps?'

'No thank you.'

Two healer-priests came in between the pillars. One was elderly and dark-skinned, with a beautiful countenance. He went and sat by the man on the other mattress. The other was young, and her heart fell. Coming over, he sat cross-legged by her bed, his hands folded peacefully in his lap. She could smell lavender on him and sacred herbs. Nervously she waited for him to speak. He was silent, meditating. Slowly he opened his eyes and smiled. 'Greetings, Zaidan,' he said.

'Greetings,' she replied, looking up at the ceiling again, two spots of red in her pale cheeks. *In the name of God,* she thought, *why on earth did they give me a novice?*

'How are you feeling?' he asked.

'I'm all right.'

'If there's anything you want at any time, tell me.'

'I don't want anything.' She fell silent, her fingers picking nervously at a loose thread on her blanket. She was an attractive woman, but there was a soul-hardness in her expression, and shades of pain and sleeplessness about her hazel eyes. She looked older than she was.

They remained quiet, while the fire in the brazier crackled, and the smoke gave off a sweet incense.

'I suppose I have to tell you my life history,' she said, after a while. 'That'll complete your education.'

'You don't have to tell me anything,' he said, and she could tell from his voice that he was smiling. 'All you have to do is sleep.'

'I know. It was all explained.' She sighed and turned away, tears sliding down her cheeks. 'But I seldom sleep. I can't. And when I do, I dream that I'm being drowned in dark water. Every time I close my eyes, I drown.' For a long time she wept, and Gabriel waited, and the peace of the place soaked into them both. Presently he began talking very quietly, and Zaidan closed her eyes and listened. Soon she slept, and the old nightmares stormed over her. But through them she heard a voice, calm and compelling, and she followed the words into places glorious and empowering, and filled with light.

There was a long underground passage leading from the Infirmary to the Sanctuary of Healing Dreams. It was used by patients who needed to sleep in the sanctuary, and by Myron now, on his way to see his brother. The tunnel led to a back room in the sanctuary, where families of patients could wait if they wished to. Myron had been in the room only a few seconds when a slave accosted him.

'Are you a patient, sir?' asked the slave.

'No. I wanted . . . I hoped to see Gabriel. Is he busy?'

The slave's face broke into a wide smile. 'You must be his brother, sir.'

'Yes.'

'You look so alike. I'm sorry, but he cannot be disturbed. He's with a patient. It's vital that people in the sanctuary are not interrupted, except in dire emergencies. Can I give him a message for you, in the morning?'

'Not really. I just wanted to see him. I haven't seen him since he entered the Citadel. I was visiting a friend in the Infirmary, and I thought it might be possible to see Gabriel on my way home.'

The slave was thoughtful. 'I have a brother of my own, sir,' he said. 'I haven't seen him for many years and would give my right hand to look on his face again. I know what it means. Come. But you must be totally quiet.'

Myron followed the slave through several passages to a wide place bordered by high pillars. Beyond the columns stretched a vast room, aglow with lamplight. Across the floor, his face in profile and misty with the smoke from a brazier, sat Gabriel. His eyes were closed, but his lips moved as he prayed. For a long time Myron looked at him, while the slave waited. Then Myron turned away, and the slave showed him the way to the front door of the sanctuary.

Outside, Myron stood for a few minutes on the terrace, looking up at the starry sky. There was no wind and there had been only a light snowfall during the day, but the air was bitter. Myron breathed on his hands to warm them and smiled to himself, thinking of Gabriel. Then he looked out at the long road back to the city, deciding he would enjoy a walk. He was used to walking in the city at night, between the gymnasium and Eva's home, and had never yet been assaulted or robbed. Besides, he had his sword.

He pulled his cloak closer about him, ran down the sanctuary steps, and made his way towards the trees. As he walked under the overhanging branches, sniffing the richness of pine and damp grass, a man stepped out from behind a tree. Myron could hardly see him in the darkness.

'You've finished early tonight, healer-priest,' said the man. His voice was muffled, for he wore a scarf over his lower face. 'Walking back to the Citadel?'

Myron noticed the flash of a blade in the man's hand, and he drew his sword. A twig crunched on the earth behind him, and as he spun around something smashed into the side of his head. Blinded by pain, already falling, he slashed out wildly with his sword.

Gabriel remained beside the sleeping woman, softly chanting prayers for her. While he prayed, a sudden dread fell on him. He saw trees tall and black against the stars, and a naked sword. He opened his eyes and leaned close to Zaidan, pressing his forehead lightly against hers. There was no fear in her, only peace. Gabriel sat upright and continued meditating. But the images returned, and he could not shake them off. He covered himself with protection again, praying light over his body and mind. He wondered if he was picking up dream-images from the old man across the room and imagined a wall of light down the centre of the sanctuary, shielding him. But still the visions came.

He saw wheel ruts on a road, very close to his face, and stones gleaming with ice, and heard a rumbling in his ears. Pain went through him and he doubled over, crying out. His own voice startled him out of the vision, and he glanced at Zaidan. She was asleep, tranquil. Still the pains tore through him, cramping his bowels and making him retch. He staggered to his feet and rushed out to the latrines. Crouching over the deep drain, he vomited. Then he leaned against the white stone walls, his eyes closed. His head ached, and he felt a crawling down his left cheek, as if blood ran there. Before him rose the face of the demon in Jaganath's painting, and that other visage behind it, terrifying and predatory. The rumbling came nearer, surged over him, and all was thunder and chaos and pain. He opened his eyes. On the wall beside him a lamp sputtered, and a slave came in to replenish the oil in it.

'Can I help you, sir?' asked the slave, concerned. 'Are you ill?'

'I'm all right,' said Gabriel. 'A bit of a headache, that's all.'

'Should I call a chariot to take you back to the Citadel?'

'No, thank you. I'll finish here.'

The slave went out, and Gabriel walked slowly back to his place by the sleeping woman. He sat down, his gaze fixed on the glowing brazier. Sweat ran down his face and into his eyes, and he shook with the agony that went through him. He rocked slowly, trying not to cry out. Darkness surrounded him. He felt as though he were floating above his body, high above a winding road. He saw himself lying on stones. He was covered in blood. But when he looked more closely, it was not his own face he saw. It was Myron's.

He closed his eyes and covered Myron with shielding light. Then he tried to pray, but wept quietly instead. He was still crying when Sheel Chandra came over to him in the early dawn, and whispered that there was a message for him.

Gabriel nodded and stood up. He felt exhausted, but incredibly calm. Zaidan was asleep, smiling a little. Gabriel spoke a blessing over her, then followed Sheel Chandra out. The Master gazed at Gabriel with sorrow, knowing that he already knew.

Before the Master said a word, Gabriel asked, 'Where is he?'

'In the Infirmary,' Sheel Chandra replied. 'He's still alive, but he cannot live long.'

Myron was in a private chamber in the Infirmary, not far from Eva's. He was the colour of parchment and breathed as if every breath were agony. His eyes were closed. He was naked under the linen sheet, and the sheet was stained with blood. He had bandages about his chest and abdomen, all spreading with scarlet. His skin was deeply bruised, and grazes covered him, glistening with ointments. His left cheek and ear had been split open, and there was a deep graze on his forehead. On a table near his bed were his clothes, torn and bloodied and covered with dirt and stones, but carefully folded. Across them lay his leather belt and beloved sword, bent as if it were a child's toy. Beside the table, close by the bed, a brazier burned. Above, a wide window let in the pale morning sun.

Gabriel sat on the edge of the bed, and Myron opened his eyes. He struggled to lift his head, to speak.

'Save your strength, brother,' said Gabriel. He took Myron's hand, and Myron's fingers closed tightly about his. Myron collapsed, his eyes fixed on Gabriel's face.

'By God, it's good to see you,' said Myron hoarsely. His lips were cut, and they bled afresh as he spoke.

'Good to see you, too. But not in this state.'

Myron grinned. 'I wanted to feel your healing touch. Went a bit far, though. Falling out of a chariot would have been better than being run over by one.' Pain went through him, contorting his face. He waited until it passed, and said, 'There's something important. About you. I have to tell you. Can't remember.'

'Don't worry about me, Myron. Don't think of anything.'

'Have to. I wish I could remember. How's Eva?'

'She doesn't know yet that you're here. They'll tell her soon.'

'Give her my medallion.' He was referring to a silver coin he had found years before, that he had always worn for good luck.

'You'll be able to give it to her yourself,' said Gabriel.

Myron shook his head. His eyes, always so lucid and blue,

were dark and lustreless now. He tried to speak again, coughed, and cried out in agony.

'Don't talk,' said Gabriel, leaning over him. 'I'll stop your pain.'

Myron's scalp was sticky with blood, and Gabriel's fingers shook as he searched for the vital energy pathways at the back of Myron's head. He found them and applied pressure there, but the healing forces in him, usually so strong and controlled, were chaotic now, unfocused and ineffective. He bent his head on the pillow beside Myron's, so Myron could not see his despair.

'No hope, is there?' said Myron huskily. 'The physicians told me. Don't leave me.'

'I won't leave you for a moment, I swear.'

The moments, the hours, crawled on. Salverion came, and Gabriel watched with hope while he examined Myron. But even the Grand Master could do no more than relieve the worst of Myron's pain. Afterwards he put his arm about his disciple's bowed shoulders, said a prayer for him and for the dying youth, and went away.

It was the longest day the brothers had ever endured. By noon Myron was too weak to speak or move, but his eyes followed Gabriel. In the evening he became restless, obviously in great pain. He tried to speak but could not. Gabriel lay on the bed beside him, holding him in his arms. Suddenly Myron's breathing changed; his breaths became very deep and slow, with long spaces in between, and his eyes glazed over. Gabriel gave a great cry and held him close. Weeping, he kissed Myron's face and hair, all the time speaking words of love and farewell.

A huge stillness, utterly silent, overshadowed them. As in a vision, Gabriel saw a valley, long and straight under lightless skies. All was grey, without colour or gravity or air; it was a neutral place, a shadow place between the worlds. Wraithlike beings moved in the awful cold, and there were bodiless howls and obscure, half-glimpsed terrors. It was supernatural, frightening. At his left walked Myron, his face resolute, though he stumbled a little. On Myron's other side was a very tall man, supporting him. Gabriel saw the man clearly, saw hair like white fire, and a face full of goodness and beauty and light, and heard him say to Myron, with indescribable love, 'Don't be afraid, beloved; there are only shadows here. Death is evil's last great illusion.'

Gabriel felt suspended, beyond feeling, beyond everything but the knowledge that he was in a place unearthly and profound. The wraithlike beings vanished, and there was only quiet. He walked on with Myron, deeper into the valley. After a while Gabriel became aware of a physical presence standing behind him, touching his shoulder. Somehow that tiny pressure kept him back, reminded him of his own world, and when Myron gave a joyful cry and began to run, Gabriel could barely keep pace with him. They were rising upward; there was a sense of incredible lightness, of a mighty wind, of silence, of unutterable peace and joy. The only sound was Myron breathing, long moments between each breath, impossibly long. Several times Gabriel thought his brother had died. And then Myron would exhale again, and be another step beyond him. Yet they were more than steps; each breath was the crossing of a universe, a journey to infinity and light. With every part of his being, Gabriel was aware of the nearness of another world; he felt the awesome peace, the presences of people waiting for Myron, the power and the rapture. And then Myron breathed one last time, a sigh. And he was there.

With everything in him Gabriel yearned to go on, to be with Myron in that place, but there was a wall ahead of him, like a blindness. The hand on his shoulder drew him back, back through endless winds and shadows and distances immeasurable. He returned sobbing, gasping, not wanting to breathe, his arms tight about his brother's body. He felt numb, as if his spirit had flown with Myron's, and this existence were no longer real. The glory of the other world was still on him, powerfully.

Slowly he moved off the bed, and lay Myron flat on his back. Myron's skin was waxen, his lips the same pallid yellow as his face. He was still, so still. Gabriel crossed Myron's arms over his chest and placed his fists on his shoulders, like a soldier. Then he turned and confronted Salverion.

'Why?' Gabriel demanded, brokenly. 'Why did you bring me back?'

'It was not your time,' replied the Master.

'And it was his?'

For a few moments Salverion was silent. Then he said, with extreme gentleness, 'There's something you must be told, about his death. Will you come with me, out to the service rooms?'

'If it's to do with Myron, tell me here.'

'It's painful, my son.'

'Just tell me.'

So Salverion told him, and when Gabriel shook his head and screamed, the Master took him in his arms, holding Gabriel's face against his chest to muffle the sounds of agony and rage.

10 The Meeting

SUBIN BALANCED ON the wooden gate and peered down the bare road to the hills. Behind her the new wooden house stood golden brown in the barren field, its dark sloping roof powdered white by the last light fall of snow. Smoke rose from the wide chimney, straight into the crystal air. In the nearest farms dogs barked and children shouted as they played. In Subin's home were ten extra children, all her cousins, but they were playing quietly in one of the bedrooms, out of the way of the adults. The house was hushed.

She thought of the spare bedroom, cleared of its boxes of old clothes and Gabriel's things, with the low funeral bier and the white cloth, and Myron lifeless on it. She had only glimpsed him, then fled screaming from the room, and even her uncle Egan had not been able to catch her. She had run down the little track between the farms, right to the edge of the Shinali land, where she was never supposed to go. Shaking, she hid behind the snow piled up beside a fence post and watched the strange people wearing heavy skins, as they hunted in the snow with little slings and stones. They killed two rabbits, and one of the animals struggled a long way, with its back legs dragging, before a boy got to it and broke its neck. Subin had cried then and gone home again. She would not go into the house but waited here on the gate, her eyes fixed on the road.

Lena came out, wrapped a blanket around the child, and put

a bowl of hot soup into her hands. 'Are you sure you won't come in, Subin?' she asked. 'He may not be here until tonight.'

'I'll wait,' said Subin, and her mother, knowing how determined she was, hugged her and went inside again.

An hour later Subin saw two dark spots on the road. They came closer, and she made out two horses with riders. As they neared she saw that one man had streaming hair of gold, and she flung off the blanket, leaped off the gate, and rushed to meet him.

Gabriel halted his horse, leaned down, and swept her up on to the saddle in front of him. He hugged her close, cherishing the smell of her, the smallness of her body wriggling against his. Her face was cold, and she was shivering as she nestled into him. He enfolded her in his fur cloak.

'How long have you been waiting?' he asked.

'All day,' she said. She sighed blissfully, stroking the velvet fabric of his crimson robe and the strange, slight roughness of his chin. Then her arms wound about his neck, and she pressed her face into his shoulder, sniffing the incense in his clothes, and feeling the smoothness of the seven embroidered silver stars. She noticed the other rider waiting nearby, his face dark and striking, his eyes like jade. He wore all black.

'Who's he?' she whispered.

'My friend Ferron,' said Gabriel. 'Ferron, this is my sister, Subin.'

Ferron greeted the child, but she stared at him reticently, wishing he had not come.

Gabriel walked Rebellion towards the house, glad of the quiet time to nerve himself against the fuss ahead. Ferron followed, his sword flashing at his side.

'Are there many people at home, Subin?' Gabriel asked.

'Heaps,' she said, lifting her head. 'All our tribe, even Jorn.

He's already broken that little wooden horse you sent me. I have to sleep with him too, which is worse. Him and his sister. There are beds everywhere, except in the spare room. There's only . . . Only him, there.'

'Have you seen him?'

She nodded, and hid her face again. 'I wish he would wake up,' she whispered.

Fighting to control his feelings, Gabriel kissed the top of her head. He wanted to say, 'So do I', but he thought of Myron's horrific injuries and suffering, of his last breathtaking earthly moments, and the place where Myron had gone, and he could not.

Ferron took the horses to the barn while Gabriel went to the house. He felt strange standing outside the door to his new home, not knowing whether to knock or walk straight in. Subin decided for him, taking him inside and pulling him by the hand down an arched and timbered hall. A door opened, and a hum of conversation trickled into the hall. Lena came out, closing the door behind her. She saw Gabriel and gave a little gasp. Then they were embracing, and she was crying, half laughing, touching his hands and face and hair.

'Oh, Gabriel!' she said. 'It's good to see you again. I wish you were here just for a visit, and not . . . Not for this.' She held him at arms' length, her hands on his shoulders. 'You look wonderful. Tired, but wonderful.' Then her eyes clouded over, and a deep grief settled over her face. 'I have to talk to you,' she said. 'Go and play with your cousins for a while, Subin.' She took Gabriel into a bedroom where a baby slept, and closed the door. Lena sat on one of the beds, her hands twisted tightly together on her lap. The way she sat, so tense and still, reminded him of the day he had arrived home from the Academy, and she had been waiting with Salverion. It seemed a lifetime ago.

'The city sentries brought Myron's body here,' she said. 'They told me something, said I wasn't to discuss it with anyone else. I haven't. But I need to know whether you know.' She hesitated, tears spilling down her cheeks. 'Did they tell you how he died, Gabriel? Why he died?'

He sat beside her and took one of her hands in his. 'Salverion told me,' he said, making an enormous effort to remain composed. 'Whoever did it thought Myron was me, leaving the sanctuary. That's why he was found halfway to the Citadel. They tried to make it look as if I'd been accidentally run over on my walk back. They would have got away with it, except that they had the wrong person.'

'Why, Gabriel? I hear marvellous reports of you. I've even heard that the Empress herself favours you. So why have you made enemies?'

'It's because the Empress favours me. There are jealous people at the palace, Mother.'

'Jealous enough to do murder?'

'They're very influential lords. They'll be brought to justice in the end. But it may take time.'

'And in the meantime, do they plot again, and next time get the right person? Am I to lose two sons?'

'I'm careful. I go nowhere now without Ferron. He's an excellent swordsman.'

'So was Myron.'

Gabriel stood up and began pacing angrily. 'I'll be careful, I swear. I won't walk home alone again, and I'll vary the routes when I go running. But I refuse to live in fear. Fear messes up my energies, lessens my ability to heal. If I give in to fear, they win more surely than if they cut my throat.'

'You went away to be a healer-priest, to study as Salverion's disciple, but, from what I hear, you seem to spend more time at the palace than at the Citadel, getting yourself tangled in dangerous politics, and making enemies. What's our Empire coming to, when nobles are exempt from justice, and even an Elected One isn't safe? Do you have to carry on with your Citadel work, Gabriel? I'd rather have you alive and not healing.'

'If I can't heal, I'd rather be dead.'

Lena covered her face with her hands. 'How can you say that?' she said, weeping.

He sat down beside her again, his anger spent. 'I'm sorry. I don't know what I'm saying half the time. I haven't slept for three days. I feel as if my brain's been removed. I can't remember names of acquaintances, or how to mix a simple medicine.'

'I'm sorry, too. This must be harder on you than on any of us.' She gave him a pale smile. 'I hope you can remember the names of your relatives. They've been waiting all day for your arrival, though not so faithfully as Subin waited.'

Seeing the relatives again was a trial. The moment Gabriel entered the room, the talking stopped, and all eyes turned in his direction. Before, he had been the family failure, the son who refused to take over the great business his father had built up; now he was regarded with such esteem, he was embarrassed. He shook hands with all the men in the Navoran way, embraced the women, and tried to ignore the whispers. He was surprised when his female cousins blushed wildly when he hugged them, then giggled later among themselves.

One young woman he had never seen before turned away from him with tears in her eyes before they could be introduced. Someone whispered that she was Eva, and he probably reminded her too much of Myron. Then Gabriel was cornered by aunts curious about his training and was relieved when Subin interrupted, tugging at his hands and begging him to come and see the rest of the house. As graciously as he could, he excused himself and went with her, closing the door on the undertones and the stares.

'Thanks for rescuing me, Subin,' he said, hugging her. With shining eyes, she led him from one room to the other. Myron had been right, in his letter: Gabriel did love the house, with its earthy timber smell and long windows overlooking the ploughed fields. Upstairs, Subin showed him her tiny room under the eaves.

'You can see the Shinali land and the mountains,' she said.

He bent low to look out. Past the farms, halfway along the plain, was a large mound in the earth. It was near the river, and there were trees nearby, stark and black against the snowy land. Smoke drifted from a hole in the mound's centre.

'That's the thatched roof of their house,' Subin said. 'They live under the ground, Topaz said.'

'Who's Topaz?'

'Mama's friend. He sold her this land. He's coming tomorrow, when they . . . when they . . .' She bit her lip and stared out of the window.

'Are they burying him in the family crypt?' asked Gabriel gently.

'No. They're burning him. We saw the Shinali once, burning a body. Myron was visiting us and saw them too, and said that's what he'd like. So that's what we're doing. I heard Uncle Egan telling Mama she was wrong, that she should put him in the crypt with Father. But she won't, because Myron said.'

'She's right, if that's what Myron wanted. Have you ever talked to the Shinali, or been to visit them?'

'No. We're not allowed on their land. Only the army. That's in the treaty, Topaz said.'

Suddenly she scrambled up on to her bed and opened a small cupboard up by the ceiling. 'I keep my secret things in here,' she said. 'No one else is allowed to look, only you.'

He glanced in, his hair brushing the timbered ceiling. There was a bird's nest in there, a tiny turtle shell, and all the gifts he had sent her since he had been away. There was also a stack of letters, their broken seals the blue wax of the Citadel.

'You keep everything,' he said, smiling.

She bounded off the bed, falling on to the mattresses and blankets placed on the floor for her cousins. While down there she took the opportunity to lift the gold hem of his gown, and peered at his legs.

'You *do* wear pants underneath!' she said, grinning like an imp. 'I heard the girls arguing about it, so I said I'd look.'

'Well, now you can announce it to the whole family, and put an end to the gossip.' He chuckled, hauling her to her feet. They went out, and she showed him the rest of the house. Outside a closed door she stopped, and took his hand.

'Would you like to go in with me and see him?' Gabriel asked. She nodded, and he held her near as they pushed open the door and went in.

The room was bare, except for a few bowls of the wild blue irises that grew along the river banks. In the centre, on a low bier covered with white linen, lay Myron, his eyes closed. He was dressed in trousers and an old embroidered shirt he had loved. He looked different from the way he had looked in the Infirmary. His body had been embalmed, and there was colour in his cheeks, his scars had been made almost invisible, and his hair had been washed. He looked tranquil and very beautiful.

Gabriel crouched down by the bier, his arm around Subin's small shoulders. 'He looks different. He's empty,' she whispered.

'What you see there *is* empty, Subin. It's only his body, left behind like old clothes he doesn't need any more. Myron himself is somewhere else.'

'With Father?'

'I suppose so.'

'Is it a nice place?'

'Ten thousand times better than this world, Subin. It's awe-inspiring.'

'How do you know?'

'He took me there with him. To the edge of it.'

'I wish we didn't have to burn him. I like his old clothes.' She began to cry, and he held her close and wept with her, his sobs deep and anguished. Afterwards he mopped her up with her handkerchief, and she giggled when he asked if he could borrow it too, though it was soaked. Then, their arms around each other, they went to the kitchen to join the family for a meal.

To Gabriel, the funeral had a sense of unreality. He did not weep; even when the flames engulfed Myron, he thought of the shadowed valley and the journey and the breathtaking peace, and his face was steadfast and calm. He watched the ash falling on the frozen earth, then turned his eyes to the pillar of smoke curling high in the cold morning air. Afterwards, while the body smouldered and the last shreds of smoke drifted over the fields, everyone went to the house for goblets of mulled wine.

'How's the healing business going, Gabriel?' one of the uncles asked.

'The healing business is continuing, as it always will,' Gabriel replied.

'Unlike some of its customers, eh?' said the uncle, with a laugh. Then he realised what he had said. He choked, and added earnestly, 'I hope you're enjoying it, though, Gabriel.'

'He ought to be,' said Egan, 'since he sacrificed his father's business for it.'

Another uncle cleared his throat, and said, 'Give him a chance, Egan. He's done well, you have to admit it.' He turned to Gabriel and said, 'You look very fine in those clothes, Gabriel. Very fine. We all got a surprise when we heard you'd been elected for the Citadel. Your father would be proud of you.'

'He wouldn't be proud of today's little performance, though,' remarked Egan, grimly.

'What do you mean?' asked Gabriel.

'The burning,' said Egan. 'It's not a proper funeral. I'm very disappointed with Lena. She's made a lot of important decisions, all wrong.'

'The burning wasn't her idea, it was Myron's,' said Gabriel angrily. 'It's what he wanted. And none of Mother's decisions have been wrong. You only think they are because they haven't coincided with what *you* want.'

There was an uncomfortable silence. Then one of the other uncles said, 'It'll be time to plant the corn soon. With so many farms growing it, won't there be a drop in prices?'

The talk turned to farming. Gabriel looked out of the window at the funeral pyre still smouldering, and excused himself.

He leaned in the kitchen doorway and watched Topaz give instructions to the slaves, for the funeral feast to be held that evening. The surveyor had one arm around Lena, and she had both arms around his waist. Gabriel could not remember ever seeing his father embrace his mother, or helping with domestic things.

Lena glanced up at her eldest son. Her eyes were red

rimmed, and she was very pale, but she looked serene. She came over to him, and he gave her a hug. 'Do you want me to do anything?' he asked.

'No. It's all under control. Why? You want to go for a run?'

'Would you mind?'

'Of course not. I'd come too, if I could keep up with you.'

'I'll run slowly.'

'I was joking, love. You go, and send me back some of the silence.'

'I'll do that,' he promised, kissing her cheek. She went back to Topaz, and Gabriel went upstairs to the room he and Ferron had shared last night with his brothers and several male cousins. He found a chest of his old clothes, and pulled on a pair of warm leather trousers, a thick woollen shirt, and a sleeveless quilted tunic edged with fur. Then he pulled on some comfortable boots and went outside.

Running slowly at first, he followed the path Subin had taken yesterday, that divided the farms lying between theirs and the plain. On the edge of the Shinali land he stopped. Between the stretches of unmelted snow the grasslands were brown, the grasses coarse and tough. The plain was deserted, and he guessed the Shinali were all in their house, warm by the fire. He touched the bone under his shirt, feeling its smoothness and power. It was the first time he had stood on Shinali land, and he knelt and spread his right hand flat on the earth, not noticing the ice, but feeling a deep awe and a hunger he could not name.

Standing, he turned right, southward, and jogged beside the farm fences until he came to the forested hills that lay between the Shinali land and the coast. Here an old road skirted the Shinali land, then turned sharply inland, running beneath the foothills of the mountains towards the ancient Taroth Fort.

There it crossed an old bridge, then wound eastward through the Taroth Pass to the ports and towns beyond the mountains. Once busy with traders, it was seldom used now, as most people came to Navora by ship. Avoiding the cracked stones and deep ruts, Gabriel ran eastwards beside the road on the smooth Shinali land. Between the hills a sea breeze blew in, tangy with the scent of salt. He pictured Lena and covered her with peace.

Lifting his eyes to the mountains, he increased his pace, thinking of Myron running ahead of him down the long grey valley. His eyes streamed in the morning sun. For a long way he ran, the cold air hurting his throat and biting through his clothes. He ran as if the pain were pleasure, his teeth gritted, his deep breaths like mists before his face. At last he stopped, leaning over with his hands on his knees, breathing hard, and sobbing. When he straightened he noticed a figure standing between himself and the sun. The person's face was shadowed and obscure, but the light behind made a halo of the long dark hair and shone in the rough edges of the brown woollen cloak.

Gabriel wiped his hand across his eyes and looked again, half expecting the presence to be gone. But the person was still there, standing motionless, watching him. He realised, with alarm, that he had wandered from the road, deep into Shinali land.

'I'm sorry I'm trespassing; I didn't realise I'd left the road,' Gabriel said, walking farther ahead, and drawing alongside the figure so he could see without the sun in his eyes. Then he felt foolish, realising the Shinali would not understand the Navoran tongue.

'You're welcome here,' said a woman's voice. He moved past her, and she turned so the light was full on her face. He stared at her, his heart thumping in his ribs.

She was almost as tall as he was, with a self-reliant, fearless look. Her skin was brown and perfect, her face beautifully shaped, with high cheekbones and a firm chin slightly cleft. Her eyes were like amber, lustrous and warm, framed in lashes of deepest black. She smiled, and his heart missed a beat.

'I didn't think you'd understand Navoran,' he said huskily.

'I'm knowing enough to talk,' she replied, openly studying his face, his hair and clothes, even his boots. There was something forthright and honest about her curiosity, and it did not embarrass him, though his face was streaked with sweat and tears. He had a feeling she was well acquainted with both. Besides, he was studying her, too – and enjoying what he saw. After a while their eyes met again, and they smiled.

He glanced across the plain at the Shinali house, at the smoke twisting into the blue. 'I like your home,' he said. 'It must be warm underground.'

'It is.' With an unconscious grace, she put down the bundle of sticks she had collected and sat on the grass between the scattered snow, her arms around her knees. Her cloak fell open, and he saw that she wore a white woollen dress, handwoven, with long, wide sleeves painted in ochre with moons and stars. She looked up at him, her lips still curved, and he sat beside her.

He stole a glance at her face and decided that perhaps she was his age, maybe a year or two older. It was hard to tell.

'I saw you leaving your house,' she said, looking at the farms. 'It was the one with the funeral pyre. Time gone there was a funeral, but the farmers didn't burn the dead.'

'It's not a Navoran custom, but my brother wanted it,' said Gabriel.

She made no sympathetic comments, and he was grateful. He felt suddenly shattered inside, exhausted, and close to tears again.

'Are you knowing many Shinali customs?' she asked.

'No. I don't know much at all about your people. I'm sorry.'

'We have a greeting.' She pressed her palm flat against her breast, then to his. Her hand remained on him a moment or two, and she felt his heart hammering. 'It means,' she said, 'my heart and yours are in harmony.'

'I like that. We Navorans have a handshake. Hold up your right arm, like this.'

She did, turning to face him. But instead of waiting for him to explain, she moved at the same time he did, her wrist smooth and strong against his, her fingers entwining easily with his own. 'I'm already knowing the Navoran way,' she said, her smile candid and lovely. Long after the handshake was over, he remembered the feel of her skin. And when she had leaned close, a scent had come to him: earth, wool, and fire.

'What's your name?' he asked.

'Ashila.'

'Mine's Gabriel.'

She repeated his name several times, emphasising the middle syllable. He decided he liked the change. He liked her voice, too, with its unfamiliar accent and grammar, and lyrical tones.

They sat looking at the plain and the farms to their left. There was still a smudge in the sky from the smoke of the distant pyre. A few people were gathered around it, too far away for Gabriel to tell who they were.

'I have a question,' Ashila said. 'I'm being afraid to ask.'

'You can ask anything.'

'Why aren't you with your clan? Why are you out here mourning, only you?'

'I don't know all my clan very well,' he replied, 'and the conversation's a bit of a trial. I've lived away from home for a –'

'Stop, please,' she said, touching his arm. 'Your words, I'm not knowing them.'

'Sorry.' He spoke slowly, choosing words he hoped she would understand. 'My clan is big, and we don't all live in one house, like Shinali. Many people in my clan I don't know well. They talk a lot, ask questions about my life away. I can't think to talk; my heart's too full of my dead brother, Myron. Something huge has happened, and I can't just sit around drinking bowls of tea and talking about cures for illnesses and the price of corn.'

'It's strange, your clan's way of mourning,' she remarked.

'What do your people do?'

'We fast three days. We dance and cry and lament, and cut our skin and cover ourselves with ashes of the burned.'

He looked faintly amused. 'I can't see my aunts and uncles doing that.'

'Would you be doing it, if you could?'

'For Myron, yes.'

They were silent, and she pulled up some grasses and plaited them into a band. Her fingers were deft, and, when she twisted the band into a circle, Gabriel could not tell where it began and where it ended. She gave it to him, and he slid it over his wrist. 'Thank you,' he said. 'It's beautiful.'

'We wear those when we're mourning,' she explained. 'They help us remember the body of our beloved is part of the earth now, part of the grass. And their spirit's . . . ah . . .' She could not think of the word, so she made an arc with her hands towards the sky, and finished, 'there, but not far and far away.'

'I'll wear it always,' he said.

She smiled, her eyes shining. A cool wind blew across from the plain, whipping her hair across her face. He was acutely conscious of everything about her – of the richness and rhythm of her voice, her gracefulness when she moved, the glimmer of sun on her skin, the blue-black sheen of her smooth hair, the slightly upward slant of the outer corners of her eyes, the contours of her throat, the curve of her lips. Never had another human being awoken such intense awareness in him, or evoked such a sense of astonishment and delight. Even her handmade shoes and garments, with their leather ties and painted designs, entranced him.

This is madness, he thought. *I should go home, get back to the real world, fast.*

'If you like,' she said, 'you're welcome in our house for a time. It's not . . . ah . . . not hushed, with us all inside, but you won't be drinking tea or talking on corn.'

No way. You could change my life forever, Shinali woman.

'I'd like that very much, thank you,' he said.

'I know you're mourning, and I'll tell the others, if you like.' She added, with humour in her eyes, 'We won't ask you to be singing and dancing for us.'

I'd do the Navoran fire-dance with you right now, if you were willing.

She stood up and swung her bundle of sticks over her shoulder.

'I'll carry that for you,' he offered, standing with her, and reaching for the firewood.

'No. Men don't carry wood. Men carry the food.'

'I don't have any food to bring.'

'That's good. Guests don't bring anything, only themselves.' She began to walk across the grass towards the house. It was a long way off, and on the other side of the river. She strode quickly, and he hurried to keep up with her. She was beautiful to watch.

'Is the wintertime hard for your people?' he asked.

'For the old ones, it's hard. If their boots break, and the cold kills bits of their toes and feet. A high lot of pain they have.'

'That's what we call gangrene,' he said. 'The diseased skin should be cut off.'

'Are you a healer?'

'Yes.'

She suddenly stopped, staring at him with amazement and joy. 'So I am! That's how I'm knowing your speech. A Navoran soldier came on our land three winters past. He was prisoner with the eastern tribes. He was coming back over the mountains, and we found him. Like this with death, he was.' She held up two fingers, close. 'He stayed with my clan two winters, and I and my mother healed him. He showed us his speech, and how to make a stone smokehouse for our fish. Now we smoke many and many at one time, instead of only little lots over the fire in our house. That's what we eat in the winter. Smoked fish. And we eat new-dead deer and rabbits, if we can get them.'

'Did your whole clan learn to speak Navoran?'

'No. But the soldier got knowing of a lot of our words.'

They began walking again, the wind raw in their faces. Gabriel noticed the shapely form of Ashila's thighs against the fabric of her long dress, as the wind blew against her. She was slender, womanly. He tore his eyes away.

'I and my mother,' she said, 'we learn to speak Navoran. And our chieftain and his family. A little of the others. But some were being angry with Navorans and wouldn't be knowing the man's talk or his ways, though they gave him welcome, and helped him.'

'Why were they angry?'

'Because of the chieftain's daughter. She went to live in the stone city, to be knowing Navoran ways, and to be peacemaker.

They killed her and didn't give us back her body. We couldn't mourn her. It was long time past, but some of the warriors in our tribe still don't . . . ah . . . believe on Navorans.'

The Shinali bone burned against his breast. 'Perhaps I'd better not visit your house, then,' he said.

'If you're my friend and I ask you, you'll be welcomed.'

'Are you sure?'

She looked bewildered, so he added, '*Sure*. Certain. Know in a strong way.'

'I'm being this sure,' she said, making a fist of her right hand and driving it hard into her left palm.

They walked for a long time without speaking. Several times he saw sticks on the ground and picked them up for firewood. Each time she took the stick from him and poked it into her bundle. As they drew near to the centre of the plain and the Shinali house, he realised how big the river was.

Immediately opposite the Shinali house the waters were placid, but farther west, where the river rushed towards the sea, they were white as they tumbled over rocks and down small waterfalls. Just past the farms the river divided into three, its tributaries cutting deep ravines through the coastal hills. Its most southern branch ran close to Navora, and was the city's water supply. But the city could not be seen from here, only the Citadel in the hills, its windows winking in the sun.

There were flat-topped rocks forming a natural bridge across to the Shinali house. Ashila crossed them first, the firewood balanced across her left shoulder, her feet sure and quick. Gabriel removed his boots so his bare feet would have a better hold on the icy surfaces, and followed her. On the other side he sat on the grass and chafed his feet to get the feeling back in them, then pulled on his boots again.

Through the black web of her windblown hair, Ashila watched him. Never had she seen anyone so fair. His hair was like the wheat at harvest time, his eyes like the sky in high summer. And his rays were green and blue and mauve, the colours of healing and spirit-unity. She had seen Navorans before, the soldiers with their red shadows and their soulless eyes. Even the soldier who had stayed had his shadowed side. But not this man. This man was all light, and beautiful. As he stood he caught her watching him, and his feelings ran like fire across his skin. Ashila smiled, half afraid and wondering, then walked on again.

As they traversed the flat area of grass between the river and the dwelling, and the roar of the waters diminished, another sound came to Gabriel. It was the carefree music of flutes, and the wilder, rasping notes of instruments he did not know. The tune was spirited, and accompanied by laughter and shouts. The flutes were familiar to him, and he touched the bone under his shirt and remembered ancient dreams. But there came to mind, as well, a face. A woman, wounded and imploring. Guilt tore through him, and his heart thundered as he neared the house in the earth.

11 Day of the Soul's Return

ONLY THE THATCHED roof and a small portion of the house wall were above ground level. At intervals along the wall were windows, protected from the weather by wide overhanging eaves. Next to the large smoke hole in the roof was an upturned boat, used to cover the hole in times of snow or rain. The smoke from the outlet blew towards him, winding about him aromas rich with roasting meat and burning wood. He closed his eyes and breathed it in deeply. The smoke was like incense, a holiness, easing his terrors.

Ashila touched his arm, and he opened his eyes. 'You don't have to come in, if the noise worries you,' she said, thinking he grieved. 'They were sleeping when I left. I'm sorry.'

'Don't be sorry,' he replied. 'I'm not.'

She led him down through the opening in the ground. They descended a flight of dirt steps, and Gabriel bent his head as he passed under the entrance roof. An air of excitement enveloped him, with smells of fire, smoked fish, dried grass, earth, fish oil, human sweat, and warm wool.

A group of men danced around the central fire, and the rest of the clan sat in a circle around them, clapping. The dance seemed to have no predetermined steps, and the men whirled and leaped, their movements uninhibited and frenzied. It took the clan a few moments to notice Gabriel. Several of the dancers hesitated, and the music missed a beat. Then they continued as wildly as before, while Gabriel and Ashila waited on the lower step.

The women all wore simple woollen shifts painted with simple designs, and the men were in woollen or leather trousers and sleeveless sheepskin vests. Many of the children, and some of the male dancers, were naked. Several of the men had painted their skin with coloured clay or ash, and their decorated ochre and blue faces shone weirdly in the firelight. The scene was alien, and for a moment Gabriel's fear returned, and he was all Navoran and in a place he had no right to be. Then he felt Ashila lean close. 'They are waking up the strongness in themselves,' she explained, her mouth close to his ear because of the din. 'They're going on a hunt little time. Or a canoe race on the rapids.'

He nodded and relaxed. The music ended in triumphant discord, and everyone cheered.

In the quiet, while a few of the elders whispered and the children giggled, Ashila removed her shoes and left them by the steps with dozens of other pairs. She went to the fire, dropped her bundle of sticks on the hearth, and approached a very old man sitting on the floor. Kneeling in front of him, she spoke in Shinali. Gabriel recognised his own name several times. Some of the adults looked directly at Gabriel, their faces curious but friendly.

Ashila came back to him. 'Our chieftain, Oboth, is wanting to talk to you,' she said quietly. 'When you greet him, kneel and put your –' she touched his forehead, and continued – 'on the floor. Then do the greeting I showed you. Don't hold his hand the Navoran way.'

Gabriel removed his boots, left them next to her shoes, and began to follow Ashila across the dirt floor to Oboth. The men who had been dancing moved aside to make a path for him, but no one spoke. The last man in the group moved to let Ashila pass, but then stepped back directly in front of Gabriel. The Shinali was in his mid-twenties, tall and magnificent, with a mass of black ringlets decorated with beads and leaves. A blue stripe was painted down the centre of his face, from his hairline to his roughly trimmed beard, and there were ochre lines on his cheeks. He looked overbearing and fierce, and he considered Gabriel suspiciously, from under lowered lids. He was stark naked, and sweat poured down him from the dance. The paint on his face, mixed with fish oil, smelled rank.

Ashila came back and angrily slapped her right hand hard on the man's chest, as if to push him away. He did not budge. 'He's breaking the treaty,' he said in Navoran, his eyes holding Gabriel's. 'The farmers, forbidden on Shinali land.'

'He's not a farmer,' said Ashila.

'What is he, then?'

'A high lot better well mannered than you,' she replied, and several people laughed. 'He's my guest,' she added. 'Give him way, Tarkwan.'

Tarkwan grunted and stepped aside.

Breathing easily again, Gabriel went and knelt in front of the chieftain as Ashila had told him to do. His action caused an undercurrent of surprise among the people. He made the greeting, then sat cross-legged, as the chieftain was sitting, and waited. He noticed, with a shock, that the chieftain was wearing a bone carving identical to the one he wore himself. Memories rushed over him, sharp with guilt, and he realised that the Shinali woman he had failed to help had been Oboth's daughter. Anguished, he closed his eyes against the painful childhood images, against the kindliness in Oboth's face.

Seeing the mourning bracelet on Gabriel's wrist, and

misreading his obvious distress, the chieftain said gently, 'I am sorry for your pain, my friend. I hope the All-father is being kind to the one you mourn.'

'I know he is,' Gabriel replied, looking up at last and studying the chieftain's face.

Oboth was a small, wrinkled man with a decisive expression. He had no hair on his head, and his snowy beard was thin. He looked to be well over eighty years old. Gabriel noticed that the whites of his eyes were an unhealthy yellow, and that he trembled constantly. But in spite of whatever pain he endured, the chieftain smiled warmly.

'What are you, Gabriel,' he asked, 'besides well mannered?'

'I'm a healer,' said Gabriel. 'I study at the Citadel. That's the white building standing by itself in the hills.'

Oboth nodded. 'We know it. You must be a good healer. Only the best go to the Citadel.'

Embarrassed, Gabriel shook his head. He was surprised that the Shinali knew about the Citadel. 'I'm only learning,' he said. 'My Masters – they're the best healers.'

The chieftain smiled again, liking the youth's humility. 'Your parents, what farm?' he asked.

'My father died some time ago. My mother and family have the farm nearest the hills, on the other side of the river. It's not the one immediately by the river, but the farm next to it.'

'Good flat land, for crops.'

'Yes.'

Oboth launched into a detailed description of which seasons were best for planting particular vegetables, and Gabriel struggled to understand.

'I'm not a gardener,' Gabriel said finally, when Oboth had finished talking about full moons and sickle moons and new moons. 'But I'm sure if you were to visit my mother, she'd welcome you and be very glad of your advice.'

'She'd be a rare Navoran,' said Oboth, with a twinkle in his eye. They talked a little longer, while the musicians started their music again. The children began playing a game, one of them hiding a pebble and the others looking for it, while several elderly women started cooking flat unleavened bread on hot stones in the fire's ashes.

After talking to the chieftain, Gabriel went with Ashila to the far end of the house, where it was quieter. There he met Ashila's mother, Thandeka, the clan healer; a woman with a forceful, indomitable look like her daughter's, and a warm smile. She asked him about his work at the Citadel and surprised him by knowing Salverion's name. She also knew of Amael, the Master of Herbal Medicines. Gabriel wanted to talk more with her, but others came over to meet him and he was claimed by a group of boys eager to hear about the great city of Navora.

Many spoke Navoran, but in broken words and jumbled sentences. He was moved that they wanted to speak his language at all, and asked them to teach him some Shinali words. So they did, laughing when he made mistakes, and applauding when he got words right. Even the ones who could not speak Navoran were eloquent, using hand signs and other mimed movements to communicate with him. They all touched his clothes, fingering the thick quilting of his vest and the fine weave of his shirt. Several of the young women stroked his hair, admiring its alien colour, and sniffing at the scent of the soaps he had used. He blushed, far more self-conscious than they were.

An old woman hobbled over and shooed the girls away. 'Stop touching him,' she growled, in Navoran. 'He's not a horse you're going to be trading for.'

One of the girls said something in Shinali, and the whole clan broke into laughter. 'What did she say?' Gabriel asked Ashila, but she buried her face in her hands, her shoulders shaking with mirth, and would not tell him.

They were left alone and sat on the dirt floor to watch the men dance again. Examining the interior of the house, Gabriel saw that it was bigger than he had imagined, and dim but for the firelight and the beam of sun streaming through the smoke hole. In the centre of the house the fire burned in a large pit lined with stones. Gourds of water, clay bowls, and cooking pots stood on the wide stone hearth. Around the walls of the dwelling was a raised area like a platform, spread with flax matting and covered with blankets traded from Navora, as well as sheepskins and furs. They were the sleeping places. Above them rose the excavated walls, covered with flax woven into patterns, and adorned with the clan's treasures: carvings, drums, bows, and spears. Long wooden beams, gracefully curved, rose from the walls and formed the domed roof, expertly thatched with grass and flax. Through the dimness he glimpsed looms holding partly finished fabrics, and noticed that several people spun wool or flax while they sat talking.

Looking again at the sleeping places, Gabriel had a strong impression of lying in warm furs with the fire crackling across the room. It was like a fleeting memory, disturbing him, filling him with yearning. So many things here seemed to evoke memories: the weapons that looked familiar though he had never seen them before, the haunting music of the flutes, the mingled sounds of the river outside with the Shinali speech and guttural chanting of old men, and the smells of wool and ash. All were familiar, loved, the stuff of childhood images.

He realised that Ashila was watching him intently, her eyes

shimmering in the smoky light, her face very grave. 'What's on your mind, Gabriel?' she asked.

'Everything here,' he said. 'I dreamed about this place when I was a child. And sometimes since.'

'We believe that when we dream, our soul journeys. Maybe you've been here before, and today was the time chosen for your return.'

'For what reason?'

Her eyes held his, and a beautiful smile crossed her face, as if she recognised something joyful and profound. In that moment he knew she had the Vision. He looked away, afraid in case she saw what drew him here.

Across the room the men had finished dancing and were wrestling one another, shouting challenges. 'They're going to race the canoes,' said Ashila, standing up. 'Come and watch.'

With all the clan, they went outside. The people shouted with excitement, and Ashila explained that they were placing bets on who would win. They bet their prized possessions – favourite clothes, spears, painted pottery.

Though the wind remained keen, most of the competitors were naked, obviously intending to stay that way for the rough ride through the rapids. Six canoes lay on the riverbank, two paddles in each. Already the men had divided into pairs, though Tarkwan stood alone. Slowly the tall Shinali picked up a paddle from the last boat and went over to Gabriel. Almost casually he threw the paddle to him. The action was a challenge, and as Gabriel caught the paddle, an uneasy silence fell. The clan watched, squinting against the light, while the wind tugged at their hair and tossed their cloaks.

Ashila said to Gabriel, quietly, 'Tarkwan goes the high dangerous way, all times only him. Even our warriors don't like to go in his canoe.'

Gabriel's eyes met Tarkwan's. The Shinali was smiling a little, almost laughing. 'The Navorans, they have no bravery, *haii*?' Tarkwan said.

'I'll go with you,' said Gabriel, though his voice shook. 'I was brought up in boats.'

Tarkwan's smile widened. 'Are you getting your clothes wet, healer, or are you taking them off?'

Gabriel swallowed nervously. He had not thought of this. Deciding to compromise, he removed only his vest and shirt. As he took off his shirt he remembered the Shinali bone he wore. Carefully he removed the talisman with his shirt, and rolled it tightly into the clothes. He gave the bundle to Ashila and hoped she would not unroll it. Wearing only his trousers and carrying the paddle, he went over to the canoe. It was hewn from a single log, pointed at the bow and stern, and ornately carved.

Tarkwan bent to pick up the bow of the canoe, and Gabriel lifted the stern. 'Afraid the women will see you, and laugh?' asked Tarkwan loudly, glancing mockingly at Gabriel's trousers.

'I'm afraid,' Gabriel replied, equally loud, 'that if the women see me, they'll be laughing at you.'

The clan roared with merriment, and Tarkwan grinned as they carried the canoe down into the water. The river closed about Gabriel's legs, instantly numbing them. Tarkwan held the boat while Gabriel got in, and gave him instructions. The other canoes were already waiting, the men paddling to hold them stationary in the current. Oboth stood on the bank, his arms raised. Shivering with terror and cold, Gabriel stared past Tarkwan's back at the foaming water ahead. Then Oboth's arms went down, and the canoes shot forward.

Tarkwan chanted, and Gabriel paddled in time with his rhythm. The work was easy at first, as they sped through the deep pools and skimmed over barely submerged rocks. Gabriel noticed that the other canoes kept close by the shore far to his left. Soon the waters became swift and treacherous, and he fought to keep control, his knees pressed against Tarkwan's back. They plunged through churning rapids, and the last glimpse Gabriel had of the other canoes was of dark shapes still far to his left and falling fast behind. Behind them, too, were the farmlands and the plain. They had entered a steep valley sliced between the hills, and there was no time for anything but watching the seething water and responding to Tarkwan's shouted commands.

Thunder filled his ears and the canoe pitched, tilting, over the edge of a waterfall. There were breathtaking seconds of weightlessness, then turmoil as the boat hit the water again. Icy forces surged over them and Gabriel thought, in that strange timeless calm at the core of supreme danger, how ironic it was that one half-mad Shinali should accomplish what the most cunning men in the Empire had failed to do. But he did not die; the canoe bounded up into the light and rushed on again.

Tarkwan's arms worked powerfully, the paddle flashing in the sun in time to his chant. Sweat and water poured down him, and he punctuated his chant with shouts of pure pleasure. Without realising it Gabriel shouted with him, then they were plummeting down another waterfall, and beyond that through deep swirling pools. Gabriel roared at Tarkwan in fury as the canoe spun fast, seemingly out of control, and overhanging rocks flashed perilously close to their heads. Then they shot forward again, fast as an arrow, the waters thundering about them. Suddenly the river widened, became flat and quiet, and the race was over.

They were the first through. Risking a glance behind him now, Gabriel saw four of the other canoes still battling the last rapids, close to the far shore. A canoe had overturned under the second waterfall and the men had abandoned it and were downriver, swimming ashore where the waters were easier.

Breathing hard, exultant, Gabriel and Tarkwan paddled to the shore, then carried the canoe up on to the stones. As they emptied the water out of it, Tarkwan said: 'Not bad work, for a well-mannered Navoran.'

'A mad Navoran, you mean,' said Gabriel, his teeth chattering. He was blue with cold and shaking so much he could hardly talk, but his grin was as big as Tarkwan's.

They were met by people who had walked here earlier, bearing blankets and clothes. At first the group was disconcerted to see Gabriel, but they greeted him courteously, since he had paddled in Tarkwan's canoe, and congratulated him. Because they had not expected a newcomer, there were no dry trousers for Gabriel, but they gave him a thick blanket and a sheepskin jacket painted with Shinali designs. Still shivering, Gabriel stood beside Tarkwan and watched the other canoes finish. Tarkwan hugged his friends as they came ashore, and he and Gabriel graciously accepted their praise.

Carrying the canoes, they started the long walk back, keeping to the pebbly shore along the steep river valley, then skirting the farms and crossing the grasslands towards the Shinali house. It was late afternoon when they got back. People ran to meet them, and when they were told who had won, there were hugs and cheers. Gabriel found himself going from one embrace to another. All the young people hugged him, kissing both his cheeks and laughing at his blue lips, and the elders congratulated him in Shinali, briefly touching his chest with their palms.

He looked for Ashila. She was standing a little way apart from all the excitement, her arms around an elderly woman who could only shuffle along. But she smiled at him, her dark eyes fervent and admiring, and she got the colour back in his face again.

In the house he found his shirt and vest exactly as he had rolled them, but warming on the hearth. Tarkwan's younger brother, Yeshi, pressed a pair of trousers into his arms. The trousers were soft brown leather painted with red-and-black animals, and were Yeshi's best. Gabriel thanked him, found a quiet space near the sleeping platform, and removed the Shinali jacket and his own soaking trousers. Entranced by his pale skin, a group of children stood watching him, creeping closer and closer, until he felt little fingers in his hair and down his back. He tolerated them until they got too familiar, then he growled suddenly like a dog, and the children fled, shrieking and laughing. He pulled on Yeshi's trousers and his own shirt and vest, luxuriating in the warmth. Unobserved, he hid the bone carving inside his shirt. When he went back to the fire a woman took his leather trousers and hung them over a stick to dry. He thanked her, found a space by the hearth, and sat there to thaw out.

Tarkwan offered Gabriel a drink of wine in a rough clay bowl. 'It was part of the payment for the land,' Tarkwan explained, sitting beside him. 'The best Navoran wine, they said.'

Gabriel tasted it; it was like vinegar. 'To the river,' he said, raising the bowl. 'And to excellent canoes.'

As Tarkwan lifted his bowl as well, Gabriel noticed a blue spiral tattooed on the Shinali's left breast. He stared at it, old memories flashing back. He saw the Shinali woman again, wounded on the rocks: the spiral tattoo on her breast, and her face, beautiful and strong, and so like Tarkwan's. She had been his sister. Again remorse and fear tore through Gabriel. *He'd kill me if he knew*, he thought.

Tarkwan finished his wine in a few thirsty gulps, then wiped his hand across his dripping chin. 'It's good wine?' he asked.

'Not the best,' Gabriel replied.

Tarkwan laughed, but the sound had a bitter ring. 'They cheated us, *haii?*' he said. 'Navoran dogs.'

Other people sat down to drink. Besides the wine, pottery bowls of hot herbal tea were passed around. Offered, too, were the flat cakes of steaming bread. Relaxing a little, Gabriel realised that he was hungry. After the bread came warmed meat and generous chunks of smoked fish. There were vegetables, too: yellow roots cooked in ashes, and salads made of cress and wild mint. The musicians started playing again, and people began to sing. Since they sang between mouthfuls of food and sometimes while chewing them, the sound was not consistent or wonderful, but Gabriel enjoyed it. Several times he thought of Myron, and a tight feeling went across his chest. But most of the time he forgot, and listened to the flutes and singing and talk, cherishing the rumbustious company. Often he sought Ashila and glimpsed her talking to friends or feeding someone's child, or just sitting across the fire observing him. Many times their eyes met, and they smiled, and there spun between them something fine and strong and unforgettable.

When the feasting was finished, a crowd of children dragged Gabriel over to the sleeping platform, gave him a bowl of thick black dye and a point of deer antler, and begged him to paint canoes on their clothes and to make his own sign. When finally they raced off, splattered with black dye and with Gabriel's initials and wobbly canoes on their chests, their hero pulled on his boots and went outside to find Ashila.

12 Prophecies and Destinies

BEHIND THE SHINALI house he discovered the holes used for latrines concealed by a group of trees and, beyond that, a stone enclosure obviously used to shelter the sheep at night. Now the sheep were out on the plain, guarded by children. Each young shepherd carried a sling, and fired tiny stones to keep sheep from straying. Never striking the sheep, the pebbles hit the dirt beside the animals' heads, startling them back towards the flock. Gabriel admired the shepherds' skill.

Close to the house, on the side nearer the farms, were vegetable gardens. Gabriel saw Ashila working there, beside the old woman Gabriel had seen her with after the canoeing. The woman was laughing to herself as she shuffled between the cabbages, and Gabriel realised that she was sick in her mind. Seeing Gabriel, Ashila stood up and came to meet him.

'She's in her own world,' Ashila explained, looking across at the old woman, still chuckling and talking to herself. 'Her name's Domi. She knows nothing in this world, except the garden. All times, she's being with her children, though they're dead.'

'At least she's happy,' said Gabriel, and Ashila nodded. He added, with regret in his voice, 'I have to go home now, I'm sorry. My family needs me.'

She looked disappointed, though she smiled. 'I'm being sorry, too,' she said. 'Will you be visiting us again?'

'I don't have to go back to the Citadel until the day after tomorrow. Could I come tomorrow? I could return Yeshi's trousers.'

'You are not needing a reason to come,' she said.

Together they went into the house, and he got his damp trousers from the stick by the fire, then said goodbye to Oboth and other members of the clan. They urged him to stay longer, but when he said he had to go, they looked at his mourning bracelet and understood. Ashila walked with him to the edge of the Shinali land.

'I wish we could have had more time to talk, you and I,' Gabriel said.

'There's a time for all things.'

He wanted to tell her that there was no time – that these hours, and maybe an hour or two tomorrow, were all they had, but he could not.

'Sometimes,' she said, 'it's not the longness of a time that matters, but the goodness in it. And your time here is good.'

'It's good for me, too,' he said. 'I needed it. I needed your Shinali ways.'

'Tell me on your ways, Gabriel. On your life. What it's like to live Navoran.'

So he did, and she listened, often laughing in amazement, sometimes putting her hand on his arm as a sign for him to stop and explain. Laughing and talking, their heads close, with Gabriel sometimes gesturing in signs, they came to the fence that bordered the first farm. Here the farmers had built a stone bridge across the river, for themselves and wagons to cross. Gabriel and Ashila were so intent on conversation, they did not notice at first that someone waited on the bridge. Then Gabriel looked up and saw Ferron. The keeper was wearing a hooded cloak, wrapped tight against the chill air, and he looked tense and agitated.

'I was worried about you,' Ferron said angrily, striding down off the bridge and coming over to them. His sword, swinging at his side, glinted in the pale afternoon sun. 'But I see my concern was unnecessary.'

'This is Ashila,' said Gabriel, resenting Ferron's attitude. 'Ashila, this is my friend Ferron.'

Ferron pushed back his hood and studied the young woman's face. Her eyes still shone from laughter, and her cheeks were flushed. 'Greetings, Ashila,' Ferron said. 'You've obviously cared for him well. He looks happy enough, in spite of his grief.'

Ashila did not know what to say to that, so she whispered goodbye and turned to go. Gabriel caught her hand. 'I'll see you tomorrow,' he said. 'Does it matter when I come?'

'All times, you are welcome,' she said, smiling again, though her eyes looked past him to Ferron and were wary.

'I'll come in the afternoon.'

She nodded, and her fingers tightened briefly about his before they parted. He watched her go, walking quickly, with that easy grace of hers, then he turned and began walking back to the farm with Ferron.

'There was no need to come after me,' Gabriel said. 'I was fine.'

'Were you?' asked Ferron. 'Why are you wearing Shinali pants?'

'Mine got wet. I went canoeing.'

'Good God, man!' cried Ferron. 'We were watching the canoes! That ride was suicidal! Have you gone mad?' He glanced back at Ashila and muttered, 'Don't answer that.'

'It was a race,' said Gabriel. 'I was challenged by the chieftain's son. I had to take part.'

'And I have to look after you. I risk my own life to guard you against Jaganath. I don't know why I bother, when you rush off and invite the Shinali to do the job for him.'

'You're going too far, Ferron.'

'That makes two of us.'

They walked for a while in silence, rapidly, then Ferron said: 'You know you won't ever see her again.'

'I don't need a lecture.'

'Someone's got to tell you. You're making an idiot of yourself, Gabriel. You came here for your brother's funeral, and you end up fooling around with a native girl. What is it between you and the Shinali? I bet it's something to do with that damned amulet –'

'Enough!' shouted Gabriel, gripping the front of Ferron's cloak. 'You've said enough!'

Ferron shook him off, and they stood looking across the Shinali land, their breathing deep and their breath misty in the cold air.

'I'm sorry,' said Ferron quietly. 'I'm concerned, that's all. I don't want to drag you back to the Citadel lovesick.'

'You won't.'

'That look you had when you said goodbye to her – it was just brotherly affection?'

'Yes.'

Ferron looked at him sideways, his green eyes dancing with humour. 'You're a bad liar, brother.'

It was mid-afternoon when Gabriel visited the Shinali the next day. The children saw him coming and ran to meet him. The women, gathering in their washing from where they had spread it on the grass to dry, stood up and called greetings to him. There were no men about. As Gabriel passed the garden he noticed old Domi working alone there, laughing and chatting joyfully to her dead loved ones.

Ashila was on the riverbank, placing fresh fish in the smoke house the Navoran soldier had helped the Shinali build. It was like the smoke houses Gabriel had seen as a boy, on the beach near his father's boats. Leaving her friends to finish the task, Ashila washed her hands in the river and came up to meet Gabriel. She pressed her hand against her own chest, then his. Then, laughing because they both moved at exactly the same moment to do it, they shook hands the Navoran way.

'I've brought these back, for Yeshi,' he said, giving her the trousers.

'He'll be thanking you. Will you come and have a drink with us?'

He wanted to spend all the time today alone with her, but knew nothing of Shinali traditions of hospitality or welcome, and was afraid of offending. So, accepting her offer, he followed her into the house. The older women had already boiled water and made their pungent herbal tea. They sat around the hearth and chatted to him while they drank, and if they spoke Shinali, Ashila interpreted. Sometimes Gabriel misunderstood and gave answers that sent them into peals of laughter. He laughed with them, feeling embarrassed but never humiliated, self-conscious because he was the only adult male present.

'The men are in the forest, hunting deer,' an old woman explained. 'Smoked fish, we're being tiring of it, after the snowtime. And all the old sheeps, we've eat.'

'I told my mother about your smoked fish,' Gabriel said.

'The farmers would like to trade, your fish for their goats. Soon they want to farm sheep and cattle. Maybe then you could trade for beef.' They looked bewildered, so he added, 'Red meat, different from deer.'

They talked of various foods, and the women explained what herbs they used and where they found them. Children bought some of the herbs to show him, tricking him into eating the bitterest leaves, and laughing at the faces he pulled. And all the time they touched his unfamiliar fine-woven shirt, and stroked his pale hair and skin.

Afterwards, when he and Ashila went outside again, she asked, 'Would the champion like to come for a walk today? Or, if you're thinking that's too dull, we could take spears and hunt mountain lions.'

'A walk with you sounds a high lot exciting,' he replied.

A crowd of children begged and howled to come with them, but Ashila sent them back, promising to tell them stories that night if they were obedient. Reluctantly, the children stayed. Walking close to the river, Gabriel and Ashila set off towards the mountains. Again he was struck by her unaffected beauty and grace, and last night's dreams paled in the light of her presence. He tried not to stare at her, concentrating instead on the view before them. Directly ahead, where the river cut through the ranges, was the gorge where the Taroth Fort had been built. Gabriel remembered the conversation at Jaganath's house.

'Does the Navoran army go through your land often?' he asked.

'The last time was two summers past. They get prisoners from the Hena tribes, or the Igaal, on the far side of the mountains.'

'Why didn't those tribes sign a treaty, the way your people did?'

'It would have been hard for them to sign a treaty; their tribes are too many, too . . .' She flung out her hand, as if scattering grain.

'Widespread?' he suggested.

'Yes. Too widespread. They're nomads, following deer herds. They attacked us sometimes, for slaves. Warlike, they were. They attacked the Navorans too, so our storytellers say, while the stone city was being built. To stop them coming through the mountains, the Navorans made Taroth Fort. That was long time past, even before our chieftain, Oboth, was born.'

'And your people – were they warlike?'

'Not at first. We were fisherfolk, full of peace, and a great people. The coast lands were ours – all the land, this side of the mountains. The Navorans came, and for a time we lived together, our boats on the water side by side. And side by side we fought the Igaal and the Hena, before the fort was made. But the Navorans grew, became strong and too many, and wanted our waters and our lands for themselves. They broke holes in our fishing boats, and sank them, and made life hard for us. Then we became warlike. Then we fought hard battles – for our waters, our land, and our lives. Oboth was a great warrior in those days, and he and the old ones, they still have the scars. But the Navorans killed many of us, and the ones left they beat back to this plain, to this last place before the mountains and the desert lands of our enemies. Trapped between two foes, we were. In the end we made peace with the Navorans and settled here by the river. The soldiers in Taroth Fort protected us from the Hena and Igaal, but also they watched us, like a lion watches the deer. We were never easy, under their eyes. After a time, they left the fort.'

'Was that when you signed the treaty?'

'The fort was empty three, maybe four summers, before we

made the treaty. When I was being a little girl, Oboth signed it. It made strong our peace, and said forever we keep our land. But all we have now is this plain, and our people are not great any more. We become less and less. Eight winters past there was a bad sickness. It came soon after the Navoran trader came. It killed nearly us all who were left. Now there are only ten times ten of us. That's how many the soldier counted. Since, some have died, some been born. One houseful now, that's all.'

'That sickness must have been the bulai fever. The trader should have known better than to come here, with the disease in Navora. What was he trading?'

'Blankets, for smoked fish. He had his family, old ones and children. He was going on a journey, he said, far and far from the city. He didn't say things on the fever.'

'Was he the only one who crossed your plain?'

'No. There was a high lot of them, but they didn't visit us. Most stayed on the old road, where you ran yesterday. They were going over the mountains.'

'There's no fever now,' he said, 'but it comes every six or seven years and is due again. If you see many people leaving Navora, don't have anything to do with them.'

'This fever,' she said, 'what are its signs?'

'I've never seen it. But Salverion, my teacher, says it looks like other sicknesses, and is very hard to recognise. That's why it's often widespread before it's found. The only symptom that gives the plague away is grey patches deep in the back of the throat. Once you see those, you know it's bulai fever.'

'How does it spread?'

'Very quickly, in the spit and in the blood, and it always kills.'

'One man killed nearly all our people?' she asked.

'Maybe. I don't really know. But it seems that way.'

'Just as well our house is being in the middle of the grasslands,' she said. 'It's a long way to spit, even for a Navoran.'

They laughed, then walked in silence for a while, looking at the savage ravines and snowy peaks ahead. In the gorge dividing the ranges, the ancient fort looked huge and impressive, its sheer walls the same tawny colour as the mountain rock. As he looked at it, Gabriel asked, 'Where would your people go, Ashila, if you didn't have the plain?'

She shrugged. 'The mountains are too hard and dry. Not good for farming or growing vegetables. And the Hena and Igaal are still unfriendly. Yet there are old prophecies that say time to come we'll leave our land and go to the lands of the Igaal and Hena, and become one with them, and make a great nation again. The old prophets said other things, too.'

'Can you tell me what those things are?'

She thought before answering, not wanting to offend him. 'The prophets say Navora will rot from the inside, like a tree with a worm in it. Not all of it will rot. But the part that does, that has no strongness, will be cut down by the new Shinali nation. We'll wipe the Navoran city into the sea and take back the lands that were ours. But one part of the Navoran tree will remain, a good branch that will fall to the ground and become a new tree. It will grow side by side with the Shinali tree, the roots separate and strong, but the leaves and branches will weave together like one tree. The eagle will make its nest in the branches of both.'

'We have a similar prophecy,' said Gabriel. 'My Master, Salverion, told me of it. It will be a time of cleansing for our nation, a beginning again.'

Ashila looked across at the farms, towards his house. 'There is the good branch,' she said. 'People already wanting harmony with us, with our life on the land. People like your mother. Like you. In the Time of the Eagle, you'll be the tree that grows beside ours, on this land.'

He smiled. 'I wouldn't complain about a Shinali way of life. But why call the new time the Time of the Eagle?'

'The eagle is the sign of our people. It's the sign carved on the sacred *torne,* the bone that Oboth wears. The *torne* holds great power, all the memories and wisdom of our clan. It also tells a prophecy, that our victory will begin with one man, a man with a high lot of braveness, who does one thing great for us. It's his face on the *torne*, with the eagle. We won't be knowing who the man is; the prophets say he'll come and go, and most of us won't even recognise him, or know what he does. But he will begin the Time of the Eagle. It's ancient, the *torne*, and is passed down from chieftain to oldest son, and from chieftain's wife to the women of the family. Oboth's daughter had one, but it's lost with her.'

Abruptly, Gabriel turned and walked on. But Ashila had seen his azure eyes darken like the skies when the sun was gone, and she followed, confused, sensing more in him than sorrow for the huge change to come in his people's destiny. There was something else, something deep and lifelong and secret, and it disturbed her profoundly.

Eventually Gabriel stopped and waited for her. He looked distraught. 'Maybe I shouldn't be here,' he said.

'Why? Because our people, yours and mine, were old enemies?'

'Not that. You don't know me, Ashila. I have no right to be here on your land, a guest in your house.'

'You are having the right. Your spirit has long visited our house, our land. You dream Shinali dreams. You have more right than you know.'

'What do you mean?'

She hesitated, then said quietly: 'There's another thing, about the face on the ancient *torne*. The man who will begin the Time of the Eagle . . . he's Navoran.'

'What's that to do with me?'

She was silent, solemn, and he realised what she implied. Astounded, he shook his head, then laughed a little. 'You don't know me, Ashila! I dream Shinali dreams, that's all. But as for being the one to bring about the rebirth of your nation – by God! You couldn't be more wrong! That man will be a far better person than I.'

'He will bring about the rebirth of the Navoran nation, too. A man who loves both peoples, both ways. He will unite them, make them one.'

'He'll be a good man, Ashila. Brave. True. Not me.'

'You're brave. You went with Tarkwan in his canoe. And your heart is true. I see it.'

'No, you don't.'

'I see pain. That is different from not-truth. Why are you here this day, Gabriel? Are you thinking it's chance?'

'You're terribly mistaken. I'm not the person you think I am.'

'My knowing is never wrong.'

'This time it is wrong.'

'My knowing is this right,' she said, driving her right fist violently into her left palm.

Gabriel looked away from her impassioned face, appalled at this sudden disunity between them, at what he thought was the huge folly of her belief.

Ashila sighed deeply and made a graceful sign with her hand, as if to apologise. 'I'm being sorry, Gabriel,' she said quietly. 'You're my guest, a friend on our land. Also, this is your mourning time. I'm being sorry I shakened your canoe.'

'I don't mind you shaking my canoe,' he said, 'just don't turn it upside down.'

'That is for the All-father to do, not me,' she replied. 'I would be happy if we could paddle our canoes together, side by side.'

He smiled, and it transformed the strong angles of his face, banishing whatever tormented him. They began walking again, close, and came to a group of trees beside the river. One had fallen, its colossal trunk and tangled branches making a natural shelter from the wind. Ashila leaned against it, facing the mountains. The tree had obviously fallen a long time ago, and the ground around it was trampled smooth into a comfortable hollow.

'We're not the first to stop here,' Gabriel observed, putting his cloak down so they could sit on it, and noticing stylised pictures of animals and weapons cut into the trunk beside his head. There were flocks of birds, each one the same.

As she sat down with him, Ashila explained: 'This place we call *Ta-sarn-ee*. It means 'The place where no one sees.' This is where people come to get away from the clan.'

'I suppose there's not much privacy, all of you living in one house.'

'Arik, the soldier who lived with us, he told us that Navorans have one family in one house. It must be hard for you, in our place. So much noise.'

'Yesterday I needed the noise,' said Gabriel. 'I enjoyed my time with your people, Ashila.'

'Will you eat with us tonight, before you go?'

'I'd like to, but it's my last night with my family for a long time.'

'Oboth is pleased someone from the farms has come to us. He wants Navorans to meet with us, though the treaty forbids them on our land. That's why he sold a little land for farms: he hopes to trade, and that Navorans who love the land will be our friends. He'll be glad that you've talked on these things with your mother.'

'What's wrong with the chieftain? He's in a lot of pain.'

'He doesn't tell me that, and I can't help him till he does.'

'What kind of healing do you give?'

'With medicines from plants and trees. And sometimes, if I'm feeling very strong, I can heal just from here.' She placed her fingertips on her forehead and watched his face, expecting him to laugh.

'I heal that way too,' he said.

Ashila looked astounded. 'Arik said the only way for healing was with a knife, and strong drink to kill the pain.'

'That's the way it is for most of the physicians in Navora, especially the ones who travel with the army. Though they also use herbal medicines. I think your mother's met some of the healers I know. I'd like to talk to her again and find out.'

'What other healings are you knowing?'

'At the Citadel we learn to stop pain so people feel nothing if they have to have surgery.'

'What's surgery?'

'Healing with the knife.'

'How do you stop the pain of that?'

'I can't tell you, I'm sorry. We make vows that we won't ever teach our skills.'

'Can you show me? Not show me how to do it, but only what happens.'

He hesitated. 'I don't know. I've never done this.'

'Not even for another healer, whose heart is like yours?'

'You make it hard to say no, Ashila. If I stop the feeling in your hand, is that all right?'

'Yes.'

'It's best if we stand so you can have your spine perfectly straight.'

She did as he suggested, and he explained that he would touch the back of her neck and her shoulder. She turned her back to him and waited, relaxed and trusting. Gently he brushed aside her hair, then moved his fingertips across her spine. Her neck was long and lithe, her skin like warm satin, and he had trouble keeping his thoughts on his work. When he had finished blocking the necessary pathways, his hands stayed there and he had an almost irresistible urge to move his mouth over her skin. Never before during his work had he felt such an impulse, and it shocked him.

'Have you finished?' she asked, because his fingers were still.

'Yes. Try to make a fist of your right hand.'

She tried, then turned to face him, her eyes wide with wonder. 'I can't!' she cried. 'I can't move it.'

'The paralysis will wear off by tonight.' He lifted her hand and squeezed each of her fingertips in turn, hard, until her nails were bloodless.

'I'm feeling nothing,' she said. 'You could sew up a cut on my hand, and I'd be not knowing it.'

'That's why we learn that skill.'

'And you're not allowed to show me how?'

'I'm afraid not.'

'How long did it take you to learn?'

'I can't tell you that either. I can't say anything at all about the healing arts I learn. I'm sorry.'

'I understand. Thank you for showing me this.'

He was still holding her hand, massaging it gently to hasten back the feeling. 'Can you tell me how you heal with your mind?' he asked.

'Words are hard. When a person is sick, say with fever, I sleep with them, see their pain and sick-being, but not with these eyes. Then, with a high lot of strongness, I see them well. You're knowing what I mean?'

'Yes, I know. Did your mother teach you healing, Ashila?'

'Yes. And an old woman gave her the knowing when she was being young.'

'And you'll teach someone, one day?'

'That's our way.'

'Who will you teach?'

'My daughter, when I have one.'

'Do you have anyone in the clan you want to marry?'

'I was loving Tarkwan, long in time.'

'All your life, you mean?'

'No. Long time past. I was six summers old, and he was twelve.'

'What happened?'

'He was being a man before I was being a woman. He chose Moondarri.'

'Are they married?'

'Since they were fourteen summers old. He's always bringing her to *Ta-sarn-ee*, and the people laugh at them for it. Tarkwan carved all the birds in the tree, a bird for every time they're being here.'

Gabriel was still holding her hand, lightly stroking her fingers and palm and wrist. She withdrew it, and gave him the other.

'You want me to numb this one, too?' he asked, puzzled.

'No. But if you're pleasuring my hand,' she said, her lips curled, 'I'd like it on skin that can feel.'

Reddening, he laughed softly and let her go. 'Sorry,' he said.

'I was forgetting myself. Forgetting a lot of things.' He picked up his cloak and flung it around his shoulders again, and stood looking at the mountains. The snowy peaks shone, turned golden by the sun setting on the far side of the sky.

'Sometimes forgetting is good,' Ashila murmured. 'Do you want to walk on?'

'For a little way.'

They walked up out of the shadows into the dazzling light and on towards the mountains. They stopped after a while, looking at the peaks.

Ashila was wearing only her woollen dress, and she shivered, putting her paralysed hand under her arm. Gabriel stood behind her and enfolded her in the cloak with him. Their shadows merged into one, stretched out in front of them across the bright Shinali land. The evening was serene. The only sounds were the calls of homeward-bound birds and the chuckle of the river as it rushed across the stones. The mountains were breathtaking, their valleys streaked with misty purple, their summits on fire with the last light of the day.

'What do you call the mountains?' Gabriel asked.

'The highest one, on the other side of the river, we call Sharnath. It's our sacred mountain.'

'Why is it sacred?'

'The All-father lives there.'

'You go there to worship?'

'This word . . . worship?'

'To pray. Talk to the All-father.'

'No. We worship wherever we are. But we journey to the mountain, one time in a turning of the seasons, those of us who need to. We have a time we call the Moon of the Seventh Sacrament. It's the seventh season, the little last one, only one new moon to the next. It comes at the ending of the winter, in the time of the yellow flowers.'

'What do you do, on the Moon of the Seventh Sacrament?'

'It's our holy time, when we let go things of the old seasons and prepare for the new. The earth-changes are also in the spirit world. If we need to, we can journey up the sacred mountain and make a sacrament to the All-father.'

'Like a sacrifice?'

'I'm not knowing that word.'

'Sacrifice means to give something up.'

Ashila repeated the word several times. 'It's like that, like a sacrifice,' she said. 'On the mountain we leave a sign of whatever we want to forget, and when we return home it's finished. We can leave there anything, and it's a secret between ourselves and the All-father. It may be a debt we can't pay, a hurt we can't forgive, a guilt, a grief. Anything that's heavy on our hearts, that we can't carry. The sacrament is a letting go. It's a work of the All-father, not of ourselves, something we leave with him to finish or mend.'

'It's a beautiful belief.'

'Do you have anything like that in Navora?'

'I suppose the nearest thing is our Sanctuary of Healing Dreams. People sleep there who need healing in their minds.'

Without warning, images of his last night in the sanctuary crowded into his head, and he thought of Myron being there, wanting to see him; saw Myron standing on the sanctuary steps, running down them, going to his death. To the death that should have been Gabriel's. Grief went through him, deep and hard like a physical pain.

Ashila felt his arms tighten about her, felt him press his face into her hair, and heard his breath, broken and distraught. She wanted to turn around and face him, but he held her too firmly.

So she moved her arms until they were lying over his, and their hands were clasped. She held him that way until he was quiet again, and the skies were dark and velvet blue, and a sliver of silver moon hung in the sky. Even then he did not move away but stayed close, his breath warm across her hair.

'My brother died for me,' he said. And he sighed deeply, as if speaking the words eased an agony.

'That makes your life twice sacred,' she said.

'I hadn't thought of it that way. I feel guilty for being alive.'

'Our destinies are written,' she said. 'Don't sorrow for anything, Gabriel. Our birthing time is chosen by the All-father, the parents we have and the home and all the days and big happenings of our lives. Don't you think he also chooses with high carefulness that day we walk the shadow-place between the worlds and see his face?'

Gently Gabriel released her and turned her to him. He lifted his hand and stroked back her hair, his fingertips lingering on her cheek. 'I know he chose this day,' he said.

'I know it too. But this day's almost gone, and your people are needing you.'

'My people,' he sighed, looking back along the grasslands towards the farms and the winking lights of the houses there. Beyond, coppery in the dusk, were the Citadel hills, and, hidden from view, the mighty city of Navora. He said, with sorrow and bitterness, 'My people are a tangled brood, Ashila.'

He put his arm and the cloak around her, and they walked back to her home. He went inside to say goodbye, and the people did their best to persuade him to stay for the night, or at least for the evening feast. The men were back after a successful hunt, and they were celebrating. 'We'll be showing you how to dance the Shinali way,' said Tarkwan.

'And I'll be giving you Shinali clothes, and be painting your face,' Yeshi promised.

Gabriel was very tempted but declined as graciously as he could. They all shook hands with him, and many embraced him. Lastly he went to say goodbye to the chieftain, Oboth. 'May I speak to you outside, for a moment?' Gabriel asked.

Oboth went up the steps with him into the freezing night, and they stood for a few moments looking up at the stars while Gabriel chose his words.

'I was at a dinner in the city a little time past,' Gabriel said. 'One of the guests was the commander of the Navoran army. He'd been drinking wine and said a few things that probably he shouldn't have. He said the army was going to cross the Shinali land again soon, and mentioned something about walking through your house. He said other things. I can't remember them word for word, but I think the treaty isn't going to be honoured much longer. Also, they're going to restore Taroth, make it strong again.'

For a long time the chieftain said nothing, but his eyes were moist as they gazed across his land. He looked suddenly incredibly old and frail and tormented.

'I wish I could help you, Oboth,' Gabriel said.

'You just have. More than you know.'

'I mean, your sickness.'

'Nothing can help that.'

'At least let me stop the pain.'

Oboth nodded, and Gabriel stood in front of him and held him close and moved his hands over the chieftain's bowed spine.

Ashila came out of the house. Unnoticed, in utter silence, she watched. In the starlight Gabriel's hands seemed luminous as they moved down the chieftain's back, and his hair was like silver, his face inexorable and frightening and beautiful. His eyes were closed, and drops of sweat rolled down his forehead, as if huge forces were being drawn out of him. At last he sighed, and at the same moment Oboth lifted his head. In wonder the chieftain touched his own chest, moving his hands down as if searching for something he had lost. Then his face broke into a smile, and he took Gabriel's hands and chanted a blessing in Shinali.

Gabriel glanced up and saw Ashila waiting for him. She looked away as soon as he saw her, and started walking along the grasslands towards the farms. Gabriel and Oboth embraced, the chieftain thanking him again in Shinali and in Navoran, telling him to come back whenever he wished. Then he went back into the house, and Gabriel ran after Ashila.

She was striding fast, and he thought she was angry again. He could not see her face; she kept it averted or managed to walk just ahead of him. He wanted to rest, to gather back his energies, but she seemed in a hurry. He wiped his arm across his face and noticed that his hand trembled.

'Are you angry with me?' he asked.

She shook her head.

'Why so fast? Why won't you look at me? If it's because of Oboth, I didn't heal him. That's for you to do your way. I just stopped his pain, that's all. I'm sorry if you feel that my helping him was wrong.'

'Oh, Gabriel,' she said, stopping and gazing at him. Her face was wet with tears. 'How could it be wrong? It was beautiful. Like a holy work.'

'It was just nerves.'

'Nerves?'

'Yes. I block them, so the pain messages don't get through. I shouldn't be telling you this. I'm breaking my vows. But don't look at me like that, Ashila. I'm nothing special.'

'Yes you are. What are nerves? Devils?'

'No, I'm not. And they're not. Devils, I mean. Nerves. Can we walk slowly? I'm tired. I can hardly think. I get like this when I've healed.'

'I'm sorry,' she said softly. 'I'm not understanding you well. Next time, perhaps, I will.'

'I think you understand me very well,' he said, walking on again. 'But there's something I've got to tell you, Ashila. I won't be coming back. Not for a long time. I can't. I'm pledged to stay at the Citadel and can't make journeys or visits to friends. I was allowed to come to the farm only for two days, because of Myron. Tomorrow I go back to the Citadel.'

'You had only two days for your family, and you gave pieces of them to us?'

'I suppose I did.'

She looked at him straight, and her smile changed the pulsing of his heart. 'Thank you,' she said. 'I thank you, with *sharleema*.'

He stopped walking. 'What does *sharleema* mean?' he asked, tensely.

'What's wrong, Gabriel?'

'What does it mean?'

'I'm sorry if –'

'Tell me!'

'It has many meanings. There isn't a word in your language like it. Arik said it meant with all the force of my soul. It can be a word of high thanks, or a strong asking, or a vow. If I said something to you and I wanted you to know the words were powerful to me, I'd add *sharleema*. To say *sharleema* at a promise end is to make the promise strong for life. If I asked you to do something, and added *sharleema,* it would be a crime for you not to do my asking. When I said *sharleema* just now, when I thanked you for giving us pieces of your days, I was telling you that I have a debt to you, and you have the right to ask anything of me, and I'll do it. We don't use *sharleema* unless we mean it. Are you all right?'

'Yes.' But his face was drawn and pale, and she worried. They walked for a long way without speaking. Beside them the river boomed, the rapids foaming white under the brilliant stars. Nearer the edge of the plain the river widened as it sighed and gurgled idly over the stones.

'How is your hand?' he asked suddenly, remembering.

'I can move it now,' she answered, flexing her fingers and turning her wrist.

'You have all the feeling back?' he asked, taking her fingers and squeezing them gently.

'I'm not knowing. Bite it and see,' she joked.

He lifted her hand to his mouth and took one of her fingers between his teeth, biting it softly and sliding his tongue about it, deliciously. She moaned and laughed and tried half-heartedly to pull free. He lowered her hand but did not let it go and was elated when she entwined her fingers with his. Too soon they came to the bridge. They walked up on to it, and Ashila leaned on the wall, looking down into the water. Gabriel leaned beside her, his shoulder touching hers.

'I haven't stood on the stone place before,' Ashila said. 'We don't come this close to the farms.'

'Maybe you should.'

'The treaty forbids it.'

'A treaty's supposed to be a covenant, an understanding. Ours divides, splits people apart.'

'It didn't keep you away.'

'I was invited on to your land. But there's something I don't understand. Your chieftain, Oboth, he welcomed me, and seems to want friendship with the farmers. But Tarkwan is still hostile. Unwelcoming.'

'Tarkwan will welcome the farmers, time to come. He will see that the farmers are the new Navorans. He will remember the prophecy and see that already the good branch is putting out its leaves.'

'It's the rest of the tree I fear for,' he said, his eyes on the twinkling lights of the city. 'It won't be easily cut down, not without a great battle. I fear for your people, too.'

'Think on the time of peace that will follow. A high lot of nights, I dream on that time. If you dreamed on it, Gabriel, what would your dreams be?'

'Radiant, if you were in them,' he said softly.

'What does radiant mean?'

'Shining. Joyful. Beautiful. Triumphant. Glorious. Do you want me to go on?'

'Only if you have easy words. The last two, what do they mean?'

'They mean "radiant".'

'Of course. How quickly I'm forgetting.'

'I won't. Forget quickly, I mean.'

'Neither will I,' she said, her voice low and eloquent. 'I've been loving this time.'

'I'm sorry it was only a morning and an afternoon.'

'It was worth a high lot.'

'I can't leave the Citadel again for six years.' He had not meant it to sound brutal, but it did. He began to apologise, but Ashila lifted her hand and placed a finger on his lips.

'Don't speak of it again,' she said. 'Just say farewell, and go.'

'Do you have a Shinali way of saying goodbye?'

'Yes. The act is the same as our greeting, only the words are different.'

'Will you show me?'

She placed her hand over her heart, then on his. 'My heart and yours will always be together.'

With a solemn look he touched his fingers to his chest, then to hers. His palm brushed the warm swell of her breast, and stayed there. Slowly he pushed aside her cloak and moved his hand over the rough fabric of her dress, up to the smooth skin of her throat. He caressed her, stroking his fingers in the warm hollows of her collarbone and along the contours of her neck. Then he drew her to him and very softly kissed her, his mouth unsure, tender.

Her hands slid about his waist, holding him close. When he moved away, neither of them was breathing calmly.

'I think I messed up the Shinali farewell,' he said huskily.

'I liked your messed-up way.' She smiled. 'Do you have a Navoran farewell?'

'That was it. Shall I do it again?'

Her eyes shimmered and her smile became uncertain. 'My heart says yes, but my wisdom says no.'

'Which one are you listening to? I'll accept whichever it is.'

She considered for a while, then said very quietly, 'My heart.'

They kissed again, and it was a long time before they moved apart. 'I have to go,' he whispered, caressing her face. 'I must.'

'I know,' she said, tears shining on her cheeks. 'May the All-father go with you.'

'And with you.' This time he made the Shinali farewell

properly, brief and full of meaning. He started to walk away but stopped and looked at her again, his eyes wet.

'Go,' she said. 'But keep me in your knowing. I'll keep you in mine. *Sharleema.*'

He tried to speak, and took a step towards her. She shook her head, and he turned abruptly and went away. He did not look back.

13 Hauntings

THE WINTER WORE ON. People said it was the longest and worst winter for a hundred years. In the hills around the Citadel the snow was deeper than a man was high, and the roads were impassable. Even in the city, snow and sleet fell, and the cobbled roads and ancient steps were treacherous with ice. Water froze in the aqueduct, and the city was without clean water. Every day people were taken to the Infirmary with winter illnesses, injuries from falls, and diseases from contaminated water. Travel became dangerous, and only messengers carrying mail braved the roads. Many businesses and public places closed, and people stayed inside huddled by their fires, waiting for the storms to abate.

In the Citadel the disciples studied with the Masters in the Library, and for leisure played sports and held friendly contests in the Citadel gymnasium. On the most bitter days the disciples, and often the Masters as well, gathered around the massive fireplace in the recreation room, to play chess and complex Navoran card games. Always Gabriel was there with his friends, and they marvelled at the serene way he endured both the grief of his brother's murder, and the strain of the long and fruitless investigation that brought no arrests and no justice.

Gabriel did not always feel serene. At times he felt a sense of joy, almost of elation, knowing where Myron was. If he wept it was for himself, because he missed Myron's letters and the huge pleasure his brother had been in his life. But there were times of unbearable longing, when he would have given half his life to see Myron one more time. The torment was not helped when he received a letter from Jaganath, full of compassion and apologies, and with hints that he had seen Myron and that the veils were thin. Jaganath offered again to teach Gabriel the skills to communicate with the dwellers on the Other Side and ended his letter by saying that he and Gabriel shared the same power, and he did not offer anything Gabriel did not already possess in his own heart. Though seeming warm and empathetic, the letter made Gabriel more suspicious than ever, and he burned it. But in the bad times he doubted his judgement, and Jaganath's words haunted him.

There were other letters, too, that disturbed him. Occasionally his lawyer wrote about the investigation, and the reports awoke in Gabriel a great rage and helplessness. He never spoke of his anger and thought he was dealing with it well, but there were nights when he dreamed he was hunted by shadowy beings, inhuman and terrible. Sometimes he turned and fought his pursuers, hacking them to shreds with a sword, until they were no more than bits of hair and flesh in pools of blood. Then the pieces would mingle together, would smirk and clatter their pointed teeth at him, and he would mutilate them again and again, until he woke screaming, with Ferron leaning over him. For hours afterwards he would shake with the fury and violence and terror of the dream, and Ferron would stay and hold him until he was quiet.

Not all the dreams were fearful. There were shining dreams in which he saw Myron again, fully alive and glorious, and they talked together or walked in childhood places they had loved. In the dreams he was aware that Myron was not his earthly self, and he always woke with a feeling of rapture and deep peace, as if it had been not a dream but something more.

And there were the visions of Ashila. She filled his nightly thoughts as completely as she filled his mind by day, and every hour was illuminated by the love of her. He had never known such feelings, such sublime joy and yearning and agony. She became his hope, his reason for being.

In his free time and when the weather was less brutal, Gabriel wrapped himself in furs, climbed the narrow steps to the top of the Citadel wall, and looked out towards the Shinali lands. In the ploughed farms the furrows ran in dark lines, and the trees stood stark and bleak against the brooding sky. The Shinali plain was cloaked with snow, divided by the blue-black wintry river. Herds of deer, their bodies dark and delicate, left trails across the white. And far out, in the heart of the land, was the snowy mound of the house, and smoke torn in the wind.

There was not much free time. Most of his days were spent with Sheel Chandra in the small and beautiful meditation room near the top of the Citadel tower. There, with the wind whistling about the white stone walls, Gabriel learned the deeper powers of healing with his mind, and the limitless forces of faith. Sometimes he and Sheel Chandra were days at a time in the meditation room, their bodies so still they barely breathed, their minds dimensions away.

One morning, just before daybreak, Gabriel opened his eyes and saw Ashila. She was standing by one of the narrow windows in the meditation room, a saffron-coloured blanket around her, her hair blown as if by a strong wind. The dawn light was on her, and she was watching him, her face tender and radiant. He gave a low cry and stood up. Ashila remained. A gust of wind blew the blanket aside, and as she drew it closed again he noticed a mourning bracelet about her wrist. The image of her was so vivid, so real, he went to her and reached out to caress her face. But as he was about to touch her skin, she vanished.

He stared at his raised hand, aware of the earthy scent of the grasslands and the pungent smell of wood smoke. Crouching, he touched the floor where her feet had been. It felt warm. He moved into the place where she had stood. Until the grey daylight filtered in through the thick glass he stood there, feeling the strength and joy of her, and being blessed.

As he went back to Sheel Chandra, he saw the Master's dark eyes open and shining on him. 'Don't ask anything, Master,' Gabriel whispered, sitting down again.

'I don't have to,' murmured Sheel Chandra, with his beautiful smile. 'Your mind has been full of her all night. I'm not surprised she visited.'

'How did you know what was in my mind?'

'It's hard not to see your memories when they're so strong.'

'You've been well entertained, then, Master,' said Gabriel, blushing. 'I hope you enjoyed yourself.'

Sheel Chandra chuckled, and the sound was rich and warm. 'Oh, I surely did,' he said.

The sick man opened his eyes. The light hurt, his head throbbed intolerably, and he was so tired he had no strength even to turn over in bed. He sweated and shivered, feverish, his whole body aching. A young man bent over him. Like the other physicians, he looked weary from overwork, and there were dark smudges under his extraordinary blue eyes. He was covered from neck to foot in the loose white garments all the physicians wore in this clinic where infectious diseases were treated. But, unlike the others, he was unhurried, his cool hands methodical and sensitive as they moved over Biorn's abdomen and under his ribs, gently probing the swollen tissues there.

'You're Salverion's disciple, aren't you?' Biorn whispered, wincing as Gabriel found a painful spot.

'Yes.'

'You come a long way every day in this weather, for the pleasure of poking and prodding us.'

Gabriel smiled, and examined the man's eyes. The whites were slightly yellow, as was his skin. 'I don't travel far at all, actually,' he replied. 'Salverion and I share a small apartment attached to the Infirmary. Do you have nausea and fatigue?'

The man nodded. 'You've been here since first light this morning. And I thought I saw you last night. Don't you rest?'

'Occasionally,' Gabriel replied. 'There are over four hundred people in here at the moment, with fever from polluted water.'

'Is that what I've got?' asked Biorn anxiously. 'Just fever from the water?'

'Yes. It's caused an infection in your liver. You'll recover, though it'll take time. You'll have to get plenty of rest for some months.' As he turned to go, Gabriel added, 'And you may have to give up wine, I'm afraid.'

'You've just ruined my life,' joked Biorn. His voice was slightly hoarse, and Gabriel stopped. He felt an uncomfortable dizzy sensation in his head, like the intuitive warning of impending danger. He turned back and stood contemplating the sick man.

'Do you mind if I examine you again?' he asked. 'I might have missed something.'

'I'm not going anywhere,' Biorn replied.

Again, Gabriel examined him thoroughly, from his feet to his head. It was the disease from contaminated water, surely. Yet still the suspicion persisted, that it was more. For the second time he checked Biorn's tongue, then asked a slave to bring a lamp, and he looked carefully inside Biorn's mouth at the back of his throat. There, for the first time, Gabriel saw the dreaded grey patches of the bulai fever.

'Does the light hurt your eyes, Biorn?' he asked.

The patient nodded. 'And my head aches,' he said, 'though they said that happens with fever.'

Carefully, Gabriel washed his hands in the bowl of water between Biorn's cubicle and the next one. 'Change this water,' he said quietly, to the slave. 'Put in twice the amount of antiseptic herbs, and have a bowl and towel to each cubicle, not one between two. Until you hear from Salverion, don't change any dressings, or touch any patients with cuts or boils or anything that bleeds.'

'We haven't got enough bowls for every patient, sir,' said the slave. But Gabriel had already turned away and was going towards the physician in charge of the ward. He spoke to him for a few moments, and the physician nodded gravely as he looked in Biorn's direction.

Gabriel left, dropping his white outer garments in the large bucket at the end of the ward. He put on his cloak and gloves, then went out through the freezing grounds to the main surgery, where Salverion worked. As he pushed open the heavy doors, he was met by a breath of warm air from a hundred braziers. He stamped the snow off his boots, and a slave came over to him. Bowing low, the man told him that Salverion had already left.

'He finished the operation so soon?' asked Gabriel.

'The child died, sir,' replied the slave.

Gabriel sighed and went back out into the storm. This time he walked in another direction, to the accommodation block and his own small apartment. It was deserted, but the lamps were lit, and logs blazed in the large fireplace. The wood smoke was fragrant, unlike the usual smell from coal. The winter storms had prevented ships bringing coal from the mines in the far north, and trees were being felled on the Citadel hills for the city's fuel. Gabriel sniffed deeply, remembering a different fire.

Ferron had prepared a simple meal, and on the table beside it was a small package. Gabriel went over and picked it up. It was addressed to him, and the writing was his mother's. It was the first letter since Myron's funeral, and it was crumpled and stained from travel, though the seal was unbroken. At any other time he would have opened it immediately, but now he tossed it on his bed to read later and began pacing the tiny room. Stopping in front of the window, he looked out at the swirling snow. Darkness was drawing in already, though it was barely evening. He could see the lights in the Infirmary, blurred by the storm. A slave struggled across the snow, carrying a bundle of firewood for one of the wards. Gabriel thought of Ashila and ached.

The door opened and slammed shut, and Salverion came in. He looked incredibly tired as he took off his snow-speckled cloak and hung it on the hook behind the door. He slumped in his chair by the fire, his fingers spread before the heat. 'The child died,' he said.

'I know, Master. I went to the surgery to find you. I'm sorry. I know she was the daughter of a friend of yours.'

'I've just been talking to him and his wife,' said Salverion, sighing heavily. 'She was their only child. They adored her.'

Gabriel sat on the edge of the chair opposite him, leaning forward a little, his fingers clenched between his knees. The Master noticed that he was still wearing the strange bracelet woven from the tough grasses of the Shinali plains. Always he wore it, except when he was helping in the operating rooms.

'Why don't you relax?' asked Salverion. 'You've been working since dawn, and, if I know you, you haven't even stopped to eat. Why don't you bring over that table there, with the bread and cheese?' When Gabriel did not move, the Master frowned. 'What is it, my son?'

'I think I've found bulai fever,' said Gabriel. 'The fungal infection in the man's throat was grey. His voice was slightly hoarse. He had a form of liver sickness, too, that confused the diagnosis. I think you should check him.'

Salverion stopped chafing his hands and sat very still. 'Where is he?' he asked.

'In the third ward. The man called Biorn. I've told the physician in charge –'

But Salverion had retrieved his cloak and was already out of the door. Gabriel went into the bathroom to fill the large bronze bowl so he could wash. Never had he been so tired, or so deadly afraid. Before summer a third of the population of Navora could be dead. Which of his friends? Which members of his family? Images of Myron in death rose before him. The waxen face changed, became Lena's, then Subin's, then -

He shook his head, and the images vanished. But he longed suddenly for Myron, and the longing tore at his heart like a pain. He bent his face in his hands and wept. Jaganath's voice whispered in his ear: *I can give you the skill to see beyond the veils of death, and to bring back visions of those who dwell there. I can give you the power to communicate face-to-face with the dead . . .*

'No!' Gabriel cried, picking up the bronze bowl and flinging it hard against the tiled wall. The clang reverberated through the small apartment, and a servant knocked on the door and called out to see if he was all right. 'I'm fine!' Gabriel yelled. Shaking, he picked up the dented bowl and filled it with cold water. Then he stripped and poured the water over himself, over his hair and shoulders and all his body. The cold struck him like ice, stunning him, numbing him to the soul. Afterwards, shivering and unfeeling, he dressed in a pair of his own soft leather trousers and a woollen shirt that had been Myron's. Then he sat by the fire, his head in his hands. Never had he felt so alone, so abandoned. For more than an hour he sat there, unmoving, and did not notice that the room grew dark and the fire fell to embers in the grate. He saw only Myron's face, bloodless and still, and for the first time he doubted the reality of the place where Myron had gone.

Again he heard the voice, soft and seductive: *In the last great human experience, you're impotent. But I can change that* . . . With a huge effort Gabriel shut out the voice. But he remembered, too, the letter he had received from Jaganath early in the winter, the letter in which the High Oracle hinted that he had seen Myron, and that he was willing to help Gabriel communicate with his brother through the veils of death. The offer was so tempting . . .

Gabriel groaned and wept, knowing that if he were not so utterly exhausted, this night he would have gone to see Jaganath.

At last he roused himself, poked the fire back into life, and drew the curtains. The light, the growing warmth, gave him a kind of peace and eased his pain. He was drying his hair by the fire when Salverion returned.

The Master looked ashen and suddenly very old. 'It is bulai fever,' he said, dropping into the chair and rubbing his hands wearily over his face. 'You did well to recognise it, Gabriel. It's hard to do when there's another disease present. I've had every other patient with fever checked. We found four more cases, all in the first stage of the disease. As soon as the weather clears we'll have Biorn and the others taken with the trained physicians to the island. That way we may contain the plague. Tomorrow you and I go back to the Citadel with the other Masters of Healing, and all the healer-priests.'

'Why?' asked Gabriel, puzzled. 'Why right now, when we're most needed here?'

'Because we can't risk getting the fever.'

'Why not? Other healers have to.'

'Use your brains, my son. All the Citadel healers, all Navora's top teachers, lawyers, politicians, and the Empress and her advisers – we all have to be kept in total isolation. We have no choice; it's Navoran law. I don't think you realise how contagious bulai is.'

Remembering something, Gabriel said, 'Shouldn't the whole city be isolated? Do you realise that the last time we had the epidemic, people fled Navora? Most went along the old road, and left through the mountains, but one man visited the Shinali on the way, and wiped out nearly all their clan.'

'How do you know this?'

Gabriel picked up his tortoiseshell comb and began tugging at the knots in his damp hair. He replied, almost carelessly, 'When I was on Mother's farm for the funeral, I went for a run on the edge of the Shinali plain. I met one of the people. She told me.'

Salverion contemplated his disciple's bent head. 'Is she the reason you're not sleeping?' he asked softly.

Gabriel gave up on the tangles and stood. 'One of them,' he admitted.

'What else bothers you, my son?'

'Jaganath,' said Gabriel, after a while. 'And what he offered to teach me, about the Other Side.'

Salverion made no comment, and Gabriel added, with a faint

smile, 'In my weaker moments, I imagine that he knows more than we know.'

'Maybe he does know more,' said Salverion. 'But would you trust him to tear holes in the veil for you, and to give you control over whatever comes through?'

Gabriel thought again of the painted demons on Jaganath's wall, and shook his head.

'Do you remember that prophecy I mentioned once, about the rebirth and rise of the Shinali nation, the cleansing of Navora, and the one great unified people?' asked Salverion, and Gabriel nodded. The Master went on, 'I told you that the prophetic vision was seen by three Masters of the Citadel, at the same time. This was a great confirmation that the prophecy was true. One of those Masters was Jaganath.'

Gabriel stared at him, astounded. 'Jaganath! Jaganath was a Citadel Master?'

'Yes. We don't speak of it often. He was the only one to ever break his vows, to betray us and the wisdom we shared. He was one of our finest Masters, and the closest friend of Sheel Chandra. Jaganath was a great favourite with the Empress. At the time she had a small son, the only human being she ever truly loved. He drowned, and Petra was desolate. Jaganath contacted the boy in the other dimension, gave Petra visions of him, and messages. Petra came to rely on Jaganath for her happiness, even her sanity. He soon realised the great power this gave him, over her – and, through her, over the Empire. Slowly that power corrupted him. The vows he made with us restricted him, and he left the Citadel to become her chief Oracle and adviser. Over the years his control over her has strengthened. If she complies with his wishes, she sees her son. If she does not, she is haunted by her worst nightmares, by demons and intolerable fears. Sheel Chandra and I have done our best to help her, but Jaganath's hold on her is very strong. His hold over many people, including the army commander, Kamos, is strong. I fear that one day Petra will challenge Jaganath over something he won't tolerate, and he'll declare himself Emperor, supported by Kamos and the army, and all the other influential people he manipulates.

'He's a constant reminder to us of what pride can do, or greed, or lust. None of us are free from temptation, Gabriel, and corruption has very subtle beginnings. We must remain vigilant. You do well to resist him.'

'It isn't always easy,' said Gabriel.

'I'm always here,' said Salverion. 'Everyone at the Citadel is behind you. We give each other strength. But our bodies need strength, as well as our souls – especially with bulai fever to be dealt with. Get yourself some food. I'll go and see the High Judge, Cosimo, and ask him to pass a law forbidding travel in and out of the city, to contain the fever. Guards should be put on all roads. It won't be difficult preventing people leaving, with most of the city walled, and the grasslands and Taroth Pass the only way out. And everyone must be told of the grey patches on the back of the throat, so cases of the fever can be recognised early, and isolated. Ignorance is our worst enemy.'

'Could I go and see Cosimo for you, Master?'

'Thank you, but no. His wife has not been well, lately; I promised I would see her again as soon as I could. Now is the last chance I may have for a while. I won't be long.'

He left, and Gabriel collapsed in a chair, drew the lamp closer, and broke the seal on the package from his mother. Inside were several folded pieces of parchment, and something wrapped in a square of soft leather that smelled of Shinali fire.

Inside the leather was a small design woven of grass. It was like a figure of eight, but was more complex and intricate, and woven, like his mourning bracelet, without beginning or end. Smiling, he held it in his hand while he unfolded the letter. It was dated almost two months earlier.

Greetings, dear Gabriel.

I have no idea when you'll get this – if you receive it at all. I'm sure half our letters aren't delivered these days, or they're simply dumped in the snowdrifts if the messengers can't get through. However, I need to write, and writing a letter to you is better than trying to write morbid poems. I've been doing that a lot lately – writing poems. Topaz says they're good, though I suspect he'd say that if I wrote recipes for poison. There isn't a lot to do these days when we're all kept in by the snow. I teach the children, since we didn't bring our own tutor when we came here, but it's more like a carnival than a classroom. Normally I teach the children of some of the other farmers as well, though of course the weather's too bad at the moment for them to walk, even between farms.

Before the weather got bad Subin and Jayd visited the Shinali, and took them blankets they'd collected from around the farms. I thought two children bearing gifts would hardly be accused of breaking the treaty. They also took a piglet. I hope the Shinali wait until it's bigger before they eat it. I was afraid they would take the children out in the canoes, and was ready to go and risk strong words with them if they did. But Subin said they danced around the fire instead, so I guess that wasn't so dangerous. They came home with their faces painted with clay mixed with fish oil. Subin wouldn't let me wash hers off, and she stank for days. And the Shinali gave them a flute each and seeds for us. We have to wait until the sickle moon to plant them, whatever that is. I have a lot to learn.

I enclose a gift for you from one of the Shinali. A woman called

Ashila asked Subin to give it to you, and told her the meaning of it. Subin is breathing down my neck at this moment, making sure I get the meaning right. It's the Shinali sign for dreams, and it means (word for word direct from Subin, this!): 'The spirit world and the earth world both the same.' By the way, Subin says Ashila is very beautiful. Should I be worried? Are you worried, or are you at peace? All your life you've chosen the difficult way of doing things. If I can help by taking messages to the Shinali for you, I will. Or at least Subin will; there isn't much appeal for me in dancing around a fire with fish oil all over my face. Several farmers have taken the Shinali gifts of extra blankets and food, because of the extremely bitter winter. I hope that when the weather is better we may become friends with them. Certainly the children want to be friends. Not only mine; other farmers' children, too, relish the idea of hunting rabbits with little stones in slings or dancing naked by a fire. I suppose there's something of that freedom and wildness in all of us.

The children are restless now that we can't go out. Jayd breaks the boredom by carving animals in the doorposts. I was angry at first, then decided I quite liked them. He's doing the doors now, and the banisters down the stairs. We'll have the most decorated house in the farmlands.

I feel very distressed and angry that Myron's murderers haven't yet been found. Aren't those strange words to write? It all seems so unreal. I have awful dreams that I'm killing things. It's my craving for vengeance, I suppose. I remember what you said about powerful men being behind this, and I can't understand what's happening in our Empire. Are high lords really so powerful that they're above the law? I remember years ago there was a controversial court case, and many people thought the judge had been bribed, but everyone was too afraid to speak out. Your father was very angry over it. He said that the Empire was going rotten at the heart. He cried when he said it. It was the only time I ever saw him in tears, ever saw him not strong, not proud and sure and fiercely Navoran. He said if he had the courage, he'd expose the rot himself. But he didn't, and now the evil's spread. I never thought the rot would come so close to my own heart.

There is still plenty you can do, I suppose, even if you are confined to the Citadel. At least you have lots of company.

Talking of company: I have something to tell you, and I hope you won't think badly of me. Topaz is living here. He was going to build his own house nearby in the hills, but we want to get married in the summer, and it didn't make sense for him not to be here in the meantime. I would love to have discussed this with you face-to-face. I hope you're happy about the marriage.

Do you think Salverion would let you come? The wedding will be here on the farm. And you could bring a friend. I don't mean your bodyguard, either.

All the children send their love, and Subin says to tell you she is making a present for you, for your birthday. You'll probably already be nineteen, by the time you get this. I think I'll save your present until I see you. I don't want to risk sending it by messenger, not in this weather. I hope you're happy. I pray every day for God to bless your life. I love you more than you know.

Lena.

14 THE HONOUR-FEAST

FERRON KNOCKED ON Gabriel's door. 'Gabriel?' he called. 'There's a message for you.' There was no answer, so he went in, picking up scattered clothes and straightening rugs and cushions as he went. The bedroom was in disarray, the floor strewn with letters Gabriel had received, and half-written notes he had begun and abandoned. Above the disorder, fixed to the wall over Gabriel's bed, was Myron's sword, diagonally crossed with the scabbard. It had been restored by the best smith Ferron knew, and it looked splendid again, bright and enduring.

Ferron began with the letters, putting them in a tidy stack on the table. He noticed one that Gabriel had begun and not yet finished. It was addressed to someone called Arik, care of the headquarters of the Navoran army. Glancing over the words, Ferron realised that Gabriel was asking Arik to teach him the Shinali language. The keeper shook his head in bafflement and placed the note with the others. Under one letter he found a small leather bag stitched carefully with surgical silk. A blue cord was threaded around the neck of it, drawing it tightly closed. The knot in the cord had frayed and broken. Ferron had never seen the bag except around Gabriel's neck. Curious, he opened it and shook the contents on to his palm. There was the bone carving Gabriel had always worn, with its etching of the eagle and the man combined; the grass bracelet, frayed till it had broken, and a strange, harmonious pattern also made of grass. Ferron replaced the things carefully, made the bed, and put the amulet bag in the centre of the cushions. Then he picked up the boots lying on the floor, placing them in the clothes cupboard. He noticed that Gabriel's old shoes, which he wore when he went running, were not there.

The weather had cleared, and only a light powdering of snow remained on the ground. In the garden the trees were in bud, and a fountain made tinkling music. Outside Gabriel's window two people, unseen, were walking in the fresh evening air, and Ferron recognised the rich accent and resonance of Sheel Chandra's voice. He was talking about the epidemic in the city, saying that the island quarantine had been most effective, since only four hundred and seventy had died. Ferron strained to hear more, but Sheel Chandra and his companion had moved on.

There was the sound of stamping and heavy breathing in the doorway, and Gabriel arrived, coming in through the door from his garden. He wiped his arm across his sweating face, pulled off his damp shirt, and dropped it on the bedroom floor. Then he noticed Ferron and picked it up again. 'I see you've just ruined my mess,' Gabriel said. 'I'll never find anything now.'

'How were the Shinali?' Ferron asked.

'Too far away to see well,' said Gabriel. 'They were hunting deer. I didn't see any weapons, but I suspect they were using slings and stones. Whatever they used, it was deadly. They killed three deer. I saw them carry the bodies back.'

'Feasting time tonight,' announced Ferron, taking a crimson robe from the cupboard and placing it carefully across the bed.

'What's that for?' asked Gabriel. 'I'm not going out.'

'Yes, you are. For a feast,' Ferron replied.

The strangest expression passed over Gabriel's face: a mixture of absolute bewilderment, hope, doubt, awe, and joy. 'With the Shinali?' he croaked.

'Come back to this world, brother,' said Ferron. 'It's only the Empress. You're invited to the palace.'

Gabriel sighed heavily and sat down on the bed, running his hands through his damp hair. His fingers were shaking. 'I was thinking of the deer,' he said. 'Of the Shinali feasting. My mind's still out there.'

'As well as a few other vital organs,' remarked Ferron.

'What do you mean?'

'Your heart, for one. And your soul, if it's an organ. Not being a healer or a priest, I'm not sure.'

'How come I'm going to the palace? No one's authorised to leave the Citadel yet. Travel in and out of the city is still banned.'

'We're authorised, you and I. I've already spoken with Salverion. The epidemic's over, and travel's no longer prohibited.'

Gabriel glanced at the cushions and picked up the leather bag. 'Where was this?' he asked, pleased. 'I turned the place upside down, looking for it.'

'I noticed. It was on the floor under some parchments. You'd better hurry and get ready to go out. The Empress's chariot is already waiting for us at the gate.'

'What are you wearing?'

'What I'm in. I won't be feasting. I'll wait in the outer courtyard for you, same as usual.'

'Are you sure? If it's a feast we'll be there for hours. I could invite you as my friend; I don't think the Empress would mind.'

'Thanks, but I'll wait as usual.'

As Gabriel picked up a towel and headed for the washrooms, he felt a deep sense of unease. Over the next hour it intensified. By the time he was ready to leave for the palace, he felt ill.

*

The palace was ablaze with lamps, and there were musicians playing in the courtyard, their flutes and harps festive in the late winter air. Gabriel and Ferron stopped in the courtyard, looking up the steps towards the great entrance hall to the palace, where braziers burned between the fountains, and people wandered, sipping wine from goblets and laughing softly as they talked. They all were dressed gloriously, with jewels winking in their hair and on their hands. The women were heavily made up and wore silks and fine linens, ignoring the cold for the sake of fashion.

'It's going to be quite a party,' observed Ferron, moving into the shadows behind a large potted tree. 'Good luck. I'll wait here.'

'I wish you were coming with me,' said Gabriel, trying to smooth down his hair. It was still damp from the bath, and tangled from the windy ride through the hills. 'I'll be like a crow among the peacocks, with that lot. I don't know what I'll talk about. I'll probably make an absolute fool of myself. Do I look all right?'

'Too perfect for your own good,' said Ferron. 'The Empress will adore you.'

A slave approached to greet Gabriel and take his cloak, but Gabriel pushed the fur into Ferron's arms. 'You hold it,' he said. 'Just in case. And don't move. Wait right here.'

'What's wrong with you?' muttered Ferron, suddenly alarmed. 'You're shaking like a leaf. Are you all right?'

The slave bowed low to Gabriel. 'Her Majesty wants to see you, sir,' he said. 'Please come with me.'

He was taken up the steps to a secluded part of the interior gardens, where the Empress sat on a cushioned bench by a fountain. She turned as he approached, and he bowed low. As he stood, he looked straight into her face and was shocked.

Paint and powder could not hide the sharper angles of her face, nor the heavy shadows about her eyes and the lines of strain around her mouth. She smiled when she saw him, but there remained in her look something desperate and haunted. She was also very drunk. She staggered a little as she came towards him, and he could smell spiced wine on her breath.

'I've been looking forward all winter to seeing you, my dear,' she said, almost falling against him as she kissed his cheek, her lips too close to his mouth, leaving a scarlet stain there. She had not been so familiar with him before, and he blushed deeply, surreptitiously wiping off the sticky make-up with his fingertips. She did not notice but clasped her hands firmly about his right arm, and led him along the marble court under the lamps. She was wearing white silk, with a necklace of amethysts to match her eyes. Her eyes were still beautiful, in spite of the anxiety in them.

'It's been the most terrible winter,' she said, slurring her words. 'I've had shocking dreams, Gabriel. So many times I've wanted to see you. But you were unable to travel or busy at the Infirmary, and then locked up in the Citadel again because of the epidemic. You know how to deal with bad dreams, don't you? You're trained to do that sort of thing.'

'I think you should sleep in the Sanctuary of Healing Dreams, Lady,' he advised. 'And Sheel Chandra is far better qualified to deal with nightmares than I am.'

'But I want *you* to deal with them,' she said, with an alluring smile. 'And we can do better than the sanctuary.'

They walked on, the Empress leaning against him, her steps unsteady. He did not feel too steady himself, with the sudden nausea and horror that surged over him.

'You have many guests, Lady,' he said. 'I feel that I'm keeping you from them. They've looked forward a long time to seeing you, I'm sure.'

'And you, Gabriel? Have you looked forward to seeing me?'

'I've often wondered how you are, Your Majesty.'

'That's not what I asked.'

Gabriel said nothing else, and the Empress sighed and became agitated. 'Oh, Gabriel! I've never been so lonely in all my life as I have in these weeks while travel was banned. I was a prisoner here, locked in with Sanigar and Kamos and that dreadful Jaganath. He used to be so kind, so compassionate. I trusted him with my life. But he's changed. He terrifies me now. Sometimes I feel that my mind isn't my own, that he somehow overrides my will with his. I refuse to consult him any more – to consult any of them. They're plotting something. I know it. Still, they'll come to grief. I've had a very vivid and prophetic dream, and *that* will put an end to it.'

Dizziness swept over Gabriel again, and all his nerves jangled. 'You should talk to Sheel Chandra about this, Lady,' he said.

'Not him. I'll talk to you about it later, my dear. In the meantime, I suppose I shouldn't keep you all to myself. Come and meet everyone.'

He took a deep breath and allowed himself to be led back to the courtyard. Gradually his dizziness and confusion passed, and he managed to make polite and attentive conversation with most of the guests. He saw Jaganath again, for the first time since the fateful night at Jaganath's house, and the man was suave and very charming. 'May I borrow our healer-priest for a moment, Your Majesty?' Jaganath asked. 'I would like to speak with him about a personal matter.'

'One moment only,' she replied, and Jaganath bowed and took Gabriel aside.

'I trust you received my letter,' the High Oracle said.

'I did.'

'I had hoped for a reply. You rob yourself of a great joy, Gabriel, in this mad refusal to allow me to help you contact your brother. You have no idea how thin are the veils between you two. You could have the most wonderful communion with him.'

Gabriel said nothing, and Jaganath added, in his most persuasive tones, 'You are still angry with me, and I understand that. But the powers we have must transcend personal differences. And I know how you yearn to see your brother again. You were very close to him, and his death was such a tragedy.'

'That it was,' agreed Gabriel, trying to keep his voice calm. 'You must have been devastated when you heard they'd killed him instead of me.'

Jaganath's eyes narrowed, but his expression did not alter. At that moment the Empress interrupted, closing her hands firmly around Gabriel's arm. 'You've had your time with him, you old fox,' she said sweetly, to Jaganath. 'He's all mine now.'

Clinging to Gabriel's arm, she led him away. 'Beware of Jaganath,' she murmured. 'He hates you. He hates anyone he can't control. Oh, look – there's my darling old Konral! He used to tell me stories when I was a child. Come and meet him.'

Gabriel wished she would leave him alone so he could go and speak with a few people he recognised, but she gripped his arm as if she were drowning, steering him erratically between her friends and introducing him with unrestrained flattery. Often she whispered witty comments in his ear, and several times she stroked his hair back off his cheek. Many of the guests were whispering, and some of the women gave him sly glances when he was introduced to them. He realised what they all were thinking and felt hot with shame.

He saw the High Judge, Cosimo, and persuaded the Empress to excuse him for a while.

Cosimo was with his scribe, a slave called Izben. Gabriel had met them before, when he visited Cosimo's home with Salverion. Cosimo was a well-built, handsome man, though his blind eyes, pallid and shimmering, were disconcerting at first. His curly brown hair was greying at the temples. He was quiet-spoken, with an air of serenity that invited trust. He spoke softly now, as he greeted Gabriel, embracing him warmly and shaking his hand in the Navoran way. 'I hear that Her Majesty is being especially congenial this evening,' Cosimo remarked.

'Too congenial,' Gabriel replied. He greeted Izben as well, then said to Cosimo, 'Do you mind if I stay with you for now, and sit by you for the feast?'

'Of course not. We'd be honoured. How is Salverion?'

'He's very well, thank you, after our enforced holiday. How is your wife now?'

'Much better. And your family? How is your mother?'

'They're all fine. No one at the farms caught the fever. Neither did the Shinali. Your travel ban was very effective, my lord.'

'It pleases me to know that.' Cosimo hesitated, listening intently to determine that they were quite alone. 'Izben said you were talking to Jaganath before,' he murmured. 'Your lawyer is certain that Jaganath was behind your brother's murder. Have you anything substantial that could implicate him?'

'Only my intuition.'

'I appreciate that, but intuition, even that of a healer-priest with the Vision, isn't enough to warrant an arrest.'

'What happened with the two men you were questioning?' Gabriel asked.

'They admitted nothing. As we had no real evidence against them, we had to release them. I'm sorry. I've interviewed over two hundred people who work at the palace, and not one will speak a word about the High Oracle. But if I find the smallest bit of evidence against him, I'll have Jaganath arrested so fast he won't have time to predict his own prison term. That I promise.'

The musicians stopped playing, and the Empress's steward announced that the feast was prepared. Everyone moved into the dining room. There were three long, low tables with cushions on either side. Bowls of exotic fruits stood on the purple cloths, and each place was set with an elegant Amaranian glass, a silver-handled knife and spoon, and a golden plate. Over the head table hung a rich canopy. Slaves waited to serve, wearing white flowers in their hair and in garlands around their waists. Guests milled about the tables, vying politely for the honoured places closest to the canopied area. With Cosimo and Izben, Gabriel stood behind sumptuous cushions at the table farthest away, and waited for the Empress to enter.

'Have you been at a feast like this before?' Gabriel whispered to Cosimo.

'Several times. I always leave with a craving for a walk in fresh air, preferably in the places where the working people live.'

'When can we leave?'

'When the Empress says we can. In the morning, probably.'

Gabriel groaned, thinking of Ferron.

A hush fell and the Empress came in, accompanied by her high lords. She took her place at her table, the chief steward standing behind her. The cushion next to hers was vacant. She sat, and there was a rustle of silk and a ripple of colour across the room, as all her guests sat as well. They were silent while the High Priest, Kanyiida, stood and said a blessing over the occasion. Afterward the guests waited, no one moving.

'Before the first course is brought in, the Empress makes a speech,' whispered Izben to Gabriel. 'Never long, fortunately.'

But this time the Empress did not speak immediately. She beckoned her steward to her and whispered something to him. He nodded, then walked down the full length of her table and along the strip of crimson carpet towards the back of the room, his footsteps soft in the silence. He came all the way to the last table, and walked along behind the guests until he came to Gabriel.

'Gabriel, son of Jager?' he asked, bowing low.

Gabriel's palms sweated, and he could not speak. He nodded.

'Her Majesty would like you to sit with her, sir.'

Shaking and feeling sick again, Gabriel got up and prepared to follow the steward. But the man bowed again and indicated that Gabriel should go first. Gabriel took a deep breath and faced the long lamp-lit carpet to the canopied grand table. Never had a walk seemed so long, nor had he felt this conspicuous, this naked under so many curious eyes. At the end of the walk was the Empress, flushed and smiling graciously, and looking amused. Gravely, he bowed and took his place beside her.

'My dearest friends,' the Empress said, still sitting, 'this dinner is a celebration for me. I celebrate dreams, and the wisdom and warnings they give. I celebrate true friendship, honesty, and the gift of knowing what dreams mean. I honour bravery and trustworthiness.' She had a little trouble getting her tongue around the last word, and some of the guests smirked behind their hands. She went on, her voice raised: 'In this feast we honour my new interpreter of dreams. One I trust above all others. One who has never lied to me, never tried to exploit me, never let me down. We honour Gabriel Eshban Vala.'

With a fond and triumphant smile, she picked up Gabriel's limp hand, and kissed his fingers. 'You could look pleased, my dear,' she whispered, leaning her head close to his. 'This is your honour-feast, not your funeral.'

Dimly he heard applause. He realised he should get up and bow, make some kind of speech himself, but his limbs felt paralysed.

'We'll forgive him for his beautiful bewilderment,' said the Empress, so all could hear. 'And we'll excuse him from making a speech. Until later.'

There was courteous laughter and applause, and the Empress nodded to her steward. People began to talk, and slaves came in bearing large trays of steaming fish and bowls of tangy sauces.

The smell of the rich food made Gabriel's stomach churn. He glanced across the table, and saw Jaganath sitting directly opposite. The Oracle's lips were frozen into a smile, bloodless and deadly.

Somehow Gabriel got through the first four courses. He noticed that all the food served to the Empress came in separate dishes with sealed covers, doubtless already tasted for poison by a slave. Sometimes, as a special favour, she offered him morsels from her plate. The food was rich and spicy, and he thirsted for cold water. But the slaves kept on filling his glass with wine, full-flavoured and heady, and he tried not to drink much. Music and laughter mingled in his ears with the Empress's murmuring, and often he missed what she was saying. At one stage she told him to call her Petra. He did, though her name felt alien on his lips, the intimacy dangerous.

Kamos, the army commander, sat with Jaganath on the other side of the table, and Sanigar was beside him. Nagay, commander of the navy, was absent, and Gabriel assumed he was somewhere on the ocean. Mostly they ignored Gabriel, but during the fourth course Kamos said to him, in a voice so loud he was heard throughout the entire room, 'We heard that you visited the Shinali, Gabriel. Friendly with the barbarians, are we? Or is there a kind of wild challenge in defying our treaty?'

Gabriel reddened, and the Empress asked, 'Are you friendly with them, my dear?'

'I was invited on to their land, Lady,' he said. 'When I was home for my brother's funeral, I went running on the edge of the grasslands, and the Shinali saw me and invited me to their house.'

Slowly the Empress smiled. 'I can imagine you wearing nothing but paint, and dancing around a primitive fire,' she said. 'Or were you doing something more serious, like studying their medicines?'

'Our worthy Elected One wasn't studying their medicines, Your Majesty,' said Jaganath, softly. 'He was being extremely sociable, canoe racing down the rapids.'

'Very brave of you, Gabriel!' said Petra. 'Did your canoe win?'

'I was with the chieftain's son,' replied Gabriel. 'Together we won.'

'And what else did you do, to impress the natives with our Navoran excellence?'

'Nothing, Lady.'

'Nothing? None of your wonderful healing? None of the famous skills Salverion has been teaching you?'

'I wasn't there to impress them, Lady. I talked with one of

their healers. They use many of the skills I learn at the Citadel. Our Navoran knowledge isn't so superior.'

There was an uncomfortable silence, then Sanigar said, 'These little strips of meat really are delicious, Your Majesty. Are they pork?'

'They're strips of defiant slave, my dear Sanigar,' the Empress replied, straight-faced, but with her eyes twinkling at Gabriel. She offered him some, and he shook his head, his cheeks colourless. Across the table, Jaganath and his friends laughed.

Desserts were brought in, and the Empress placed tiny fruit pies and choice glazed fruits on Gabriel's plate. Suddenly most of the lamps were extinguished, and the dancers arrived. The music became high and passionate, and the performers began a spectacular rendering of the Navoran fire-dance, dancing in the dark with burning torches, their semi-naked bodies licked by the flames.

Petra leaned close to Gabriel, her arm around his neck, whispering something he did not hear. Her skin felt warm, and her other hand was on his knee. He shifted his position so her hands were no longer on him.

'I brought the dancers in just for you, my dear,' she said.

The music changed, became a stirring throb of drums. The dancers were in pairs, moving close, their motions ecstatic and wild, and very erotic. It was the fire-dance as Gabriel had never seen it danced before. It was too much for some of the guests, and they grabbed slaves and pulled them down on to the cushions with them, and the fervid dark filled with the fragrance of the crushed white flowers. Gabriel looked down at the table and toyed with his wineglass. He felt overwarm, and his hand shook. Ashila filled his mind, his blood.

'Well, do you like them?' Petra whispered. 'They'll dance again for us later, if you like. Just for you and me.' Her hand was on his thigh again, moving not so subtly.

He could hardly breathe, and his head ached. 'I can't stay, Lady,' he said. 'I have to go now. Salverion and I have surgery in the morning. It'll be a long day, we haven't been to the Infirmary since the epidemic started. I must sleep.'

'But my dear, you're sleeping here,' she said.

'Thank you, Lady, but no.' He stood up and bowed to her. The drums still pulsed, and the guests, apart from the High Judge, had their eyes riveted on the dancers or were occupied with the slaves. No one noticed what was happening under the silken canopy. 'Thank you for the dinner, Your Majesty.' Gabriel bowed again and began to walk out. He had not passed the first row of curtains, when the Empress called him back.

'Gabriel!' Her voice was shrill and furious, and he stopped. Everything stopped: the music, the dancers, the rapt murmuring of the guests. All eyes turned in his direction, and there was absolute quiet. Very slowly Gabriel stopped walking. He seemed to hear his mother's voice, from a time way back in his childhood: *There are times to run, and times to stand firm. You'll learn the difference* . . .

But he did not know the difference, not this time. The Empress made the decision for him. 'One more step,' she said, 'and you're exiled.'

He turned around and bowed again. 'I have to leave, Lady. I'm sorry. I have work in the morning.'

'Gabriel, you are walking on the very edge of propriety,' she said, her voice shaking and low. 'I forgive you, allowing for your youth and inexperience. But your behaviour is unacceptable. Anyone else walking out against my will, I'd have whipped. I order you to come and sit down. I have a dream I want you to interpret. I want all these present to hear it.'

'I cannot interpret dreams as a public entertainment, Your Majesty. I'm sorry.'

'Come and sit down!'

He obeyed, his face hard and furious.

'Don't ever defy me again,' Petra murmured, as she smiled and waved at the musicians. They began playing again. Amused, and making quiet comments to one another, the other guests returned their attention to the dancers. Gabriel picked up his wine and finished it in a few gulps. A slave filled the glass again. As if nothing had happened, the dance went on. Suddenly the music stopped, and the dancers bowed and waved their torches, and left. The guests hooted and howled for more. When they were quieter, the Empress clapped her hands and there was silence. Slaves lit the lamps again.

'A short time ago,' said Petra, 'I called you all my friends. My dearest friends, I said. But this was not quite correct. Not all of you are my friends. One of you is my enemy.'

The silence was profound. Gabriel held his breath, over-powered with a sense of catastrophe. He glanced at Jaganath: the man was looking directly at him, his black eyes glittering.

'Ten nights ago I had a dream,' Petra continued. 'It was a special dream, vivid and unforgettable. I have my thoughts on what the dream means, but I crave an accurate and honest interpretation. I'm going to tell you all my dream, and Gabriel will give us the true meaning of it.'

'Your Majesty,' began Gabriel, but she held up her hand to silence him.

'In my dream,' she said, her voice clear and strong, 'I saw a great field of golden wheat. The sky above it was blue, serene.

There was a feeling in my dream that everything was fine and good. But then I saw, growing among the stalks of wheat, a poisonous weed. Larger and larger that weed grew, putting out long tendrils that reached to all the golden stalks. Soon it overran the whole field, affecting all the wheat. Its roots spread, and new weeds sprang up, sometimes within the very wheat itself; there was no separating the wheat from the weeds, they were so entwined. Then the skies darkened, and a great storm came. An eagle flew across the field, with claws long and sharp like sickles, and it cut down the wheat and the poisonous plants with it. Fire flew from the eagle's claws, and all the field was burned clean. But some grains fell into the ashen soil, and they grew. The eagle watched over them, and spread its wings over them, and guarded them. Out of its feathers new seeds dropped. These seeds grew up with the grains from the old field, and a new harvest came into being. The new crop was strong, better than before, and there were no weeds.

'And after that dream was another one. In the second I was lying in the field of wheat, while the skies were still blue, just at the time the first weed sprang up. Its very first tendril wrapped itself around me, entangling me, choking me. At last I struggled free, and when I stood I saw how the whole field was ruined by the weed. I grieved, and as I grieved I heard a great cry. At the sound of it the skies darkened, and the eagle came. I saw no more.

'And now Gabriel will tell us the meanings of these dreams. Won't you, my dear?'

Gabriel was sitting staring at the plate in front of him. The gold dissolved, re-formed in the shape of fallen stalks of wheat. As clearly as if they were before him in reality, he saw the images of the dream. And with the images came the meaning, clear and unmistakable and devastating.

'Well?' Petra cried, when he was silent for too long. 'Tell us, Gabriel! Tell us what the dreams mean.'

'I'm not the one to interpret these dreams, Lady,' he said. 'Please call Sheel Chandra.'

'You *are* the one,' she said. 'And as your Empress I command you to tell us the meanings of these dreams.'

'It will disturb you, Lady,' he said.

'I'm fully aware of that. Tell us.'

So he told them, his voice low and unfaltering, and audible to every person in the room. 'The field of wheat is the Navoran Empire,' he explained. 'The beginning of the dream, when the field is pure and the skies are blue, signifies the early greatness of Navora, the laws and the creeds and the integrity and truth of the people. But in time, as the Empire grows, the golden wheat becomes contaminated. The weed is the corruption, the poison that begins secretly at the roots and grows up to choke and destroy the wheat, plant by plant. In the end the whole field is ruined.' His voice broke, and he wiped his eyes and tried to control himself. He was no longer conscious of the guests, or even of the Empress. He saw only the dream, and knew an awful grief. For the first time, sitting here in the supreme splendour of the Empire he belonged to, he realised the shocking devastation the prophecy foretold.

'The eagle is another power, another civilisation,' he went on. 'It comes, sees Navora already weakened, corrupted, and easily it conquers, levels the whole field. The fire signifies a cleansing, a purification, making the way for a new beginning. For not all is destroyed. Some of the wheat, the best of Navora, remains, and it grows alongside the new people represented by the eagle, and a new field comes into being, made of two nations unified, equal, and at peace.'

The listeners stirred, and there were angry mutters of treason.

'And myself, half strangled by the weed?' breathed the Empress. 'What does that mean?'

Gabriel raised his head, looked at Petra, and tried to focus his eyes clearly. 'Please don't ask, Lady. I can't tell you that. Not in this place, here. Not now.'

'Why not?'

'Because it's not for everyone to hear. I beg of you, don't ask.'

'But I do ask, Gabriel. I know what it means, that part of the dream. It means that, out of all these treacherous people around me, there is one who plots my death. It means there's going to be an attempt to assassinate me, doesn't it? And that one demonic act is the beginning of the ruin of our Empire. Tell us, Gabriel. Tell us what the dream means. Point out the person who will do it.'

'I can't, Your Majesty.'

'I command you. Tell us.'

'If I tell you, Lady, it will endanger my life.'

'No it won't. The person named will be arrested in moments, and you'll walk out of here free, I swear. Now – speak.'

For the first time since he had begun to explain the dreams, Gabriel looked at the guests. They were white-faced, appalled. The High Judge, Cosimo, was sitting very still, his face turned towards Gabriel. He was shaking his head very slightly, and his cheeks were streaked with tears. Gabriel dared not look at Jaganath. He took a deep breath. *Sovereign Lord, give me courage,* he thought.

Facing the Empress, he said in a voice that was heard by all, 'The second part of the dream is nothing to do with assassination. The weed that tries to choke Your Majesty is the corruption that begins the fall of our Empire. There is one weed in the beginning: one man, very powerful and evil, and insidious at first. He tries to entangle you in his powers, to control you, and through you the Empire. The second part of the dream is a warning, lady. You must free yourself of him.'

'His name?' asked the Empress. 'You must tell me, Gabriel. I command you.'

'It is Jaganath, Lady.'

The silence was absolute.

Then, in a voice like silk, Jaganath said, 'The son of Jager lies, Your Majesty. He lies and deceives, to protect himself.'

'I think not, my old friend,' said the Empress. 'It distresses and grieves me to say it, but I believe he is right.'

'He is not right, for he speaks only half the truth, interprets only half the meaning in your dreams,' said Jaganath, with lethal calm. 'He conceals truths crucial to the survival of our Empire. This night he has done you an unforgivable wrong.'

'You had better explain yourself, Jaganath,' said the Empress, her voice shaking. 'And if you lie – if just one word is a lie – you will be dead by dawn. That is my solemn oath.'

Jaganath spoke again, every word softly laden with power. 'Your dreams, Lady, are the reappearance of a great prophecy. It was first seen many years ago by three Masters of the Citadel. That vision, too, was of the field of wheat, and the time of the eagle. I know: I was one of those who saw it. This dream you had is to remind us of that great prophecy, to warn us that these are fateful times. But Gabriel has lied about the interpretation, told you only a part of it, concealed the central truths.

'One truth he conceals is that the eagle means the Shinali people. These he did not name, because he is their friend. They are the destroyers who will tear down our Empire. And the other truth – the crucial warning in your dream – Gabriel failed to mention at all. A part of that prophecy, signified in your dream only by a human cry, is that a Navoran is the catalyst in bringing about this huge change, this destruction to our Empire. The cry you heard in your dream is the call that summons the eagle to the golden field. It's the cry of the traitor, the friend of the Shinali, the betrayer of us all. That cry is the danger, Lady, not me. We are in gravest peril from the Shinali nation, and from the Navoran traitor who would help them rise against us. That traitor, Lady, is Gabriel himself.'

There was stunned silence. Then the Empress asked, 'Tell me, Gabriel, is this true? Is my dream the prophecy, and will a Navoran begin the Time of the Eagle?'

Speechless, he nodded.

'And is that Navoran you?' she asked.

'Of course it's Gabriel!' cried Jaganath, smashing a fist on to the table. 'He's a friend to the Shinali! We all heard how he went canoeing with them, how he honours their ways, says they're equal with ours! He wears a sacred Shinali talisman, Lady – a bone carved with the image of the Navoran who will awaken the Shinali eagle. He's allied his dreams with them, his very soul.'

'Is this true?' the Empress asked Gabriel. 'Do you wear a Shinali talisman?'

Gabriel stared at her, tried to speak, but could not. Guilt flooded his face. He fumbled with the cord around his neck, drew out the small leather bag, and removed the bone. The Empress took it, examined the images carved there, then stared long and hard at Gabriel's face. 'Jaganath is right,' she murmured. Then she gave the bone back to him, and he put it away.

All around them people broke into an uproar. They no longer whispered of treason or treachery, now they screamed the accusations. Some, stirred up by Jaganath, called for the death penalty. Through the tumult Gabriel was aware of Jaganath, overpowering and triumphant. Words spoken long ago by Jaganath echoed in his head: *The day will come when you'll interpret another dream and cause another death – and that death will be your own. You'll wish, then, you'd allied yourself with me.*

At last people were quiet. The Empress opened her mouth to speak, but Jaganath spoke first. 'We may not stop the rise of the eagle,' he said, 'but the cry that begins its fatal flight we can – and must – silence. According to our laws, Gabriel Eshban Vala is guilty of treason and must die.'

'I will not pass that sentence,' said Petra, her voice shaking. 'You will not command me, Jaganath. I am your Empress. And Gabriel has not betrayed us.'

'Not yet, Lady,' said Jaganath, his tone ominous. 'But he will.'

The Empress pressed her hand on Gabriel's arm. 'Will you swear to me, my dear, in front of all these witnesses, that you will never visit the Shinali again?'

For a long time he thought, his head bent. Then he said, very low: 'I can't promise that, Lady. I'm sorry.'

Again there were cries of treason.

The Empress lifted her hand for silence. 'I too am sorry, Gabriel,' she said. 'I cannot help you. But I said that you would leave this place freely, and that promise I will keep. Go now. I grant you one hour, before another soul leaves this room.'

He glanced at her face, saw that she wept. 'Your Majesty, I cannot forswear my friendship with the Shinali,' he said. 'If respect for another people is a crime, then I am guilty of that, and will die for it if necessary. But I am not guilty of treason. My interpretation of your dreams was true, and my warning to you remains. The weed is strangling us both.'

'I will not forget. Go. Please.'

Shakily, Gabriel got to his feet, bowed, and walked out. He dared not glance back. Quickly he passed the rigid guards, the pillars and statues and curtained doorways. For a few panic-stricken moments he thought he was lost. Then he saw the dark plants in the courtyard and the still, cold light of the stars. He began to run. Ferron stepped out from the shadows, and Gabriel gripped his arm. 'Get me out!' he cried.

15 Traitor's Flight

WITHOUT A WORD Ferron tossed him his cloak and led him out of the courtyard by a side corridor, unfamiliar to Gabriel. Breathing hard, feeling sick again, he ran after Ferron down steps, along other passages, and into a large kitchen. Ferron grabbed a burning torch and a few candles and a box of flints. The candles and flints he stuffed down the front of his black tunic, tightening his belt so nothing would fall through.

'What do we want those for?' asked Gabriel.

'Where we're going, if we lose our light we're finished,' Ferron replied. Then he led Gabriel to the back of the kitchen, where a small doorway led down a flight of stone stairs. The air was freezing, the stairs pitch black. Ferron held the torch high as they descended, their breathing and footsteps echoing.

'Where are we going?' asked Gabriel, stumbling on the stairs and almost falling. He felt dizzy again and leaned, gasping, against the wall, but Ferron grabbed his arm and dragged him on.

'We're under the slave quarters, going to the cellars,' Ferron replied. 'The vaults lead to catacombs underneath the palace. They'll take us out to the coast.'

The stairs seemed endless, the air cold as a tomb. Again Gabriel staggered and gripped Ferron's shoulders to support himself. Ferron smelled the wine on him, and swore. 'You're drunk, aren't you?' he snapped.

Gabriel turned away, leaned against the passage wall, and

vomited. Ferron waited, sympathy mixing with his irritation. 'I thought you'd have been more careful,' Ferron said. 'So what did you do to enrage Her Majesty – throw up all over her table?'

Gabriel wiped his mouth on his sleeve, and shook his head. 'Worse,' he said.

'It doesn't get worse than that,' said Ferron.

'Believe me, it does.'

Ferron shook his head in disbelief, and hurried on. They came to a natural cavern in the rock. It was used as a storeroom, and was filled with discarded furniture, old curtains, abandoned statues, and cracked urns. The air was stale, and the flames of the torch sputtered and hissed. Ferron went to the end of the cavern, to where ancient wooden screens leaned against the rocky wall. Gabriel followed, his face sickly in the flame light. Ferron pulled aside the wooden screens, and through the cloud of dust Gabriel saw an entrance to a tunnel.

'I helped slaves escape through here,' Ferron said, thrusting the torch into the gloom. 'I found this by accident when I was putting stuff in the storage room.'

The darkness was so complete, it seemed to crawl out of the tunnel and glide over them, covering their faces like a shroud, foul and suffocating. Gabriel felt the dark, felt the oppressive walls, the intolerable weight of untold depths of rock, the poisonous smell. He drew back into the cavern, leaning against the dusty remains of the screens. 'I can't,' he said, choking. 'I can't go in there, Ferron. There's no air.'

'There's less in a tomb,' said Ferron, gripping his arm and dragging him through the gap. He pulled a screen back over the hole and pushed past Gabriel into the tunnel. It stretched before them, its near walls glimmering in the red light. Beyond were only vague shadows, and then the utter dark. Ferron began walking, dragging Gabriel after him. He could hear Gabriel breathing hard and moaning and felt him stumble sometimes on the uneven floor. But he forced him on, while the torch spat and waned in the stifling dark. They came to a large cave, and the torchlight showed two tunnels leading from it. Ferron took the one on the left. Gabriel hesitated. 'I've been down here a dozen times,' Ferron said. 'I won't get us lost.'

They entered the tunnel, bending their heads under the low roof. 'How many did you help to escape?' asked Gabriel, hoping conversation might control his rising nausea and panic.

'About fifteen, in the two years I knew about the tunnels, and before Salverion gave me my freedom.'

'Why didn't more want their liberty?'

'Freedom isn't so easy for a fugitive slave. For most, freedom means poverty, homelessness, starvation, and the terror of being caught and punished. The lucky ones find labour in the coal mines in the north, if they make it that far. The mines are worse than bondage at the palace, from what I've heard. Only slaves in dire trouble wanted to escape.'

'You were never tempted to leave?'

'Sometimes. But I was in a high position for a slave. Besides, before I knew about these catacombs, I met Salverion. He'd seen my wall paintings and was impressed. He promised to obtain my freedom for me. A good freedom, with work and a home. So I waited.'

'Why didn't he simply buy you?'

'I wasn't for sale.'

The tunnel divided into two again, and they went to the right. The passageways began to slope upward, and in places where they widened were signs of human habitation: ancient burial crypts, remains of primeval fires, and fragments of pottery from bygone tribes. There were crude drawings carved into the walls, and fossils of shells and strange sea creatures. Gabriel realised the tunnels and caves had been carved out aeons ago by the sea, and lived in down the centuries by primitive fisher-folk. Unfamiliar images flashed across his mind, and sometimes he could have sworn he glimpsed people leaning over fires or heard snatches of ancient chants. But it was only strange reflections on dripping walls, and echoes of waves booming on distant rocks. He hurried after Ferron, sweat trickling down his face in spite of the cold.

At last he saw a glimmer in the blackness ahead, and he pushed past Ferron and ran towards it, gulping the fresher air, smelling salt, and hearing the roar of the sea. The glimmer became a filmy grey, and he came up into a spacious cave. On the far side of it, unbelievably bright after the total dark, was a cave opening and a starry sky. The ocean below sounded tumultuous, thundering against the base of the cliff.

On the cave floor were remains of a fire, flat stones that had been used for seats, and a few bones. Gabriel went to the entrance, breathing deeply, watching the waves foaming over the rocks, luminous and white.

Ferron stood beside him, the wind tearing at the torch's fire.

'Are you going to tell me why we're fleeing?' Ferron asked.

Calmly, feeling as if he were speaking of someone else and not himself, Gabriel told him.

When he had finished, Ferron said, 'You took on a mighty opponent, accusing Jaganath. Surely you realised he'd twist your words, turn the blame on to you? Why didn't you defend yourself?'

'I had no chance. He was cunning, lied about me being the Navoran in the prophecy, but mixed the lie with enough truth that everyone believed him.'

'Did he lie?'

'I'm not a traitor, Ferron!'

'Neither is the Navoran in the prophecy. From what I can see, he rights a great wrong. A cleansing won't be a bad thing, for an empire built on slavery and the seizure of native land.'

'Don't *you* start! I've had all this from Ashila.'

'Hold your peace, brother. I'm only trotting out my thoughts.'

'Trot out something useful. What's going to happen now?'

'I'm going to take you along the coast, and up the cliff to the hills and a cave where I used to hide fugitive slaves until it was safe for them to travel. Then I'll go and see Salverion, ask him what we should do.'

'I meant, after that?'

Ferron did not reply, but began climbing down the rocky slope from the cave, turning left towards the harbour, the rugged bluff and the hills.

Gabriel lay sleeping in the dirt alcove carved years ago into the cave wall. It had been the bed of slaves, and their terrors and griefs mingled with Gabriel's own, in troubled dreams.

Rain slashed the leaves over the cave entrance, and there was an echoing tumult of waters splashing and trickling and surging all around. Thunder boomed, and lightning tore jagged strips across the skies. Waking suddenly, Gabriel stared at the dirt roof above his head. For a few seconds he had no idea where he was, or why; then, like a fist slammed into the pit of his stomach, the events of last night hit him.

Groaning, he rolled out of the alcove. He stretched, feeling cramped and tense, then went and stood in the cave entrance, gazing through the leaves at the storm-ravaged hills. Bushes and a colossal rock blocked most of his view and shielded the cave from anyone outside. Cupping his hands beneath a rivulet of rain than ran off the rock, he drank thirstily, then washed, wishing the cold water would ease the throbbing in his head. It was hard to tell the hour, with the skies so glowering and dark. Late afternoon, maybe.

'Where are you, Ferron?' he muttered, going back into the cave again and sitting on the flat rock in the centre, that for years had been used as a table. Gabriel's crimson robe was torn and stained, and very damp. Rain had started to fall before they got to the cave, and Gabriel was cold now, and aching all over. Ferron had warned him against lighting a fire, though there was dry wood and kindling in the cave. Pacing to get warm, Gabriel considered the fire. Ferron had left the candles and flints, and the temptation was great. Gabriel was about to reach for the flints when he heard a rustle in the leaves outside. Rigid with fear, he peered through the dimness.

Ferron appeared, rain streaming off his thick cloak. He was carrying two full leather bags, oiled against the rain. He was breathing hard, and his face was white and strained. Coming into the cave, he dropped the bags on the rock.

'What's happening?' demanded Gabriel. 'What took you so long?'

Ferron leaned on the rock, his head bent. 'It's not good news, brother.'

Gabriel's heart sank. 'I can't go back yet?'

'No. Palace guards and sentries have already been to the Citadel. They were there when I arrived. I saw their chariots outside the main gate. They searched the place, though it's sacrosanct. They even went into the Great Library. I waited in a farm shed until this afternoon, when they left.'

'Well? What did Salverion say? I have to wait a few days, until it all blows over?'

'It's not going to blow over.' Ferron hesitated, then said in a low voice that shook, 'You're wanted for treason, Gabriel. If you're caught, it's the death penalty. The Empress did her utmost to revoke the law, with Cosimo's help – and she might have succeeded, but she needed the agreement of all her other advisers. Jaganath refused to bend. If you had only sworn that you would never visit the Shinali again, all would be well. But you refused, and Jaganath insists that in your refusal you have sworn alliance with our enemies. He wants you dead. You have to leave the Empire.'

Gabriel shook his head, stunned, his face ashen. Ferron opened one of the leather bags and took out a change of clothes and some rolled letters, sealed with the blue wax of the Citadel.

'I've got letters from Salverion and Sheel Chandra,' he said. 'And there's this.' He held out to Gabriel a leather bag with a drawstring cord. Gabriel did not move, so Ferron opened the bag and poured gold coins across the dark rock. Each coin was worth five hundred hasaries. The bag held a fortune.

'It's enough to buy you a passage on the ship *Endurance*,' Ferron said. 'It leaves in six days, from the port at Timano. It'll take you four days to walk there. I wanted to bring Rebellion for you, but Salverion said a horse is too easy to track. So you have to walk. Leave the day after tomorrow. The *Endurance* sails to Shanduria, Sheel Chandra's country. In the letter is the name and address of a friend of his who speaks a little Navoran, and who'll help you. He's a qualified physician. You can work with him and finish your training in surgery. At the same time you'll learn the language and get to know the people. Shanduria is outside the Empire, so you'll be safe there. You have enough money to buy a house and later a clinic of your own. There's food in the bag for you, and a few clothes. I hope they're all right. I didn't have much time to think. And there's a packet of seeds there, for you to crush and mix into a dye. You'll have a better chance if your hair is dark. I've put in your shaving things, too, and some soap. You won't be able to grow a beard if your hair's black. Make up a false name for yourself, and a family history. Your life now depends on your ability to lie, so for God's sake get a talent for it. I also brought you this.' From his belt he drew Myron's sword, adding grimly, 'You might need it.'

Gabriel took the sword in both his hands and ran his fingers along the beautiful etching of the scabbard. He tried to speak but could not. The world seemed to spin around him, fast out of control.

'I wish I could come with you,' said Ferron, his voice catching in his throat. 'But I'm going home to Amaran.'

Gabriel looked at him, his eyes like those of a man drowning. 'Why?' he asked. 'Why do you have to leave, too?'

'I was seen at the palace with you,' said Ferron. 'They're looking for me, as well. I'd be interrogated. I'm not staying around for that. Salverion's given me money, too.'

Carefully, Gabriel placed the sword across the stone. Then he turned to the keeper, distraught. 'I've ruined both our lives, Ferron! I'm sorry. I'm so sorry.'

Ferron shook his head. 'Not ruined them,' he said. 'Just changed them.' He went over to Gabriel and hugged him. 'I'm going now, brother, while there's still light. My ship leaves tomorrow from the next port around, between here and Timano. I'll be there in time if I go now and walk all night. Will you be all right here?'

Gabriel nodded and wiped his face on his sleeve.

'There's food in your bag,' said Ferron, 'and some red wine. Don't forget, your ship leaves in six days, from Timano. You'll be safe here until you go.' He searched Gabriel's face and added gently, though the words were a warning, 'Remember that if anyone shelters you they'll be breaking the law, and be liable for punishment. It's better if no one knows where you are, then they don't have to lie.'

'I know,' said Gabriel. He tried to say something else but shook his head instead. Suddenly they were embracing again, hard, and crying. Ferron kissed both Gabriel's cheeks, said an Amaranian blessing over him, then picked up his bag and went out again into the rain. Gabriel watched until his dark figure faded and vanished in the grey landscape; then he went into the cave, sat on the stone, and gave in to grief.

Much later he lit one of the candles Ferron had left, and read the letters from Salverion and Sheel Chandra. Often, while he read, he wiped his eyes on his sleeve, and sometimes he smiled.

You will always be in my heart, Salverion ended. *If you are able to write, please sign yourself Darshan. It was the name of my only son, who died some time ago. I think he would be proud for you to borrow it.*

Please destroy these letters, your Citadel clothes, and everything by which you might be recognised. You are, of course, absolved of your vows of obedience to us. Your vows of healing are between you and God. May He go with you. My prayers will cover you, every hour.

Sheel Chandra's letter was similar, full of concern, sound advice, and love. Gabriel memorised the name and address in it, then burned the scroll, with Salverion's, in the candle flame. The parchments curled, flamed briefly, and darkened to ash. The sealing wax melted on to the rock, two shining pools in the dark.

Then, by the flickering candlelight, Gabriel took off his crimson Citadel robe. He folded it carefully, and looked at the firewood on the floor of the cave. He stroked the rich crimson and the seven stars, and could not bring himself to destroy it.

Hiding the purse of money deep within its folds, he pushed the robe to the end of the leather bag, and pulled on a pair of his own trousers and a green quilted tunic. He ate a piece of bread and cheese, and drank a few mouthfuls of wine. Then he packed his bag again, blew out the candle and placed it with the others in the bag, pulled on his cloak, and strapped Myron's sword to his leather belt. He left the cave as he had found it, except for the tiny pile of ashes on the rock, and the pool of wax hardening to Citadel blue.

Outside, the storm had passed. The first stars glimmered, and a crescent moon rode between the tattered clouds. Slithering on the wet grasses of the steep hill, Gabriel began walking.

16 Sanctuary

Ashila woke and lay looking at the thatched ceiling. It had stopped raining, and the men on watch had dragged the upturned boat off the smoke hole. The sky was clear, the stars bright. It was quiet after the storm. She could hear the men on watch talking quietly, and smell the smoke from their pipes. They were sitting on the roof, rustling the thatch as they moved.

Ashila turned over to go back to sleep, but a sense of urgency and gladness swept through her. Careful not to disturb her mother next to her, she got out of bed. She pulled on her dress, wrapped a saffron-coloured blanket around herself, and went up the dirt steps on to the grasslands.

The eastern skies flushed pink behind the mountains, and the plain shone after the rain. The river was the colour of silver, and swollen with the rain and melted snows. Ashila looked towards the sacred mountain and saw someone walking along the riverbank, coming her way. Though he was far off and coming from the direction opposite Navora, she knew who he was. She guessed he had crossed to this side over the old bridge by the fort and knew he must have travelled all night. She walked quickly to meet him, her bare feet making soft imprints on the grass.

He began to run. As they drew near to each other, they stopped. She could hear his breathing, hard after his run, although his face was shadowed and indistinct. He was troubled, the light around him variable and not as shining as it had been, but he smiled as he came to her. They stood close, looking at one another, not speaking. At the same time they lifted their right hands and joined them in the Navoran handshake. After it he did not let her go, but lifted her hand to his mouth, kissing her fingers and the back of her wrist. Then he held her hand to his breast, tight, drawing her to him. He kissed her forehead and cheek, his lips gentle.

'I think you messed up the Navoran greeting,' she said, smiling.

He laughed a little and released her hand. Suddenly he was serious, and she felt a pain go through him. 'I've messed up a lot of things Navoran,' he said.

'I'm knowing you're in trouble,' she told him. 'Last night men came looking for you. They were all dressed the same but were not soldiers. They went first to your mother's house. They were there a little time, then they came here.'

'They were sentries. They uphold the laws. What did they say?'

'That they were wanting you for treason. A strange word. What does it mean?'

He looked away, over towards the Citadel hills. The Citadel was rose-coloured, its windows and golden domes glinting in the first light. 'It means I have no loyalty to the Navoran Empire,' he said, his voice broken and hoarse. 'It means I'm a danger to my nation, and for that I have to die.'

'Why are you a danger, Gabriel?'

'At a feast the Empress commanded me to tell her the meaning of a dream. So I did. I warned her about the evil, the rot at the heart of the Empire. I even named the rot – it's her chief adviser, Jaganath. But he pointed the finger at me, twisted everything I said, said I was the evil one. Because he's powerful and cunning, everyone believed him.'

'Oh, Gabriel.' She came close and rested her head on his shoulder, her hand on his chest. 'Your heart, it's like a Shinali's,' she said. 'Brave, and full of strongness.'

'That's not bravery you feel beating there,' he said. 'It's pure terror.'

'Braveness isn't being not afraid,' she said. 'It's being afraid, and still doing what we must.'

'I have to leave, Ashila. There's a ship sailing in six days, from a port farther east. I have to start walking there tomorrow.'

'Will you be staying with us until then?'

'I can't. I'm a fugitive now. If I'm found here, it'll be an excuse for them to confiscate your land. Or worse.'

'I'm not knowing all your words.'

'If you shelter me, that'll anger powerful people in the city, and they'll send soldiers to take your land by force, as punishment.'

'I'm thinking they won't be coming again looking for you,' she said. 'If they do, our watchmen will see. We watch all the days and nights now, since what you told Oboth. He died in the winter. We'll ask Tarkwan if you can stay. He's chieftain now.'

She started to walk back, but Gabriel remained where he was. His eyes, full of despair, were fixed on the distant Citadel. Ashila came and took the bag from his hand, slipped her arm about his waist, and led him away to the Shinali house.

Tarkwan dipped a piece of bread in the fish stew, sucked the dripping morsel into his mouth, and chewed thoughtfully. Over their breakfast meal Gabriel had told him and all the clan what had happened. His words had been simple and straightforward, and they had listened in silence, not looking at him when he wept, and honouring his truthfulness.

When he had finished Tarkwan said, 'You stay with us today and tonight, if none speak against it.' Then he waited, looking at the faces of the people around him. No one spoke, though one old man threw his uneaten bread into the fire and walked out.

'I can't stay,' said Gabriel, his own bread like a lump in his throat. He felt sick again, his nerves on edge. 'If I'm found here, you'll all be in trouble.'

'We're in that now,' said another man from across the fire. He was elderly. 'Oboth told us soldiers would come, go through our house. All the time we have men on the roof, watching.'

'We've had fever in Navora, and no travel was allowed,' Gabriel explained. 'But they could come any time now, if they still plan to.'

'We're ready for them,' said Yeshi, 'thanks to you. The right's yours, to sleep in our house. So I say.'

Tarkwan looked at one of the elders across the fire. The man was lean and stately, with heavy-lidded eyes that saw deep. He wore necklaces of ancient human bones and animal teeth, and his long woollen tunic was painted with many signs and symbols. He was the clan holy man.

'What are your words on it, Zalidas?' Tarkwan asked.

Zalidas answered, in Shinali, 'He protected us. We're owing him the same. And I'm thinking he should read us the treaty, so we're clearly knowing it. A long time ago we heard its words, and it may be that we have forgotten some of it.'

One of the old women pulled up a hearthstone, and from the hollow underneath drew something wrapped in leather. She passed it to Tarkwan. 'It's the treaty,' Tarkwan said, handing it to Gabriel. 'Will you remind us what's in it, every word?'

The leather was warm, the parchment within dry and well preserved. Gabriel read it through to himself first. There was silence while he did so. Even the children were quiet, solemnly chewing their bread and stew, the juices running down making their chins shiny in the firelight. The house was dim in the early morning.

'It's hard to understand,' Gabriel said. 'It's written in legal terms. But it says that the side of the river where your house stands is protected. They can use the other side of the river for a route to the mountain pass. It says they can even build a road through, if they wish. But the treaty clearly states that they won't come on the land where your house is. And it says the plain is yours forever – unless you give them reason to confiscate it. That means that if you do something they don't agree with, they have the right to take your land by force.'

'What if they do a thing we're not agreeing with?' asked Tarkwan.

'I don't know,' said Gabriel. 'The treaty doesn't mention that.'

'They were being wrong yesterday, coming in our house,' a young man said with rancour.

'That was a bit different,' said Gabriel. 'They would have been sentries, looking for me.'

'They broke the treaty,' said Tarkwan. 'But not again. I swear it, with *sharleema*.'

'What will you do when the soldiers come?' asked Gabriel.

'Fight them.'

'They're trained fighters,' Gabriel said. 'Their crossbows shoot farther than you can throw your spears. You can't possibly win, their weapons are better. I'm sorry, but that's the truth.'

'We have another weapon,' said Tarkwan. 'One we all use,

even the children. We're ready.' He offered no further information, and Gabriel did not ask. But he was afraid, as he rolled the
treaty within the leather and passed it back to the old woman.

Later, when the breakfast was over, he went down to the
river with the large bowls that had held the stew and helped
Ashila wash them in the shallows. The day was cloudy but fine,
and on the branches overhead a few leaves had burst. In the
flaxes on the river bank tiny yellow flowers bloomed. In the
garden behind them the old woman Domi crouched alone
between the plants, rocking back and forth in delight, chuckling.

They washed the bowls quickly in the freezing water, rubbing
sand on the smooth wood to scour off the fat. Several children
crouched on the rocks watching them, and Gabriel noticed that
one little boy lovingly cradled a small pig. As the children watched
him, they giggled and made comments in Shinali.

'They're laughing on you helping me,' Ashila explained,
smiling. 'This work, it's woman's.'

'What other work are you going to do today?'

'I'm all times looking for firewood. And some of the old ones,
their toes hurt a high lot from the snow. I'll help my mother make
more medicines for them from the roots and leaves we've dried.'

'If you've time, would you help me do something?'

'Yes.'

'I have some seeds and pods I have to crush, to make a dye
for my hair. I have to change my appearance.'

She swilled the water around a clean bowl, her head bent.
'I'll help you,' she said.

'Thanks. Would you let me help you mix your medicines?'

'If you like. But the men are going hunting today. That would
be a high lot more exciting for a hero, than helping me.'

'I don't think so.'

She looked at him sideways through her tangled hair, her lips curved. 'One more day, *haii?*' she said.

They finished cleaning the bowls, and Ashila gave them to the children to carry to the house. Then she went slowly back with Gabriel. As they walked he stole a long look at her profile, calm and strong and beautiful. Countless times he had imagined this, longed for it – walking with her again on the Shinali land, seeing the golden brown of her skin, the sheen of her hair, that graceful way she moved. He yearned to touch her skin again. As if she knew, she moved near to him and slid her palm softly down his inner wrist and into his hand. Her skin was cool from the river, her bone bangles smooth and cold. They walked close, shoulders touching, their fingers entwined. Joy, bittersweet, soared through him.

Back at the house, Ashila's mother, Thandeka, spread blankets and furs near Tarkwan's sleeping place and insisted that Gabriel rest. Exhausted as much from emotional trauma as from the long night's walk, he slept so heavily he did not notice the laughter of the children, or the chatter of the people as they went about their morning tasks. When he woke, he found Ashila and her mother mixing dried herbs into medicines. He was surprised at how many parts of the trees and natural plants they used, and the variety of the medicines they made. While Ashila gave medicines to the people who needed them, Gabriel asked Thandeka where she had heard of the healers at the Citadel.

'The healer Amael, he came here once to ask on our ways,' Thandeka replied. 'We gave him some of our barks and leaves. He gave us his plants, and the knowing of how they worked. Most are finished now. He was telling about the Citadel, and the healers there, and Salverion. He said the house is high beautiful. I'm being sad for you, Gabriel, having to leave it.'

Ashila came over to them, with a request for Gabriel.

'The people, they're wanting something,' she said, 'and they're being afraid to ask.'

'They can ask me anything,' he said.

'The old ones with the dying feet, they ask if you'll heal them with the knife.'

Gabriel looked at Thandeka. They were crouching by the hearth mixing poultices for boils and minor wounds. 'Do you mind if I help your people?' he asked. 'You're their healer, not I. If you don't agree, I'll understand.'

'How could I be not agreeing?' she said softly. 'Our healings, they'll work together.'

To Ashila, Gabriel said: 'I'll stop the pain for them while I cut off the gangrene. Do they understand what I have to do?'

'Yes.' She hesitated. 'And one of the boys has a high lot of pain in his tooth, and a woman's hand is cut deep. Another woman is having a . . .' She struggled for words, holding her hands in front of her as if around a hard ball.

'A baby?' he prompted.

'No. It's looking like that, but it's not.'

'A tumour?'

'I'm not knowing the word. And there are a little lot of others wanting your healing.'

'I'll help the ones I can, Ashila. I'm not fully trained; I can do only simple surgery. Do you have plenty of clean cloth, sharp knives, needles, and some tendons I can use for thread?'

She nodded. 'Will you be letting me help?' she asked shyly.

'I can't do it without you,' he said, and was touched by the gladness in her face. She hurried away to put into an ordered line the growing number of his patients, the ones with the most urgent needs being first.

*

Ashila put the bowl of cleaned knives into a bronze bowl of water ready to be boiled before they were used for food again. She threaded the precious bone needles safely into a piece of cloth and put it away, then stood watching Gabriel. He was with the people he had healed with the knife, checking them as they lay wrapped in blankets on their mats by the fire. All the time he talked to them, while Thandeka interpreted. Last, he checked an old woman whose foot had been amputated. As he examined her bandages he explained that the release from pain that he had given would soon be over, and she would have to take Thandeka's medicines. His voice was gentle, loving, as if she were his grandmother. Thandeka translated for him. The old woman nodded gravely and touched his hands, thanking him in Shinali and adding, '*Sharleema*.'

Gabriel came back to the fire, and Ashila gave him his soap and a bowl of warm water. He washed his hands carefully and dried them near the flames, his expression pensive.

'You're being tired, Gabriel?' Ashila asked gently.

'A bit,' he answered, smiling. 'Thank you for giving me this time to heal your people, Ashila. It means more to me than you know.'

'I'm glad. Will you be resting now, or would you be liking a walk with me?'

'I'd love a walk with you.'

Gabriel got his fur cloak, had a few words with Thandeka about the ones recovering, and followed Ashila out of the house. As they went up the steps they passed the weapons standing in an alcove by the entrance. Among the bows and stone axes and spears stood Myron's sword, alien and shining.

As they walked along the riverbank towards the mountains, a large group of children started to follow them. All afternoon the children had watched the operations, making noisy comments of encouragement or revulsion, one or two of them getting sick and having to be carried outside. They had been a boisterous audience, after the dignified witnesses Gabriel was used to at the Navora Infirmary. As the children followed him now, he turned and waved his arms at them, telling them to go. They shrieked with laughter and ignored him, until their elders called them back. He walked on with Ashila, blissfully alone with her at last.

'Thank you for helping me today,' he said. 'You were excellent.'

'It's a word I'm not knowing,' she said.

'It means wonderful, praiseworthy, perfect, a high lot good.'

She laughed, and, for the first time, he saw her blush. 'I'm not being any of those,' she said.

'You're all of them.'

'I'm wanting to ask you something.'

'Then ask.'

'In the house, when you were saying it was a high lot to you, healing my people, what were you meaning?'

He was thoughtful for a time, before answering. At last he said, 'There's an old reason, and a new one. The new one is that you gave me back my work, my purpose. Until today I couldn't see beyond leaving the Citadel, couldn't see myself healing anywhere else. I couldn't imagine going on a ship to another country and beginning again. Now I can. You've given me hope, and I thank you, with *sharleema*.'

An icy wind was blowing off the mountains, and Ashila drew her blanket more closely about her. She made a small sound like a sob, and he took her in his arms, holding her close and kissing her hair. 'I can't stay, you know that,' he said. 'I'll be put to death if I'm found.'

She tried to speak, but the words were lost in deep sobs, heartrending and terrible. He held her closer, struggling with his own emotions, not knowing what to say. After a while she pulled away, wiping her face on her hands. 'I'm being sorry,' she said. 'I mean to be helping you, not sorrowing you.'

'I didn't mean to be sorrowing you, either,' he said. He took her hands in his and kissed them, tasting her tears. 'Let's make a rule. We don't think about tomorrow. Only today. Now.'

They started walking again, their arms around each other, and came to the place called *Ta-sarn-ee*. The hollowed earth was full of mud after the rain.

Ashila began collecting branches that had broken off the tree during the storm, piling them on the grass for collecting later, and Gabriel helped her. 'Tonight we're feasting,' she explained. 'That's why the men are hunting. It's the last moon of the winter, the time of the yellow flowers. It's a high rich feast, and we all go joy-wild. Will you dance tonight, the Shinali way?'

'If you show me how,' he replied.

'I will. We can be painting your face, too, then if the soldiers come they'll be thinking you're Shinali.'

'I doubt it,' he said. 'Not with my hair.' Suddenly he remembered the vital thing he was supposed to do. 'Do you mind if we go back now and dye my hair?' he asked.

She picked up the firewood but would not let Gabriel help her carry it.

Back at the house, Gabriel got the bag of seeds and pods Ferron had given him for the dye. He poured them all into a wooden bowl and crushed them, then mixed in a little water. 'It's looking like something the sheep did,' Ashila said, peering over his shoulder and wrinkling her nose at the fetid paste. 'Aren't you fearing it'll make a mess, Gabriel?'

'I'm terrified,' he confessed, standing up and giving the bowl to her. 'I'll probably end up green. And smelly. After the dyeing, we'll wash out the mixture with my Citadel soap. Where shall we do this?'

'Out by the river. Are you being sure, Gabriel?'

'This sure,' he replied, striking his right fist hard into his left palm.

He took off his shirt and dropped it on the floor by the hearth. Immediately one of the children pounced on it and pulled it on over his own clothes. Gabriel left on the small leather bag with his amulets. Ashila noticed it and looked curious, but asked nothing. As she and Gabriel went outside the children followed again, eager to see what marvellous bewitchment the Navoran would do next. But Ashila ordered them all to go away, and led Gabriel down to a secluded part of the river where smooth rocks edged deep pools. By the river she made him lie down on his back with his head over the water, and she crouched down and wet his hair. The water was glacial, and he yelped, shuddering. Then she worked the stinking mixture over his scalp.

'What colour is my hair?' he asked.

'I can't be knowing yet,' she replied. Her voice sounded strange, and he thought she was laughing.

'It's green, isn't it?' he cried, alarmed.

'No,' she said. 'No, it's not green. Keep still. The dye, you're getting it over both of us.'

So he lay passive, and she worked in silence, painstakingly, hardly seeing for tears as she rubbed the thick black dye through all the gold.

Afterwards, when he went into the house, the people gathered about him, awed at the transformation. Many of the young people touched his hair, and the old ones shook their heads, muttering and mystified. Ashila had done her task well: his hair was evenly coloured, deep brown with warm red lights, and his eyebrows, too, were dark. To complete the change, he warmed some water over the fire and had his first shave in three days, removing the red-gold stubble that looked odd now. Ferron had forgotten to give him a mirror, and he cut himself twice. When she saw him, Ashila licked her forefinger and wiped the two places on his jaw where he bled. She looked very grave.

'Do I look different enough?' he asked anxiously. 'Will anyone know me, do you think?'

'I'm hardly knowing you, myself,' she replied, her dark eyes shimmering.

Shortly afterwards the men came back from the hunt, carrying two deer. They were dumbfounded when they saw Gabriel, though Tarkwan laughed and gave him a handful of bone beads to thread through his hair. 'Make a good Shinali,' Tarkwan said.

'A better Shinali than I do a Navoran, I hope,' Gabriel replied.

Ashila was busy helping the women prepare vegetables for the night's feast, so Gabriel went out and helped the men cut up the deer. It was a work, he discovered, almost as skilled as surgery. Nothing was wasted. The bones and antlers were kept for making jewellery or pipes, the tendons would be used for sewing clothes, and all the meat was for eating. Even the hooves were kept, to be hollowed for small containers in which to mix paint and dye. The first steaks and the offal were given to the women to cook, but darkness had fallen before all the work was done. Gabriel enjoyed his part in it. Though he understood none of the words, he liked the cheerful banter of the men as they worked, and the way they took care to show him how to make the cuts properly. Yeshi worked with Gabriel, and asked him about Navora and the Citadel. Gabriel told him, his voice husky at times, his head bent low over the butchered deer.

Inside the house the fire was roaring, and hot bowls of tea had been prepared. Gabriel went to see the people he had healed that afternoon and found them all comfortable. They thanked him again and joked with him about the magic way he stopped their pain. Then he went and sat by Ashila and Thandeka, to drink his tea. Every now and again Ashila stole a long look at him, her expression wistful.

'The man's heart is not in his hair,' Thandeka said to her daughter, in Shinali. Ashila just sighed, tore her eyes off Gabriel's strange dark locks, and sipped her tea.

In one part of the room the men were having their faces painted. A girl came to Gabriel and shyly asked if he would like to be painted too. He agreed and went with her to the painting area. He sat by Tarkwan, who was having his face decorated by his wife. Gabriel noticed that Moondarri had a tattoo on the back of her left wrist, identical to one that Tarkwan had on his. It was a stylised picture of a stag and doe leaping over the sun. Moondarri noticed Gabriel looking at it. 'It's our wedding mark,' she explained. 'When Shinali marry, a mark is made in their skins for life. The deer are us, together long as the sun remains.'

The girl who was going to paint Gabriel brought him tiny pots with several colours, and told him to choose. He returned to Ashila with half his face a stunning red, and with a fine white zigzag down his chin. Ashila gazed at him, her eyes admiring and disturbed. 'Why are you choosing those colours?' she asked.

'I like them. We wore red at the Citadel.'

'It's our colour for love and sacrifice,' she said.

The feast was almost ready. Iron pots, traded years ago from Navorans, hung on sticks over the fire, and stew bubbled enticingly, while steaks cooked on bone skewers over the embers. A flax mat was spread with baskets of unleavened bread, and bowls of salads made with wild herbs and cress. When the meat was cooked, it was put into bowls. Everyone chose their bowls and put in them the bread and salad they wanted. As chieftain, Tarkwan chose first, then Gabriel, as the clan's guest. Next the children came forward, then the elders, and last everyone else. Silence fell as Zalidas blessed the food, then they began eating.

Gabriel had not realised until now how hungry he was. He had hardly eaten at the breakfast, and his last proper meal had been the fateful dinner at the palace two days ago. He frowned a little, thinking of it, and Ashila noticed. 'There's something you're not liking?' she asked.

'No. I like it all, thank you,' he replied. 'I was just thinking of the last dinner I had, at the palace.'

'I'm fearing this is poor besides that,' she said.

'No. This is a high lot better,' he said. 'The company's better, too.'

After the feast the bowls and baskets were cleared away, then hollowed gourds of cold river water were passed around and shared by everyone. Then it was time to relax while the meal digested, and to tell stories and jokes. Gabriel delighted in the Shinali talk, with its soft accents and lilting rhythms. He enjoyed it more when Ashila interpreted, her head bent close to his, her exquisite hands describing in signs the words she did not know.

Then a drummer began to beat a throbbing tattoo. The pipes and flutes joined in, and several of the people got up to dance. The men and women danced together, stamping, clapping, whirling, leaping, moving with the tempo of the drum. At times the dance was violent, fierce; at times slow and incredibly sensuous. It was not unlike the Navoran fire-dance, except that this dancing, uncomplicated and spontaneous, had a kind of innocence that was more appealing to Gabriel. As he watched, he beat time with his hands against his thighs. Ashila smiled sideways at him. He caught her gaze and smiled back.

'We can dance if you're wanting to,' she said.

The children hooted and cheered as they joined the dancers. Gabriel felt suddenly self-conscious and clumsy, knowing he was watched. But gradually the music got into his blood, reached back to some deep, primeval part of him, and he gave himself to it, dancing instinctively, impassioned, his Navoran inhibitions abandoned for the first time in his life.

Later he sat with Ashila and the other young people and watched the last couple dance.

Tarkwan and Moondarri looked good together, both tall and lithe and beautiful. Perhaps because the drumbeats slowed, perhaps because they were the last, they danced close, watching one another, smiling. Their skin glistened with sweat in the firelight, and Tarkwan's painted face shone. They never touched, but the energy between them was dynamic.

When the dancing was over and the drums and flutes put away, the people spoke a night blessing to one another and moved to their sleeping places. Before they retired each person took a small bowl of warm water and, by their own bed, stripped and washed all over. No one watched anyone else, and the ritual was unselfconscious and strangely private. Ashila brought Gabriel a bowl and two pieces of soft cloth. 'Your sleeping place is by Tarkwan's,' she said. 'Is there anything else you're needing before you sleep?'

He hesitated a moment, then shook his head.

She leaned across the bowl and kissed his lips. There was applause and whistling from across the house. Wiping the red paint from her mouth, and ignoring the jests, she went over to her own bed. It was several sleeping places along from his. Gabriel took the bowl over to the place beside Tarkwan's and, as nonchalantly as he could manage it, removed all his clothes, and washed. The paint from his face turned the water the colour of blood.

Soon everyone was in bed. Across the firelit house a child sobbed, and a mother crooned to it. Elders talked, their voices hushed. There was the muffled grunting of a little pig as it was cuddled under the blankets. Unable to sleep, a girl sang to herself, very low, making shadows on the firelit wall with her hands. Tarkwan laughed at something Moondarri said, and they kissed and murmured lovingly together. Feet padded between the beds where the young people lay, and there was furtive giggling. Gabriel listened, watching the firelight glimmer on the thatch. He thought of Ashila across the room and yearned for her.

After a while the clan was silent, except for the sounds of sleep. Gabriel tossed restlessly in the furs, a hundred fears gnawing at his peace. He got out of bed, wrapped his cloak around himself, and went up into the night. There were no stars now, and the air was heavy with the scent of impending rain. From behind the Shinali house came the bleating of sheep, safe in their sheltered fold. Above the farms and hills the western skies glowered red from the lamps and fires of Navora. Someone called softly to him, and Gabriel looked up and saw three watchmen sitting on the roof.

'You're coming to wake us up?' one of them joked, his voice low. 'You're thinking we sleep, *haii*?'

'I'm thinking I wish *I* could,' replied Gabriel, and they chuckled.

'The soldiers, how many?' a watchman asked.

'I don't know,' Gabriel replied. 'Not many, I think. They were only going to give your people a fright, not make war with them.'

'We'll be giving them fright,' they said.

Rain began to fall, splattering softly on the thatch. The watchmen lifted the upturned boat over the smoke hole, then sat down again, dragging a flax mat over their heads and backs. 'Go inside,' they told Gabriel. 'They won't come without our knowing.'

Gabriel went down the steps into the house, and returned to his bed. He lay tensely on his back with his hands linked behind his head, listening to the drumming of the rain on the upturned boat. Someone else got up, wrapped a saffron-coloured blanket around herself, and came and stood at the foot of his bed.

'Are you fearing?' she whispered.

'Yes,' he whispered back.

She crept on to the matting that made a space between his bed and Tarkwan's. Clutching her blanket about her, she moved up to lie beside him. He was motionless, gazing at her, his sapphire eyes unsure and hungering.

'I'm coming here to wake up the braveness in you,' she said, in hushed tones.

'If you stay here, you'll wake up more than my braveness,' he replied, moving an arm around her neck. He kissed her forehead, his heart pounding, his whole being in turmoil.

She leaned up on her elbow, and looked at him. She was relaxed, her eyes dancing though her face was serious. 'Am I having the right man?' she asked, sliding one slender arm out of the blanket, and stroking his dark and unfamiliar hair.

'I don't know.' He grinned. 'Who were you looking for?'

'Are you Gabriel, from Navora?'

'I think so.'

'I'm worrying you are not. You danced joy-wild tonight, like a Shinali. Are you being sure you're Navoran?'

'No.'

'What are you, then?'

He thought for a few seconds, and replied, 'A Navali.'

She laughed softly, bending her head over his chest, her hair cool and silken on his skin. Her hand brushed the leather bag around his neck, and she fingered it, curiously. 'What's being in here?'

'Things precious to me.'

'What?'

'Guess.'

Gently her fingers probed the leather. Suddenly she smiled. 'I'm knowing. A mourning bracelet, and a dream-sign. And a piece of something hard. A bone. A Shinali bone?'

'Yes.'

'Who was giving it to you?'

'I found it when I was seven years old.'

'You were being a Navali long time since?'

'No, only since tonight.'

'You have nothing Navoran, precious?'

'Just Myron's sword. It's a bit big to wear around my neck.'

'You can fight with the sword?'

'No. I can hardly raise it, it's so heavy.'

She laughed again and settled down with her head on his shoulder. The rain babbled and sighed more densely on the thatch, and thunder rolled over the grasslands.

'Now that you've woken up my braveness and everything

else, Shinali woman,' Gabriel said, 'are you going back to your own bed?'

'Are you wanting me to go?' she asked.

For a few seconds he hesitated. 'No.'

She slid under the furs with him, her blanket still around her. He turned on his side and faced her, moving the yellow cloth off her shoulders, off all of her. He held her close, feeling the full length of her body against his, skin to skin, and he moaned aloud with amazement and desire.

'Hush,' she whispered, smiling, pressing her fingers over his lips. 'You'll be waking all the clan.'

But he had forgotten the clan, forgotten everything but her, and he kissed her over and over again, on her neck and face and hair, until she was as lost as he was in their love. And the rain spilled, hissing, over the Shinali house, covering their cries of abandonment and awe and ecstasy.

17 Killings and Healings

Gabriel stood by the fire. In his hands was his crimson Citadel robe, rolled for burning. On his bed, beside Myron's sword, was the packed bag, the purse hidden in a shirt at the end of it. The bag was fragrant with the smell of Shinali bread, left over from the clan's breakfast and put into a soft flax basket for him. He had also been given strips of smoked fish, and one of Thandeka's best blankets for when he slept in the open. All was ready for his journey. There remained only the burning of the Citadel robe, the last vestige of his identity as healer-priest, and the farewells.

He glanced across the fire at the people he had healed. They lay in their sleeping places, silently watching him, their eyes beaming. It was peaceful here, the calmness contrasting with the anguish in his heart. Outside, the younger children were releasing the sheep to graze on the spring grass, and the bleating of the animals and shouts of the young shepherds were homely and cheerful. Gabriel could hear the voices of the women working in the garden, and the talk of the men as they sat in the sun and smoked their pipes. On the other side of the house, towards the mountains, the youths joked with one another as they scraped clean the hides of the deer they had killed yesterday.

Ashila waited beside Gabriel, her eyes luminous and sad.

'Don't be burning that,' she whispered, touching the Citadel robe. 'Let me have it.'

'I have to burn it,' he replied. 'If the sentries come here again looking for me and find it, they'll know you sheltered me.'

He held the garment out over the fire, and the golden threads on the hem shone in the shaft of light from the smoke hole above. At that moment there was an unearthly hush. The children stopped shouting, and the women ceased talking in the garden. The elders became silent, and the youths stopped joking. On the thatch above there was a rustling sound as the watchmen stood. Gabriel glanced at Ashila. Her eyes were wide with fear. Then the most terrible noise broke out: a piercing wail, trilling and high, like an alarm. Other cries added to it, and the clamour filled the house and plain, and echoed back from the mountains.

'What is it?' Gabriel asked.

Ashila could hardly hear him. 'The soldiers!' she cried.

At that moment a group of children came rushing into the house. They raced across to the people recovering, and leaped on to the beds with them. Men and women came running in, went to their sleeping places, picked up small bags, tied them to their belts, and raced out again. The men grabbed spears or stone axes from the alcove on the way. Someone bumped into Gabriel. The crimson robe flew from his hands on to the floor and was trampled by urgent feet. Distraught elders carrying babies came in, and went and sat with the children and the sick. There were people everywhere, hurrying, their movements purposeful. Gabriel looked for Ashila again. She had collected whatever she had needed from her own sleeping place and was by the door selecting a spear. He rushed over to her.

'You can't fight!' he cried.

'I fight excellent!' she replied fiercely. 'The old warriors, they were showing us how, all through the cold time. All of us.'

A group of youths came in. They seized axes and spears, and hurried out. Tarkwan's brother, Yeshi, stayed, going over to guard the sick ones and the children. Then it was only Gabriel and Ashila in the doorway.

She stared at him, agony in her eyes. 'Go,' she said, crying. 'If they find you, they'll be killing you. Hide in *Ta-sarn-ee*, and when it's safe, when the soldiers have gone, go to your ship.' She kissed him, and pushed him towards his sword and bag. 'Hurry! Run!'

He swept up his bag and slipped the sword through his belt. 'Run!' she cried, urging him up the steps. Outside, Gabriel glanced across the plain towards the farms. The soldiers had come down the new road across the hills and were crossing the Shinali ground in front of the farms. He could not see clearly how many there were, but they were only a small company, thirty soldiers perhaps, and at their rear were four wagons drawn by horses.

Ashila pulled at Gabriel's clothes, forcing him towards the river and the group of trees. He felt her hand pressed against his heart, her lips on his cheek, his mouth. 'Go! Now!' she cried.

He kissed her one last time, flung his bag over his shoulder, turned towards the sheltering trees, and ran.

Behind him, Tarkwan went into the house and removed the treaty from its hiding place. When he went up on to the grasslands again, his people were gathered around their house as if nothing was amiss. Women were gardening again, and the young men were scraping hides. They all had slings tucked into their belts, and smooth river stones in their pouches. Other people stood or sat in groups, as if taking pleasure in the first day of the spring. Tarkwan walked among them, giving encouragement and instructions. Spears lay concealed in the grass; knives and axes were hidden in the thick sheepskin clothing. Only a few minutes had passed since the alarm had been given.

In the house Yeshi waited, his right hand already swinging the leather sling with its lethal stone. Children began to whimper, and the elders hushed them. Through the ground ran a throb like a distant drum. It grew to a constant beat, insistent and heavy. The marching of feet.

Outside, the women stopped working in the garden and stood up. Only old Domi worked on, chatting happily, and unaware. The youths left their hides stretched out on the ground and joined the rest of the people. Tarkwan stood before them all, straight-backed and undaunted. The soldiers marched on. The wagons rumbled closer, heavy with equipment for restoring Taroth Fort.

The gardens lay directly in the line of the march. Nearer the soldiers came, marching in ordered lines, eyes straight ahead and faces expressionless. They wore bronze armour on the upper part of their bodies, with plumes on their helmets and shoulders. The plumes were snow white in the morning, and the sun shone on polished breastplates, and on daggers and swords. Across their shields pranced the blood-red horses of the Empire, proud and conquering.

As the soldiers approached the garden, the women moved back. No one noticed that old Domi still crouched there among her precious cabbages, muttering and nodding. Even when the soldiers marched on to the garden, crushing the work of years, no one noticed her. Tarkwan was running beside the men at the front, waving the treaty. Shouting for their leader, he implored them to stop and talk. The soldiers marched on, inexorable and heedless. There was a startled cry: a scream, confused and angry, then full of pain. And then they saw Domi, her arms over her head, rolling helplessly among her ruined cabbages, soldiers' boots in her hair and on her back and legs, until she was covered in soil and blood. Then she lay still, and the soldiers tramped, uncaring, over her body.

Then Tarkwan raised his arms and gave a piercing call like the earlier warning-wail. The next moment the air was full of the strange whirring of leather slings, and a hail of deadly stones shot into the soldiers' ranks. Many were hit from behind, on their legs or the backs of their necks. The stones hit hard, sinking into flesh. The soldiers stumbled, many fell, and the orderly ranks broke. Not knowing what had hit them, they had no time to organise themselves. Drawing their swords, they whirled to face the Shinali, and the next volley of stones thudded into their faces and necks, breaking teeth and tearing into windpipes and eyes.

The company, trained to fight in unison, became disarrayed, confused, and the Shinali took full advantage of that. When their spears broke on the bronze shields, they used their axes and knives. Behind the hand-to-hand fighters were Shinali with their slings, sending shower after shower of stones, each missile accurate and lethal. The army captain roared his commands, tried to regroup his men into a fighting force, but his orders were lost in the strange, high war cries of the Shinali, and there was only chaos.

In the place called *Ta-sarn-ee*, Gabriel crouched in hiding, his arms covering his head. But he could still hear the soldiers shouting as they wielded their swords, and the high-pitched wails of the Shinali as they hurled their spears or stabbed deep with their knives. And always there were the screams as steel or stone sliced into flesh, and the agonised cries of the dying.

After a while he heard a call in Navoran: 'Retreat!' Then the terrifying Shinali war cry again, cut short as if Tarkwan forbade it. After that the only sounds were the rumble of the wagon wheels as they went away, and the moans of people in pain.

Slowly, shaking all over, Gabriel got up, dragged himself down a track to the river, and was violently sick. He washed his face and hands, went back to the hiding place, and picked up his bag and sword from where he had thrown them. He staggered up on to the grasslands, and faced the mountains and freedom. Behind him an unearthly hush lay over the land. He dared not look; even with his eyes closed, he could see the dead and wounded, the unspeakable suffering. And another image, old and even more powerful: a Shinali woman, her body naked and broken, her hand outstretched, pleading, her eyes imploring him. *Tortan qui, sharleema.*

By the Shinali house, Ashila stood gazing in disbelief at the horror about her. Dead and dying lay all around, Navoran soldiers and Shinali together. People lay in pools of their own blood, some crawled in agony, others lay groaning and pleading for help. The ground was scattered with Shinali slain, cut down as they fled, their weapons flung aside, or lying open-eyed, defiant, their slings and knives still clutched in their hands. Survivors bowed on the bloodstained earth beside them, lamenting. Others, wounded or deep in shock, roamed aimlessly. They seemed lost, trapped in a nightmare they could not comprehend.

The sun, hardly higher now than when the strife began, glinted on abandoned weapons and discarded bronze shields with their red horses. Everywhere the grass was stained with scarlet. Beyond the battleground the soldiers retreated, leaning on the wagons or on each other. People had left their farms and were running to help them.

Ashila stumbled across the devastated earth, calling her mother's name. She saw Tarkwan walking among the wounded, praying over his own people, but cutting the wounded soldiers' throats. She turned away and went on searching, hardly able to see the faces for her tears. At last she found Thandeka, alive but with a deep cut to her right shoulder. Ashila knelt down, took her own blood-smeared knife from her belt, sliced a strip of cloth from Thandeka's skirt, and bound her shoulder to stop the flow of blood.

'I'm all right,' Thandeka whispered, pushing her away. 'But I can't be helping you. You have to heal them. On your own.'

Ashila stood up. Numb and despairing, she walked among the wounded, binding on makeshift tourniquets to stop the most severe bleeding. By a dying youth she crouched down, trying vainly to block the outpouring of blood from his chest. While she strove to save him, a wail louder than all the rest pierced the morning. It was more a scream than a lament, a passionate cry of intolerable sorrow. She looked across the grasslands and saw Tarkwan kneeling, Moondarri dead in his arms. When Ashila glanced down at the wounded youth again, he too was dead, his open eyes fixed on her face. She bent her head, her reddened hands upturned on her lap, and wept. *Tortan qui,* she prayed. *Help me. Give me strength.*

She looked up and saw Gabriel. He was standing just in front of her, his bag and sword dropped on the bloodied ground beside him.

'I've come back to help,' he said.

The Shinali woman lay on a blanket waiting to be taken to the healer. Her name was Taslim, and she was the first in a long line of wounded waiting for Gabriel's healing. She had a sword wound in the chest, and breathing was difficult and excruciating. The world seemed shadowed and far away, made dim by pain. Someone sat with her – her son, only thirteen summers old. She spoke her husband's name, asking after him, but her son only wept aloud and said nothing. Taslim sobbed, and it was agony for her. Ashila came, moved aside Taslim's upper clothes, and washed her skin with antiseptic liquids. Then men lifted her up on the blanket, and carried her to the healer.

Taslim was placed on a grass mat by the river. Beside her was the young man from Navora. Taslim could smell smoke from a nearby fire, and turned her head and saw knives with their blades heating in the flames. Trembling with terror, she tried to crawl away. '*Kaath sharleema*,' she said, weeping. '*Mercy, I beg of you.*'

The healer put his hand on her forehead, and spoke his alien words. She understood few of them, but his voice was gentle, and she listened. Then his hands, strong and tender and very warm, were on the back of her neck. Power came from his hands, and after a time she felt as if all the pain and fear were being swept away in a mighty river of light that poured through her. She felt weightless, almost joyful, and she relaxed, looking up at his face. He smiled, and she saw that his eyes were radiant, like the holy man's when he entranced himself and moved in the realms of the All-father.

Taslim licked her lips and relaxed, and even when he lifted the smoking knife over her and she felt a curious pressure on her chest and smelled her own flesh searing, she made no sound. The peace deepened, and she floated in it, barely aware of the sound of steel against her own bones, or the smell of the salve-soaked strips of cloth he packed into the wounded space of her lung. When she opened her eyes again, the healer was holding a bone needle threaded with deer tendon and was sewing up the wound. Ashila was helping, cutting the threads as he tied the knots. Taslim felt only the soft pull as he drew the tendons tight, and the release as Ashila cut them. Their hands, his pale and hers brown, worked in perfect unison, like the sounds of two flutes playing. Then his hand was on Taslim's forehead again, cool and refreshing as the wind, and Taslim slept, unaware that she was bandaged, then taken to the house to be looked after by the elders.

The day wore on. There were more than thirty needing surgery. Many of the wounds were minor, simple cuts needing sewing, but some people had injuries that were deep and complex, and Gabriel was unable to help them. He simply stopped the worst of their pain and left them with their loved ones to die as peacefully as possible.

The sun was almost gone when the work was finished, and Gabriel and Ashila washed their hands in the river for the last time. As he crouched there by the coppery waters, Gabriel looked along the shore towards the mountains. Zalidas was painting the dead with sacred signs and chanting prayers over them, ready for their burning. The row was long: twenty-two Shinali had died, and more would probably join them before tomorrow. Past them, lying on the grass and covered with their shields, were the dead soldiers. Nine shields there were, blazing like fire under the evening skies. High above them wheeled birds of prey, ominous and waiting.

Gabriel looked the other way, towards Lena's farm. He longed to go and visit his family, but one of the army wagons was outside. He guessed that Lena, along with other farmers, was looking after wounded soldiers until wagons came from the city to take them to the Navora Infirmary. They would know

now, in Navora, what had happened. Kamos, the army commander, would know. He would be with the Empress now. The image Gabriel had of the Empress with her advisers was very strong. Most clearly of all he saw Jaganath, domineering and inexorable, urging the Empress to send the entire army on to Shinali land to wipe out the mutinous natives.

Ashila watched Gabriel's face, saw his eyes narrowed against the low sun, weary, yet still full of light. He seemed to see beyond the hills, to something far that troubled him. As if to wipe the vision from his mind, he scooped up a handful of glittering water and splashed it over his face. Ashila noticed again the silver ring he wore, shaped like a snake.

'What is that ring?' she asked, touching it.

'It's from the Empress,' he replied. 'A pledge-ring. When she gave it to me she promised that if I returned it to her in a time of need, she would do whatever I asked.'

'She promised that?' asked Ashila. 'Like our promises, with *sharleema*?'

'With the greatest Navoran *sharleema*,' said Gabriel. 'But she gave me the pledge-ring before I was accused of treason. If I use the ring now, I'd be letting them know where I am, and they'd come and drag me off to Navora for execution.'

'You'll never use the ring?'

He smiled faintly and touched her cheek. 'Only if I have a request worth dying for.'

As they walked back to the house, they smelled stew cooking and heard some of the women singing a lament. They stopped to listen, watching the first stars come out. Past the house, beyond the funeral pyre, a lone figure stood by the river bank, facing the sacred mountain. It was Tarkwan.

'I have to talk to him,' said Gabriel.

The chieftain was chanting quietly, his eyes wet with tears and fixed on the snowy slopes of Sharnath. He finished his lament, then, without taking his eyes off the sacred place, he asked, 'What are you thinking your people will do now, Gabriel?'

'I think the army will come in full force,' Gabriel replied. 'I know it's wrong and unjust, but you'll be blamed for what happened today. The authorities in Navora want your land; this will give them the excuse to take it.'

'I'll die before I leave my land,' said Tarkwan.

'If you stay and fight,' said Gabriel, 'you'll all be massacred. You'll lose your lives as well as your plain.'

'So we run like rabbits before the hunter, and leave our land to be taken?'

'Better your land than your lives.'

'You're not knowing what you say, Gabriel. Our life *is* our land.'

'No, it's not. And I do know what I say. I've lost everything, not just my land but my right to live in any place that's called Navoran. But it hasn't killed me. I still breathe, still live, can still heal and hope and love. Life and land are separate, Tarkwan.'

'You talk like a Navoran,' said Tarkwan angrily. 'You say that because you have no land, except what you took from us. So you trade it away, and keep it or lose it, and you don't love it with your heart because it's not yours and never was.' Tarkwan bent and scooped up a handful of soft dust. He shook it in front of Gabriel's face, his voice rising with grief and rage, and he wept as he spoke. 'My ancient ones, their blood and bones, are in this dust! We were living here when your forefathers were sitting on far beaches dreaming on what lands they could go and steal. In distant time past, the All-father gave us this land. We were being here with the first grass, the first beasts. From when he made the sun, he made us for this land. All this land, far as you can see. And now we have only this, this plain where I stand. Today our kinsmen and kinswomen died on this land, they gave their blood to guard and keep it. And you say give it up, it's not life. If this land isn't my life, what is?'

'I'm only telling you what will happen if you stay,' said Gabriel. 'If you want to die for your land, that's your right. But I think you should ask your people if they want to die. I think you should ask the mothers if they want their children to die. Ask the husbands if they want their wives to die. Even though you're chieftain, I don't think you have the right to make those choices for them.'

'They'll be doing what I say,' said Tarkwan.

Gabriel opened his mouth to say something else, thought better of it, and went back to the house. Just before he went down the steps, he looked again in the direction of Lena's farm. The lamps had been lit in the farmhouses, and smoke rose from the chimneys. They heartened him, those signs of homely life and the memories of his family, but as he went down the dirt steps into the Shinali house, his heart grew heavy with foreboding.

Outside, in the darkening night, Tarkwan walked alone beside the rows of dead waiting to be burned. They had been covered with flax matting. He came to the last body, knelt beside it, and folded back the covering. Even in death Moondarri was beautiful, her eyes closed as if she slept, her countenance assured and serene. On her forehead Zalidas had painted the most sacred sign, because she had died for the land, and because she was kinswoman to the chieftain. It was the sign of the eagle flying. Tarkwan looked at her this last time, his face streaming with tears. He bent and kissed her hair and lips and eyes. Then he folded the covering back over her and walked a short distance away. Chanting, crying, he lay flat upon the ground, his arms spread wide, his face and body pressed against the earth. It was an act of oneness, of worship; an embracement of the land he loved more than life, almost as much as he loved Moondarri.

The night was dark when he went into the house. The food was keeping hot on the hearthstones while the people waited for him. They looked at him as he stood on the lowest step, their faces uplifted and trusting. His voice was hoarse from grief as he spoke to them, and sometimes it broke, but it was still commanding. At his words Yeshi cried out angrily, and some of the other young men also shouted. The elders silenced them. When Tarkwan had finished talking, many of the people wailed and lamented. Ashila went and sat by Gabriel. She began to translate what Tarkwan had said but shook her head and wept, unable to speak for her despair.

Fear tore through Gabriel. 'He wants us to stay and fight, doesn't he?' he said.

She shook her head. 'No,' she sobbed. 'He's wanting us to leave our land, and flee.'

18 Moon of the Seventh Sacrament

THE SHINALI DWELLING was emptied of everything that could be carried away. The only things remaining were the heavy looms, the largest cooking pots, the wall carvings, and the canoes, which had been placed around the barren sleeping place. The fire burned low, its hearth desolate. In the embers was a fragment of crimson cloth embroidered in gold – all that remained of Gabriel's Citadel clothes.

A sorrowful lament filled the vacant house, as the people carried in the dead to be burned. The soldiers, too, were brought in and placed side by side with the Shinali, and they all were covered with the firewood that remained. Then the clan gathered around, and Zalidas sang a prayer. Afterwards he asked Gabriel if he wished to pray for the souls of the dead soldiers. Gabriel did, trying to remember the prayer said over Myron's body before it was cremated. Ashila stood by him, her hand in his.

Then, with all the people, they went out into the night. Tarkwan left last, bringing with him a branch with one end aflame. The clan's priest hung a skin over the doorway and drew a sacred sign over it with red paint. Then, while his people watched, Tarkwan ran the burning branch along the low eaves of the house. The thatch caught quickly, and flames and sparks and pieces of blazing straw flew high into the dark. Within moments the beams caught alight, and wood cracked and spat. Some of the thatch collapsed, igniting the wood over the bodies inside. A pall of black smoke, rank with the smell of burning flesh, drifted across the stars.

The people mourned, their wails and chants rising with the increasing flames and smoke. A little way apart, out of the way of smoke and falling fragments of burning straw, lay the sick, surrounded by the clan's possessions. As the house blazed, the mourners went over to them and prepared to leave. Tarkwan was the last to walk away. His face streamed with sweat from the fire's heat, and with tears. He picked up his sleeping mat and spears and slung his roll of clothes across his back. Without a word he started to lead his people away, towards the mountains.

His clan trailed behind him, carrying their wounded and dying in stretchers made of sleeping mats. Many carried children, and they all were burdened with blankets, clothes, eating utensils, food in flax baskets, traps, and hunting weapons. Gabriel and Ashila walked together, both bearing heavy bundles. Myron's sword hung at Gabriel's side. Thandeka walked with them, her right arm in a sling. With her good arm she carried her sister's child, orphaned in the fight. The child struggled as they left, screaming for his mother and holding out his hands towards the blazing house. One youth carried two cooking pots, and they clanged together, ringing mournfully in the frosty dark. Most of the people walked alone, too laden with belongings to have hands free to touch or comfort one another. They made slow progress, because some of those carrying hurt loved ones were themselves wounded and weary, and often had to rest. Smoke swirled about them, blown by the night wind.

Ashila wiped her eyes on her sleeve and glanced at Gabriel. His face, too, was wet. She looked quickly away, anguished.

'You're not having to walk with us,' she said. 'I understand if you're wanting to hurry on.'

'Why would I want to hurry on?' he asked.

'To your ship,' she replied, her eyes straight ahead. Gabriel put his roll of bedding down on the grass and touched her arm, stopping her. She would not look at him, so he turned her to face him, tilting her chin upward gently with his hand. She was crying. Fervently, tenderly, he kissed her, unmindful of the people trudging past. When at last he drew away, she whispered, 'Is that your Navoran farewell?'

'No,' he replied. 'It's to tell you I love you. And that, no matter what happens, I want to be here with you and your people. I'll never leave you.'

She dropped her things on the grass and flung her arms around his neck. 'All night I'm being afraid,' she choked. 'All night I'm thinking . . .'

He kissed her again and they clung together, half laughing, half crying. Lifting his head he looked over her shoulder, past the burning house to the farms. He raised his right hand and blew a kiss towards his own home. Then he released Ashila and they picked up their bags and bundles, and walked away towards the mountains and Taroth Pass, and the far Hena lands.

Subin sat by her little window, watching the Shinali house burn. Her eyes glimmered in the light of a candle on the sill, and her face was red and swollen from crying.

Lena came in with a pile of freshly washed clothes and put them on a shelf. 'Will you make the soldiers some bowls of coffee, Subin?' she asked. 'I have to tear up some more bandages. Some of them won't stop bleeding. And I told you not to light candles in your room. This is a wooden house, not a stone one.'

'The Shinali house is on fire,' said Subin.

Alarmed, Lena bent and looked out. 'God help them!' she said softly.

'They're not in it,' said Subin. 'They're leaving, see? They put all the dead people in their house and set it on fire.' She started crying again, and Lena sat down and held her, stroking her hair to comfort her. 'I suppose they have to go, darling,' Lena said. 'They must be using their house as a funeral pyre. Whatever happened today, the Shinali are going to be blamed for it. The whole Navoran army will be crawling over that plain tomorrow.'

'But it wasn't their fault!' cried Subin. 'Topaz said the soldiers were wrong! It's not fair! Who's going to look after the sheep, now, and put them in the fold at night?' She wailed in renewed fury and sorrow, and Lena hugged her. Subin went on, distraught: 'Everybody's gone! Father. Myron. The Shinali. Gabriel.'

'Gabriel will write to us,' Lena said, making a mammoth effort not to weep herself, failing, and hiding her face in her child's hair. When she could speak again her tone was low, though the soldiers were downstairs. 'It'll be fun getting his letters, Subin. They'll be all about some strange country. And he writes wonderful letters, doesn't he?'

Subin did not reply but stared out of the window at the house devoured by fire. Suddenly a feeling of total peace came over her, and with it a knowing, undeniable and real. She sighed deeply and said, 'He won't write. He can't. He hasn't got parchment and ink.'

'They have those things on ships,' Lena told her. 'He'll send the letters when he gets into ports, and have them brought back here on other ships.'

'He's not going on a ship,' said Subin.

'Yes he is, darling. Salverion said so, when he brought us Gabriel's things yesterday. He won't be on the ship just yet, but he will be soon.'

But Subin's eyes remained fixed on the burning Shinali house and the people, misty in the smoke, fleeing across the firelit plain. She said, 'He won't go on the boat. He's too late for it.'

'How do you know?' whispered Lena, a weird feeling crawling down her spine.

'I just do.' Suddenly Subin flung her arms about her mother's neck and kissed her cheeks. 'I think he doesn't want us to worry about him, Mama. No matter what happens, he doesn't want us to worry.'

Lena laughed a little, half amused, half wondering. But she too felt the peace, as she looked out at the fire on the Shinali land and the people setting forth on a journey. Above them the stars blazed around the moon. It was a crescent moon: the moon of new beginnings, of holiness and hope – the Moon of the Seventh Sacrament.

Tarkwan stood on a flat rock and watched his people toiling across the stone bridge. Behind them stretched the bleak ravine called Taroth Pass, with the gigantic fort looming in its entrance. Before them rose the rocky slopes of Sharnath, dark against the stars.

Burdened with his own belongings and sleeping mat and furs, Gabriel walked up and down the line speaking words of encouragement and touching those who moaned in pain. As he came off the bridge and passed Tarkwan, he asked, 'How's your leg?'

'It's holding me up, this far,' Tarkwan replied, glancing down at his bandaged thigh. 'Your clever sewing, it's working.'

At the foot of the mountain, the people dropped their bundles and placed their sick carefully on smooth places on the ground. Many lay down on the blankets with them, falling instantly asleep. Gabriel and Ashila made their bed and lay down, their arms around each other. Somewhere in the darkness a child cried for its dead mother, and other mourners sobbed quietly. In a singsong, guttural voice an old man started singing a lament, and it wound about them in the dark wind, haunting and sorrowful.

Gabriel looked across the river and back along the plain. The Shinali house was only an emptiness in the earth now, with embers dying. Smoke drifted up, smudging the stars. Turning his gaze to the old bridge they had just crossed, Gabriel studied Taroth Fort. It was huge, its boundary walls built of rock and inclining slightly inwards. The wooden gate was massive. At the four corners stood lookout towers. It was like a castle, lofty and impregnable. He guessed there were lodging places inside, and kitchens and utility rooms for the army that had once lived there and guarded the pass while the city of Navora was established.

On the lower mountain slope behind him, a man began to lament, his voice wild and tormented.

'It's Tarkwan,' whispered Ashila. 'His pain and his guilt, they are too big for his heart to hold.'

'Why should he have guilt?' asked Gabriel. 'He fought well to keep his land. You all fought well.'

'But we lost,' she said. 'As chieftain, Tarkwan bears the guilt of that, and guilt for his people who died.'

'But there's no need for guilt. He can't blame himself for things beyond his control.'

'Can't he?' she replied. 'Have you never laid guilt on yourself, Gabriel, for what you could not help?'

He lay silent, very still, while the weight of the ancient bone *torne* grew heavy on his breast. At last he said, very quietly, 'I do have guilt, Ashila. And no matter what I've done – no matter how hard I've tried to forget it or wipe it out – it's always there.'

'Some things we can't wipe out ourselves,' she said. 'That's why we have this time of the sacrament. Up on the mountain, we give to the All-father our secret hurts and griefs and guilts, for him to finish or mend. It is better than holding on to them, trying to forget them. The holy rite, it's an outward sign of what is happening in our hearts, and it is strong and true.'

Gabriel was about to ask something else, when they heard a small landslide of stones from higher on the mountain. Glancing up, they saw that Tarkwan had begun clambering up the slope, following a twisting path. He limped badly.

'I'll go with him,' said Gabriel, removing his arm from about Ashila's neck.

Ashila kissed him, saying, 'He goes for the secret rite, Gabriel. The prayers, they're said in solitude.'

'I'll remember.' Getting up, he ran quickly between the people sprawled over the shingle and stones, and began climbing the track Tarkwan had taken. The rocks were steep, and he was panting by the time he reached the chieftain. Tarkwan, too, was breathing hard, his inhalations long and torn by pain, or grief. The bandage on his leg was soaked in blood. Without a word Tarkwan put his arm across Gabriel's shoulder and leaned on him as they ascended the mountain together.

The sun was coming up by the time they reached the holy place. It was a flat rock overhanging a sheer precipice. Far below, the eastern desert glimmered, and the sun's rim trembled on the verge of the world. To the west the Shinali grasslands lay shadowed. In the south stretched the jagged coast and the sea.

Looking straight out, Gabriel saw only sky, waiting for the dawn.

Tarkwan went and knelt on the rock, close to the edge. Gabriel waited against the cliff, torn between respect for Tarkwan's privacy, and the fear that he might throw himself over.

The chieftain had forgotten Gabriel. He knelt and touched his forehead to the rock three times, chanting in Shinali. While he chanted, he opened a hide pouch he carried, taking out a wisp of thatch from the house and a handful of earth from Shinali land. Crouching over the emblems, touching them lovingly with his fingertips, he cried out his shame and defeat, his intolerable guilt for failing to save his people's home and land. As his chant rose, he took his knife from his belt.

Gabriel stepped forward, stopped, hesitant and afraid. Tarkwan placed the blade edge on the back of his wrist, along his wedding tattoo. Between the two deer he made a cut, then laid the blade flat and sliced away the skin beneath the doe. The place where she had been became a hollow pool of blood. He placed the film of skin on the dust beside the Shinali soil, his chanting anguished and terrible. Several times he spoke the same word, and Gabriel guessed it was the name of the All-father. Often he heard the word *sharleema*, and then Moondarri's name, over and over, in tones hoarse with despair and love and grief.

Slowly, while he chanted and cried, Tarkwan picked up the emblems of all that he had loved and lost and flung them over the edge of the precipice, surrendering them to the All-father. They fell just as the sun leaped up, orange and blinding. Then the chieftain lay down full length on the rock, his face to the dust, and lamented.

Without a sound Gabriel went and knelt beside him, a few paces away. As Tarkwan had done, he bent his head to the ground three times, then smoothed away the stones and grit on the edge of the rock. Tarkwan remained motionless, his eyes closed and his forehead bowed against the dirt. Gabriel lifted his arms and removed the bag from about his neck. From it he took the Shinali bone and laid it on the edge of the precipice. The ancient *torne* shone, its etched symbol stained still with the blood of the woman he had abandoned, stained still with his guilt. A guilt too heavy for his heart, though a hundred times he had atoned for it – and more than atoned. It was not even guilt, now, that bound his soul to the Shinali people, it was love. But behind that love, behind all the understanding and joy and healing, was the Shinali woman still wounded on the stones, and his silence when he might have gone for help. It was time, this holy morning, to let it all go.

Quietly, he spoke an old Navoran prayer for forgiveness, a prayer of trust and relinquishment; then, blinded by the sun, he picked up the bone carving and threw it far out over the edge. It spun, golden and shining, and was lost in light.

Long after, he turned his head and looked at the chieftain. Tarkwan's *torne*, threaded on a leather thong around his neck, glowed on the dust close by his dark skin. A small pulse beat in Tarkwan's throat, and he was breathing easier now. He lifted his head and looked at Gabriel, and they both smiled. The chieftain's face, dusky and beautiful and almost joyful in the dawning sun, was like his sister's.

Without a word they both stood and, with their arms about each other, began the walk back down the mountain. Above them the skies were turquoise, glowing with the promise of a new season.

'Do you have knowing of our great Shinali prophecies?' Tarkwan asked.

'Yes. Ashila told me about them.'

'This day they begin to come true,' said Tarkwan, his face alight and full of hope. 'This day begins the Time of the Eagle. This day we begin our journey to the lands of the Igaal and the Hena. We'll live as wanderers, following deer for food, making strong our peace with those who once were enemies. Then, time to come, as one great people, we'll return and take back what was ours.'

They rounded a bend and saw the people below. Smoke from cooking fires rose in the tranquil morning air, and the young people were fishing off the bridge, catching breakfast. Then someone screamed, and others called out, their voices shrill with alarm. Gabriel and Tarkwan lifted their eyes from the dusty track and looked across the Shinali grasslands. On this side of the river, pouring down from the new road through the hills from Navora and spreading out across the plain like a dark approaching sea, deadly and organised and inexorable, came the entire Navoran army.

Tarkwan halted on the path, his arm tight around Gabriel's neck. Gabriel glanced at the chieftain's face, could not bear what he saw there, and looked down at the people again. The clan was in confusion, people gathering up the sick in their blankets and running, fleeing hopelessly in all directions, hauling children by the hand, leaving weapons and food and clothing strewn across the rocks.

The chieftain cupped his hands around his mouth and called down to them. People stopped running and looked up. Letting go of Gabriel, Tarkwan made a sign with his arms, and people stayed where they were. Limping, stumbling, sometimes falling, Tarkwan ran with Gabriel down the rest of the rocky path. As they reached the clan, the army crossed the halfway mark of the plain, opposite the ruined Shinali house. The soldiers were all on horses. The morning sun struck swords and bows like fire, and the horses' hooves made thunder in the earth.

Hushed, the clan waited, their faces ashen and without hope. A few children began to cry, their frightened sobs loud in the stillness. All eyes were on the chieftain. He seemed at a loss, while the horses' hooves drummed closer. He turned to Gabriel. 'Your knowing of Navorans is a high lot better than mine,' Tarkwan said. 'What are they wanting? Our lives?'

'I don't know,' said Gabriel. 'But it's pointless to run. I suggest we put all our weapons, even our hunting knives and slings and fishing spears, in a pile on the ground. Then, as a sign of surrender, we should kneel with our hands folded on our foreheads, and our heads pressed against the earth. They may show mercy. I don't know.'

Tarkwan looked at his people and gave them those instructions in Shinali. Then he took his knife and sling and put them on a flat rock between the mountain and the plain. All his people did the same, until there was a great pile there. Tarkwan cried out something else in Shinali, folded his hands against his forehead, and knelt down to wait. Slowly the people knelt behind him. Beside them were their earthly goods, bundled into blankets or rolled in sleeping mats. Many knelt on the blankets on which the wounded and sick lay, bewildered and helpless.

Gabriel looked for Ashila. She came to him, dragging their belongings. She gave him Myron's sword, and he took it over to the pile of weapons and placed it on the top. He thought of Myron wanting a Shinali funeral, and had the feeling he would not mind his sword being among the spears with their bone heads and the knives with their rough antler handles. Even so, it was hard leaving it.

Then he went back to Ashila. As they knelt together, he delved in his bag for the purse of gold pieces. Inconspicuously, he took out the coins and pushed some into his boots. He gave a handful to Ashila, and she concealed them in a pouch sewn along the inside of her wide belt. Gabriel left just two coins in the bag, and replaced it. The pledge-ring he took off and placed in the amulet bag around his neck, hiding it within his clothes. Then he and Ashila crossed their hands on their foreheads and they bent their heads to the ground.

The earth shook with the rumble of the approaching army. Boulders were loosened on the mountain and crashed, booming, down the canyons. The air seemed full of thunder, though the skies were impossibly serene. The Shinali people waited, quiet, only a few children crying. The army came closer. The tumult became unbearable, the trampling hooves too close. Just as people were about to leap up in terror and run, it stopped. There was quiet, only the shifting of restless hooves on stones, the snorting of horses, and the creaking of leather. The sound of a man dismounting, of stones crunching under boots. And a voice, loud and harsh and echoing. Gabriel recognised it.

'Who's the chieftain here?' Kamos called.

They heard the stones shift as someone stood.

'I'm chieftain,' Tarkwan replied, his voice steady.

'Come here,' said Kamos.

Saddles creaked and stones crunched as more soldiers dismounted. There was the smack of flesh on flesh, and a low cry, and the noise of someone falling on the stones. Grunts and painful breathing as Tarkwan was lifted up, hit again and again. Groans of agony, then a man's scream. Someone in the clan stood up, and a soldier shouted at him to get down again. He refused, stumbling through the rows of bowed Shinali to his chieftain. There was the hiss of an arrow, and the man fell. People cried out as he collapsed over them, and at the back of the clan a woman started to wail. The soldiers shouted. After that no one moved. The shot Shinali lay jerking, his blood running out across the stones. After a while he lay still. And the beating of Tarkwan went on.

Ashila wept, and Gabriel risked reaching out and touching her. She gripped his hand hard, until her fingers hurt his. They both tried to pray, to cover Tarkwan with light and protection, but the thud of fists and boots, and the groans, were hard to envision against.

Finally it was over, and they heard him dragged away. Some of the soldiers rode over the bridge. Then the commander spoke again, ordering the Shinali to stand. Some in the front did not understand and were kicked until they obeyed.

Gabriel stole a long look at Kamos. The man looked grand in his army uniform, his bronze breastplate burnished and gleaming, his white plumes fluttering in the breeze, his cloak in proud folds about him. He glanced in Gabriel's direction, but did not recognise him. Kamos looked slightly bored as he glanced over the shabby band. They did not look like fighters.

'For rebellion and crimes against the Navoran Empire, your lands have been confiscated!' he shouted. 'You're to be imprisoned in the Taroth Fort. There, your commander will be Officer Razzak. Your sentence will last for as long as Her Majesty sees fit. Go quietly. If anyone runs, they'll be shot. That includes children. Move.'

In orderly lines, not risking a whisper, the people traversed the bridge and the gravelly gorge to the fort. As they approached, the walls towered over them, brown like the mountain rock, solid and overpowering. Only one gate was open. On the outside of the other gate, rusty iron rings were fixed with chains into the wood. They had been used for punishment in years gone by, when prisoners or rebellious soldiers were transfixed spreadeagled on the gates to hang in the relentless sun, sometimes until they died. Now Tarkwan was fastened there.

People sobbed as they went past. His face, once so lordly and beautiful, was a bloodied pulp. The soldiers had stripped him, and every part of him was bruised and torn. The long wound on his leg had ripped open, and the bandages dripped blood.

Several people tried to go to him as they went past, but a soldier stood by with a sword, and every time they came too close he placed the naked blade against their chests. So Tarkwan hung helplessly, still conscious and fully aware of his people as they came into their prison, his breathing harsh and tormented and full of a terrible wrath.

19 The Spirit That Lasts

INSIDE THE FORT was a vast courtyard, used in former days for practising battle manoeuvres. Derelict now, the courtyard was littered with broken timber and spiralling grass-heads blown in on gales from the eastern desert. Some had taken root, and there were clumps of grass where once skilled men had marched. On the far side of the courtyard were the barracks, three storeys high, with the courtyard walls left open to the air. In past winters wooden shutters had closed off the arched openings, but the timber had rotted and now the wind whistled among the pillars and abandoned straw mattresses. Along the west wall were the kitchens and bathrooms, and on the upper floors more barracks. A porch with stone pillars fronted the kitchens, and outside it was a well, broken now. The east wall, facing the mountain pass, had slits where archers had waited with their bows. The place was colossal, desolate, with an awful air of forsakenness.

Soldiers stood just inside the gate, searching the Shinali for concealed weapons. All knives and slings were confiscated, as well as bone sewing needles, and the pointed pieces of deer antler used to paint lines on faces and clothes. Zalidas's tattooing equipment was taken.

As he neared the soldiers, Gabriel frantically thought up a

story, a new name, a reason for being here. He repeated the lie in his mind, trying to be composed, while warnings buzzed in his head. The woman in front of him had her comb taken, as well as the bone pin she used to fasten her cloak. Then it was Gabriel's turn. His heart thumped as he held out his bag. The soldier, hardly older than himself, glanced up. He stopped, astounded. 'You're Navoran!' he said.

Gabriel nodded, and the soldier called over one of the others. He gave him Gabriel's bag, and they whispered together. The second soldier was an older man with a burn mark down his face, and eyes amber and piercing, like a hawk's. His expression was hard, uncompromising. He wore the red shoulder plumes of an officer, and Gabriel guessed he was Razzak, the commander in charge of the fort.

Without speaking, Razzak indicated for Gabriel to follow him. Gabriel glanced back at Ashila. 'If they ask you, my name's Darshan,' he whispered, then followed the officer to a place just beyond the Shinalis' scattered belongings. Razzak opened Gabriel's bag and emptied it on to the ground. All his belongings rolled out on to the dust. The officer picked up the purse and emptied it on to his palm. The two gold pieces, each worth two months' wages for a soldier, glinted in the sun.

'Don't you worry about thieves, boy?' asked Razzak, his astute eyes searching Gabriel's face.

'Not with the Shinali, sir.'

The officer grunted. 'What's your name?'

'Darshan.'

'Who are your parents?'

'My mother was Navoran; she's dead now. My father is an Amaranian physician. He has rather unconventional methods of healing. He's training me but wanted me to study with the

Shinali while he's visiting relatives in Amaran. In return, I'm teaching the Shinali some of our ways.'

'You were with the Shinali yesterday, during the fight?'

'Yes.'

'Why didn't you get out of it, after the trouble? You must have known the army would be back.'

'I stayed to help clean up the wounds, after the fighting.'

The soldier put the coins back in the money purse and handed it to him. 'You're free to go,' he said.

'I'd rather stay, sir.'

'You can't.'

'The Shinali are my friends, sir; I've been with them most of the winter. I'd like to be here as their physician.'

The officer sighed. 'Very well, since they need one. But don't expect any privileges. You'll be treated the same as the prisoners.'

'Thank you. May I ask you a favour, sir? The Shinali chieftain . . . could he be given back to them? He was only defending his people and property yesterday. You and I would have done the same, in his circumstances.'

The officer did not reply, and Gabriel gathered up his belongings and turned to go. The officer suddenly called him back. 'I'll have your shaving blades,' he said.

As Gabriel handed them over, he asked if he could borrow them each morning.

'You can shave in the soldiers' barracks,' the officer replied.

Gabriel went over to the group of Shinali and put his things on the ground by Ashila. He was trembling, and she looked at him anxiously. 'He believed you, Darshan?' she whispered.

'I think so.'

They watched as the last Shinali were brought into the fort

and searched. Outside the gates, the greater part of the army prepared to return to Navora, the day's work concluded. They were taking the horses of the small company that would remain to guard the rebel clan. While Gabriel watched, the massive wooden gate was banged shut, locked, and bolted.

With drawn swords the guards herded the people over to the barracks. Inside, the dingy stone chambers were covered in dust. The stairs to the upper chambers were narrow and steep, the wooden floors damaged and rotting. There were no windows, only the gaping archways yawning over the courtyard below. Ordered to stay on the ground floor, the Shinali climbed two steps to the lowest barracks. The floor was thick with dirt blown in from the courtyard, and there were the remains of small animals eaten by hawks and other birds of prey. Forgotten nests, blown to pieces by the winds, were strewn across the dust, and there were piles of bird droppings. At the far end were ancient latrines, holes in the ground that once had wooden seats over them. Now they were half full of debris.

Gathering in groups with their friends and families, the people spread out their sleeping mats and blankets. Voices echoed, unnaturally loud, along the stone walls, and every rustle and footstep was magnified. Children clambered up the perilous stone stairs, and were hauled quickly back. There was little space for them to play; quarters were cramped, the sleeping mats overlapping. Being sacred, Shinali beds were never walked on; here, in the desperate overcrowding, it was impossible not to step on them. But the people trod carefully around the edges, grieving anew at being forced to break time-honoured traditions.

Gabriel worried about other traditions, too, as he spread out his bedding, wondering where Ashila would place hers. To his joy, she spread her blankets with his furs, making one bed. Then

Gabriel sat down and removed the gold coins from his boots. He asked Ashila for the coins she had carried, and put them all in the money bag again. Then he went to the back of the barrack chamber, felt along the wall until he found a loose stone, and hid the money bag behind it. Several Shinali watched, wondering what he was doing. He said to them, 'If the soldiers come looking, never tell them.' They only half understood but shook their heads solemnly.

Many of the clan, having organised their meagre belongings, were standing on the steps of the barracks looking towards the enormous closed gates, where, unseen, their chieftain hung in his awful and lonely pain. Zalidas began singing a great Shinali prayer of encouragement and hope, and others took it up until the deep chant rang across the dusty yard and echoed around the high stone walls.

There was a shout in the courtyard, and one of the soldiers ordered everyone to line up. They obeyed, leaving the sick in their blankets in the cold barracks. They were commanded to stand in lines, men first, then women, then children. Many of the Shinali did not understand, so others interpreted. About fifty soldiers stood in ranks facing the Shinali. They were all heavily armed, many with the lethal crossbows for which Navoran soldiers were famous. When the Shinali were in lines, the soldier spoke again.

'I'm Officer Razzak,' he told them. 'I'm in command. You'll remain here a few days, while Her Majesty decides what to do with you. Make your food last. There's water in the well. Our quarters are forbidden to you. Anyone who attempts to escape will be punished. Give me no trouble, and this time tomorrow you can have your chieftain back. Any questions?'

There were none, and the officer walked towards them,

looking them over carefully, and calling out several of the younger women. They went forward, Ashila among them. The Shinali men tensed.

'You're cleaning the kitchens and washrooms,' Razzak said. Then he called out ten of the youths. 'You're digging out the latrines, and cleaning up the well.'

In a masterful display of Navoran military precision, the soldiers marched around the Shinali once, then over to their own quarters, where they dispersed. Several of them took up guard positions around the walls and by the gates; others led the selected Shinali men and women to the squalid kitchens and washrooms. The women were given buckets and scrubbing brushes, the men spades. The soldiers were admirably organised. They were at ease, too, now that the day's work had been so smoothly accomplished. They leaned against the stone pillars outside the kitchen, laughing and joking as they supervised the women's work. A group of them, armed with naked swords, went to oversee the men.

The remaining Shinali watched them for a while, making certain their women were safe, then went back to the barracks. Many were dazed, still lost in horror and grief, unable to comprehend what had happened. A few sat alone in the dirt, rocking and weeping quietly.

Gabriel went into the barracks and saw to the wounded. They were urgently in need of washing and clean dressings. With Thandeka interpreting, he asked their families to get water, and they returned with wooden bowls and cooking pots full of the brackish stuff from the well. Thandeka used a little of the water to make medicine from the dried roots and herbs she had brought, and gave it to those with infections. She went among the rest of the clan asking them to give clothes they could spare to be cut for bandages, and she and Gabriel spent the rest of the day cleansing wounds and rebinding them in clean cloth. As they worked, Gabriel made sure everyone was told to call him by his new name in front of the soldiers.

It was still afternoon when the sun slid down behind the high walls, and a deadly cold settled over the fort. The women finished scrubbing the kitchens and washrooms, and stopped at the cleared well to wash their hands and faces. Ashila went to the place she and Gabriel had chosen in the barracks, and dropped wearily on to her sleeping mat. Soon after, he found her fast asleep. Her knuckles were raw from scrubbing, and he gently bound them in clean bandages. Then he lay beside her, his arm across her waist, and dozed. All around him Shinali rested, some sleeping from sheer exhaustion, others lying wide awake and staring at the broken timbers above.

It was evening when Gabriel woke. People had gathered up some of the rotten timbers and lit a fire in the yard, and were stewing smoked fish and vegetables. Before the meal Zalidas sang a prayer, then, as always, the Shinali went in their ranks to choose their food. The meal restored some kind of normality to their devastated lives. Afterwards, the children collected small stones, or removed beads from their hair, to play complex games with them on markings scratched in the fire-lit dust. One of the musicians produced his pipe, and the tune was haunting and plaintive. Always the people were aware of their chieftain, and often they looked towards the gates, their lips moving in prayer.

When the fire was low everyone went to their places in the barracks, carrying their bowls of water for washing. The stone chambers were freezing now. In the blue moonlight, shivering, Gabriel and Ashila stripped and washed themselves. It was extremely difficult with so little room, and with everyone trying to confine their feet to the very edges of the bedding. People bumped into each other, and water spilled on blankets. Soon everyone was in bed, and the hollow dark echoed with whispers and sighs and the sound of weeping. Wind moaned through the stone archways, blowing in dust and the last smoke from the dying fire. Gabriel drew the furs and blankets up around their necks, and held Ashila close.

'Tell me on Darshan,' she whispered. 'Is he the Navali?'

'No. He's the handsome son of a Navoran woman and an Amaranian healer. That makes him Navoranian.'

'I'm having a hard time knowing who I'm sleeping with,' she muttered.

He laughed softly and kissed her, his hand roving. 'Who's sleeping?' he asked.

'Some of us are trying to,' said Zalidas from nearby, and Ashila giggled and stopped Gabriel's hand. They embraced quietly, constrained and aching.

'I've just thought of something,' Gabriel whispered, suddenly tense. 'You have herbs, don't you, to stop pregnancy?'

'Yes. My mother gives them to all the girls, until they're being married. And after, if they want. Why? Are you worried on it?'

'Yes.'

'Don't be.'

They lay in silence, trying to sleep. Without thinking, he moved his hand over her shoulders and back, massaging them. She sighed blissfully. 'Your hands, they're being a high lot good,' she whispered. 'They wipe away my fearings.'

'There's no need to be afraid. We have friends who can help us. One of the Masters, Sheel Chandra, taught me how to communicate with him through mind alone. I think you know that power. And if I can't reach Sheel Chandra, I'll leave here and go and see Salverion. He'd do something to help us. The Empress listens to him.'

'You can leave this place?'

'Yes. I'm not a prisoner. But I'll only go if I have to, I can't risk being recognised. There's bound to be a reward for anyone who gives the city sentries information about me.'

'You would be safer on your ship, far and far from here. I'm fearing that one day, time to come, you'll be sorry you stayed with us.'

'I made the choice to stay, Ashila, and I'm not sorry for it. I swear that, with *sharleema*.'

'I bless your swearing, healer,' said Zalidas in his deep voice, making them both jump. 'And I'll be blessing you again, if you stop talking and let us sleep.'

Several people chuckled, and Gabriel blushed in the darkness, wondering how much they had all heard. He and Ashila lay very still after that, and soon her breathing became calm as she slept. Even in sleep she looked strong, her lips and chin firm, her brow clear and steadfast. Sudden, overwhelming tenderness swept through Gabriel. He gazed at her with wonder, his heart full of joy, knowing that nothing else in his life – whatever he might have gained or lost – nothing would ever compare with her. And he knew beyond doubt that, of all the places in the Empire to which he could have fled, this place with Ashila, with these people, was right.

In the mystic and dusky edge of sleep he heard the Empress's voice saying to him, in another life, 'Do you believe in destiny, Gabriel?'

'I'm not sure,' he had replied then.

He was sure, now.

*

Ashila spread the wet clothes across the hemp line to dry, and watched Gabriel and the children running around the inside perimeter of the walls. The first time around he always ran slowly, letting them think the fastest of them were keeping up with him, but after that he ran alone, swiftly, and they shrieked with glee when he came up behind them on the following laps, gasping and staggering, pretending he was nearly dead of exhaustion and they were winning. Then he would pass them again and run on, around and around until they gave up and collapsed on the dirt so he had to jump over them. One day four of the soldiers had run with him, and they made a race of it. Gabriel won easily.

He ran without his shirt today, for the sun was warm. The children soon gave up, and counted his laps in Shinali. They cheered when he finished, because he had run two more than yesterday. He came over to Ashila, and she gave him a wet cloth to wash his face.

'I'm not knowing why you run like that,' she said.

'It uses up the strongness,' he replied, unable to think of a better word to explain tension. 'The Shinali men should run with me. They might not argue so much.'

'The hunting, they're missing it. And they're missing freedom. Ten days we are being here. It's too long. Will you talk to Razzak again, ask him why?'

'There's no point, he just gets angry with me now. He's waiting for orders from Navora. But he has requested supplies. At least we'll have more food soon. And firewood.'

Gabriel glanced towards the barracks. Most of the people injured in the battle had recovered, except four whose wounds had become seriously infected. They lay in the dimness with several other Shinali suffering from diarrhoea and vomiting, caught from the contaminated well water.

Seeing where Gabriel looked, Ashila said, 'Tarkwan's much better today, though his wound is still bad. He was talking to me while I washed him. And later the men were fighting, and he sat up and told them to wake up the . . . ah, the laughter-spirit in them. More than that. The life, the spirit that lasts, that overcomes all things. He said we have to dance, not argue. We have to remember we're Shinali and strong.'

'The musicians brought their instruments,' said Gabriel. 'We'll light a fire tonight, and dance.'

The courtyard began to fill with soldiers preparing for their exercises. They wore no armour now, but their uniforms were immaculate, each grey-blue tunic decorated with white shoulder ribbons and emblazoned on the front with the red horse. Shinali children gathered to watch, enthralled. They loved drill times with the precision marching, stunning archery, and breathtaking swordplay.

Suddenly there was a hammering on the gates, and guards opened it. The exercises stopped, and everyone watched as a wagon came through, piled with provisions. The soldiers unloaded it, laughing with satisfaction at the large kegs of army ale and the huge cheeses and hams. Their own supplies they took into the kitchen under the porch, but they threw the Shinali stores on to the dirt in the sun. When the wagon was gone, Gabriel went over and inspected the Shinali supplies: one sack of flour and a box of withered vegetables. There was no firewood. Fuming, he went into Razzak's dingy office. The officer was sitting behind his makeshift desk, reading a letter.

'There's no firewood for us,' said Gabriel. 'No decent food, just rubbish left over from the Navoran markets. It's not fit for humans.'

'It'll do for savages,' Razzak replied.

'I'll go out and see if I can get us better food,' said Gabriel, thinking of Salverion.

'That's not possible right now. You have to stay here.'

'Why, sir?'

'Some of my soldiers are sick. Just dysentery and other minor ailments, but I need them healthy. I've requested a physician, but in the meantime your peculiar methods of healing are better than nothing.'

'I'll do what I can for them, sir. Then I'll go.'

'You can go when a physician arrives, not before. This discussion is over. Leave.'

A deep fear came over Gabriel and he asked, 'Have you had further orders, sir? Are we to stay here much longer?'

Razzak shuffled the parchments on his desk, and did not reply. Gabriel turned and went out, his heart troubled.

The flames sprang high against the stars, and the thick smoke swirled across the courtyard, mingling with the glittering dust kicked up by the Shinali dancers. The soldiers leaned against the pillars of the porch and watched, their faces made ruddy by the firelight and the ale. Some tapped their feet in time to the Shinali drums and the wild strains of the pipes, longing to join in the abandonment, and secretly envying the strange young healer who spoke like someone high born and danced like a savage.

Later, while the Shinali chanted age-old songs of the land they loved, Gabriel asked a guard if he could climb one of the four corner towers.

'Do what you like,' the soldier replied. 'You're not a prisoner here.'

Gabriel went to the south-west tower, and found the door unlocked. Inside, narrow stairs spiralled steeply upward to a small room. Its walls were hexagonal, and all around were wide windows. Through them the wind came, sweet with the scent of grasslands and the sea. Leaning on the thick stone ledge, Gabriel looked out. The view was breathtaking. He was so high, he could see all the land to the ocean. Directly below lay the Shinali plain. Past that were the farms, the sown fields smooth and shining under the moon, the lights winking in the houses. Then there were the hills, and the luminous walls of the Citadel. And beyond those, spread out on the rocky coast like tiny embers aglow, was the city of Navora. He could make out the road leading into it, the lights of the Navora Infirmary, and the Sanctuary of Healing Dreams. Beyond the city was the sea, smooth and serene under the stars.

For a few moments, while he looked at Navora, he felt an unbearable longing for all that he had left behind. Struggling to forget, to embrace only the present, he stood very still, his hands folded on the stone ledge, and made his breathing slow and calm. This was the first moment of privacy he had had since being in the fort, and it was sweet. He had craved the solitude and shining silences of the Citadel. Closing his eyes, he imagined himself walking in those brilliant corridors. They would be drenched in reflected moonlight now. In his mind he walked down the pillared porch to the Great Library, beside the herb garden with its fountains and sundial. He passed through the great golden doors to the Library, crossed the luminous floors, and climbed the marble stairs to the meditation room high in the central tower. The peace of the place, the blessedness, overwhelmed him. Incense burned, its smoke musky and aromatic. On a cushion on the floor sat Sheel Chandra, his eyes closed, his body so still he seemed not to breathe. His face was lifted, fine and reposed in the starlight. He sat upright, relaxed but alert, as if he listened or waited. There was another cushion beside him, and Gabriel sat on it.

'I need to talk to you, Master,' he said, and was not sure whether the words were audible, or only in his mind.

'I'm listening, son of my heart.' These words, too, might have been only thought, but they were real enough, and the love in them was empowering.

'The Shinali are interred in Taroth Fort. I'm with them. There's little food. Everyone suffers from dysentery and minor infections, and two have liver sickness. We've been here ten days. The Shinali are peaceful so far, but I don't know how much longer they can last without rebelling. No one knows what's going to happen to them, and the uncertainty is unbearable.

'Would you please help us, Master? Would you and Salverion go to the Empress, persuade her to let the Shinali go? If that's not successful, would you please send us some supplies? Fresh food, and medicines.'

'Consider it all done.'

'Thank you. Thank you for everything, for your wisdom, your presence in my life, your love. I can't say I'm sorry for . . . for the way things have turned out. I think it was all written. But I deeply miss you, and Salverion.'

'Our love surrounds you always,' said Sheel Chandra tenderly, 'and we are as close as your next thought of us.'

Very softly, not knowing whether the Master would know, Gabriel kissed his own fingers, and placed them lightly on Sheel Chandra's upturned palm. Then, making no sound, he got up and went down the long stairs, through the shining passages, and out into the night wind rich with the scent of cultivated earth, trees, and citrus fruits. He sighed deeply, and became aware again of the window ledge beneath his hands, and of his feet firmly planted on the ancient floor of the fort tower. From the courtyard on the other side came sounds of flutes. A few minutes longer he stood there, then he went down the stairs and joined the people by their fire.

'It was good up there, *haii*?' they asked.

'Very good,' he said, picking up some meat from a bowl on the hearth and chewing on it. 'I could see all the world to the ocean.'

Later, instead of preparing for bed, he rolled the sleeping mat and blankets, and collected up his and Ashila's clothes.

'Why are you doing that?' she whispered.

'We're going to our own *Ta-sarn-ee*,' he said, 'if the guards don't stop us.' He took her hand, and they went out carefully between the rows of beds, to the courtyard.

Two soldiers were on duty by the main gate, standing to attention, their bows held ready in their hands. They watched as Gabriel and Ashila crossed the courtyard, and one of them muttered to the other, 'Shouldn't we stop them? The towers are forbidden to the Shinali.'

The other guard, an older man, shook his head. 'I had toothache, and he fixed it. He deserves some reward for what he does here. Say nothing, lad, I'll answer to Razzak if need be.'

In the lofty room of the tower, Ashila gazed out across her people's land, her eyes full of longing. 'They've not walked on it yet or changed it,' she said. 'It's still our land.'

'It always will be,' said Gabriel, standing behind her and enfolding her in his arms. For a long time they stood looking down at the grasslands.

'Your place, are you missing it?' she asked, her eyes on the Citadel hills and the smouldering lights of Navora.

'I was, but I'm not now,' he replied.

She kissed his cheek, then moved out of his arms and inspected the tiny room. Gabriel had already placed the fur and blankets on the floor, for their bed. He had brought a candle as well, and he lit it now, using the flints Ferron had left for him. The tiny flame sent a warm glow across their sleeping place.

Gabriel lay on his back on the bed, watching Ashila, his hands linked behind his head. She walked around the windows, looking out of each one, marvelling at the view. Last, she took a long look at the Shinali land, then went and lay down with him.

'It's strange, being only us two,' she whispered.

'We don't have to whisper,' he said. 'And if you're lonely I'll invite Zalidas and a few of the others up here.'

She leaned up on one elbow and caressed his hair and face. 'It's good having a light,' she said. 'I love your face. And your heart. And your spirit. And everything that is you. All my life, it seems, I've had knowing of you. When I first saw your face, it was not a stranger's. What made you come to us, Gabriel? Why did you run on our land, that day of your brother's burning?'

He did not answer immediately but lay looking at the timber beams of the tower roof. The candle flickered on the wooden floor beside him, its glow ebbing and flowing across his features. 'When I was little,' he said, 'I broke a marble statue of the Empress. I ran away, and found . . . I found a Shinali bone. That's when it all started.'

Ashila touched the small leather bag on his chest, feeling for the Shinali bone. Gently, Gabriel removed her fingers from the leather and held them tightly in his own. Beneath their hands, his heart thudded.

'It was *her* bone!' Ashila whispered. 'The daughter of –'

'Please say nothing else,' he said. 'It's gone, the bone and my feelings about it. It's gone now, to the All-father.'

'I'm wanting to ask you just one thing.'

'Then ask. But I may not answer.'

'The All-father, he has given you peace?'

'More than peace,' he replied, lifting her fingers to his lips and kissing them. 'He has given me you.'

Ashila settled down again, her head on his chest. A moth came in and fluttered around the candle flame, searing its wings. In the sky beyond their windows a night bird shrieked, and the wind from the sea sighed around the tower.

In that huge, beautiful, silent solitude they loved one another, freely and with joy. Afterwards they lay in each other's arms, watching the stars traverse the sky, and Ashila sang an old Shinali prayer for restoration and tomorrow.

20 HOPE

GABRIEL CROUCHED BY Tarkwan, and inspected the unhealed wound in his thigh. 'I need to clean this with a heated knife,' Gabriel told him. 'If the infection goes unchecked, your whole leg may go bad.'

'Do what you must,' said Tarkwan. 'I'll be needing my legs for walking on my land again, in freedom.'

'I'll ask Razzak if I can borrow a knife. Ashila will help, and I'll stop what pain I can.'

'If Razzak's in a good mind, ask him for our spears and slings, as well,' said Tarkwan, with bitter humour.

Gabriel grinned and got up to go to Razzak's office.

He returned shortly, accompanied by two armed guards, and carrying a cloth containing a small pair of scissors, a needle and thread, and a knife. Ashila was with him, with a bowl of water and her medicinal herbs. Other Shinali gathered around, silent and watchful, as the guards positioned themselves one at Tarkwan's right shoulder and one at his left, their swords bare. Zalidas crouched at Tarkwan's feet, chanting a prayer for his spirit to journey in a good place while his body endured pain. In the courtyard, not far away, Thandeka had lit a small fire. Gabriel was about to give her the knife to heat, but one of the soldiers forbade it. 'Only you touch the knife,' he said to Gabriel.

Gabriel placed the blade across the flames and returned to Tarkwan. Kneeling by his head, he moved his hands behind the chieftain's neck, his fingers tracing deep pathways to block the pain. Tarkwan relaxed, his eyes closed. With one hand he held the bone *torne* on his chest.

'The pain, it is gone?' Gabriel asked Tarkwan, in Shinali.

Tarkwan nodded, and Gabriel picked up the scissors and began cutting the stitches that remained across the gaping wound. It would all have to be scraped and burned back to the healthy flesh before he washed it out with lotions made from Ashila's antiseptic herbs, and stitched it closed again. Sunlight poured over his hands, for he worked in the bright light at the edge of the Shinali barracks. A few flies buzzed over the wound, and Ashila brushed them away. Then Gabriel got the knife from the fire and began cutting away the infected parts, at the same time sealing the blood vessels with the heated blade, preventing fatal bleeding. All the time the Shinali clan watched, and the guards waited, tense and suspicious. Not understanding Gabriel's way of stopping pain, the soldiers marvelled at what appeared to them to be the chieftain's incredible self-control and endurance.

Suddenly there was a commotion near the gates, and several of the Shinali shouted that someone had arrived. Fearing authorities from the city, Gabriel glanced up but could see only Shinali people gathered on the steps. Then he remembered his communion with Sheel Chandra last night, and fear changed to hope.

'Keep working,' said one of the guards, seeing Gabriel's hands still. 'The sooner that knife gets safely away from these savages, the better.'

Gabriel continued, while Ashila used clean rags to wipe away the gathering blood and the bad tissue he cut free.

Some of the children came running in, yelling about women

from the farms, and baskets of food. Understanding some of their words, Gabriel thought of his mother. Had Salverion been to see her, told her he was here? Again, his hands faltered. With cries of delight other Shinali raced to the gates. Only the elderly stayed to share their chieftain's healing, to give him the strength of their presence. Zalidas chanted on, quietly, and Tarkwan remained motionless, though he smiled a little, hearing his people's pleasure. Gabriel worked on, cutting away the last of the infected flesh. Then he heated the knife again and burned the wound clean. Just as he began to suture it closed, a guard came up the barrack steps, with one of the visitors. 'This woman wants to speak to a healer,' the guard announced. 'Says she's got medicines and ointments.'

Not moving from his position at Tarkwan's side, Gabriel looked up. His eyes met his mother's, and for a moment they both smiled. Astonishment crossed her face as she saw his dark hair. Very slightly, warning her, Gabriel shook his head. Then he looked down again, hoping his joy did not show. 'If you don't mind waiting, I have to finish here first,' he said. 'I won't be long.'

'I don't mind waiting,' she replied. 'At least it's relatively quiet here, compared to my house. It's full of rowdy children whose father loves them too much to discipline them. It'll be chaotic there when I get back. But I shouldn't complain. I ought to be thankful they're all healthy and happy. And free.'

Having told him that much of his family and her recent marriage, she fell silent. Gabriel continued his task, not knowing what to say, longing to look again at her face.

Lena waited, the basket of medicines in her arms. Trying to appear casual, ignoring the guards with their drawn swords, she watched her son as he sutured the Shinali's wound. Never had she seen him heal before, and she marvelled at his swift skill and the surety with which he worked. A scene came back to her from long ago: that terrible day of Jager's funeral, the argument with the uncles, and Gabriel's startling announcement that he wanted to help people. She smiled to herself, remembering the look on his face that day, so fiercely determined. And here he was, doing the work he had always longed to do. She felt inexpressibly blessed to see it, to witness at last a part of the life he had chosen.

Tarkwan groaned, and Gabriel asked him in Shinali if his pain had come back. Tarkwan nodded, and Gabriel touched the base of his skull again, and the upper part of his spine. 'I'm near finishing,' Gabriel said, also in Shinali. 'The woman here, she's my mother. Soldiers, they must not . . . ah . . .' He groped for the right words.

Ashila said, also in Shinali, 'We're all knowing, Darshan. Don't be fearing.'

Lena listened, thinking how strange it was to hear Gabriel speak Shinali. She remembered Myron's funeral, and Gabriel's visit then to the Shinali, and she remembered the name of Ashila, the one he had grown to love. She looked at the young woman who helped him now, wondering. The girl glanced up at Lena and smiled, and Lena knew. A great joy went through her, and a sorrow. She thought about the Shinali carving she had seen sometimes around Gabriel's neck when he was a boy, and wondered if he still wore it. What was the connection? Lifelong it was, powerful, and she could not even begin to understand it.

She looked past him, to the interior of the barracks. Beds were spread on woven grass matting, all in tidy rows, with narrow pathways left between. Several Shinali lay there sleeping, and Lena wondered if they were ill. There were cooking pots and bundles of clothes piled tidily along the walls. Dust lay over everything, and the place was grubby, despite the obvious attempts at cleanliness. From somewhere came the smell of latrines, and the warm air was full of flies. They buzzed around Lena's head and crawled over Gabriel as he worked.

Tarkwan's eyes opened a slit, and he studied Gabriel's mother. 'Were you one of the farmers who sent us blankets and food, when the winter was a high lot bad?' he asked.

'Yes. I organised it,' she replied. 'I hope you didn't mind that we came on your land.'

'Your blankets warmed our bodies as much as your kindness warmed our hearts,' said Tarkwan. 'I thank you. We'll not be forgetting.'

'I hope . . . was hoping that this spring we'd be able to trade seeds for crops, and that you would show us how to care properly for sheep,' said Lena. 'I was hoping we could be friends, living together in peace. I want you to know that I love the land I bought from you, and will look after it well.'

'The time of peace will come,' said Tarkwan, 'and we will be helping you.'

One of the soldiers gave a hard laugh and lowered the point of his sword to Tarkwan's throat. 'Keep your mouth shut, dog!' he spat. 'The only peace you'll get is in the grave.'

Fortunately, just then Gabriel finished. 'It's done now, Tarkwan,' he said, standing up and leaving Ashila to wash the wound and bind it. Thandeka brought him a bowl of water, and he washed his hands, and also the scissors and knife. He handed the instruments to the guards, hoping they would leave. But they did not.

Not daring to ask them to go, in case it aroused suspicions, Gabriel said to Lena, 'Thank you for waiting. You'd better show me these medicines you've brought, and explain what they are.'

'Just simple herbs and potions, all labelled,' Lena replied, taking the cloth off the basket, and picking up a small pot of ointment. She handed it to him, and for an instant their fingers touched. Longing to embrace, to speak freely, they simply smiled. 'It's good of you to bring them,' Gabriel said. 'My helper here, Ashila, she's grateful, too.'

Ashila stood, and Lena saw that she was almost as tall as Gabriel himself. They looked fine together, so fine. Lena bent her head over her basket, hiding her emotion. 'There are other things here,' she said, fumbling with the contents. 'There are bandages, too. But no soap. I wish I'd bought soap. I should have thought . . .'

Conscious of the soldiers, Gabriel put his hand across Lena's, steadying her, giving her peace. 'What you've brought is priceless to us,' he said. 'Thank you. It was thoughtful of you to come. It means more to us than I can say.'

'Other farmers came with me,' she said. 'We've brought food for the Shinali, clean clothes, and some games for the children. I don't know if we'll be able to come again. The commander said we weren't to make a habit of it. But if we can come, is there anything else you need?'

'News,' he said. 'Do you know how long we are going to be here?'

One of the soldiers stepped forward. 'This isn't a social visit,' he said to Lena. 'Just hand over the medicines and go.'

As Lena handed Gabriel the basket, she said, 'A friend of mine, also a healer, visited me early this morning. He is going to talk to the Empress. He said –'

'Enough, woman!' said the soldier. 'And I'll have the basket. I'll search it first.'

It was given to him, and he rifled through it, removing a pair of scissors and a needle.

'They were for simple surgery,' protested Lena. 'They're hardly weapons.'

'With the Shinali,' said the soldier, 'even little stones are weapons.' He gave the basket to Gabriel and indicated with his sword that Lena should go.

One last time she gazed at Gabriel. They were both near tears, both longing to speak. Suddenly, before they could give themselves away, Lena turned and hurried back to the gates. As she crossed the courtyard a Shinali child ran up to her and shyly thanked her for the apple he was eating. Lena took the child's hand and they walked together to the gates. It was the last image Gabriel had of his mother – that walk of hers across the yellow dust, hand-in-hand with the Shinali child. He thought of the Time of the Eagle, the prophecy of the renewed nations; of what Ashila had said about the farmers being the good branch, that part of the old Navora that would survive and live in unity with the restored Shinali people. For the first time he realised the full worth of his mother's dreams and decisions and insights. Overwhelmed with gratitude and hope, he watched as she walked through the gates with the other farmers and disappeared into the brightness outside.

A month passed, and spring blazed into summer. Every five days supply wagons came to the fort, bringing firewood and food, but if Razzak received new information about the fate of the Shinali, he kept it to himself. The physician he had requested never arrived. Several times Gabriel pleaded with Razzak to let the Shinali wash in the river and drink fresh water, but the commander refused. He also refused Gabriel's request that some of the soldiers hunt deer in the mountains, to supplement the paltry supplies allocated to the Shinali. Adult prisoners often went hungry so children would have enough to eat, and they all suffered diarrhoea and vomiting from the contaminated well water. Moved to pity, some of the soldiers shared their rations with the Shinali children, and often brought them fresh drinking water from the river. But even this was a mixed blessing: one of the soldiers, suffering from measles, passed it on to a Shinali child. Having never known measles before, the Shinali had no natural resistance to the disease; it spread like wildfire, killing four of the children and two adults. Several more remained seriously ill.

Twice more the farmers came to the fort, bringing baskets of fresh fruit and vegetables, along with medical supplies and bundles of firewood, but Razzak did not let them through the gates. Gabriel did not see his mother again.

Almost every night Gabriel meditated, trying to commune with Sheel Chandra. Though he could move in his mind within the Citadel and once saw Salverion slumped wearily in a chair, his head bent in his hands, unreachable, he never found the Master of Mind-power. After a time he no longer tried, saving his energies for healing, and to assuage the unrest and desperation he sensed in the Shinali. Healing was becoming increasingly difficult, as his body became weaker.

One morning, exhausted after sitting with a boy critically ill from dysentery, Gabriel left the stifling barracks to go and rest. The morning was only half gone, but already the trapped air between the high stone walls was close and suffocating, and the flies were intolerable. As he crossed the courtyard, Gabriel stepped carefully between the rows of Shinali bedding and sleeping mats spread out to air in the sun. The children played as near to the shade of the porch as they dared, and some of the married soldiers, missing their own children in Navora, were showing them tricks with cards, or telling them stories. The young people were gathered in a shelter in the back of the fort, where firewood had once been stored. It was little more than a broken tile roof propped up by wooden beams, but it gave shade and was their own place.

All the healthy adults were busy. Some washed clothes, while others made a fire with wood salvaged from the rotting upper floors of the barracks. Using sharp stones, others skinned a rabbit that had come in the last wagon, and threaded vegetables on sticks, for roasting. Ashila was with them. They joked with Gabriel as he went by, asking whether, with his strange powers, he could freshen mouldy turnips. 'Not turnips, sorry,' he said, 'only flowers. Find those, and we'll be having a feast a high lot good.' Their laughter followed him as he climbed the stairs of his tower.

A wisp of breeze came into the high room, and Gabriel stopped for a few moments to enjoy it, and to look at the distant sea. He could see, on the far side of the farmlands where the wooded hills bordered the coast, the old road he had run along that day when he first met Ashila. Then the road had been deserted, but now it was dotted with people. Dust rose about them, and they seemed to hurry, as if they fled something terrible.

As Gabriel stared down at them, a terrible foreboding came over him. Sheltering his eyes with his hand, he looked at Navora. The city slumbered under the blazing skies, appearing, as always, majestic and serene, but outside Navora's walls many fires burned, their smoke drifting black across the dazzling towers and domes.

For a long time Gabriel looked, uncertain, full of dread. Did the smoke come from funeral pyres for the dead, too many to be buried in the city's mausoleums? But if the plague was so bad, why were people leaving? What had happened to the ban on travel, to prevent the sickness from spreading? Was there no law and order any more?

A sound in the courtyard below made Gabriel turn around.

Far below, Tarkwan was limping near the barrack steps, his voice raised in anger. Several youths went over to talk to him, and he shouted at them in Shinali. Gabriel did not understand everything that was said, but realised Tarkwan was looking for something and accusing the youths of taking it.

A soldier began to walk across the courtyard, treading carefully between the rows of bedding. Halfway across, he crouched and picked up something from the dust. Gabriel could not see what it was. The soldier glanced up at Tarkwan, then turned and took back to the porch whatever he had found.

Outside the barracks Tarkwan shouted again, and one of the youths answered brashly. It was Yeshi. Other Shinali men joined them, with the youths Tarkwan had accused before. The chieftain's rage was becoming ugly, the argument violent. Soldiers were leaving the shade of the porch, their swords unsheathed. Officer Razzak stepped out into the courtyard and called Tarkwan's name.

Tarkwan turned towards the gathered soldiers. Between them, vivid in the sun, lay the Shinali blankets and frayed sleeping mats. Three of the soldiers started walking over them, towards Tarkwan. Gabriel shouted down a warning, to remind the soldiers that sleeping mats were sacred and not to be walked on, but he was too high up, and they could not hear him. In horror, Gabriel watched as Tarkwan strode down the gaps between the blankets, reached the first soldier, and hit him hard across the face. The soldier collapsed. His two companions flung themselves at Tarkwan, and the three of them fell on the blankets, fighting. The Shinali men rushed to Tarkwan's aid, and soldiers ran at them with their swords, yelling threats. One of the Shinali was wounded, and he fell to his knees on the blankets, clutching his abdomen and screaming.

Something broke in the Shinali, broke in all of them, and suddenly there were men fighting everywhere, and shouts and tumult, and swords slashing through the rising dust. Everywhere people screamed. Appalled, helpless, Gabriel watched from the tower. As quickly as it began, the clamour subsided. Then there was silence, but for the wailing of children. Through settling dust Gabriel saw the jumbled bedding, and several Shinali men fallen across it. Already Tarkwan was being dragged away, still fighting, restrained by six soldiers. Across the courtyard the women were standing by their pots of washing and the fire, their faces ashen and full of disbelief. The fight had lasted only a few seconds.

Shaking, Gabriel rushed down the stairs. Numb with horror and grief, he walked among the wounded, bending over them tenderly, finding their wounds. Across the trampled bedding five men lay dead, cut down helplessly as they had rushed to help their chieftain. Two of them were the youths who had argued with Tarkwan only moments before. Three others lay injured, Yeshi among them. Gabriel went and knelt by them, tearing strips from their clothes and making tourniquets to stop the worst of their bleeding. Ashila came and knelt beside him to help, her face streaked with dust and tears.

Behind them the massive gates were opened, grating on the parched dust. Gabriel and Ashila looked around and saw Tarkwan being dragged out by six soldiers. Other soldiers went with them, and the gates were shut. Soon afterwards they heard a cry, defiant and full of rage, and then only the sounds of an awful beating, and helpless struggle, and chains rattling on the sun-scorched wood.

'Do you know anything about this, Darshan?' Razzak asked, as he placed a bone knife into Gabriel's hands.

Gabriel turned the knife over, inspecting it. It was cleverly made from animal bones. The handle was roughly shaped to fit securely into a man's fist, but the blade was sleek and smooth, the edges honed from hours of polishing with dust and ash. It was unsophisticated and deadly, and strangely beautiful.

'I don't know anything about it,' Gabriel said, handing the knife back to the officer.

Razzak placed it on the table between them. His eyes, uncomfortably shrewd, searched Gabriel's face. 'If you're lying to me,' he said, 'and I find out, I'll have you and every Shinali male flogged.'

'I'm not lying,' said Gabriel evenly, meeting the soldier's eyes. 'I don't know anything about this knife. I don't know who made it, or how, or when.'

'They were plotting a revolt,' said Razzak.

'I knew nothing about that, sir. I swear it. If I'd known, I'd have talked them out of it.'

Razzak sat down and reached for some parchment. On the shelf behind him were stacks of his daily reports, scrupulously kept.

Gabriel looked out of the window and saw the women taking the bedding back into the barracks. Two youths staggered about, clutching injuries that dripped scarlet on the dust. Inside the barracks, Thandeka and Ashila were laying the wounded out ready for healing.

'You'd better go and stitch the fools up,' said Razzak.

'May I see Tarkwan too, please sir?'

'No.'

'Will he be given water?'

'No.' Razzak dipped his pen in a bottle of ink, preparing to write his report on the day's rebellion.

Gabriel steeled himself for an argument. 'He'll die in this heat, sir. I beg you, in the name of everything fine that Navora stands for, to bring him back in.'

Razzak almost laughed. 'Why? So he can stir up his rabble again?'

'They're not rabble. They're a nation.'

'They're rebels against Her Majesty's army, and he's the main agitator. If you bother me again about him, or I have any trouble from his people, he'll die of something worse than heat. Now go.'

Not for the first time, Gabriel thought of his hidden gold, and of bribery. With any other commander it might have worked, but Razzak, with his almost obsessive allegiance to order and army regulations, was beyond corruption. Furious, frustrated, Gabriel left the office.

For the rest of the morning he and Ashila sewed up wounds. Thandeka helped, while Zalidas chanted his desperate prayers. People sat in the sun on the steps and looked towards the gates, their eyes dry and blazing with helpless outrage. Six soldiers guarded the gates, their crossbows ready with arrows laid in place. Guards, fully armed and alert, were everywhere.

When Gabriel's work was done, he lay on an empty bed by the wounded and dozed, trying to ignore the flies and the stench from the latrines. Ashila came and sat down by him.

'Tarkwan was plotting to use that knife he made, wasn't he?' Gabriel asked, in Navoran.

'Yes. We had a plan. But everything happened before time, and we weren't ready. The knife, it was hidden in Tarkwan's blankets, and he was angry that his bed was being moved without –'

'Why didn't you tell me about this?' he demanded, sitting up to confront her.

'Because you would have forbidden it.'

'You see why?'

'No,' she replied angrily. 'I'm not seeing why, Gabriel. Why would you forbid us to fight for our freedom?'

'Because you'd all die.'

'And we're not dying now?' She looked around at the sick, and cried, 'You think this is life, Gabriel? You think this slow dying from sickness and heartbreak is better than a quick death in a fight for freedom?'

'Keep your voice down.'

'I'll speak as I wish! We'll *all* do as we wish. You're not our chieftain. If my people choose to fight for freedom, we will. If we die in that fight, that's dying with more honour and purpose than the way we die now, locked up in this stink.'

'Be quiet! You'll end up out there with Tarkwan!'

'I'd be more glad out there with him, than being in here like this. From ancient times, my people have never been inside walls. Always, we've had some land, some part of earth and sky and water to call our own. Now we're having nothing.'

'I know how you feel, but if you fight –'

'You're not knowing! You're not Shinali!'

Gabriel got up and went and sat on the steps, his back to her. He was shaking, deeply hurt. It was the first time they had argued.

Ashila came and stood beside him, staring down into his stony face. 'You never want to fight,' she said. 'When the soldiers were coming to our house and we made war with them, you ran. After –'

'That's not fair! I ran because I had to! You told me to! Because if I'd stayed –'

'You ran! And then you talked Tarkwan into making us all run! And see where we ran to? A trap in a stone cage. Your words are not all the time good, Gabriel. If we told you our plans, you'd have told us not to fight. So we kept it secret.'

'You should have told me. Don't cut me off, Ashila. I'm one of you.'

'No you're not. You're Navoran. You're afraid. You wouldn't go and see Salverion because you were afraid, and now it's too late. You're afraid of your own name, afraid of pain, afraid of death, afraid of –'

'I am *not* afraid!'

'You are! You won't fight, won't suffer for freedom, or land, or –'

'I have suffered!' he cried, standing up. 'I could have gone to the ship, I could have left for another kind of life! But I chose to be here with you! I *chose* this, Ashila – it wasn't forced on me. I chose to be locked up with your people, rather than be free. I chose it out of oneness with you, out of love.'

'I was thinking you'd be sorry for it, one day.'

'I'm not sorry!'

'Then why are you against us?'

'I'm not against you!'

'You are! We want one thing, you want another! You don't listen to us, Gabriel! You never listen! All times you know best, your Navoran way must be our way. But you're wrong. This time you're wrong.' She lowered her voice, and said, 'We want to fight. We want to fight for our freedom, for a part of earth to call our own, for some river and some sky. And if we all die in that fight, that's our destiny.'

'The river and sky aren't worth dying for. Nothing's worth dying for.'

'Nothing's what my people die for now. Nothing! Better to die for freedom, for hope.'

'That's madness.'

'It's Shinali braveness. Something you don't have.'

She turned and went over to the tower. Gabriel sank down on the step, his head in his hands. Minutes later Ashila was back, her bedding and spare clothes in her arms.

'What are you doing?' he asked, as she brushed past.

'I'm being with my people again,' she said, 'and no more above them.'

21 Visions of Fire

THE DAY WORE ON, and the heat in the barracks became intense. People lay on their beds, inert. Even the sick stopped groaning, and an awful hush fell across the fort. In the room in the tower, Gabriel sat and tried to gather his scattered energies. But he was tired, tired in his mind and body and soul, and it was a long time before he reached the point of stillness and replenishment.

Outside, on the gate, Tarkwan moved his lips in the form of the All-father's name, and fought to gather his strength. His wrists and ankles were raw and bleeding from the iron rings, and the weight of his body on his outspread arms cramped his chest muscles, making breathing difficult. Blinking the sweat out of his eyes, he looked across the river at the sacred mountain. Its brown slopes blurred in the scorched air, and the fierce light crashed and thundered in the sky. Images wavered in the heat: the face of a young man, fierce and resolute, with long hair that flowed and became the feathers and wings of an eagle, the engraving on the ancient *torne*, the forerunner, the one who would begin the Time of the Eagle, the fulfilment of the great Shinali dream to win back all they had lost. Marvelling, Tarkwan realised who it was. The images burned in the sun, melted. Tarkwan's body throbbed, became a part of the heat and brightness and pain that filled the universe. Lowering his gaze, he saw the road with people walking along it. A wagon came, drawn by horses. Dust rose, and the river glittered. Tarkwan half fainted, his mouth parched.

There was a rumbling in the earth, and voices echoed. A darkness passed in front of him, and something cool touched his lips. Water. Water cold and blessed, running down his face and body, and into his mouth, on his tongue. He drank, sobbing with joy and release, thinking he was in the realms of the All-father. He gave a great soundless cry: 'Moondarri!'

A hand touched his face, and a bowl was pressed against his cracked lips. He opened his eyes. A Navoran man stood there, holding the bowl up to him. The man's eyes were grey, his face red with the heat or a fever, and sweat ran down his cheeks and into his beard.

'Take a bit more,' he said kindly. Tarkwan drank, crying, his lips bleeding against the stained bowl.

Behind the man stood a woman with two children. She tried to hide their faces in her dress, but they peeked at the naked Shinali transfixed on the gate, and wondered at him. Behind them was a wagon, and in it another woman, lying sick. When the man had finished giving water to Tarkwan, he went to the wagon and dropped the bowl into a bucket of water near the sick woman. Then they all got on the wagon again, and went on.

Tarkwan closed his eyes against the light, and wept for the vision of Moondarri and Paradise that had come, and briefly shone, and vanished again.

Evening fell, and Gabriel went back to the Shinali barracks to check the wounds of those who had been hurt that morning. Each one in distress he sat with for a while, his hands on the great nerve pathways of their pains, easing them, freeing them. Afterwards he found Ashila sitting on the barrack steps. They had not spoken since their argument that afternoon, and he was afraid she would get up and leave. But she stayed where she was, so he sat with her, and together they watched the yellow moon rise above the old fort walls.

'I'm sorry for not understanding you better,' Gabriel said. 'I've lived inside stone walls all my life, I've got no idea what this must be like for you and your people. I'm sorry.'

'I'm being sorry, too,' she said. 'I was wrong. Your heart, it's half Shinali.'

'More than half,' he said.

'I know. I'm being sorry I hurt you.'

'What hurt most was your saying that I had no bravery. All my life I've been called a coward. First by my father, then Salverion, and Jaganath. And now you.'

'I was wrong. What you told the Empress, that took bravery.'

'Did it? I had no choice then, Ashila. The times I have had a choice, I've always run. What you said was true: if it comes to fighting, to risking pain or death, I'm a coward.'

'You didn't always run. You spoke truth before: you stayed here with us, out of love. I'm thinking love and braveness, they weigh the same.'

The moon rose higher, and Ashila yawned and leaned her head on Gabriel's shoulder. 'I put my things back in the tower,' she said.

'Why?'

'I chose you.'

'I don't want you to have to choose between your people and me. I wanted the room in the tower because I need privacy. If you like, we'll sleep back in the barracks again. I don't care, so long as we're together. I can't bear being out of tune with you. I love you, Ashila. You're my life. Without you, I have nothing.'

'You're my life, too,' she said. 'I was angry today, I was

shaking your canoe the hardest way I could. Then I realised it was my canoe, too.'

'We'll keep our *Ta-sarn-ee*, then?'

'We'll keep it,' she said. 'But tonight I'm so tired you'll have to push me up the stairs.'

'You're the strong one,' he replied. 'You should push me.'

He slipped his arm around her shoulders. His fingers stroked her neck, then wandered down, gentle and pleasuring, inside her clothes. The feel of her skin, her womanness, still amazed him. Suddenly his hand stopped, cupped over her breast.

'This used to be a smaller handful,' he said.

She smiled and kissed him. 'You miss a lot, for a healer.'

'Ashila? Are you . . .?'

She nodded, her smile brilliant.

'But how? You told me you were taking your herbs, to prevent this!'

'I said we had herbs. I didn't say I was taking them.'

He started to laugh, astounded, his face flushed in the moonlight. Hugging her, laughing, he picked her up in his arms and carried her across the dust towards their tower. He was almost dancing, joy-wild.

'You said you were tired,' she reminded him, her lips against his.

'That was a hundred years ago,' he said, kissing her ardently, 'before I knew we're pregnant.'

'And you're being strong, now?' she asked.

'You've no idea how strong. I'll show you.'

'You'll push me up the stairs?'

'I'll fly you up on eagle's wings, and then I'll love you like I've never loved you before.'

He tripped and almost fell with her in the dust. 'Careful,

eagle-man,' she said, clinging with her arms around his neck. 'You'll be messing up your feathers.'

He pushed open the tower door and staggered with her up the first few stairs. Gradually he stopped, gasping, and put her down. His limbs were trembling from weakness and hunger. 'Sorry,' he said. 'I think I've crashed before I've even taken flight. I seem to mess up all the great events.'

'I'm hoping you don't mess up this next one,' she said, getting behind him and pushing him up the stairs.

Early next morning one of the soldiers banged on the door of the tower where Gabriel and Ashila slept, and began climbing the stairs. He was about Gabriel's age, and the two were friends, for Gabriel shaved in the soldiers' barrack room every morning. Bleary-eyed, his hair still tousled from sleep, Gabriel met him halfway down.

'A woman from the farms just brought this,' the soldier said, handing a basket to Gabriel. It was covered with a white cloth. 'Razzak checked it. It's medicines.'

Gabriel took the basket, smiling. The cloth was embroidered with blue irises, Lena's favourite flowers. He remembered watching her make the cloth, when he was very small. 'God knows, we need them,' he said. 'Thanks, Embry.'

'The woman came just as I was out getting river water for the children,' Embry told him. 'I talked to her for a while. She was upset at seeing Tarkwan on the gates like that. She wanted to give him water, but he was unconscious, so we didn't go near him. She also wanted to come in and see you, but there's bulai fever in the city again, and Razzak won't let anyone in except the soldiers with the supply wagons. I said I'd make sure you got the medicines and the instructions she wanted to give you.'

'Are the farmers all right?' asked Gabriel, alarmed.

'Yes, they're all fine. Like us, they're safely isolated. She asked me to tell you that the physician who gave her the medicines mixed them especially, so you could treat the dysentery and liver sickness. She said the drugs are strong, and you need only a few drops in water. Also, the physician has given you a book on the treatment of infectious diseases. He's written a few notes himself in the back, which he thought might be helpful. I'm sorry you couldn't see her, I had the feeling she had other things she wanted you to know. I asked Razzak twice if she could see you, but he was unbending, as usual.'

'Thank you. You're a good friend,' said Gabriel. 'Not just to me, but to the Shinali.'

'I wish I could do more.' Embry sighed. 'I never thought, when I joined the army, that I'd be stuck in a fort guarding prisoners, half of them children.'

'Did the woman tell you any news from outside?'

'Only that there's plague, and political unrest. Maybe the Empress has forgotten we're here.' He grinned ruefully, and went back down the stairs.

In the tower room, Ashila was still in bed, sleeping fitfully. Gabriel sat in a patch of early morning sun and unwrapped the cloth in the basket. His hands shook a little, and he touched the contents lovingly, knowing his mother had packed them. He noticed the book Embry had mentioned and picked it up. It was a tattered medical textbook, similar to one he had used often in his first medical training with Hevron, in the Navoran Infirmary. It seemed a lifetime ago. Recalling Embry's words about a message, he turned the pages. Written inside the back cover were brief notes on isolating the sick. The handwriting was Salverion's.

Hardly able to breathe for apprehension and joy, he examined the book more closely. The back cover was unusually thick, the leather on the inside torn partway down the spine. Carefully he worked his fingers into the tiny gap, felt parchment, fine and smooth. Gently he drew it out, unfolded it. He sniffed it, smelled the scents of the Citadel, the mingled fragrances of incense and gardens. The handwriting, small and dense to cover the single page, was also Salverion's.

Dearest son, the Master had written. *With all my heart, I wish I could visit you and see your face one more time. But I cannot risk betraying your identity, and this letter is hazardous enough. I hope it gets safely into your hands. Please burn it immediately when you have finished it.*

It grieves me deeply to warn you that the judgement against you still stands, and Jaganath has offered a fortune for information leading to your arrest. If he finds you, even the Empress will not be able to save you. Remember this, in whatever you decide to do.

There is much to tell you, and I must be brief. Perhaps you know that people are fleeing the city. There are two reasons. Bulai fever is here, and all physicians, including the Citadel healers, have been called upon to fight it. Panic is widespread, and people ignore the ban on travel. The other reason people flee is Jaganath. His influence grows stronger by the day. All are intimidated; those who challenge him disappear or are murdered. Even those once utterly loyal to the Empress now follow Jaganath, afraid that if they do not he will have their wives and children killed. No one who threatens his influence is safe. Even at the Citadel we do not escape his wrath: he has seeded rumours, slandered many of the Masters, and created distrust and doubt. No one trusts anyone. The whole city is divided; people live in suspicion and fear, and there is no way we can unite against him.

There is no plague in the Citadel, or among the farmers. You will be safe in the fort, as you are isolated. Safe from plague, at least. But there is another danger, and I must tell you about it. Whether or not you tell the Shinali is your decision.

Jaganath's power over the Empress is very great. She dares not defy him, for fear of the demons that he causes her to see. I have visited her several times, and she has pleaded with me to release her from the appalling apparitions, but in spite of all I do for her, she still perceives the demons as being alive. I can do no more. The only person who can help her now is Sheel Chandra, and he has suffered a heart seizure and is himself quite ill. Perhaps that is why, if you have been trying to contact him again, you have not been able. The mind-force is much weakened if the body is ill or overstrained. So the Empress remains in her terrors, and Jaganath rules Navora through her. But in one thing she stands strong against him: he wants the Shinali wiped out, and she is determined to save them. The Shinali, and the prophecy of the Time of the Eagle, are all that come between Jaganath and his ambition to be Emperor.

The Empress believes that the Time of the Eagle is near at hand. She has told me she sees the Navora she loves falling under Jaganath's influence, and longs for the cleansing even though it means the end of her rule, and the end of the Empire as we know it. She would have the Shinali freed, so the prophecy may be fulfilled; Jaganath would have the Shinali utterly destroyed, so that he would hold unrivalled power over the Empire. And so the Shinali have become trapped in the middle of this terrible struggle.

The genocide of their race would not be difficult: Razzak has committed such acts before, on strong nations scattered across land and well able to fight. This tiny nation trapped in stone walls, already weakened by hunger and disease, and disarmed, would be an easy matter for him. He waits only for Jaganath's command. I do not know how much longer the Empress can withstand him, before she abdicates the throne and leaves everything in his power. I think it is only a matter of days.

I tell you this only after a great deal of prayer, having searched my heart and soul. It is not by chance that your bond with the Shinali has been a driving force in your life, not by chance that you are with them now. I wish I could help, but the solution lies in your hands. It is the supreme joy and honour of my life to have known you and worked alongside you, and, in my small way, to have shared your remarkable destiny.

You will know what to do, when the time is right. Be strong: all heaven stands about you.

I love you well.

Salverion.

Three times Gabriel read the letter. Then he took a flint, and struck a tiny spark on to the parchment. As it burned he dropped it over the edge of the tower window, and it floated down, ash white, and fell to dust across the Shinali land.

He went over to Ashila. Her dress, damp with sweat, clung to her thin form, and her face looked pale and strained. Anxiously he knelt and put his hand on her forehead. She was feverish. She moaned in her sleep, and turned to him. Without waking her he lay down, holding her in his arms. After a long time he got up, went over to the window again, and looked out. Along the road from the city people still fled, smaller groups now, many of them alone, the last survivors, perhaps, of families.

From the barracks behind him rose a loud wail, and people mourned and lamented, and he knew someone else had died. He looked at Ashila lying curled up on their bed, her hands clenched, her face beaded with sweat.

He sat on the wide window ledge, leaned against one of the pillars supporting the tower roof, and looked across the hills, across the Citadel and the sprawling city, to the skies. 'Sovereign

Lord,' he prayed, 'give me wisdom to know your dream for me. Give me courage to live that dream. Give me strength to fulfil the task before me, knowing it was designed for me alone. Give me peace in the knowledge that I have been given everything I need. So that what I do has value in your sight, give me love. Make me a worthy son of yours.'

Then he closed his eyes and rested. Afterwards he was never sure whether he dozed and dreamed, or whether he had a vision, but he saw fire in the sky, and vast clouds of smoke torn by gigantic winds. Out of the confusion came a fiery red horse, wounded and furious, slashing with its hooves at something in the cloud. After a while the horse disintegrated, and Gabriel saw an eagle drifting in its smoke. The bird was so huge he could see its eyes burning like amber, and the sheen of individual feathers. It was magnificent, breathtaking. Far below it, the fort gates were open wide, and outside there was no road, no farmland, or city, or sea, only a pure light and a glorious white wind. And Gabriel knew, although he saw nothing in that whiteness, that beyond the gate were two destinies, two nations, and that the deliverance of one, the cleansing and restoration of the other, and the prophetic rebirth of them both, depended completely on what he did now.

At long last he faced the truth of who and what he was. He groaned, overwhelmed, fighting the truth, not wanting it, yet knowing it was inescapable, long destined, and he wept, plucking at the small leather bag that hung against his heart.

When he opened his eyes again it was late afternoon. Behind him Ashila still slept, her lashes dark and wet on her cheeks. A great peace fell across him. He knelt and kissed her lips, and she smiled in her sleep and murmured something loving in her native tongue.

'I love you, Shinali woman,' he whispered.

She did not wake, and he went down the stairs and along the porch towards Razzak's office. As he went, he pulled open the leather bag and removed the pledge-ring.

Parchments were spread across the makeshift desk in the office, and a bottle of ink was opened. Officer Razzak was writing his daily report. He looked up as Gabriel came in. 'What is it now, boy?'

Gabriel placed something on the desk. Razzak leaned across and picked it up. 'Where did you get this?' he asked, astounded.

'From the Empress,' said Gabriel. 'It's a pledge-ring.'

'I know very well what it is. I also know there are only ten of these in the whole Empire. Did you steal it from a corpse, or did she really give it to you?'

'She gave it.'

Razzak was silent, his sharp eyes narrow as he scrutinised Gabriel's face. Then he asked, 'What's your request to her?'

'That's my business, sir. May I have parchment and ink, so I can write to Her Majesty?'

Razzak pushed a few sheets across the desk. Gabriel selected a page that was cleaner than the others and picked up the pen. Dipping it in the ink, he began to write. His hands were trembling, and he dropped blobs of ink on the parchment. He took another page, shook the excess ink from the pen, and began again.

To Her Majesty, Petra, Empress of the Navoran Empire: Greetings, he wrote.

A year ago, Lady, you were good enough to give me this pledge-ring. I return it now, with the request that the Shinali people in Taroth Fort be allowed to go free.

I implore you with all my heart to grant me this favour, and to hold true to your pledge-promise.

I know this will be difficult, because of the strangling weed that threatens you, threatens everything we both cherish. I beg you also to remember, Lady, that in your dream you freed yourself from the weed; you were not overcome. I pray that you will be strong. The final word is yours, to set the eagle free.

For as long as I live I remain your faithful servant,

Gabriel Eshban Vala

He put down the pen and stood up. 'I'd like Embry to take this, please,' he said. Carefully he rolled the letter, and began to leave.

Razzak moved in front of the doorway. His hand was held out, palm up, and his face was inexorable. 'I'll give it to Embry,' he said.

'It's private, sir.'

'Nothing leaves this fort without my approval and permission.'

'You've no right to read this. You have no authority over me.'

'My authority over you began the moment you asked to stay in here. Either hand that letter over, or tear it up. It won't leave this fort without my consent. Neither will your pledge-ring.'

Gabriel gave Razzak the scroll and the pledge-ring, and left the office. He went back to the tower. Ashila was still asleep, and for that he was grateful. Silently he removed all his gold from its hiding place between broken floorboards and placed it within her roll of precious herbs. Long ago he had told her the value of the gold, and what it could buy from Navorans greedy enough for it. He hoped she would remember and use it wisely. Then he sat to wait, fighting to still the storm in his heart.

From the courtyard below, a soldier called Gabriel's name. He kissed Ashila while she slept, and stroked her hair and the cherished contours of her face. Then he got up and went downstairs.

Razzak was alone in the dim office, standing in front of his desk. Gabriel waited, his throat dry and his heart thundering in his ears. Very slowly Razzak came over to him. Without warning he lifted his left hand and hit Gabriel hard across the face. Before Gabriel could regain his balance, he hit him again. Gabriel collapsed on the floor, and Razzak kicked him in the abdomen. He was about to kick him again but thought better of it.

'I'd break your neck, if there wasn't a price on it,' Razzak spat. 'Traitor.'

Groaning, retching, Gabriel rolled on to his knees. The room seemed to whirl about him, and there was a ringing in his ears.

'I asked my men if any of them had heard of Gabriel Eshban Vala,' said Razzak. 'One of them had. He remembered hearing about a healer-priest who spoke treason against the Empire.'

'It wasn't treason,' said Gabriel hoarsely, gripping the edge of the desk and hauling himself to his feet. He tried to add, 'It was truth,' but his voice failed him.

'You disgust me,' said Razzak, with loathing. 'I thought you cared for the Shinali, and all the time you've been using them, hiding here with them, so you could escape the death penalty. What I can't understand is why you're not asking for your pardon. Do you realise you have only one request?'

'I know. It's for Shinali freedom.'

'In that case, you'll become my prisoner and I'll take you back to Navora for execution. Now tell me, do you still want your filthy savages to go free?'

Gabriel nodded, and Razzak shook his head in disbelief. 'If that's the way you want it,' he said, 'I'll send Embry to the Empress with your pledge-ring and appeal, and I'll keep you here under arrest. Since we'll be leaving soon, I'll have the chieftain brought in off the gates. I'll have the pleasure of returning to

Navora with two political prisoners – a traitor and a rebel leader. You can die together. Meanwhile, you and he will stay under that old wood shelter, opposite the Shinali barracks, away from the clan. Your girlfriend sleeps with the rest of the natives, in their barracks. As soon as we're out of here, I personally will deliver you, and the chieftain, to the Navoran authorities.'

22 Transfiguration

GABRIEL GAVE TARKWAN a drink of water, then sat back on his heels and watched as the chieftain slept again. Over them was a small tile roof, supported on wooden poles. Tarkwan lay there in the purple shade, his washed skin oiled and shining. Beads of sweat gathered on the oil and trickled down on to his clean sleeping mat. His wrists and ankles, cut and bruised by the iron rings, were bandaged. On his chest glowed the carved bone, with the sign of the eagle and the man.

Briefly, Gabriel touched Tarkwan's brow, felt the skin burning. His fever was unlike that of other people, and it worried Gabriel. He glanced across the bright courtyard to the Shinali barracks and saw Tarkwan's brother, Yeshi, talking to the clan's priest. Were they plotting another revolt? Gabriel sighed and rubbed his temples where his head ached. Whatever was happening, he could do nothing. He and Tarkwan were isolated, and visitors were forbidden. Guards brought food and water. Gabriel left the shelter only to visit the latrines, and to go once a day to check the Shinali sick. He hated the separation from Ashila, the long desperate hours, the uncertainty.

Embry had left the fort two days ago, and Gabriel's nerves were stretched. Someone shouted across the courtyard, and he jumped, upsetting a bowl of precious drinking water. Frantically he tried to scoop it up with his hands, but it soaked in a moment into the parched earth. He swore foully, and Tarkwan's lips pulled back in a grin. 'You're talking like the soldiers, Gabriel,' he said. He kept his eyes closed now, for the light was intolerable. His voice was very rough, and Gabriel frowned. An appalling thought crossed his mind, and he shook as he crouched beside the sick man.

'Will you let me look in your mouth, Tarkwan?' he asked.

Tarkwan's cracked lips bled as he opened them. Covering his own nose and mouth with a cloth, Gabriel carefully tilted the chieftain's head towards the sunlight. There, as clear and vivid as those he had seen in the Infirmary in Navora, were the grey patches of bulai fever.

Long moments passed, and Gabriel sat there stunned, wondering why he had not thought of it before.

'Can I be shutting my mouth now?' asked Tarkwan, with difficulty.

'Yes. Yes, of course. Tarkwan, when you were hanging on the gate, did anyone from Navora come near you?'

Tarkwan was thoughtful. 'Yes, I'm thinking they did. Water. They gave me water. They were saving my life.'

Gabriel said nothing, but he smoothed Tarkwan's hair back from his hot cheeks and placed a damp cloth on his forehead to cool him. He checked the bandages on Tarkwan's wrists and ankles, to make sure there was no blood leaking out. His mind in turmoil, he looked at his own hands to see whether he had any cuts or broken skin, trying to remember bathing the blood from Tarkwan, panicking about what he had done with the bloodied cloths.

He washed his hands in the wooden bowl of brown well water kept nearby for that purpose, and stood up.

'Wait!' said Tarkwan, opening his eyes. 'Speak the truth, Gabriel: it wasn't life they gave me, was it? It was the killing fever. The one you call bulai.'

After a few seconds, Gabriel nodded.

'Has anyone else got it?' asked Tarkwan.

'I don't think so. I'm going to check them now. I don't think it'll spread; not so long as I'm the only one looking after you, and we're kept separate from the others.'

In the barracks Gabriel went among all the sick, examining their mouths. Leaning against the barrack wall just out of the sun, Ashila watched him. 'What are you looking for?' she asked.

'I'm just checking them,' he replied, adjusting the cloth across his lower face, and kneeling to inspect someone else.

Ashila frowned, troubled, but she asked nothing more.

'I'm missing you at night,' she murmured, when he had finished examining the sick, and came to stand by her. 'Why can't we sleep in the tower now? Why won't Razzak let my mother look after Tarkwan? Why always you?'

'He doesn't want Tarkwan talking to any of his people and stirring up trouble again,' explained Gabriel. 'He's commanded me to look after Tarkwan, and no one else.'

He caressed Ashila's face, and she turned her lips to kiss his palm, but he moved away before she could.

'Something is great in your heart,' she said. 'I'm not knowing whether it's heavy or light.'

'It's both,' he said.

'Won't you tell me what it is?'

'I can't. Not yet.'

'Is it to do with Embry leaving the fort?'

He looked out across the courtyard, his eyes suddenly moist. They shimmered in the shade, blue and burning as the sky. 'Please don't ask me,' he said.

She placed her hand on his breast, directly over the bag he wore. Inside were the two things she had given him, woven of

Shinali grass: the worn-out remains of the bracelet, and the symbol woven like a figure of eight.

'Only a mourning bracelet left,' she said softly, 'and a Shinali dream.'

A tension lay across all of Taroth Fort. Soldiers argued often, and fights broke out. Gabriel noticed that the soldiers who had entertained children before now yelled at them to go away, and they did not bring in fresh water from the river for people to drink. The Shinali were ostracised.

Four days had passed since Embry left with the pledge-ring, and Tarkwan was dying. Gabriel washed his face for him and massaged his limbs and took away what pain he could. Then he crouched on the edge of Tarkwan's sleeping mat, looking across the courtyard, his head aching with suspense and fear. It was sunset, and the last strip of tawny light flamed on the dust. In the courtyard people sat around their fire, and the children gnawed on rabbit bones left over from the last meal.

Soldiers sat under the porch outside their barracks, quarrelling as they cleaned their bows and checked the bowstrings, and sharpened and polished swords. Many of them were packing their few belongings into knapsacks, ready to leave. Gabriel's heart pounded, and he felt a darkness worse than night descend across the fort.

'Death, I think it comes,' Tarkwan whispered, opening his eyes.

'It's only a shadow,' said Gabriel, touching Tarkwan's cheek. 'I'm here. I'll be with you. And Moondarri, she's waiting.'

Tarkwan closed his eyes, and his breathing became even and deep as he slept. Gabriel stroked his arm, touching the smooth scar where the doe had once leaped over the sun, and the image of the lone stag. A shadow fell across them, and Gabriel looked up and saw Razzak standing there.

'You've finished with the chieftain now,' said the officer. 'Come over to my soldiers' barracks. You're sleeping there tonight, under guard.' He was dark against the flaming sky, and Gabriel could not see his face.

'Why?' Gabriel asked, apprehensive.

'Because it's an order.'

'Who'll look after Tarkwan?'

'I don't particularly care, now.'

'What's happening, sir? Your men are preparing to leave. Are the Shinali leaving too, or is another company coming to relieve you?'

'I think you know very well what's happening,' said the officer. 'We've got plague here in the fort.'

'Who's got plague?' asked Gabriel, his voice steady, though he shook with fear. 'I haven't seen any.'

'Everyone's got it,' said Razzak, jerking his head towards the Shinali barracks. 'The place is full of it. People are too sick to move. They die nearly every day.'

'There's no plague in the barracks, I swear it,' said Gabriel. 'The people have liver sickness from the water, measles, and dysentery. They die because they're not used to such illnesses.'

'Is that what your chieftain's got? I think you lie, Gabriel. He's dying of bulai fever. Him, and the others in this stinking place. My men and I were told what to do if plague broke out here. I'll carry out those orders before daybreak, and then we'll leave. The chieftain will stay here, but you I'm taking with us. There's a massive reward offered for you, and I may as well have it. Now are you coming quietly, or do I drag you?'

'What orders?' asked Gabriel, hardly able to breathe.

'To eliminate the Shinali. They can't be freed to carry the pestilence to other places. And soldiers of the Navoran army are not expected to stay and catch it from them. Our time here is over.'

'You can't kill all these people.'

'I can, very easily.'

'What about the pledge-ring, and word from the Empress?'

'We won't hear from her now. She's got more to worry about than a traitor and a few barbarians. I've waited in this hell long enough. I'm not staying, especially with the fever here. We leave at dawn.'

'You're making a terrible mistake.'

'Am I?' said Razzak, with a bitter laugh. 'If you're so sure these people only have measles and diarrhoea, prove it to me. Otherwise tonight I carry out the final order.'

For a few moments Gabriel was silent, watching the children playing in the shimmering dirt, and the men and women talking on the steps. He looked at Yeshi, with his cares and dreams and fierce hopes; at Thandeka, with her serene optimism; at Zalidas, who held the clan's spirit in his hands, and kept it aflame. And there was Ashila, beautiful and strong and steadfast, who shared his dreams, his heart, and was more beloved to him than all else on earth.

'You can't prove it, can you?' said Razzak, impatiently. 'They're all dead, Gabriel.'

'No, they're not,' said Gabriel. 'I can prove there's no plague among them. You know how the pestilence is spread, where it comes from?'

'I know it's in the spit,' said Razzak, 'and in the blood.'

'Give me your knife,' said Gabriel. 'That little one, on your belt.'

Puzzled and hesitant, the soldier handed it to him.

Gabriel looked at Tarkwan's face. He was sleeping, perhaps unconscious. Gabriel lifted the chieftain's arm and made a long scratch underneath, on the side opposite the scar of Tarkwan's sacrament. Without faltering he scratched his own arm, from his inner wrist almost to his elbow. The blood sprang up, and he took Tarkwan's arm in a Navoran handshake. Tarkwan's eyes flickered open and he tried to speak, to pull free, but Gabriel held their wrists hard together, mingling their bloods. When he let Tarkwan go, he carefully wiped the knife blade clean and handed it back to the officer.

'By God, you're mad!' Razzak muttered, sheathing his knife. 'Mad, but convincing. I can't argue with the sharing of blood. Your measly Shinali can have the pleasure of Taroth Fort a little longer. But if we haven't heard from the Empress in two days, I'm carrying out the final command – and next time nothing will make me change my mind.' He turned and strode back to his office.

There were two bandages near the foot of Tarkwan's bed, and Gabriel took them and wound one about his right arm. His fingers were clumsy, and he could hardly see for the sweat that ran down his face and into his eyes. He bandaged Tarkwan's arm as well, and when he had finished Tarkwan whispered something in Shinali, and gripped his hand hard. While the chieftain slept again, Gabriel sat looking up at the fiery skies.

Never had they been so beautiful. Even the walls of the fort shone, and the dust in the courtyard was like gold. He looked across it at Ashila, and she glanced up and saw him watching her, and smiled. Love and peace and terror swept over him, and he covered his face with his hands, and wept.

A crescent moon came up and sailed slowly across the walls

to the west. Then the new day dawned, and still Tarkwan breathed, and still Gabriel sat by him.

Later in the morning Ashila asked permission to take water to Gabriel and Tarkwan. To her surprise, the guards allowed it. Gabriel stood in the sun with her while he drank, though the light hurt his eyes, and his head throbbed. He finished drinking and stood for a long time gazing at her face, thinking she had never looked so lovely. Lifting his right hand, he ran his fingertips down her cheek.

'What did you do to your arm?' she asked.

'I scratched it.'

She noticed the bandage on Tarkwan's arm, too, and remembered seeing Razzak with them last night, talking.

'An old woman died in the night,' she said. 'I watched while Yeshi and Zalidas buried her. There are fifteen graves outside the gates now.' Gabriel hardly heard her words; he was listening more to the rhythms of her voice, to its richness and the accent he loved. 'I talked to the guard who was with me,' Ashila continued. 'I told him it's bad that so many of us die in here. He said a strange thing. He said we Shinali don't know how lucky we are that we're not all dead by now. I asked him what he was meaning, but he wouldn't say. I'm thinking you've done something, Gabriel, and you're keeping it secret.'

He put the bowl on the ground and looked at her, aching to take her in his arms. She smiled a little, wondering why he did not. He started to say something, but at that moment there was a hammering on the gates, and the guards opened them.

A rider came in, wearing the uniform of a palace envoy. Ashila turned around to watch his arrival, and Gabriel slipped his arms about her from behind, his cheek against her hair as he looked over her shoulder. She folded her arms over his, the way she had in a time that seemed long past, when they had looked across Shinali land at the sacred mountain, and he had wept for his dead brother. Now they could see the same mountain through the open gates, and he wept again, and she was deadly afraid.

The envoy was taken into Razzak's office. Moments later Razzak came out, shouting for Gabriel. Unwillingly, he let Ashila go and began walking across the bright ground to the office. The earth seemed to rise and fall, and he had difficulty walking. Ashila ran after him and took his hand. Together they went into the office. Only Razzak and the envoy were there, the envoy looking impossibly clean and dignified. His eyes were on Gabriel.

'Are you Gabriel Eshban Vala?' he asked.

Gabriel nodded, and his hand tightened about Ashila's.

'I have something for you.'

The envoy pressed a scrolled letter into Gabriel's hand. Its wax seal was purple, stamped with the Empress's royal sign, and a purple ribbon bound it. Gabriel shook, and he could hardly break the wax. Turning away to face the window, he unrolled the letter. The words were indistinct, and he could not hold the parchment still. It was clean, so clean. A faint smell came to him, of incense and flowers. God, were there still flowers in the world?

Ashila took a corner of the page, holding it steady for him, and he read it aloud to her.

'To Gabriel Eshban Vala: Greetings.

'I have received your letter, and the pledge-ring. I had hoped that you were in a remote part of the Empire, safely away from the turmoil here. Yet when I think about it, I am not surprised that you are still here, and with the Shinali. The timing of your request is extraordinary; another day would have been too late.

'The weed has overrun the field, choked all the wheat, even noble sheaves I thought would stand strong. It threatens most of all to destroy the Shinali. I have wanted to give the command to let the Shinali go, but Jaganath's spies are everywhere, and I have not been able to send a command to Kamos and the army, without Jaganath obstructing it. Neither could I leave the palace, for demons sat in doorways, barring my way. I have felt totally defeated, a prisoner in my own palace, and could give no orders for anything except through Jaganath. But then your pledge-ring and letter came, delivered directly into my hands by a courageous young soldier who defied half the guards and Jaganath, in his determination to hand them over himself.

'Your words reminded me of something wonderfully empowering, that I had forgotten: you reminded me that in my dream I freed myself from the weed, I was not overcome. With all my heart, I thank you for that. I thank you, too, for the pledge-ring request to let the Shinali go, though I know the cost to you is great. The promise of the pledge-ring transcends all laws and edicts, and even Jaganath cannot stand against my word in response to your request. The pledge-promise, at this strange time in our history, is the one thing that can save the Shinali nation.

'And so your Shinali shall go free. This order I give, for their unconditional and enduring freedom, is the last command I give as Empress. I have abdicated my throne to Jaganath. By the time you read this, I will be in a ship leaving Navora. My one true adviser, Cosimo, will be with me, along with his family, and the few servants who remain true to me.

'I have no wish to see what Jaganath will do to this Empire I have loved; neither can I bear to think of its future collapse. However, I believe that when the eagle returns in full strength, it will bring not destruction, but a cleansing, and the restoration of what was best. I also believe you are the voice, the cry, that calls the eagle and begins the reformation. Your last words to me were that the weed had entangled us both; I prefer to think that you and I are in the wind that blows across the field of wheat, that we fly freely above the storm and, in spite of the chaos, play out our destined parts in the fulfilment of a great and splendid prophecy.

'I have always held you in my heart as a true friend. I wish now that I could ensure your safety, but the pledge-ring, as you know, was for one promise only. Know that in asking what you have, you have saved not only the Shinali, but also, ultimately, Navora.

'I wish so much to write more, to give you words of comfort and encouragement, but already my faithful steward stands waiting to help me prepare for my journey. It is a deep grief to me that I will not see your face again.

'With love and gratitude,

'Petra.'

Gabriel rolled the letter and tried to tie the ribbon around it. Ashila helped him. He placed the letter into her hands. 'Guard it well,' he said. 'It's your people's guarantee of freedom. Go and show it to Tarkwan.'

He walked with her to the office door. Before she went he whispered to her, 'Do you remember everything I told you about looking after someone with bulai fever?'

Dismayed, she nodded.

'Only Tarkwan has it,' he whispered. 'Take care, love.'

'I'll see you before you go?' she asked.

'Of course. And, Ashila – please don't tell the others about the pledge-ring. Not yet.'

She walked away across the shimmering dust and sat in the shade by Tarkwan. The chieftain opened his eyes, and she unrolled the parchment and held its strange scented whiteness in front of his face. 'It's from the Empress,' Ashila said. 'Gabriel sent her the pledge-ring, in trade for our freedom.'

Tarkwan nodded. 'He did more than that, to save us,' he said hoarsely, and told her. She listened, motionless, tears rolling down her face. When he had finished speaking, Tarkwan slept, fatigued and at peace.

Ashila looked past him, past the searing dust and the people waiting within the fortress walls. High above, an eagle soared on the summer wind, its wings dark against the sun. Her vision intensified: for a few breathless moments she could see the form of a man with a steadfast face and eyes that looked beyond, and red-gold hair that flowed and became a part of the wind and the sky, part of the joy-wild beating of the eagle's wings. She saw people on a journey, and a meeting of tribes; then a great nation, unified and strong, on its way to victory. She saw a battle, dark and terrible. When it cleared there was the Citadel, shining, gathering to itself the golden remnants of an empire, of many empires, and below it stretched vast grasslands where animals grazed and crops flourished, and people harvested together. She felt a huge sense of peace, of restoration, and rightness. Touching the sacred *torne* on Tarkwan's chest, she tried to tell him, but he was past hearing. She had the feeling he already knew.

From the porch across the courtyard Gabriel watched them until their figures blurred in the brightness, then went back into the office. The room was pitch black after the sunlight. He staggered and almost fell, and someone put a chair behind him so he could sit down. There was shouting outside: Officer Razzak was calling the Shinali and soldiers to an assembly. There was silence, and the people waited. Then came the announcement, the words loud and echoing around the old stones. 'The Empress Petra has given her final command. You are free to go.'

There was stunned silence, for a moment, then a mighty cheer, and sounds of celebration.

Before the cheers had faded, the palace envoy said to Gabriel, 'Gabriel Eshban Vala, I pronounce you prisoner of His Majesty, Lord Jaganath, eleventh ruler of the Navoran Empire. Do you understand the charge against you, and the sentence?'

'Yes.'

Razzak pulled Gabriel to his feet and forced his hands roughly behind him, crossing them at the wrists. The envoy started to bind him.

'Is this necessary?' asked Gabriel. 'I want to go back to Navora of my own free will. I won't try to escape, I give my word. Besides, I haven't the strength to run.'

The envoy thought for a while. 'Very well,' he said at last. 'I'll ride, you walk unshackled. But if you do try to escape, I'll do the executioner's job for him.'

There was the sound of the colossal gates being pushed open, clanging back against the stone walls. The envoy left the office. Gabriel followed him, though the light blinded him and he stumbled on the step. People were dark shapes moving across the shining dust. He could just make out someone being conveyed on a blanket towards the open gates. His eyesight cleared a little, and he saw that it was Tarkwan being carried. As the people took their chieftain into freedom, they sang a Shinali love song. They were still singing as they placed him by the river, overlooking the land he had loved. Soon afterwards the song turned to a lament, and Gabriel, listening, knew Tarkwan had died.

The envoy touched his prisoner's shoulder, and Gabriel went ahead of him across the courtyard to where the horse waited. It seemed strange to have the gates open wide, and people going back and forth. The soldiers were already leaving. Shinali men were raiding the soldiers' barracks, looking for their slings and knives and hunting weapons.

In the courtyard the people were preparing to leave. Not realising Gabriel had been arrested, they called cheerfully to him as he walked past. He wanted to speak their names, but could not see their faces clearly in the violent light. Everything was hazy. The sounds of happy voices intermingled with the brightness, and the clang of cooking pots sounded loud and harsh, like Navoran temple bells.

People were gathering just outside the gates, raising their hands and praying. Others were running down into the river, plunging into the cleansing coolness, rejoicing. Beyond them was the ancient fort bridge, and the road to the coastal hills and Navora. The road was well worn now, with wagon ruts deep in the dust.

The envoy mounted his horse. 'Say your farewells,' he said to Gabriel.

Gabriel looked for Ashila but could not see her. People came over to him, asking questions, their faces anxious. They remembered his trouble with Navora, and that he was accused of doing a great wrong. He did his best to encourage them, praying that his voice was steady. 'I'm not being a prisoner of this man,' he said. 'I'm going where I choose. Where's Ashila?'

Reassured, they made jokes about a half-Shinali in the city and touched his chest with their palms, honouring him, loving him. He avoided embraces, though it was hard, and his friends looked hurt. 'You want us to wait for you?' they asked. 'Our journey, there's no hurry for it. We'll be staying here and getting fat on fish and mountain goats, until you come back.'

'Don't wait,' he said.

Behind them, Yeshi and Zalidas and some of the elders were already preparing a pyre. Tarkwan's body lay wrapped in a sleeping mat, ready for cremation. People had found their stone axes and were chopping down the fort gates for wood for his funeral fire.

Yeshi came over, wearing the bone amulet, sign that he was chieftain now. Gabriel touched the bone, stroking with his fingertip the carved images of the man and the eagle merged. In the fort, musicians played, mingling funeral chants with songs of celebration. The flutes echoed in Gabriel's memory, and for a few moments he was a child again in Navora, lying hurt in bed with the Shinali bone clenched in his hand.

'Leave this place quickly,' Gabriel said to Yeshi. 'The Empress gave you freedom, but it was her last command as ruler. An evil man is emperor now.'

'We'll be gone by high moon tonight,' said Yeshi. 'I'll keep you in my knowing, brother. When we come back, in the Time of the Eagle, when the battles are past, people of your blood will tend the lands beside people of my blood.'

Gabriel thought of his mother and family, even now tending the land, loving it. And he thought of his child, Shinali and Navoran blood mixed, the unity already begun.

Yeshi touched his own chest, then placed his palm on Gabriel's and spoke the Shinali farewell.

Ashila stood nearby, and, seeing her, the new chieftain and his people went back into the fort to prepare for their great journey. Gabriel and Ashila were alone, but for the envoy waiting on the bridge.

Lifting his hand, Gabriel lightly touched her cheek. She moved closer, her face uplifted, her mouth near to his, but he shook his head and stepped back.

'Not even one farewell kiss?' she asked.

'I can't, love.'

She was certain then, and gazed along the bridge, down the

long road he would walk, but she saw only white light and a great unknowing. She bit her lip, trying to control the grief. For a while they stood like that, longing to embrace, to say a thousand things that were on their hearts.

'No one is taking my life from me,' he said. 'I lay it down myself.'

'I know,' she whispered. She looked into his eyes and saw that he was smiling, radiant, and there was so much love in him, so much triumph and joy, that she looked away again, unable to bear it.

The envoy called to Gabriel, his voice impatient.

Ashila placed her right hand on her left breast, then on Gabriel's. 'Our hearts will always be together,' she said.

'Keep me in your knowing,' he said in Shinali.

'I will, and in our child's knowing. *Sharleema*.'

They linked hands one last time, their eyes full of tears. Then he walked away.

When he was far down the road, he looked back.

Ashila saw him turn around, and she lifted her hand in a final farewell. He waved back, then walked on. She watched until he vanished in the light, until all that was left were his footsteps in the dust, and his child beneath her heart, and the happiness in her knowing.

She returned to the fort and climbed the tower and looked along the road, but saw only the sun. She sat on the bare wooden floor where they had loved, and she wept, and it was sunset when she went down again to the river, to the fish cooking on hot stones, and the funeral fire, and the nation he had saved.

The envoy walked his horse slowly, so his prisoner could keep up. But Gabriel fell often, and finally the envoy lost patience. He stopped his horse under the trees beside the road, where the evening breeze blew in from the coast. He looked back, and watched as the young man staggered in the dirt, and fell again. This time the prisoner was a long while getting up. Then he stumbled on, at last drawing alongside the horse.

'At this rate,' said the envoy, 'we'll never get to Navora.'

Gabriel tried to speak, but his voice was cracked and rasping, and no words came. Slowly the envoy dismounted. Trained in safely diagnosing bulai fever, he covered his mouth and nose with a thick cloth, then commanded Gabriel to turn his face to the light and open his mouth. Keeping at a safe distance, Gabriel obeyed, and the envoy peered at the back of his throat.

'You've got plague,' the envoy announced. 'You have a day left, I'd say, not much longer.'

Gabriel said nothing, but his eyes shone with an unearthly fire, and the envoy looked away, afraid and swearing. 'There's no point in delivering you now,' he said. 'Lord Jaganath wouldn't thank me for taking plague into his palace. Have you anything I can give him, some token, by which he'll know you were indeed my prisoner?'

Gabriel removed the small leather bag from around his neck. Jaganath had seen the bag that fateful night at the Empress's feast, when he had publicly accused Gabriel of wearing the Shinali amulet; now he would see what else it contained – the small symbol in the shape of a figure of eight, made of grass from Shinali lands, intricate and endless and strong: the sign of Shinali dreams.

Taking it, the envoy mounted his horse again and rode away, galloping fast, dust rising about him like powdered gold.

Darkness melted into light, and light to dark. Somewhere Gabriel lost the road and found himself on cliffs overlooking the sea. There was grass here, sweet and warm under his bare feet. He lay on it and watched the gulls wheeling overhead, crying. There was an eagle, gliding close, its eyes like fire. And flames in a Shinali hearth, and Ashila watching over him, smiling while she wept.

Then the sun again, and heat, and thirst.

And an evening. Or was it dawn? The skies soft, the colour of pearl. Oysters, rotting on a beach, and a knife flicking out the precious part, the eternal part, the beauty formed out of pain. The rest discarded like old clothes.

Heat. Stumbling in it, weary, thirsting, tearing off the garments that hampered and held back; the last relinquishment, terrible, sublime.

The earth, the sky, the sun and moon gone. Dimness, and silence. The great valley, shadowy and full of peace, and the wind, the holy wind, powerful and awesome and joyous. He raised his eyes and faced the vastness before him, not alone.

Elated, he lifted his arms to the glowing wind, and began to run.

THE BEGINNING

The Raging Quiet

The Raging Quiet is a haunting and compelling story about the power and determination to overcome prejudice and injustice in a world of witchcraft, feudalism and intolerance.

Set in Medieval times, it tells the story of Marnie and Raver each set apart from the community around them: Marnie because she is a newcomer having been brought to the seaside village by her new – and much older – husband; and Raver because he is the village lunatic.

The Raging Quiet – though embedded in a historical setting – has undiminished relevance today; Marnie and Raver are singled out because they are different.

ISBN 0 689 82706 7